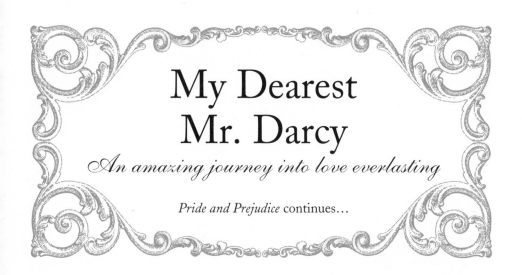

My Dearest Mr. Darcy

An amazing journey into love everlasting

Pride and Prejudice continues…

Sharon Lathan

sourcebooks
landmark

Copyright © 2010 by Sharon Lathan
Cover and internal design © 2010 by Sourcebooks, Inc.
Cover images © Bridgeman Art Library

Published by Sourcebooks Landmark, an imprint of Sourcebooks, Inc.
P.O. Box 4410, Naperville, Illinois 60567-4410
(630) 961-3900
FAX: (630) 961-2168
www.sourcebooks.com

Library of Congress Cataloging-in-Publication Data

Lathan, Sharon.
  My Dearest Mr. Darcy : an amazing journey into love everlasting : Pride and prejudice continues / Sharon Lathan.
       p. cm.
  1. Darcy, Fitzwilliam (Fictitious character)--Fiction. 2. Bennet, Elizabeth (Fictitious character)--Fiction. 3. Married people--Fiction. 4. Marriage-Fiction. 5. England--Social life and customs--19th century--Fiction. 6. Domestic fiction. I. Austen, Jane, 1775-1817. Pride and prejudice. II. Title.
  PS3612.A869D37 2010
  813'.6--dc22

                    2009040365

          Printed and bound in the United States of America
            VP 10 9 8 7 6 5 4 3 2

The Darcy Saga

BY SHARON LATHAN

Mr. and Mrs. Fitzwilliam Darcy: Two Shall Become One
Loving Mr. Darcy: Journeys Beyond Pemberley
My Dearest Mr. Darcy: An Amazing Journey into Love Everlasting

Table of Contents

Cast of Characters... vii

Prologue: Snippets of a Physician's Memoirs.................................. 1

1. Correspondence... 25
2. A Game of Riddles... 53
3. Toes in the Sand... 73
4   Caister-on-Sea... 85
5. Magic Lantern 101
6. Sunrise on the Sand 117
7. Up, Up, and Away!... 129
8. Just Desserts 145
9. On the Road Home... 157
10. Fading of Summer.. 165
11. George Darcy 181
12. Pemberley Estate 193
13. With This Ring I Thee Wed... 209
14. A Time Apart.. 225
15. Thirty Is an Auspicious Number... 247
16. November 265
17. Bundle of Joy.. 277

18. Alexander.. 299
19. Year's End 313

Acknowledgments... 335
About the Author.. 337

Cast of Characters

Fitzwilliam Darcy, Master of Pemberley in Derbyshire: 29 years of age, born November 10, 1787; parents James and Lady Anne Darcy, both deceased; married Elizabeth Bennet on November 28, 1816

Elizabeth Darcy, Mistress of Pemberley: 22 years of age, born May 28, 1795; second Bennet daughter

Georgiana Darcy: 18 years of age; sister of Mr. Darcy with guardianship shared by her brother and cousin, Col. Fitzwilliam; companion is Mrs. Annesley

Col. Richard Fitzwilliam: 32 years of age; cousin and dear friend to Mr. Darcy; second son of Lord and Lady Matlock; regiment stationed in London

Lord Matlock, the Earl of Matlock: Darcy's Uncle Malcolm, brother to Lady Anne Darcy; ancestral estate is Rivallain in Matlock, Derbyshire

Lady Matlock, the Countess of Matlock: Darcy's Aunt Madeline, wife to Lord Matlock; mother of Jonathan, Annabella, and Richard

Jonathan Fitzwilliam: Heir to the Matlock earldom, eldest Fitzwilliam son; wife is *Priscilla*

Charles Bingley: Longtime friend of Mr. Darcy; currently resides at Netherfield Hall in Hertfordshire; married Jane Bennet on November 28, 1816

Jane Bingley: elder sister of Elizabeth and eldest Bennet daughter; wife of Mr. Bingley

Caroline Bingley: unmarried sister of Charles Bingley

Louisa Hurst: married sister of Charles Bingley; husband is *Mr. Arbus Hurst*; residence London

Mr. and Mrs. Bennet: Elizabeth's parents; reside at Longbourn in Hertfordshire with two middle daughters, *Mary* and *Kitty*

Mary Bennet: Elizabeth's sister; middle Bennet daughter

Katherine (Kitty) Bennet: Elizabeth's sister; fourth Bennet daughter

Lydia Wickham: Elizabeth's sister; youngest Bennet daughter; married to Lieutenant George Wickham, stationed in Newcastle

Edward and Violet Gardiner: uncle and aunt of Elizabeth; reside in Cheapside, London

Dr. George Darcy: Mr. Darcy's uncle; brother to James Darcy

Lady Catherine de Bourgh: Mr. Darcy's aunt; sister to Lady Anne Darcy; residence Rosings Park, Kent

Anne de Bourgh: daughter of Lady Catherine; Mr. Darcy's cousin

Stephen Lathrop: Cambridge friend of Mr. Darcy; residence is Stonecrest Hall in Leicestershire; wife is *Amelia*

Henry Vernor: family friend of the Darcys; residence is Sanburl Hall near Lambton, Derbyshire; wife is *Mary*, daughter is *Bertha*

Gerald Vernor: son of Henry Vernor; childhood friend of Mr. Darcy; wife is *Harriet*; residence is Sanburl Hall

Albert Hughes: childhood friend of Mr. Darcy; wife is *Marilyn*; residence is Rymas Park near Baslow

Rory Sitwell: Derbyshire resident and Cambridge friend of Mr. Darcy; wife is *Julia*; residence is Reniswahl Hall near Staveley

George and Alison Fitzherbert: Derbyshire residents and friends; residence is Brashinharm near Barlow

Clifton and Chloe Drury: Derbyshire residents and friends; residence is Locknell Hall near Derby

Dr. Raul Penaflor Aleman de Vigo: Spanish associate of Dr. George Darcy, who refers to him as "Raja"

Joshua Daniels: son and partner of Mr. Darcy's London solicitor, *Andrew Daniels*

Charlotte Collins: Longtime friend of Elizabeth's; married to Rev. William Collins; resides at Hunsford, rectory of Rosings Park in Kent

Mrs. Reynolds: Pemberley housekeeper

Mr. Taylor: Pemberley butler

Mr. Keith: Mr. Darcy's steward

Samuel Oliver: Mr. Darcy's valet

Marguerite Charbonneau: Mrs. Darcy's maid

Phillips, Watson, Tillson, Georges, Rothchilde: Pemberley footmen

Mr. Clark: Pemberley head groundskeeper

Mr. Thurber: Pemberley head groomsman

Mrs. Langton: Pemberley cook

Mr. Anders: Pemberley head coachman

Mr. Burr: Pemberley gamekeeper

Mr. Holmes: falconer

Mrs. Smyth: Darcy House housekeeper

Mr. Travers: Darcy House butler

Hobbes: Darcy House footman

Reverend Bertram: Rector of Pemberley Chapel

Mrs. Hanford: Nanny to Darcy firstborn

Mrs. Henderson: Midwife

Madame du Loire: Modiste in Lambton

PROLOGUE

Snippets of a Physician's Memoirs

June 23, 1817
Darcy House, London

IMAGINE MY SURPRISE TO REALIZE it has been over a month since last jotting my musings in this fine book. Of course, writing while at sea is inconceivable. Egad, I abhor being at sea! Luckily the remedies for seasickness liberally doused down my gullet by the ever faithful Dr. Raul Penaflor staved off the worst of the hideous symptoms. I even managed to walk about a bit on deck. Bracing sea air, my derriere! Nonetheless, I was abed for the bulk of the trip, wallowing too far in my personal hellish misery to complain about the narrow confines of our cabin and odiferous mattress. East India trading ships cater to the needs of cargo far above passengers. We disembarked at Ramsgate. I was quite happy to embrace the rigors of overland travel rather than proceeding up the Thames, but several days of subsequent immobility were required to restore my equilibrium ere we moved beyond that lovely seacoast town. Raul, bless his Spanish heart, rather delighted in my incapacitation as it allotted him the opportunity to ramble through the streets and relish the sights. Poor man has never seen England. How does one live? I ask arrogantly.

Eventually we set off. I did manage to post a letter warning William of my arrival. I hoped it would arrive well enough in advance, although that did not prove to be true. Apparently the mail service of my great country has not improved. Not all can be perfect. Oh well, that is the way of family! I flattered myself that his astounding joy would be profound enough to overwhelm any irritation at my besieging of the newlyweds. This did prove to be true as well as fortuitous, as William had hurt himself, again, and I am sure it was only my timely arrival that saved him from a life of handicap! Ha! However, I am getting ahead of myself, as you know, dear Jharna, I am wont to do.

This trip home has been so anticipated, sea travel notwithstanding. Naturally I was thrilled that Raul wished to accompany me, but even without his companionship I would have had to come. How many hours did I bore you with memories of my homeland, Jharna? Always wishing and praying that you would agree to travel with me. Perhaps I should have prayed to your gods rather than my own. Ah well, here I now am, and never has the green English countryside and crowded London streets filled me with such joy. It is almost impossible to recollect how anxious I was to leave all those decades ago. Perhaps I am getting old, as you would tease.

Darcy House stood shining in the afternoon sun, undiminished in her grandeur and loveliness. Moderate chaos reigned, much to my delight, when I crossed the threshold. It was a scene evocative of my youth when all us rowdy children would be tearing about the foyer: Alex sliding down the banister to Mother's dismay, Estella hiding in order to frighten delicate Mary, and James doubled over in mirth while I performed some feat of acrobatic skill. Yes, I must be aging if the frequent jaunts down the ancient paths of my memories are any indication. If the obvious affection between William and his bride are evidentiary of their marital relations, then Darcy House will yet again display such a scene. In fact, they are already on the way as Mrs. Darcy is with child.

How can I describe Elizabeth Darcy? Clinically, emotionally, or both? Physically she is a tiny slip of a girl, although actually of moderate height. Strangely, considering the stature of William, she on the one hand is dwarfed by his bulk while simultaneously looming larger than life. Sheer force of personality and presence overcomes her physicality. With chestnut hair, enormous brown eyes, dainty features, and delicate bone structure, she is a picturesque counterpart for my nephew. They complement each other well on numerous levels. However, it is the aforementioned presence that I know has captured William, as I imagine it does all who know her. She is witty, intelligent, sparkling, kind, courageous, and loving. I can readily find no faults, and you know, Jharna, what a penchant I have for divining deficiencies!

I will confess that I assumed William, like the vast majority of men in his class, had acquired a wife from the leeches of proper British society. Someone poised, of excellent family, and acceptable, but likely dull, vapid, and shallow. My years away from my favored nephew, his character largely gleaned through James's letters and later his own, fostered the theory that he would take the safe and acceptable road. I cannot claim to have an overly intimate relationship with him, but could have stated with absolute certainty that taking such a path would have rendered him miserable within a year. James always told me that his son's intelligence and restrained intensity mildly intimidated him, William possessing a nature far too zealous and exacting to comfortably fit within the confines of stifling English society. Yet, he would lament, William seemed determined to do so even to the point of suppressing his inclinations.

As I recall musing in previous journal entries while visiting home, my impressions concurred with James's. William as an adult and Master of Pemberley appeared to be fulfilling the best of James's predictions and the worst of his fears. That he was brilliant as the estate manager and guardian to Georgie was evident, but there was a sadness and stoic quality to him that even I could not crack significantly. A mere smile or laugh was a rare event, and I think he was frankly relieved when I returned to India.

Estella's letter after the wedding filled me with some hope, her impression of the new Mrs. Darcy and William's emotions all favorable. She also related that Elizabeth was neither of society nor even the best family. Lady Catherine flatly refused to acknowledge the union, *shockingly*, I write with towering sarcasm! Anyway, I am repeating myself. I guess it is just the surprise of the development that still staggers me. James, of course, had married for love, but I know how rare that is. Would even my dear brother have done so if Lady Anne Fitzwilliam were not of the highest caliber and breeding? I do not know. Regardless, William has found his match in every way in Elizabeth. Theirs appears to be the deepest of loves. I cannot be happier for them.

Ah, Jharna, how amazing it is to be in the bosom of my family! For too many years I have been adrift with only you to really turn to. Now you are gone and I have longed for the reestablishment of roots. Who would have thought it? And I know you are laughing from wherever you now reside! Be that as it may, I must attempt to smother my sentimental tendencies and write of my days here clinically, or I will fill the remaining pages with nonsense.

My dearest Georgiana has evolved into a woman in my absence. She is more beautiful and graceful then I would have imagined her awkward and skinny little-girl shape to grow into. So like Anne in every way. William's personality was always more of a melding of James and Anne, his humor and playfulness there, but reserved. More like my sister Mary or brother Phillip. Actually, as I think on it, he receives that trait from my mother! Interesting. Or, with further staring into space recollections, very like the old Lord Matlock, Anne's father. There was an intimidating man! I doubt he ever cracked a smile, as the world is yet in one piece.

No, Georgie is a straight replica of dear Anne. Blonde, blue-eyed, dainty, soft-spoken, charming, innocent, yet with a sharp humor, intelligence, and quick wit hidden behind her naïveté. It is providential that I arrived at this moment in her life. She is the proverbial girl on the cusp of womanhood: one hour a silly child and the next wise and mature. I am gleaning via oblique hints that William and Elizabeth walked a rocky course on their way to felicity, Georgiana the stabilizer for my nephew's turbulent soul. I do not know the details, although the curiosity is killing me (do not snicker, Jharna). I *will* figure it out in due time!

The first several days of our dwelling have been hectic, hence why I have yet to create an entry here until today. Within days of my arrival I met Elizabeth's entire family, Lady Catherine and her daughter Miss Anne, a number of William's friends and business associates, Mr. Bingley and Miss Bingley, and my old friend Malcolm Fitzwilliam and his family. The Darcys hosted a ball that Raul and I were in time to attend. It was marvelous to see old faces again, even Lady C. She has always been fodder for entertainment; this time it was a confrontation and subsequent dubious apology for some sort of infraction against Elizabeth. I am still working out the details, but apparently she refused to acknowledge William's marriage, basing her disdain for Elizabeth's country upbringing, as well as a misguided belief that Anne and William were destined to wed. I recall James speaking of this a time or two with humor, saying once that it would be incestuous considering how close the two were as youngsters. Be that as it may, Lady C never gave up the idea even after William made it abundantly clear his leanings were elsewhere. The boy has a mind of his own, make no mistake! Even I could have told Lady C *that*.

Mr. Bingley has matured nicely since I met him two years ago, and married Elizabeth's sister Jane! Mrs. Bingley is a blonde beauty with stunning blue eyes, far quieter than Elizabeth but well suited for Mr. Bingley. The two seem very happy, and I can only imagine how delighted all the individuals involved must feel to be so closely intertwined. Mr. Bingley's sister is a beauty as well. Striking red hair rarely seen without the accompanied poor complexion Miss Bingley thankfully is not stricken with. She, however, is the quintessential product of the English ton. Always the excellent diagnostician of character, it was clear to me that Miss Bingley fancied William and was less than pleased by him choosing Elizabeth rather than her. It was all so amusing. Of course, she is the sort I expected William to end up with, and after studying all the varied interactions, I can only be thoroughly elated that William's backbone and good sense prevailed. With each passing day I am coming to admire the boy more and more. James would be so very proud of his son. Pity how those events unfolded.

Elizabeth has a large family. Her mother is rather ridiculous, but her father is an interesting man. There is no doubt where Elizabeth gets her character from. We older gentlemen hit it off quite well, kindred spirits to a degree. She has two younger sisters, but I frankly had little time to become acquainted. The room was filled to overflowing. I am certain Darcy House has not seen such an extravaganza in years. Elizabeth was the perfect hostess, William his usual reserved self but with a foolish grin frequently gracing his features and eyes that lit up whenever he gazed upon his wife, which was constantly. I can remember James having much the same expression whenever he even *thought* of Anne. I was young enough then to tease him mercilessly about it! Now I guess I am a bit wiser and assuredly older, so these displays of affection do not annoy me as profoundly. In truth, the heart gets all fluttery, but I would not admit that anywhere but within these pages! Still, as moving as it is, even this new sentimental me is relieved to know I was never blatantly moony every time you were nearby, Jharna.

Raul charmed all the available women, and many of those who are not. That man is far too handsome for his own good! Not to mention being a royal—you know that's why I call him Raja, to his annoyance. It was requisite for me to play down his assets, so to speak, to avoid a matrimonial plot by Elizabeth's mother. I find myself curious as to what part she may have had to play in her eldest daughters wooing such eligible bachelors. No insult intended, as both Elizabeth and Jane are excellent ladies; however, their class is clearly not equal to a Darcy. Not that I ever attributed much worth to that nonsense, but it is the world we live in. Perhaps Mrs. Bennet played no part as both men are clearly smitten with their wives, but she is the type, and I have witnessed such manipulations dozens of time. More history for me to unravel. Yes, I know, Jharna, I am a busybody.

Day two was spent in the company of Malcolm. He dragged Raja and me to White's for an afternoon of debauchery and indolence. I recognized a few faces, but the truth is my years of studying in London did not allow for leisure time, nor was I one to overly hobnob with society. I could have participated more, naturally, being a Darcy, but was looked at askance for my chosen study. I was not of the Cambridge or Oxford elite, nor did I care to be, so it created a mild stigma. No one knew quite how to deal with me, and since I was never interested in another's opinion, it was easier to avoid it all. I sensed some of the same hesitation at White's. I am still a Darcy and in the company of Lord Matlock, so cannot be shunned. Yet I am also a mere doctor wearing strange clothing and toting a Spaniard in my wake! I doubt even listing Raja's pedigree would have helped! Ah well, we had a delightful time nonetheless, the liquor as excellent as always and billiard room elegant.

The remainder of the evening has been lazy. The loving couple had a prior engagement, so Raja and I stayed with the girls. Georgie's pianoforte skills have improved dramatically since I was last here. She is quite proficient. What a shame that women cannot freely pursue careers in the arts. It has never made much sense to me that our culture expects an accomplished woman to play an array of instruments, speak and read several languages, paint and draw, be expert in all methods of needlepoint, yet do nothing with any of it beyond amuse themselves and their inner circle. I can speak several tongues, having inherited that gift from my mother, but cannot play a single instrument, cannot draw beyond vague sketches of bodily parts, and can only wield a needle when sewing flesh, yet I am considered a more valued member of society! I personally think all men should be forced to observe a woman in childbirth. That would make them think twice about the weaker sex!

Rambling again. Forgive me, my faithful journal! So, here I now am reposing in my luxurious chambers at Darcy House. I am content to be home, quite delighted to be on holiday with minimal expectations on my person, not yet feeling guilty for leeching off my nephew's kindness, experiencing an odd mixture of lethargy and exuberance, sipping a fine glass of whiskey, and doing nothing more laborious then putting quill to parchment. Or rather, steel-tipped pen to parchment. Amazing invention! William seems to have inherited a curiosity of modern innovations and mechanical gadgetry from my father. I wonder if William remembers his grandfather's obsession for science and machinery? After all, the majority of the Pemberley fountains and equipment are of his designing. I shall add that to my list of topics to discuss with my nephew. For now, staring at the fire and early to bed are the only agenda items. Good night, lovely Jharna, wherever you are.

June 24
London

Spent the day trudging through the haberdasheries of Bond Street with Raul. I am exhausted! How do the ladies do this day in and day out? Boggles my mind. Anyway, Raja, noble instincts rising to the fore, decided he required a completely new wardrobe of latest English fashion. So, yesterday he inquires of William as to the best places to shop. William jumps up with unveiled enthusiasm, proceeding to jot down the finest establishments London has to offer. Raja is flushed with happiness, eyeballing William's impeccably clad figure with obvious hankering. William, while ostensibly addressing Raja, is glancing pointedly toward me and offering graciously to arrange an appointment with Mr. Renault, his personal tailor. Elizabeth met my raised eyebrow with a barely hidden laugh. Her face is so expressive!

Oddly, that particular afternoon I was wearing my most demure salwar kameez, the beige one with turquoise trim. He should be thankful I left all my dhotis behind in India! Even I did not think the English public prepared to view my legs unbound by trousers. Nevertheless, I suppose there is a logical point to my nephew's unspoken plea. All the English suits I own are woefully outdated and threadbare. I imagine there may be the occasional soiree or festivity where a proper suit will be necessary. So, alas, I did the unthinkable and allowed Raja to drag me from shop to shop, endured two hours of measuring and clucking tongues from Mr. Renault's assistants. Raja nearly bought out each establishment, any initial contempt expressed at his dark skin and accent rapidly evaporated by the wad of cash displayed. I, on the other hand, purchased lightly, acquiring only four suits and sundry accoutrements. How I will ever survive a choking cravat is frankly beyond my comprehension. Ah, the extents we will go to for love of family!

June 26
London

Raul and I reported to Company headquarters, signed the obligatory documents, and spoke with the Director (a Mr. Allison now). He was not too pleased that we refused to give a definite date for our reenlistment, or even if we will. Apparently Raja's reputation has preceded him, with his services in prime demand. This thrills me, not only because I trained him but because his skills truly are astounding and I am delighted to see this recognized. I was a bit surprised that Raja demurred regarding his conscription, he having not alluded to any uncertainty in his future. I chose to leave the subject alone for the moment, Raul mature enough to make his own choices. Whatever his decisions for the future, I am confident he will do well.

Met William and Col. Fitzwilliam for luncheon and spirits at Estad's Saloon. I cannot believe the eatery is still standing. I remember the first time I ate there: I was thirteen, still mourning Alex, and Father decided to treat me to a gentleman's outing as a way of cheering my gloominess. Additionally he thought that I was finally capable of playing the part of a gentleman. Ha! So Pearson, James's valet, dressed me in my Sunday finery complete with pocketwatch and fancy fob as well as a walking stick that I dearly wanted to wave about and poke people with, but resisted the urge! The simple fear of what my father would do to me not worth the fun I might have had. Anyway, James was in his final year at Cambridge, joining us for a few weeks while in Town for the season, and I recall that I did feel vainly dashing and arrogantly mature squired about with my distinguished father and dandified older brother. I honestly do not recollect the food served, but the atmosphere was awe inspiring to a thirteen-year-old. James acted all sophisticated and snobbish while winking at me when Father was not looking. Yes, fun times.

Of course, I have since dined at Estad's many times, although it has been a few years. Impeccable and delicious as ever. Delightful afternoon, especially as with just the four of us I had my first real opportunity to communicate intimately with my nephew. We were there for hours, sipping excellent red wine from France and engaging in lively discourse. Naturally we were approached by a dozen fellow diners who knew William. He departed the establishment with four additional commitments to the already busy schedule of him and Elizabeth. I only knew Lord and Lady Standish. He was a crony of James's who visited Pemberley a time or two with his wife; she was a dear friend of Anne's. We spent a few minutes reminiscing.

This evening William and Elizabeth have a planned engagement at the Countess von Lieven's salon. To my incredible shock, an invitation arrived yesterday for Raja and me. I suppose I should not be too surprised by the infamous Countess knowing all that goes on in the city, but why she would extend an invite to two traveling physicians is beyond my comprehension. Nevertheless, even I would be foolish to pass up an opportunity to meet the famous woman herself, so Raja and I will attend.

June 28
London

Been a couple busy days. First I must describe the evening at Countess von Lieven's salon. I contemplated wearing one of my new suits, but decided that if it was exotic foreign gentlemen the Countess wanted, then so be it! Yet to compromise and not embarrass my formal nephew, I wore my finest sherwani of grey wool. I figured that if it was acceptable for official British East India Company affairs, then it should serve. I even topped it off with matching fez, quite dashing if I say so myself. I know you would have appreciated it, Jharna, as it was the outfit you gifted to me on my fiftieth birthday. Of course, I do think it was primarily out of your desire to see me properly attired for one of your father's ceremonies! I digress, however.

The Lieven mansion on St. James's Place was stupendous, as expected. All the lights were lit, some, to my astonishment, created with gaslight! The glow was incredible, the entire Square lit as if noontime. Even though it was well after the dinner hour, the Square was bustling with nearly every house plainly hosting some soiree or ball. The Ambassador's dwelling was no exception. The door was standing open with footmen checking invitations as folks freely walked in and out. Music and laughter from within was audible without. It was so hectic and boisterous that I find it difficult to describe with any clarity.

The whole concept of salons, as popularized by the forward Frenchwomen with designs of intellectual conversation amongst artists and philosophers, has evolved with the Countess into a place to influence political matters. Much of the former reigned here as the evening's guests included writers William Wordsworth, Percy Bysshe Shelley, and Leigh Hunt, and artists

John Constable and J.M.W. Turner, among others I did not have the chance to meet or was unfamiliar with. Elizabeth gravitated to the artists, clearly enamored by Mr. Wordsworth and Mr. Constable. The latter, especially, as apparently she and William have recently viewed an exhibition of his works, purchasing two paintings.

I confess with shame that I was astonished at how easily Elizabeth mingled with the plethora of dignitaries and their wives. As I have written, I am delighted with William's felicity and good sense to marry a woman of true value. Nonetheless, aware of Elizabeth's provincial upbringing, and having had minimal opportunity thus far to talk to her seriously, I did not quite fathom how intelligent she is. Clearly William was somewhat surprised as well. Even from his perch across the room, while discussing politics with several members of Parliament including Earl Charles Grey and George Canning (would love to have been privy to that discussion!), I noted his eyes often on his engaging wife with immense pride but mild amazement. I guess I can read William so easily as his face is so like my father's, and mine to a great extent. Quite uncanny to view another who is nearly a mirror image, but I am digressing yet again!

Elizabeth did not appear the slightest bit nervous. Perhaps that is innocence to a degree, but she conducted herself with a confidence and poise marvelous to witness. I rarely had the opportunity to join into the conversation surrounding her, my own attention captured as I will relate in a moment, but it was obvious that the people around her, both male and female, were favorably inclined. Her manners were impeccable as far as I could discern, not that I am a very good judge of proper English behavior, God knows! Still, William never seemed dismayed in any way, as I am sure he would have been if there was cause; my nephew, for all his numerous excellent qualities, is still one who keeps a tight rein on propriety and social class. Poor boy!

Raja and I found ourselves chatting part of the evening with a group of East India traders and directors. Talking shop, so to speak. The politics behind the Company never fails to make me yawn, but I suppose I do have some insight, having served for nearly thirty years. Some of the politicians in the assembly joined in, even William for a spell as he, like most wealthy Englishmen, holds stock in the Company. As a physician I never have paid much attention to the trading aspects, although I too have invested monetarily. However, as long as the revenues roll in, I really do not care how. Raja argues with me endlessly as to my lackadaisical attitude, to which I counter that if I desired to be a businessman, I would have stayed home and assisted in the management of Pemberley as my father wished! So there!!

The truth is that any Englishman worth his salt can talk politics and business, after discussing fine spirits and food, that is. It is in the blood, apparently. That and horses. And gambling and cigars. Beautiful women. Hunting and foxing. Maybe billiards too. OK, I confess, I am still as much an Englishman as you would always say, Jharna, despite my love of Indian culture!

Be that as it may, Raja and I were largely occupied and fascinated by a group of inventors and physicians added to the mix. I do not know if the inclusion of Raja and I to the guest list was due to the already invited scientific folk, or if the Countess's attendees are always so varied. Of special interest was a Dr. Albrecht from Germany, Dr. Shore from Manchester, and Dr. Nomikos from Greece who all teach at my old alma mater! We compared notes for the bulk of the evening. It was marvelous to hear of the changes to the Royal Academy as well as those things and professors that are unchanged. Raja and I were extended an invitation to visit the following day. I had planned to do so anyway, wanting to show Raja where I received my education, but having a formal invitation, luncheon included, is superior to merely spontaneously appearing at the gates and declaring myself!

In between the medical discussions, Dr. Nomikos showed us his latest acquisition: one of the new stethoscopes recently invented by the French genius Dr. Rene Laennec. I know I wrote at least a page worth of my amazed excitement at the invention when I read about it last year, so will not do so again. However, actually seeing one of the devices and testing it on a live individual was a thrilling experience beyond conveying. Dr. Nomikos traveled personally to Paris to study with Dr. Laennec and now teaches dissertations on the innovative physician's discoveries of auscultation, pulmonary, and liver diseases. Without a doubt Raja and I will attend one of his classes on the subject.

There were so many other notable persons that it would be impossible for me to list them all. Naturally the Ambassador prowled through the room, although he clearly left the prime hosting role to his illustrious wife. The Countess is everything one has read about her: physically rather plain but with a wicked wit and gregarious personality. She floated about the room with apparently ceaseless energy, charming and gracious, entering flawlessly into each conversation with her Russian accented English inerrantly offering brilliant insight no matter the topic. I spoke with her only briefly, the strange woman frankly unnerving me as she seemed to know precisely who I was, how long I had been with the Company, my professional credentials, and so on. She was enchanting and amiable in all ways, yet one got the feeling that there was clairvoyance at work! Apparently not, as she did not comment on Raja's family connections, greatly ignoring him beyond a polite greeting in fact, but it was nonetheless oddly disconcerting. I was relieved when she moved on to the next group. I could readily ascertain that she unsettled William as well, but then he does not acquit himself well in many social situations, I have found. I must teach the boy to release his subdued charm. After all, if he so physically resembles me, then the personality must be akin, yes?

We tarried until two in the morning, Elizabeth clearly too fatigued to linger longer. William worries about her so, a trait I find adorable, but considering her condition, I tend to agree with him. She certainly appears healthy enough for such a minute creature, but one cannot be too careful. William shared the details of Elizabeth's recent accident with ensuing head trauma with me, the event observably yet distressing to him, while we managed a time alone last evening. The duel itself he glossed over with regulated humility, although the lingering anger toward this nefarious Marquis was clearly evident. The description of Elizabeth's fall and subsequent unconsciousness and injuries was rendered with an attempt to relay in a detached manner, but the poor boy nearly broke down several times. How horrific for him! For the first time since my arrival I saw behind the careful regulation he wears in public. I must say, despite recognizing the affection between the two, I had not fully comprehended the deep love. What a marvel! Yes, Jharna, we loved. Deeply. But I do not think even we reached these depths. I know I miss you, your death a profound shock that I will never recover from, but have I ceased to exist? No, my dear, I am sorry to say I have not. Does that make me less of a man? Less of a devoted lover? I do not know, nor do I wish to wholly consider the subject, as it may hurt too much to reveal the flaws in my character. Sometimes introspection is best avoided. I prefer to think it just how we are designed or what fate allots us. We found each other, Jharna, and were blissfully content for many years. I do not regret it, nor do I believe I have missed something better along the way.

I recall the altered tenor of James's letters after Anne died, and the one time I visited afterwards was a staggering blow. He was utterly bereft. I have never witnessed anything quite like it. I know the poets would say that love of such a consuming nature is worth all the pain. I do not know if I concur.

Maybe I simply despise pain in all its manifestations too greatly to be able to willingly place myself in its path. No, do not dwell on it! Best to be thankful for the course set for my life, thankful for the relationships I have established, and delight in the joy my dear nephew has found. What a blessing it is to be a part of it! Yes, Jharna, I am happy to be home.

July 5
London, England

Finally a positive development on the Anne de Bourgh assignment! You know how this has intrigued me, Jharna, from my first introduction to her at William's ball. Every encounter with the dear girl has further piqued my interest, but not as fully as Raja. I am not surprised particularly as he is as terrible with a medical mystery before him as I, and can never resist bringing home the wounded puppy, quite literally! Still, his focus and near obsession on the matter has stunned even me. I daresay the sadness involved with seeing a person suffering when the belief is that assistance can be offered is agonizing. I, however, have had many more years of experience then the youthful Dr. Penaflor with bizarre cultural beliefs that occasionally prohibit me performing the healing I know I could if allowed. Perhaps my heart has hardened a bit… more introspection I prefer to avoid, thank you very much!

Anyway, it was a plea from William himself that encouraged me to break my silence on the subject and put myself on the line, so to speak. I did not quite realize how close the two were, the affection real even if not of a romantic nature as Lady C desired. He approached me several afternoons ago while in the library. I love how he does this! As I have related previously, the boy's affection toward me is growing, as is mine toward him, maturing into a real relationship beyond what was anticipated for kin. A bit of a shock, actually, and faintly unsettling in its unexpectedness, but strangely comforting. Hmmm… I must dwell on the emotions a bit at a later time.

So, Miss Anne… William had picked up on Raja's absorption, overheard a smattering of conversations on the topic, and so asked me frankly what my opinion was. Naturally I gave it to him, not a problem for me to do so! He was very serious and deeply troubled. "Uncle, do you think you could really help Anne? Because if you truly do, then I would support you one hundred percent in discovering a way to overcome Lady Catherine's dominance. My cousin has suffered for too long, and if you are correct in your diagnosis, has suffered falsely. This is intolerable. What can we do?"

It was so heartfelt that I could not refuse to accept the challenge. And yes, I confess the vision of ruffling Lady C's feathers was appealing! He chuckles evilly. That aside, the question was how to wisely go about the issue. It was my brilliant idea to talk to Malcolm. The power and prestige of Lord Matlock and all that rot. He was frankly stunned at our diagnosis from afar, having only heard the conclusions from Lady C's medical hacks. He was a bit skeptical, naturally, and I was sagacious, humbly demurring that we could be in error (although I was certain we were not) but would not know until we could physically examine the girl. The more we talked I could discern that he rather savored the idea of hassling his overbearing sister, although he would never admit to the emotion, so I let it pass. Yes, Jharna, I can be politic when I deem it proper! Now we will wait and see what transpires. Raja, bless his soul, is glowing in happiness. Very odd.

July 9
London

Whew! What a week! Besides the numerous dinner engagements, musical entertainments, and so on (Egad, how do people do this year in and year out?), Raja and I finally were allowed to examine Miss de Bourgh. It would take the entire book to fully detail the drama, and even then I do not think I could do it justice. Let me attempt the highlights.

What Malcolm said or did I have no idea. Today, as we sat about after breakfast doing basically nothing, a message arrives from Malcolm insisting Dr. Penaflor and I hasten to the de Bourgh townhouse immediately. Thankfully doctors are used to such summons, so we grabbed our bags and were ready before the carriage had been brought around.

We were greeted by Malcolm, who steered us quickly into the small parlor. "I have badgered Catherine for days and she has finally relented, sort of. Actually it is Anne who called for you to be here, standing up to her mother as I have never seen before. I was unaware that she even knew of the interest and discussion of her health. Frankly I am still abashed, and I do not think Catherine will ever recover! I suppose we have for too long thought of her as a child. Be that as it may, she is waiting and Catherine is momentarily stupefied, so follow me."

The examination was proceeding well, and as we expected, until we were interrupted by Lady C's London physician barging in. Apparently she was not as stupefied as Malcolm thought. As an aside, I was dressed in my typical attire; cool and altogether comfortable as well as roguishly handsome, I might add. Raja was dressed in one of his new suits. As impeccable as William always is, somehow managing to look serene and breezy despite the scorching climate and humidity. Handsome to be sure, but one would think him Adonis incarnate the way Miss Anne's eyes roosted on him, all aglow and adoring. She ignored me completely. Maybe I am losing my charm. I was amused and disconcerted simultaneously. However, there has been no time to explore the sentiments, nor was Raja anything but the consummate professional. Very odd.

Dr. Hayes, fifties, short and obese, naturally florid and profusely veined face not benefiting positively by a bellicose fit, was quite verbose in his opinion of our medical expertise. His command of the English language was impressive, I will give him that, at least for a time that is. Eventually the silent disregard from Raja and me wore on his nerves. Either that or the screeches of Lady C began to bother him as well, because he began to splutter a bit and repeat the curses. Malcolm had a hold of his arm, to keep him from rushing us I presume, but was unable to drag him away. Poor Miss Anne was mortified, Raja and I unable to focus on her while we tried to speak rationally to the raging man. It was messy and extremely perturbing, even to me who rather wallows in drama.

I do think we were all at an impasse, no one coherently paying attention to anyone, when a sudden shrill whistle pierced the air. It was Anne! She was sitting up in bed, her face undoubtedly ruddier than it has been in years, eyes flashing, and jaw clenched alarmingly. Needless to say, we were all speechless. "You!" she snapped in a ringing voice, pointing a rigid finger at the nearly apoplectic doctor, "Will leave this instant! How you can barge uninvited into a lady's room in this manner is unconscionable! Uncle Malcolm, take him away. Mother, I wish for you to stay, but remain silent, I beg you. I need to hear what they have to say! Please, allow me this."

Then the poor dear seemed to deflate as a balloon, collapsing onto the pillows with tears falling and the rush of color fading drastically to leave her paler than ever. Broke my heart. Raja was giving her his patented empathetic face that I have seen melt many a folk. Finally the atmosphere calmed and with Lady C observing avidly from the side, Raja and I resumed. Aided tremendously by our new stethoscopes and with the knowledge gleaned from Dr. Nomikos's lecture, we confidently concluded our original diagnosis. Miss Anne, per her answers to our questions, began feeling ill in her late teens. Fatigue of a general type that gradually increased, pallor, faint tremors with exertion as well as dyspnea and vague heart palpitations, muscle spasms, loss of concentration, occasional ulcers to the corners of her mouth, and flattened brittle fingernails. Classic signs of anemia. Her heart was strong, if beating a bit too fast, although whether that was from her illness or recent distress is impossible to say. I confess that Raja and I both listened for an inordinate amount of time to her heart and lungs, the stethoscope enabling us to hear sounds crisper and simply undetectable by placing an ear to the chest. Quite amazing and far less embarrassing to the patient, but I digress.

We spoke at great length to both Miss Anne and Lady C. Anne's eyes glowed with a hope that was heart wrenching to witness. I stressed that although we were certain of the diagnosis, the cause is impossible to pinpoint. The treatments, mainly of a dietary nature with supplements of an iron-rich tonic and various herbals brewed into tea, will absolutely improve her condition but will not be a cure and the degree of improvement can vary. Lady C seized upon that unsurety, apparently gleaning some sort of bizarre joy in knowing that we could not cure her daughter. How very sad it was, Raja unable to hide his disdain. Anyway, we finally departed with the promise to check on her again and provide the tonic's formula to the apothecary of her choosing. All in all a good day's accomplishment!

July 15
London

William, Elizabeth, and Georgie will be departing on the morrow for Pemberley. I have been rather torn. My heart desires to view my ancestral home with a tangible ache, but I am also enjoying the wonders of this great city. Raja is complacent, leaving the decision up to me. Col. Fitzwilliam, however, has arranged some time away from his Regiment and was hoping we could stay around for the type of diversions only bachelors are allowed to partake in. As he put it, with a wink toward a scowling William. Under the awkward circumstances I chose not to point out that there is many a married man who continually partakes in such diversions. I do believe William would have tossed me out of the house if I had joked in such a manner. The boy has a wicked sense of humor, but not about topics moral.

Ah, William! What an amazing young man! As I have related in numerous passages, I am continually startled by his intelligence and breadth of knowledge. James and Anne would be so very proud. The past several days have allotted us many hours to commune privately. Raja has been so busy with his daily visits to Miss de Bourgh, cavorting with the friends he has made, and the lectures on Spanish and Indian medicine he has been giving at the Academy that I have not seen much of him. William has concluded the bulk of his business affairs and with Elizabeth and the girls busy most afternoons at teas or shopping or whatever else it is women do in their spare time, William and I have been left alone. As you would always say, Jharna, I do have a lazy streak in me, so lying about on the comfortable chairs in the library has been a delight. Since William attends to his business in there, and also has a moderate lazy streak I have noticed as well as a love of literature, we end up conversing without really planning it.

Today he rather haltingly asked my opinion on Elizabeth's health. She has been rather like a bustling bee, flittering from one event to the next with seemingly inexhaustive energy. However, I, like William, have noticed grey shadows under her lovely eyes. Apparently William discussed his concerns with Madeline, and her advice was to leave it be and trust. I concurred, especially as they will be leaving tomorrow for the quiet restfulness of Pemberley. The conversation flowed, and before I really know how it happened, he was telling me the entire tale of how he met the beautiful Miss Bennet and their convoluted history toward matrimony. Quite the story! No, Jharna, I did not badger it out of him! He offered it up freely, not that I can pretend that my curiosity over the subject was not high.

Further proof of what I had already surmised: this is a relationship and marriage of extreme emotion and the truest love I think I have ever witnessed, except perhaps for James and Anne. What a marvel it is! I must say, as he related his first encounters with Elizabeth and how his infatuation grew, it brought back memories of you, Jharna. Not that our liaison was remotely the same, quite the contrary in fact, which is why I found myself musing on it. There were no sparks when we met the first time at your father's fiftieth birthday gala. Lord, that man can put on a party! I was so young then, only in India for one year, and still captivated by the cultural differences. We have laughed on it often since, my dear, how you thought I was foppish and vain while I barely glanced your way. Of course you were married then, so I would have been a louse to do so! I was instead intrigued by the dozens of other beautiful women about, including your sisters! My, how things may have gone differently if any of them had paid me any mind!

No, it is not the similarities but more the oddities of how life weaves loose threads into patterns of beauty even with the knots and errors visible. I loved your husband, Jharna. Kshitij Ullas was one of the finest physicians I have ever met in all my travels and taught me more than any other single person. He was my mentor, friend, father, and companion. I grieved when he died, more than many who claimed to do so. Despite the love that grew between us, dearest Jharna, and the joy we shared, I would still to this day give my soul to have Kshitij Ullas alive and scolding me for some dim-witted mistake! Yet, at the same time, I cannot imagine the fifteen years we spent together passing in any way but in your arms. I have long since given up trying to find the logic in it. I suppose it is as William said while telling me his tale, some things are simply meant to be. Karma, you would say in that imperiously serene tone that I adored, nodding sagely.

My admiration for William grew exponentially during those hours. And my happiness for what he has built with Elizabeth. They are almost nauseating in their adulation for each other, the barely suppressed passion humorous to observe and tremendously refreshing. The man that William has become, the husband and soon-to-be father, is a man worth knowing. It comes back to timing, Jharna, or karma if you prefer. Your death nearly two years ago (Lord, has it really been that long?) was the greatest loss I have ever experienced, except perhaps for Alex. I have gone on living, fairly easily I thought, with my usual eccentric habits and optimism and jocoseness intact. Yet, my continual dreams of home and family invaded my tranquility, so much so that I reckoned a visit to the homeland was beckoning. The news of William's marriage lent credence to the excursion. The excitement to be home I anticipated, although I have been surprised at my lack of restlessness. Of course, it has only been a month. What I honestly did not anticipate was the developing relationship with William. Frankly, the staid William of my previous acquaintance was not really the type of person I gravitate towards, nor do I believe I was more than a vague annoyance to him. It is vastly different now. He is different now. As am I, I suppose. Whatever the case, I am highly enjoying our evolving friendship. And Elizabeth and Georgie! My, it has been many a year since I have been surrounded by such a wealth of female attention! Even Elizabeth's sisters are beginning to loosen up a bit and falling under the charms of George! Ha!!

Yes, I hear you laughing, Jharna.

July 25
Pemberley, Derbyshire

Home at last! We arrived yesterday, the weather precisely as I remember it being this time of year. Hot and dry, sun shining beautifully and touching the Peaks and fields below with rays of gold. Stunning. All the pastures are a vivid green that almost hurts the eyes. And Pemberley, ah, my beloved Pemberley! How beautiful she is. Mr. Clark is still the head groundskeeper, William informs me. Obviously he has followed in his father's footsteps with equal skill as the gardens are perfection. I rose before dawn today in order to meander through the pathways in solitude as the sunrise woke the flowers, the aromas rising deliciously. I was almost late for breakfast, so lost in my reverie was I! I know, me late for a meal!

I did not have the chance to write ere we departed Kent. Miss de Bourgh was finally allowed to accompany us, but it was a dramatic scene, I am told. Raja and I stayed at the inn while Malcolm and Madeline confronted Lady C. William and Elizabeth had cleverly addressed the formal invitation to Miss Anne only. I know for a fact they rendered no formal invitations to anyone else, the festival primarily for the staff, and the inclusion of family a given. That William was quite put out by Miss Bingley insinuating herself into the company was obvious, at least to me. One annoying relative is enough, so they were succinct in their invitation to Miss Anne.

She is responding very well to the treatment. I have noticed a number of revealing glances between Miss de Bourgh and Raja. Not sure how I feel about it. I would be thrilled to see both young people find love, Miss Anne especially as she deserves some reward for tolerating her mother all these years with stoic patience. However, it is easy to misplace gratitude for affection. What is surprising is that Raja seems to be drawn to her and he has never taken his innate empathy to such degrees. I will study the situation carefully, not that there is much I can do to halt it, but I do not wish to see either hurt unduly.

Elizabeth, I am relieved to note, appears her sunny, exuberant self. Her pregnancy by all appearances seems to be progressing without complications. William is walking a foot off the ground, his eyes following her every move, not that they did not do so before. The day we arrived he was retrieving furniture from the attic. I was delighted to see the old cradle. I remember Phillip lying in it, as well as William so many years later. I know it is an heirloom, probably slept in it myself, although as there were two of us I truly do not know what Mother did! Should ask William if he unveiled a second cradle in the attic. Interesting.

I am anxious for the festival. Elizabeth is being quite secretive about the planned activities, although I can readily discern from her smug expression that it is to be an extravaganza extraordinaire! I have such fond memories of past festivals. Mother vainly tried to keep us inside but we always snuck out and mingled with the servant's children, all of us getting filthy and eating until we were ill. Good times. I specifically recall that it was the day before the Festival when James turned twenty, home from University for the summer and to celebrate his birthday on June 4, and my parents invited old Lord Matlock and his family to the Manor for the party. It was the first James, or any of us for that matter, had seen the Fitzwilliam girls for a number of years. Malcolm and James were at Cambridge together and close friends, so Father decided to include them on the guest list. Anne was fifteen, I think, and absolutely stunning. So was Muriel actually. Catherine was not there, as I remember, probably married to Sir Louis, now that I consider it. Anyway, even Alex and I at twelve could appreciate an attractive female, but James? Lord Almighty! One would think by his age he had seen his share of gorgeous ladies, but apparently not. Or, more to the point, I now know in my age-earned wisdom, not the one who would steal his heart. James took one look at Lady Anne and fell head over heels. It was clear to everyone present; James completely tongue tied and goggled eyed. Ridiculous, in fact, and Alex and I loved it! Teased him mercilessly, but he was undeterred, even when threatening to beat us senseless. Yes, indeed, happy memories!

July 31
Pemberley

Visited Rowan Lake today for a refreshing picnic organized at the last minute by Pemberley's most excellent Mistress. However, before I relate the day's fun, I must jot down the astonishing and amusing conversation with William earlier in the morning.

He discovered me where I was hiding in the library, entering sheepishly and carrying an enormous book in his arms and asking if he could have a private chat. It was exactly the opening I had been waiting for without even realizing it. He had questions about Elizabeth's pregnancy and birth, all understandable and typical questions, but the very fact that he was inquiring about a delicate, female-related topic proved to me even further the superior nature of the relationship they have. I teased him a bit as it still sends me into near hysterics how a grown man, married to boot, can blush so readily! Brilliant! I was kind though, turning on my Dr. Darcy pose and launching into it.

His quick grasp of matters obstetrical did not surprise me in the least. William's intellect is no longer a revelation. Nor was I overly shocked that he would be intimately curious about his wife's condition. I suppose I should have been though, as it is highly irregular, yet for some reason I was not. Everything about the Darcys' relationship has amazed me. Their level of intimacy shared, so blatantly apparent to anyone with a moderately discerning eye, is profound in its depth, so it seemed natural that he would want to know what to expect and what his beloved wife would suffer. Nonetheless, I was stunned on two counts: One, I suggested he consider being with Elizabeth during her delivery and after only a brief moment of flabbergast, he embraced the notion utterly and with an obvious relief that was uplifting to witness. Second, and secretly for the time being, I realized that I want, more than anything I have wanted in recent months, to be the one who delivers their baby! I truly did not anticipate the emotion and was frankly overwhelmed. Luckily William was caught up with his own emotions and did not notice me swallowing repeatedly and furiously blinking my eyes! Heavens! What is happening to me? I swear I have become a sentimental old fool overnight!

We talked for a long time, covering everything I could think of about the remaining months of her pregnancy and the birth process itself. No matter how delicate or vague I attempted to be, William always asked something pointed, frequently grasping a concept yet elucidated or leaping forward several steps while I was still explaining the fundamentals! Wonderful boy! All blushing ceased, William immersing himself so fully into the topic that I think a herd of elephants could have roared through the room and he would not have flinched. I have never seen a person focus as he does, except perhaps me when dealing with a medical trauma. I was frankly exhausted, truly at a loss as to what other information to impart, but he kept on, always thinking of something or referring to some obscure line in the textbook, which I think he has memorized cover to cover. I am quite certain we would still be in the room if not for Elizabeth interrupting to drag us away for the picnic.

Her brows rose dramatically at noting the book, but she said nothing. "Uncle and I were talking," William says with dry understatement, meeting

Elizabeth's glittering gaze candidly. The humorous lilt to her lovely lips was telling though, and I swear the two exchanged a full conversation without uttering a word. Marvelous!

August 7
Pemberley

Seems as if I barely arrived and now I am leaving! Not sure what came over me yesterday, but tomorrow most of us are departing, except for William and Elizabeth, who will be touring the southern Midlands. And, if I know my nephew even slightly, most likely purchasing anything remotely infant related within a fifty-mile radius.

I feel the itch to travel, but not with the same vagrancy typical of me. No, Jharna, it is not my usual restlessness. Quite the opposite, in fact. These past weeks have been so marvelous, and being at Pemberley has filled my soul with a peace I honestly have not felt in decades, even with you, my devoted lover. It is home. Perhaps I am sensing my mortality creeping up on me, not that I plan on departing this earth anytime soon. Fifty-three is far from old, I declare with shaking fist to the heavens! No, it is still this blasted sentimentality that has invaded my person. Ga!

The simple truth is that I feel the complete opposite of restless. What would that be? Calm, abeyant, satisfied? All of the above, I suppose. So, I want to take advantage of the fine weather and visit a few more old friends in London and the surrounds, and then visit Estella. All of this traveling and imposing on other's hospitality is welcomed with great anticipation, yet also because I want to be done with it and return to Pemberley before the winter and Baby Darcy is born. I planted the seed yesterday, both William and Elizabeth surprised by my hint. I do hope they take this separation to get used to the idea because I *will* deliver their child if I have to apply my brutal strength to the task and physically evict the midwife from the room! Of course, they adore me so I do not think that will be necessary. Yes, Jharna, smug as always.

Additionally, the lovers need some time alone. I swear those two are as transparent as glass. I know a gentleman should not entertain musings of another's sexual relationship, but it is nearly impossible not to do so around them! Poor Georgiana. Good thing she is used to being on her own because I seriously doubt she sees any more of her brother now then she did before! Be that as it may, they are rather cute together—awful word but it is apropos in this case—so I am casting no negative judgments. Warms the heart, actually, which is another reason I need to depart for awhile: I am becoming far too maudlin with all this romance in the air. Time for the Colonel and me to remember we are bachelors, loose and unencumbered!

Raja, I am coming to accept with equanimity and happiness, shall likely not be counted amongst the unattached for very much longer. As I have written, the affection, nay Love… call it what it is, George… is genuine between him and Miss Anne. His plan, he tells me now, is to work his charm on Lady C. I advised him just to tell her he is royalty and that will be that; but he is far too noble, wants to earn her approval on his own merits, gain respect, etc. I just laughed, slapped him on the back, and wished him well in the endeavor. So first I absolutely *have* to tarry in Kent as I would not miss this for the world!

Malcolm and Madeline are off to tour through Wales, taking Georgiana with them. Leaves the newlyweds utterly alone, which I know pleases them. They intend to take a small jaunt through the lower Midlands, William told me. He wants his wife to be familiar with her new shire. Plus I think they plan to purchase baby essentials. I thought it odd they did not denude London of every last diapering cloth or bonnet. Apparently they have chosen to strip Derby bare instead! First, however, he asks me seriously if I felt a woman in her fifth month should travel. I assured him that pregnant women are truly not all that fragile, especially with husbands who dote and fret so ridiculously. He was not particularly amused, but reassured. Besides, what can possible go wrong in my beautiful and peaceful agricultural county?

Anyway, I am off to Kent and then Darcy House for a spell before Devon. No agendas! Absolutely not! Allow the wind to carry me wherever it sees fit. Perhaps no longer restless per se, but definitely insouciant and aimless!

CHAPTER ONE

Correspondence

THE SUN HAD LONG since set. The full moon cast a pale bluish glow over the carpet and furnishings near the widely open windows of the Darcys' spacious private sitting room. It was far too warm on this late August evening to have a fire lit, but several oil lamps and candles illuminated the area near the empty fireplace. Darcy, as always, refused to grope in darkness or strain his or his wife's eyes while they read.

They reclined on the chaise, Lizzy nestled between her husband's legs with her back pressed into his bare chest. Peaceful silence surrounded them as they attended to the stack of correspondence that had accumulated during their journey south. Darcy, especially, was still working his way through the pile that seemed to grow rather than diminish as business-related items were continually added to the top.

Tonight he eschewed any business letters, choosing to read a lengthy missive from his sister while absently toying with a lock of his wife's hair. Lizzy smiled and lightly stroked her husband's cloth-covered thigh as she read a letter from her sister Jane that had arrived that day.

> *My Dearest Lizzy,*
>
> *My heart nearly stopped as you related your trauma with the bandits! Oh, dearest sister, how absolutely awful an experience! I am trembling yet*

at the horror of it and the thankfulness in your recovery. How proud of Mr. Darcy you must be! Charles was not at all surprised. I recall him tell-ing me once that Mr. Darcy was an excellent marksman. Of course I am quite certain he never anticipated his dear friend utilizing his skills so. Has Papa written you? Undoubtedly he shall relate the episode in an amusing manner, but Mama was quite taken by your mishap. Her nervous attack was of stupendous proportions. She has been abed for two days, despite your and Mr. Darcy's assurances that all was well. Papa retreated to his library as usual, appearing only to halt the mournful letter she had penned to you! Therefore you shall necessarily be required to affect commiseration when next you write to Mama.

Thank you for relating your excursion abroad the Derbyshire coun-tryside. What a marvelous idea! I must share this tidbit of humor: Charles was reading Mr. Darcy's letter as I was reading yours when suddenly he snorted in disgust. I inquired as to his concern and he recalled Mr. Darcy boring him nearly to death while in France with the endless tours of old castles and ruins. I chuckled so, dear Lizzy, as your letter expressed such joy over the adventures! Of course, I can empathize with my husband as such diversions are not appealing to me; however, I am cognizant of how you adore them, so was thrilled you two embarked on the endeavor.

If you have received a letter from Papa, then you know he accepted the news of Charles and me relocating with serenity. I know he is sad-dened, and perhaps he has communicated his distress to you; nonetheless, he understands and has given us his blessing. Mama, shockingly, was in hysterics. Oh Lizzy, it was awful! She wailed and moaned, lamenting how all her daughters have deserted her and she would never be able to kiss her grandchildren. Poor Charles was frantic. Papa took her in hand, but it was terrible. I must confess, as horrendous as your crisis, it did succeed in deflecting Mama's anxiety from me! Hopefully for both our sakes, Mary will proffer a blessed announcement forthwith to further avert Mama's absorption and cheer her spirits.

As for Charles and me, we are proceeding as planned. I do believe Charles would have packed up and departed within the week, but I have given him pause. It is a difficult move for me, Lizzy dear. You know that change is not embraced as easily by me as you. While we were yet in Derbyshire, my enthusiasm was as profound as Charles's. Now that I am home, Hertfordshire continually draws me in with all her lures and homey comforts. Yet oddly I find that with each passing day the sense of belonging, especially at Netherfield, ebbs. Charles speaks of Hasberry daily, and I am beginning to long for the charms of the house. Mostly, of course, my heart yearns to please my husband. I am so proud of his spirit and zeal as well as the serious maturity he displays in regard to this new undertaking.

Caroline has returned to London, abiding with the Hursts for the present, although I do believe she plans to holiday in Essex with a friend next month. As you and I were discussing, Caroline continues to puzzle me. Over time the worst of her disdain for me has vanished and she actually appears pleased for Charles and me in our obvious felicity. However, try as I might, we cannot establish a sisterly relationship or a particularly friendly one. I know you shrug her attitude away, Lizzy, believing me silly for fretting so, yet I persist in wishing it otherwise. The oddest part is how her personality vacillates. She spoke of her trip to Essex with a queer expression. She almost appeared dreamy and her eyes softened. Then it was as if she caught herself and rapidly followed with a snippy comment about the dreariness of Meryton. I do wish I could laugh at her as you do. Oh well, she is gone now and peace reigns.

Lizzy, I am pleased that your pregnancy progresses without complications. The nursery as you describe it sounds beautiful. Who would have thought to have clouds painted on a blue ceiling and a pastel landscape over one wall? I confess I have difficulty envisioning the scene. How ingenious of the decorator to suggest such a masterpiece! You did not, however, mention horses grazing upon the painted grasses. Charles and I immediately noted the omission and mutually decided it was an oversight on your part as assuredly Mr. Darcy would insist on horses! I am pleased to hear of the cuckoo clock finding a home where your child will grow amid the sweet music as we all did. I believe I shall have to hint of the same when the time comes for Charles and me. The lace curtains are a perfect touch. You amaze me, dearest sister, in your sudden embracing of domesticity. Knitting and sewing! Astounding! The needlepoint pillows and pictures I can comprehend, as you have ever adored embroidery, but making your own curtains? I truly must see it with mine own eyes to fully believe. I told Mama, but she thought me jesting. Perhaps the concept of babies brings out one's creativity as Caroline did complete the quilt. I must say, it is a skill-fully wrought item and beautiful. You will love it.

Charles has finished his missive to Mr. Darcy, so I shall close for now. You absolutely cannot tell Mama or Papa, but I am so very thrilled that we shall be close, Lizzy. I miss you so very much and want our children to grow dear to each other. Before I finish I must thank you for your timely advice at our last private chat. You were right in all aspects and the results are as you presupposed. We truly are the most fortunate of women in our marriages, are we not, dear sister? If only all could be so blessed. Imagine how wonderful the world would then be? I love you, Lizzy, and yearn for your companionship. Take care on your journey to the seacoast.

Always,

Your Jane

Lizzy was smiling broadly and chuckling as she refolded Jane's correspondence. "What does your sister have to say which so amused you, beloved?" Darcy asked, his voice rumbling over Lizzy's back.

"Have you read the letter from Charles yet?" she asked, turning her head to peer up into Darcy's face as he shook his head negative. "Apparently he related with disgust the reminiscences of your journey to France. You were not exaggerating as to his feelings on museums and ruins."

Darcy chuckled. "I could almost generate some pity if it were not for his avengement."

"You never did tell me the story of your waltz experiences."

"I suppose I can now see humor in the situation. Knowing the dance has benefited me most delightfully in the present, thus easing the painful memory." He paused to stroke her cheek and lean forward for a tasty kiss.

"You were saying?" Lizzy interrupted in a throaty whisper.

"I was saying?" he repeated, brushing her lips with insistence, but she withdrew with a giggle.

"About the waltz, William. You were going to tell me the story."

He sighed theatrically. "Very well then, but do not forget where we were, my lover." She solemnly nodded, eyes twinkling. "As I told you, I first danced the waltz in Vienna. When I was twenty-five, I traveled to Austria to visit my Aunt Mary. The waltz is quite popular there, and before I hardly knew what was happening, my cousins were grasping my hands and propelling me onto the floor of their music room. You need not imagine anything untoward, love. They are all quite older than me and married." Lizzy harrumphed and Darcy grinned.

He resumed, "They considered it a hideous lapse in my education to only know the stilted dances of the English. The Austrians are looser and prefer lively, intimate dances such as the tarantella, lavolta, courante, and galliard. I shall confess that I actually enjoyed myself and, risking the label of arrogant, I learned quickly and was quite excellent! As you now are aware, I do find dancing pleasant, provided I am familiar and comfortable with my partner." He kissed her nose, stroking along her neck. "In Vienna I reluctantly was induced to dance a few times at the balls we attended, although I refused other than my aunt or cousins. They thought that was hysterical and teased me mercilessly."

Lizzy laughed. "Ah, the poor broken hearts extend all across Europe. Those woeful Austrian ladies with their sad faces moping despondently about the ballroom."

Darcy reddened but snorted. "Unlikely, Elizabeth." Lizzy smiled, again amused at how innocent and obtuse he was in regards to his attributes and allure. "Anyway, two years later Bingley and I were in Paris at a soiree hosted by the Comte and Comtesse Petain. I did not wish to attend, not surprisingly, but Bingley adores such entertainments and despite his allusions to the contrary, I was perceptive to his annoyance and remorseful for dragging him along on my adventures. During dinner the conversation turned to the ball and the anticipation for the waltz. Bingley, sweet, seemingly scrupulous Bingley, manipulated the topic masterfully. Within minutes the entire table accounted me a veritable waltz virtuoso, and I was slated to dance with five ladies, three of whom were the Comte's excessively homely daughters!"

Lizzy was laughing so hard she could barely breathe. Darcy shuddered in memory but then laughed as well. "He completely blindsided me. I do confess it was rather inspired maneuvering, and his goal of humiliating me worked brilliantly."

"Did you trip or forget the steps?"

"Very amusing, Mrs. Darcy. No, I did not. I was graceful and flawless." He grinned. "So elegant and debonair that I believe it is fortunate we departed the next day as I may have caused the entire assemblage to fall madly in love with me."

He meant to elicit further laughter, but she smiled into his eyes instead and caressed his cheek. "Yes, I am sure they did. A host of broken hearts once again." She pulled him down for a deep kiss, Darcy happily complying. The spell was broken when he reached to embrace her waist and Georgiana's letter, still clutched in his left hand, crumpled against the swell of her belly.

"Oh dear!" he exclaimed, "I should finish this before mutilating it."

"What does she have to say?"

"You must read it, dearest. Of course, it is addressed to you as well. She is having a marvelous trip. When she dispatched this, they were at Aunt Madeline's brother's home in Rhayader. I believe they have probably moved on from there to Aberystwyth by now, but she says the mansion is enormous with all sorts of secret passageways, unused wings, a bell tower, and supposedly a ghost from the twelfth century. Listen: 'Suzette,'—one of the cousins—'declares with firm belief that the ghost is a woman who died from a suspicious fall from the bell tower. She swears, brother, that she has seen her gliding about the north wing with flowing robes of white and a sad face. I asked why all ghosts are required to wear white. Is it a metaphysical law of some sort? Suzette did not find my cheekiness amusing. Needless to say, I have not seen this ghost, although despite my skepticism, I do not intend to wander the empty corridors in the dead of night—this being, naturally, according to those laws previously mentioned, the only time the ghost will appear!'"

Chuckling, Darcy paused. Lizzy read ahead to the following paragraph, asking, "Who is this Lord Gruffudd that she mentions horseback riding with?"

Darcy frowned. "A Welshman who lives in the vicinity and is obviously close friends with Mr. Dawes, Madeline's brother. That is the fourth time she has noted his presence involved in some activity partaken. Why would she remark about an old neighbor?"

"Perhaps he is not old. You came into your inheritance young, as do others sadly. Maybe she is smitten. Did you read this? 'Lord Gruffudd is nearly as excellent a rider as you, dear brother. You always told me that a person born in the saddle is instantly recognized. Lord Gruffudd has such a demeanor. It was an entertaining ride about the moor with all in high spirits despite the drizzling mist as Lord Gruffudd's wit and humor is enlivening.' Sounds like a wee crush to me!"

Lizzy giggled, glancing to Darcy. Her laughter froze at the thunderous expression on his face. His eyes skimmed over the remaining two pages, counting Lord Gruffudd's name five more times ere her best wishes and signature. Lizzy opened her mouth to ask what was wrong, but the words failed when Darcy abruptly launched from the chaise as if sprung. Her jaw clamped shut from the sudden jolt as she fell into the space vacated by his absent body, sprawled into a bizarre angle.

Darcy commenced pacing as if caged, muttering and clenching his fists. As typical when deeply disturbed or perplexed, he ended by a far window, staring sightlessly. Lizzy struggled up from the chaise, approaching him cautiously. "William, whatever is the matter?"

He did not glance to her, shaking his head brusquely before responding in a flat, icy tone. "I never should have let her go. It is my duty to protect her from such things, and I allowed my selfishness to overrule my reason."

"I do not understand, dearest. What 'things' are you concerned about? She is having a delightful time, and so what if she has an infatuation? She will be eighteen in two weeks. It is rather normal for a girl her age to notice a handsome man, assuming that is even the case here."

Darcy pivoted her direction, the anger and self-loathing on his face propelling her backward a pace. "Need I remind you how the last infatuation she experienced concluded? Think, Elizabeth! I am aware it was before your time; however, surely you know enough of the details to comprehend why I do not wish for her to suffer such heartache again?"

Lizzy's anger flared and she placed her hands onto her hips, answering him with equal vigor. "Do not talk to me that way, Mr. Darcy! Georgiana has shared all her emotions of the Ramsgate affair with me, probably to a degree not even shared with you, but that is beside the point. You are being idiotic to equate a few mentions in a letter with the Wickham incident, and you grievously insult both your sister, who is far wiser than you give credit, and your aunt and uncle!"

"Idiotic? Really?"

"That is the least harsh term I could conjure." She crossed her arms and cocked her head slightly, a tiny smile lifting her lips at the sight of her husband attempting to glower and rage while dressed in naught but his breeches. "What truly bothers you, love? That she may experience a mild heartbreak or that she is admiring a man besides her idolized older brother?"

"That is ridiculous, Elizabeth." His denial was speedy, but the tone betrayed him. He glanced back out the window, avoiding her eyes, and ran one hand through his hair. "I feel helpless so far from her. What if she needs me? What if he is a scoundrel? What if…? Aach! I shall go insane!" He dropped his hands futilely to his sides.

Lizzy smiled, planting herself squarely in front of him and placing her palms onto his chest. "I think you are worrying for nothing, William. Georgiana will not be leaving us anytime soon, although it shall happen in due course so you must prepare yourself for the eventuality." He grunted, staring over her head, but he did clasp her waist with both hands. "I promise I shall forever idolize you and need you, my husband. I will even endeavor to do something stupid now and again so you can protect me! That way you shall never feel worthless." She smiled dazzlingly, Darcy unable to maintain his vexation. With a sigh and faint chuckle he embraced her, deciding with effort to relinquish his fear and trust his uncle and aunt, although he did hastily dispatch a sternly worded response.

❧

Dear William and Elizabeth,

Greetings from Devon! Yes, I finally made it, warning Estella of my pending arrival a whole five days ere I barged in. Forgive me for not writing sooner, although I have no excuse for having not done so other than my raging irresponsibility. I trust you both adore me, worship the ground I walk upon adequately so as to not require I fabricate false pretexts or humility. In fact, be overjoyed as this will likely be the only correspondence you receive from me! In an attempt to placate, I shall endeavor to make it an extensive one with witticisms and information. Here goes:

The ride was uneventful, as you undoubtedly have heard from Col. Fitzwilliam or Mr. Bingley or Miss de Bourgh, all whom are likely to have written prior to me. We tarried at Netherfield for two days. It has been longer than I can recall since I visited Hertfordshire. Elizabeth, your home Shire is lovely. Like William, Derbyshire will always be dearest to my heart, but the lush farms of Hertfordshire are beautiful. Meryton so reminded me of Lambton that I had the most annoying sensation of déjà vu! We dined with your parents, Elizabeth. I must say again how delightful I find your father! Capital fellow. Quite an impressive library for so small a room. Be prepared, William, as he is chomping at the bit to ramble through Pemberley's bookshelves. Your mother, Elizabeth, bless her heart, seemed all atwitter by my presence. Odd, as I rarely have such an effect on folks, being so calm and serene of spirit.

Lizzy and Darcy snorted simultaneously at this blatant falsehood.

I did my best to be charming and endearing, and believe I succeeded as she actually smiled and blushed when I said my adieus. I seem to have this effect on women despite my attempts to submerge my natural magnetism. It is a Darcy trait, do you not agree, William?

Only Lizzy snorted at this point, Darcy nudging her in the ribs.

Leaving Hertfordshire we leisurely drove to Kent. Miss de Bourgh did not strike me as being too anxious to return home. She continues to thrive, her color improving daily, even the trip not upsetting her health. Raja is thrilled. I do hope you have no qualms as to the nature of the relationship between him and your cousin, William? I know how dear she is to you. I shall confess that initially I was concerned as it is not an unusual phenomenon for patients to become enamored with their physicians. Happens to me all the time! Ha!! Seriously, as the weeks progressed, I have realized that Raul's feelings are genuine. Thus, my greatest concern was that Miss Anne's feelings may not be reciprocal and that my dear friend would be hurt. I no longer entertain this notion, as I have seen the affection between the two.

Now here is the fun part! We arrived at Rosings, Lady Catherine as enchanting as always.

"I cannot imagine my aunt ever being enchanting," Darcy grunted, Lizzy opting not to respond beyond nodding her head.

Raja and I were ignored. Col. Fitzwilliam and Miss de Bourgh were both embarrassed, bless their souls, by our obvious slighting, but Raja and I found it highly amusing. I do not think either of you grew to know Dr. Penaflor well, but let me assure you, the man has a backbone to rival even you, William. We settled at the inn in Ashford, happy to bide our time for one evening. Raja, however, had a plan with no intention of being waylaid. I do not know all the details, but it was clear to me by this point that he and Miss de Bourgh had reached an agreement of sorts. I know he has not formally proposed. You see, formality and propriety are vitally essential to a man such as Raul Penaflor and nothing short of a proper courtship will do.

Lizzy interrupted to envy the fortunate Anne in enjoying a regular court-ship as befits a lady. Darcy replied that courtships are a waste of time, Anne preferring to just get married and skip to the fun part. He grinned salaciously, eyes raking over her body, which raised a blush to her cheeks and halted any further snappy comments.

You two may not quite understand Raja's circumstance. He was raised in the courts of Madrid and Palencia. His blood is as blue as it gets and his wealth transcends yours, William; radically transcends. I honestly do not know how affluent he is, but I have gathered much and it is extensive. Additionally, his connections are superb. I do not think any of these facts interest Miss de Bourgh in the least, but Lady Catherine is another matter entirely. However, I am getting ahead of myself in the tale.

So, day two: We are invited, by Miss de Bourgh, to dine. She is showing strength beyond merely physical and I do not judge Lady Catherine is wholly pleased by that development. Nonetheless, we arrived for dinner to the sweet charm of Miss Anne, the booming effervescence of Col. Fitzwilliam, who I believe intended to stay around at the risk of court-martial for abandoning his post rather than miss the spectacle and the sour disposition of Lady Catherine.

Darcy laughed aloud, certain that this was about the truth-knowing Richard and his delight in subtly tormenting his aunt.

Most delightful dinner engagement I have ever been a part of! Lady Catherine had invited her vicar, Mr. Collins, and his wife. Lovely woman, Mrs. Collins, but more on her later. Her husband, however, I am sure was included on the dinner list as an ally in the anti-foreigner and strange distant relative front.

Lizzy's comment on Mr. Collins shall not be repeated here.

Dinner itself went well enough. The food was marvelous, Raul and Miss Anne made doe eyes at each other throughout, Lady Catherine's face pruned increasingly, Rev. Collins waxed philosophical on the virtues of chastity and morality, Mrs. Collins and Col. Fitzwilliam and I hid our smiles, and the palpable tension nearly manifested physically. As I said, it was stupendous!

As we rose from the table, Raja requested to speak alone with Lady Catherine. She demurred, pointedly stating that anything he wished to say could be said in front of us all. I tried to have the good grace to look embarrassed, but simply could not muster the emotion. Raja was prepared for any eventuality, so her presumptive hope to unman him failed. Upon arrival in the parlor, he boldly asserted himself, Miss Anne sitting with quiet grace but steady strength. I think I can closely relate the entire conversation:

'Lady Catherine,' Dr. Penaflor began, 'I am sure you are aware that Miss de Bourgh and I have grown friendly over the course of our acquaintance. Although initially my interest was as a physician and strictly professional, I soon realized that my respect and admiration for her as a person had risen. With each passing day I am amazed at the intelligence, kindness, grace, and humor that are only a fragment of the positive attributes that your daughter possesses. I am beyond fortunate to have met her and would appreciate your permission to formally court her with the definitive intention of securing her hand in matrimony when, or if, she deems me worthy of her.'

"Very well done," Darcy murmured. "Yes," Lizzy responded, "well thought out as all the right things a girl needs to hear to render an affirmative response to a proposal." She laughed, patting her husband's red cheek.

'That is a wonderful speech, Dr. Penaflor. What assurance can you offer me that any of it is the truth?'

'Time, Lady Catherine, will prove the truth of my words. I am honorable and a gentleman. I would not state such praise in the presence of a lady without fully meaning it; however, I shall take no offense as you do not know me well. Therefore, time and permission to intrude upon your home is requested so all parties involved can feel certain of the relationship.'

'Tell me, Dr. Penaflor, as a gentleman claiming to care for my daughter, do you account a mere doctor as adequate to husband the daughter of a lady?'

'I suppose the answer depends on what you consider an adequate husband. My profession, my lady, is of no import in regards to my love for her, and my desire to ensure her happiness and welfare. That comes from my

heart. If you are referring to monetary issues, I assure you I can more than adequately provide for her needs.'

'What you really mean is that in marrying her you will not have to worry about money!'

'Mother!' Miss de Bourgh declared, but Lady Catherine and Dr. Penaflor ignored her.

'What I mean, Lady Catherine, is precisely what I said. I can more than adequately provide for her needs.'

'How do you expect to do that on a doctor's income? I do not know what the status of physicians is in Spain, but in England they barely scrape a living!'

'Lady Catherine, allow me to make several things perfectly clear for all our sakes. First, I am proud of my chosen profession and will make no apologies for it. I am not a doctor for the financial benefits, although I do not see that aspect as bleakly as you do. Secondly, Miss de Bourgh is a great lady and as such deserves only the best. If I did not think I could provide this, I would not offer, no matter my feelings. You asked if a mere doctor was worthy of your daughter and I would concur that the honest answer in light of English societal mores would be no. My personal opinions of this fact are inconsequential as I have qualification beyond my calling.'

'What sort of qualification could a vagabond from Spain possibly possess?'

Raul smiled, glancing to Miss de Bourgh and then to me. Here comes the humorous part, but I also know Raja, and he abhors touting his connections. Few know anything beyond that he is a Spaniard. 'Lady Catherine, my father is Duke Manuel Penaflor Aleman de Vigo. My mother is now the Duchess de Vigo, but was born an Infanta of the royal house.'

He went on for quite a bit, outlining all the various interconnections in his family, none of which I can unravel and remember. All the while Lady Catherine's face was paling further. Frankly, I drifted off for a spell as I always do when Raja elaborates on his family relationships. I was brought to wakefulness by the blessed sound of utter silence. Now, Elizabeth dear, do not read this next part as I intend to reveal my evil nature, and as you esteem me nearly god-like in your adoration, I would hate to burst your bubble.

Lizzy dissolved into laughter, wiping tears from her eyes as she gasped, "Oh William, I so adore your uncle!" Darcy smiled, offering his handkerchief.

William, your aunt was white as a ghost and stammering inarticulate noises. Col. Fitzwilliam was red as a beet in an attempt to not laugh, Mrs. Collins stared into her lap with magnetic intensity, Rev. Collins was gazing at Raul with pure worship, and Miss de Bourgh was glowing with pride. I am quite certain he could have dropped to one knee and secured her hand on the spot. Anyway, I could not tear my eyes from Lady Catherine. I have rarely known such joy! She was completely at a loss for words, so I bluntly filled the gap.

'Well, Catherine, seems to me that Dr. Penaflor outranks you. My, my, my. What shall you do? Cannot very well withhold consent to a genuine royal, can you?' Yes, yes! I enjoyed myself immensely and could only wish with all my being that James were there. Lord, how he disliked Anne's sister!

Well, there you have it. I know you continued to read, Elizabeth, so can only pray you still love me and want these hands to deliver your baby. Lady Catherine eventually consented to Raul's courtship and I departed two days later for London, leaving Raja to his pursuits. Have not heard from him since but suppose I shall need to find a new associate. Col. Fitzwilliam accompanied me, and we two bachelors managed to have a bit of fun ere my departure to Devon. Do not worry, William, Mrs. Smyth would not allow me to ransack Darcy House too profoundly. It remains largely intact.

"Better be or there shall be hell to pay," Darcy murmured with a smile. Lizzy was dazedly imagining the vision of a pestered and flustered Mrs. Smyth with no small amount of pleasure.

The family here in Honiton greets you both. They have nothing but praise for Elizabeth, to all of which I wholeheartedly concur, and entreat me to send their congratulations on your blessing. I do pray your child is half as adorable as Cousin Nicole's two. They have the roundest brown eyes and are simply sweet enough to eat! Naturally they love me and I am having a marvelous time. However, I will return to Pemberley in late September, or sometime in there. I deem it only polite to visit with Mrs. Smyth again for a spell as I am sure she misses me greatly. I do hope all is well with you both. Enjoy your holiday at the seaside. Oh, I nearly forgot! Mrs. Collins's pregnancy is progressing nicely, not that we spoke of it, naturally, but I could readily discern that all was well. She is a delightful woman. So warm and humorous. She spoke of you, Elizabeth, with tremendous affection. We had no opportunity to speak privately, not that this would have been appropriate, but I wanted you to know her status.

With deepest regard and love to you both,

George, alias Dr. Darcy for you, Elizabeth

Darcy was grinning as he folded the letter. Glancing into his wife's dreamy face, he reached to brush the backs of his fingers over a velvet cheek. "Do not fear, love. I am positive our baby shall be the loveliest on the face of the earth."

Lizzy laughed, turning to kiss his knuckles. "Yes, surely. However, I was lost in the delicious vision of a harried Mrs. Smyth." She sighed deeply, an evil twinkle in her eyes.

Darcy assumed a stern face, although his eyes twinkled as well. "How unbecoming of you, Elizabeth Darcy. I am aghast."

Lizzy merely laughed further while Darcy rose to deposit the letter onto his desk. They sat in his study, the late afternoon August sun blazing through the open windows. No breeze was forthcoming and had not been for days upon days, therefore the room was stifling. Lizzy wore the thinnest dress she could find, refusing a petticoat thicker than the sheer muslin one, which meant that her legs did show slightly, but she was tolerably cool. She observed her husband, dressed to the nines although in a light kerseymere, and wondered for the thousandth time how he could appear so comfortable. Not even a sheen of sweat along his brow. Of course, Darcy was perpetually collected and calm.

"I certainly enjoyed your uncle's version of events over Miss de Bourgh's," Lizzy said. "Although the emotion in her letter was so touching."

"Yes," Darcy replied from his desk chair where he was rifling through a stack of folded parchment envelopes, "and, if you recall, my dearest, she expressed her wish to forgo the long courtship and hasten to the marriage part."

"She did not!"

"I beg to differ. Ah! Here it is." He fluttered the pages with a flourish, smirking at his wife, and then clearing his throat as if preparing to address Parliament. "She writes, and I quote, 'In the end Mother did consent to allow

Dr. Penaflor the right to court me. Oh William! I cannot express my happiness. I must thank you for encouraging me to follow my heart and to trust. I have no doubts regarding my feelings toward Dr. Penaflor and know he feels as strongly. Love at nearly first sight! I never anticipated this happening to me. Honestly I had relinquished all hope of finding love and cannot repress the trepidation that I shall wake to discover it is all a dream. I appreciate Dr. Penaflor's design to court me properly and comprehend it derives from his esteem; however, I must confess a desire to hasten time. Is this selfish of me, William? My life has altered drastically these past three months, and my joy is nearly complete. Suddenly my wildest wishes are within my grasp, and I am aware that the natural womanly response is to revel in the season of wooing and flirtation. Nonetheless, my greatest urge is to be married to sweet Raul and begin our life together.'"

Lizzy assumed a haughty pout in the face of Darcy's smug grin. "Very well, Mr. Darcy. I shall admit my error; however, I detect only the yearning to be bonded in matrimony and no allusion to 'fun' as you so called it."

"The fun is implied, love."

Lizzy laughed and shook her head, turning to another letter waiting on the table. "Shall I read Papa's letter aloud?"

"It is addressed to you, Elizabeth. You can share with me later if you wish as I must currently attend to this boring albeit necessary business packet from Mr. Daniels."

Thereafter, in quiet harmony they concentrated on their individual undertakings while ever with an unconscious awareness of the other's presence.

My dearest Lizzy,

My beloved daughter, why do you insist on exponentially whitening my hair even further? When you were two years of age, you toddled outside and narrowly avoided falling into the duck pond, saved by Mr. Hill, who happened to be walking by. From that day onward, my precocious second daughter, I awaited the day when some brave man would assume caretaking duties, allotting me the opportunity to breathe freely. Overall I judge Mr. Darcy has adequately fulfilled the role, but armed bandits? Heavens, child!

Naturally I maintained my equilibrium, trusting in your assurance that you and the babe are well. Your mother, however, dissolved into nervous prostration, taking to her bed in a near swoon. Kitty attended to her with a diligence that surprised me. I confess to retreating to my study, having divined ages ago that my presence is in no way placating. Suffer no guilt, my dear girl, as you know your mother fairly wallows in her misery. Dear Jane was secretly relieved, as your trauma diverted her mother's flustering over their relocation.

Luckily, fortune smiled on us all as joyous news was forthcoming. I will proceed in the hope that the latest Bennet blessing is revealed by me. Three days after receiving your missive, your mother yet abed, I was visited by Mr. Joshua Daniels. As you likely have already postulated, he rode to Hertfordshire to obtain permission to wed our Mary. Naturally I deemed it my right and duty as father of the intended to toy with him a bit, make him sweat, as they say. I daresay he reacted with far greater amusement than either Mr. Bingley or Mr. Darcy. Mr. Bingley was simply too befuddled to even ask my permission for Jane's hand, an oversight I reluctantly judged merciful in light of the general mayhem of that day. Mr. Darcy, of course, captured me utterly unaware. My usually rapid mental faculties were dulled by surprise and the ungodly hour of the day. If I did not know the truth of the situation, I would hazard to guess he planned it that way! Besides, he was so disarmingly charming and pathetic that I could not muster the heart to trifle with his frayed emotions. Well, not too much anyway.

Mr. Daniels, on the other hand, was an expectation. Via correspondence from your Uncle Gardiner, I knew the courtship was progressing at a stately pace so rightly figured it was merely a matter of time. I did not anticipate his arrival on that particular day, but was prepared for the eventuality. In the end, of course, I gave my blessing as I fully intended to do all along. He is a delightful young man and I have no doubts will care for our Mary. By the way, thank your husband for his personal endorsement of and information about the young solicitor. Having not had the luxury of acquainting ourselves with him to any great degree, your mother and I are eased by Mr. Darcy's recommendation. Of course, Edward and Violet have become quite familiar and praise him glowingly. Mary is prosaic in her commentary, but there is an underlying emotion that belies her conservative pose. All in all, we are delighted with her choice.

I do not know when they plan to wed, nor where. I chose not to question Mr. Daniels on the particulars as I had no desire to have the boy faint in my study! London would be my guess, although Mary is very fond of our vicar and the Meryton Chapel. I have not yet heard from Mary as all this transpired just yesterday. So, it has been an eventful two weeks between the Bingleys' news, your adventure, and Mary's engagement. I almost, for once, pity your mother's theatrically fraught nerves. Now, luckily for us all, she has rebounded and nearly has the wedding all planned. Or at least I am assuming so as that is all she speaks of. I, as I can only confess to you, my dear Lizzy, ignore her most awfully.

Well, there you have it! Life at Longbourn treads on with the usual undulating waves consisting of valleys of monotony and peaks of drama. I have resigned myself to Jane's departure with equanimity. In truth I have long suspected they would move and am thrilled for them. We do look forward to visiting, if you will have us, at some point this winter. I must see if the Pemberley library is all I have been led to believe it is, and we wish to tour Hasberry and Pemberley. Of course, the premiere draw will be my first grandchild. Yes, Lizzy, even beyond the library!

Please take care of yourself, my darling daughter. Dr. Darcy said your pregnancy is proceeding without mishap, and as he appears determined to attend the birth, I am greatly comforted. Nonetheless, I know you, Lizzy! Do not be foolish. Rest and listen to your husband, who I know has far greater sense and wisdom than you.

With all my love,

Papa

Darcy had diligently applied himself to Mr. Daniels's correspondence, but was fully aware of his wife's constant chuckles. Therefore, he was not the slightest bit surprised when she jumped out of her seat and crossed to his desk.

"You must read this, William!"

He took the proffered letter and sat back with a contented sigh, his father-in-law's writing always amusing. Lizzy rang for refreshments, it having been over two hours since lunch and the baby demanded nourishment. She stood by the window, rubbing her belly while their son somersaulted, and watched Darcy's face as he read.

He smiled, laughed, and grunted precisely as she knew he would during certain sentences, adding an occasional comment. "Brave am I? Yes, that is true… Poor Mr. Daniels!… Pathetic? Well, I suppose so… 'Not too much' he says! The man tortured and terrified me… Hmmm… You are welcome, Mr. Bennet… There shall be the test, my love. I will have you and our son stand across from the library door and see where he goes first… Ha! 'Greater sense and wisdom.' From the mouth of your father. Surely you cannot argue with that?" He grinned up at his wife, who ignored the query.

Mary's correspondence arrived three days later. Lizzy sat on the terrace, fanning herself and praying for a breeze, no matter how faint. Darcy was at the stables. On occasion Lizzy would accompany him for a spell, but today he planned to assist with breaking a horse, and Lizzy absolutely refused to watch. The process terrified her and she fretted all day while he was at the endeavor. Darcy knew her fears and generally evaded elaborating on his planned activities, but if she pointedly inquired, he would not lie. He deplored worrying her but could not resist the lure of the corral. Lizzy recognized his love for the work so attempted to hide her anxiety and disapproval, learning it best to not ask his agenda for the day.

Therefore, it was painfully obvious when he was to train! If Darcy's docket included riding about the farms, or visiting a fishery or mill, or checking on the breeding proceedings, he was open in sharing, giving her a complete rundown of his time so she would know precisely where he was and when he expected to return. If, on the other hand, he remained mum or became vague, she knew it meant a day of vigorous and dangerous exercise with a wild horse.

Such had been the case this morning. He woke her early, the sun barely illuminating the room. Lizzy groaned and vainly attempted to ignore the sweet kisses being rained along her shoulder and the insistent hands roaming freely. Her husband, however, was in a mood and, as was generally the case, finagled matters to arrive at the outcome he wanted. Afterwards, just as a blissfully content and tingly Lizzy was drifting back into sleep, she asked groggily, "What are your plans for the day? Are you staying with me or going for a ride?"

She could tell instantly by the silence and slight stiffening of his body that the news was unfavorable. Darcy was a terrible liar and even after all this time had yet to arrive at a plausible alibi. "I shall be riding, yes, then I… have business with Mr. Thurber and… um, well, boring… issues to attend to, and… I do not know when I shall return, but certainly for dinner, my love, so do not worry. I love you."

Now, staring at the rippling water of the lake, Lizzy sighed deeply and gave up on her prayers for a cooling wind. A sudden burst of restlessness consumed her and, grabbing her bonnet, she rose to her feet, deciding that a walk among the trees was essential. She pivoted to the door, nearly colliding with the maid.

"Forgive me, madam. I was bringing these to you." She held out two envelopes. "The post just arrived."

"Thank you, Abigail. Could you please inform Mrs. Reynolds that I will be walking the north trail to the rock pond?"

The trail leading to the pond skirted the edge of the forest. The canopy of leaves coupled with the perpetually damp loam of the floor created a significantly cooler atmosphere. Lizzy immediately perked up under the shade, rejuvenated to the point of adequately relinquishing the unrelenting angst over Darcy's employment. Sitting on one of the artistically arranged and sheltered rock benches beside the pond's rim, Lizzy removed her shoes and commenced reading.

Dear Lizzy,

I am sincerely praying that my news will reach your ears via my pen rather than Papa's. Although, in the end it matters naught as long as you are made aware of a fabulous occurrence. For cert it shall be no great marvel to you as I have spoken of little else in each letter I have sent. Yes, dear sister, naturally I speak of me and Mr. Daniels. He has proposed! I feel as if I should insert the caveat "finally" although in truth our courtship has advanced speedily. Odd, is it not, how when the correct mate appears it simply fits? I imagine it must have been the same with you and Mr. Darcy as your relationship transpired in short order. Of course, you know I tend to not be gushy or emotional by nature, but Mr. Daniels does elicit sensations of tenderness and whimsy unfamiliar in me. Now I comprehend at least some of the ridiculous expressions you would share with Mr. Darcy. Hopefully we are not as nonsensical. Anyway, I should describe the proposal as all my new women friends are consistently inquiring, so I have deduced it is of vital interest to others.

I have ascertained that Mr. Daniels, albeit sensible and serious, does have a romantic disposition and can be mildly impatient. Therefore, it was of no great surprise that he rode off to Hertfordshire, unbeknownst to me, and asked Papa for my hand. Is that not sweet? Apparently Papa teased him a bit but eventually gave his consent.

That evening, just two days ago now, Mr. Daniels arrived for dinner, having conspired with Aunt and Uncle to secure a span of time alone with me. I was momentarily shocked when first Aunt left the room, followed ten minutes later by Uncle, both mumbling something vague in excuse. Naturally I am not totally dull and presumed his intent before he dropped to his knee. Oh, Lizzy, it was so very cute! Mr. Daniels, if you recall, is quite bashful in general; however, we have reached a place of relative ease with each other. So, to see him blushing and stammering was fairly amusing. I maintained my calm and waited in serene silence until he finally (and here the word applies) blurted out the actual words, "Will you marry me?"

Oh the urge to laugh! However, I did not. Despite the humor of the situation I was, and am, deeply moved and exceedingly content. I said yes, obviously, and tried to get him off his knee, but he stubbornly remained until the ring was secure on my finger. Now it is official. His family is delighted. They, I say with a slight blush, adore me. I truly care for them as well. We have yet to decide the wedding details. I wanted to write you as soon as possible. Lizzy, as generally unromantic and stoic as I am, I want you to know how blissful I am. Also, I want to thank you and Mr. Darcy most profoundly. The sequence of events that led Mr. Daniels to my side is all because of you two. I shall be eternally grateful, and I know Mr. Daniels feels the same. He wishes to thank Mr. Darcy as well and asked me to convey his heartfelt gratitude, as it would be inappropriate, his words, to personally write to a client.

One point we are mutually firm on is dating the wedding for after your baby's birth as we insist on the presence of you and Mr. Darcy. Probably mid to late February if this seems feasible for you? We need the time to plan as Mr. Daniels intends to purchase a house for us and I wish to spend a few more months in Hertfordshire. I will keep you informed. I hope all is well with you and the baby. Please take care, Lizzy. Give my sincerest regards to Mr. Darcy. I know Georgiana is traveling so have written to her via Pemberley. Feel free to share my news if you write to her prior to her return. I love you, Lizzy.

God Bless,

Mary

Lizzy reread the letter several times. Partly this was due to her overwhelming joy in her sister's good fortune. Additionally it was due to a lack of enthusiasm toward reading the second letter.

It was from Lydia.

Lydia had written to Lizzy exactly four times, including this one, since riding off with Mr. Wickham to Newcastle nearly one year ago. Lizzy had written a dozen times, considered it her duty to do so, but in all honesty did not exalt in her sister's responses. Aside from the fact that she and her flighty youngest sister had never been tremendously akin, there was the uncomfortable reality of Lydia's marriage and current living situation that drove a deeper wedge between them. Lydia's letters were typical of her personality: self-centered, erratic, and unintelligent. Top that with incessant references to "my dear Wickham" and Lizzy was nauseous and headachy each time.

To make matters worse, it was the only area of her life she did not share with Darcy. He knew that she wrote to Lydia and was aware that she received the occasional reply; however, he never asked for details. He wished no ill upon Lydia in her marriage. Rather he harbored extreme guilt over the arrangement, knowing it was his involvement that shackled her to Wickham, even though there was no alternative as she had flatly refused to leave her "sweet Wickham's" side.

Darcy told Lizzy, much later, that his original plan was to use all the considerable means at his disposal to hush the scandal and restore Lydia to her family. Wickham was perfectly amenable to taking the money Darcy offered and disappearing, but Lydia refused to leave. He could not very well drag her away kicking and screaming, although it had crossed his mind, but then the scandal would be far more difficult to smother.

Furthermore, it had not taken Wickham long after his initial shock at seeing Darcy materialize with Lydia's Uncle Gardiner to realize Darcy's involvement in the situation was attributed to an attachment to Lizzy Bennet. The two men had known each other for too many years. Wickham uncannily deciphered the puzzle no matter how bland and uncommunicative Darcy attempted to be. Therefore Darcy had been forced to increase the sum offered Wickham in order to secure him marrying her, a step Wickham patently had no previous intention of taking. Even then, Darcy had worried that he would not follow through while simultaneously praying that he would run away and save Lydia the sad fate of being his wife.

During Lizzy and Darcy's engagement the topic had come up only once in a rebuttal to Mrs. Bennet discussing the guest list. Darcy bluntly stated that under no circumstance was Wickham to be invited to the wedding. Mrs. Bennet had moaned and dithered, muttering uncharitable comments about Mr. Darcy's character until Lizzy nearly snapped, saved only by her father steering her mother out of the room for a stern lashing. It was awful, increasingly so by the intense distress and anger of Darcy. Of course, the whole episode was unnecessary as Lydia was far too involved in her own affairs to bother traveling the distance to her sister's wedding, nor would Wickham have endured Darcy's ire.

Upon the receipt of Lydia's first correspondence after Lizzy's marriage, a full one month after in fact, Lizzy finally heard the entire story of Darcy's search for Wickham and Lydia. Her husband's lingering pain over the situation, remorse for being unable to rescue Lydia, and hatred toward Wickham was profound. Reliving the episode was tortuous, augmented by a residual grief due to his belief at the time that Elizabeth was beyond his reach. The last pieces of the mystery were revealed. They hugged, kissed, and made love, then vowed to never speak of it again.

It was not that Darcy refused to utter Wickham's or Lydia's name or hear them spoken in his presence; he merely preferred to avoid the topic. Therefore, Lizzy chose to facilitate tranquility and impede any suffering touching her husband by hiding the letters received and never mentioning her sister. Fortunately it was not a difficult chore, but she still hated anything remotely secretive between her and her spouse.

"Quit stalling, Lizzy," she chided herself, opening the letter with a sigh.

Dear Lizzy,

You are pregnant! Oh Lizzy, I completely forgot. I was cleaning out my desk and ran across one of your letters, how do you have the time to write so much, Lizzy? Unbelievable! Anyway, I reread it and remembered. Congratulations! You are happy, are you? You said you were and I am sure Mr. Darcy wishes for an heir. I do not think I am at all ready to have a baby. Growing fat and being sick, oh how horrible! I do hope that does not happen to you, Lizzy. Of course you are far thinner than me so maybe it shall not affect you so. The Major's wife had her third baby six months ago, three! Can you imagine? Anyway, she is still huge, poor dear. I heard she was about my size once, so I fear that could be my fate! My dear Wickham is in no hurry to have babies, so I need not concern myself yet. So are you feeling well? Have you been sick? I do pray the delivery goes well. I hear people die when having babies! Of course Mama had no problems so hopefully you will take after her. I daresay you and Mr. Darcy desire a male? Yes? I am doing fantastically! Newcastle is a huge city, Lizzy! There are so many diversions here. The parks are beautiful, the seashore is near although far too cold this far to the north, the shopping is fantastic, and the theater is amazing! Better than London, most people say. I adore all the parties. Lizzy, the dancing is frequent and so delightful. Balls nearly every Saturday! I have made so many friends. There are so many Scots here! They talk with a strange accent, a burr it is called, and they are big and sweaty usually. Scary but intriguing. My dear Wickham is busy so often, spends so many nights working, poor darling. His superiors torture him! Work, work, work all the time. He comes home at the wee hours of the morning tired and mussed up. Luckily my lady friends keep me entertained. Everyone is so kind! I never lack for dancing partners as the officers sympathize with my sweet Wickham's absence, poor baby! You would think that working such long hours would mean he is paid more, yet we barely manage to survive! He tries so hard, my dear husband, but there is only so much one man can do. He does try to win at the tables on occasion, just to augment our income, you understand, but the scoundrels cheat so here! Of course, you do not have to worry about money! So fortunate. Mama wrote about your fine carriage and jewels and gowns. My George said it is expected as a Darcy and that Mr. Darcy would have it no other way. Well, do not worry about me, Lizzy. I admit I envy you just a small bit! Nonetheless, I am happy with my friends and my dear Wickham. See, it all turned out wonderfully despite Mr. Darcy and Uncle fretting so. Oh, I hear my dear George downstairs! I must close now, Lizzy. I know you will write me soon. You are so good! I do not know how you find the time. I thought being Mistress of Pemberley would keep you occupied. My Wickham says it is probably because Mr. Darcy does all the work himself and does not trust you to do anything. I do not believe this as I know how bright you are, but do not tell him I disagree! Give my best to Mr. Darcy. I love you, Lizzy!

> *Your sister,*
> *Lydia Wickham*

"Oh Lydia, you silly, naïve fool," Lizzy whispered, folding the letter slowly. She retrieved a handkerchief from her pocket to dab at teary eyes, rubbing her thumb gently over the parchment while losing herself in sad musings. With head bowed and thoughts drifting, she did not note the faint crunch of boot heels on sandy path.

"Elizabeth? Are you well?"

She glanced up, mildly startled, but recognizing her husband's voice instantly. He stood a couple feet away, the sun blocked by an exceedingly tall body thus throwing his face into shadow. The tone of concern was unmistakable, however, even without visualizing the creases between furrowed brows.

Lizzy smiled, brushing quickly at her eyes and flipping the letter over. "I am fine, dearest. What are you doing here?" She held out her hand and he approached, sitting onto the bench beside her.

"I was told you had walked here, and since my heart was breaking with my need to see your face, I decided to forego washing up or changing, hastening here to find my beautiful wife with teary eyes and sad face." He ran his fingers across her cheek, nodding toward the letter. "Distressing news?"

"No, no. The opposite actually. I heard from Mary. She shared her blessed news with her usual aplomb, insisting I thank you specifically for the initial introduction. Mr. Daniels considers you a matchmaker extraordinaire."

Darcy laughed. "How kind, although if I recall, I was out of town at the time and had little to do with the meeting. Still, it is an excellent match and I am very happy for her, for them both actually. Mary is a lovely girl and will make a steady, faithful wife." He continued to caress her cheek, staring intently into her eyes all the while. "However, I sense dissimulation on your part. These are sad eyes, not happy eyes."

Lizzy dropped her gaze, the intensity of his stare unnerving her. "It is nothing, William. Better if we do not speak of it."

He frowned, transferring his hands to clasp both of hers, silence falling for a brief time. "Elizabeth, I appreciate that I have no right to insist you divulge all information to me. Secrets are a natural human necessity, I suppose. However, I would hate to think you felt you *could not* share something troubling with me. That I had somehow given you reason to conclude I was disinterested or vexed with any issue related to you. If the former, then simply say so. If the latter, then we must talk about it."

Lizzy shook her head, actually chuckling slightly as she returned her gaze to his serious face. "William, you truly are too amazing. I could almost become annoyed at that fact alone if it was not so wonderful." She sighed, patting his puzzled face. "I only wish to spare you pain, my love. I... It is a letter from Lydia, is all. She is well," she hastily added, Darcy's countenance instantaneously darkening with sorrow. "Too well, in fact. Giddy with the joy of balls and friends and her dear Wickham." She shrugged, staring into the pond. "I likely read too much in between the lines as she never relates anything but her bounding happiness. I am not sure if I am sad or thankful for her perpetual immaturity and gullibility."

She leaned against Darcy's side, his arm surrounding her with a gentle squeeze. Silence fell again, the soft chirping of birds and steady trickle of water over rocks serenely persisting despite the mild tension in the air. When he broke the calm, his voice was quite low and hesitant. "Does he... harm her in any way, do you think?"

"No. I am certain even foolish Lydia would recognize and not tolerate physical violence. As I said, she seems happy. She says he works until morning and that they have little money and that he gambles, only to make money of course. I suppose it is uncharitable of me to immediately leap to negative conclusions, but I rather doubt he is working, nor that he gambles out of duty!"

Darcy released a guttural sound that clearly relayed his views on Wickham's behavior. "It is as I imagined it would be for them. I did harbor some hope that matrimony and the responsibility incurred would breed a sense of honor in Wickham, and perhaps it may yet to some degree. At least he has not abandoned her and is maintaining his post." He paused, shifting on the hard rock and pulling her tighter into his side. "Elizabeth, I have a confession. You know I do not enjoy speaking of... him, and the guilt that abides in my heart has caused you to not broach the subject. In truth I am relieved and I do appreciate your compassion. Nonetheless, I do not wish for secrets between us if at all possible to avoid."

She glanced up quickly, tears springing to her eyes. "Forgive me, William! I did not mean..."

He halted her with a kiss, smiling as he resumed, "Allow me to finish. The secret I refer to is my own. I have vast connections, as you know, and have utilized my contacts to keep abreast of Wickham's activities both personal and professional. I receive regular dispatches, in fact. So I am asking you to forgive me for not sharing what I know."

Lizzy's mouth had fallen open and her eyes were wide. Darcy kissed her cheek, holding her gaze as he continued, "It is as you have deduced. Wickham is not faithful to your sister, although I am assured that he is discreet, which is a surprising improvement. He gambles too much and drinks, but he does pay his bills, adequately fulfills his duties, has been in no serious offenses, and by all outward appearances cares for Lydia's needs. As you say she claims, my sources assure me that she is content. How much she is aware of Wickham's activities, I do not know. Many women in her place simply deny the truth, living in a state of willing blindness. I would have wished more for her in life, as I know you would as well, my love, but it is not as horrible as I envisioned." He smiled wryly. "I guess that is enough to be thankful for."

Lizzy was dumbfounded. "Why would you do this, William? Lydia freely placed herself in this situation. It is not your fault! You have no reason to exert such efforts or worry so."

"Logically I comprehend the truth of your assertions, Elizabeth. Lydia is a foolish girl to be sure; however, you know she would not be in this particular situation if not for me. My damnable pride and sense of politesse, not wanting to cause scandal to my family. It allowed a villain to roam free. To charm, flatter, and destroy young girls at will. And I was forced to see them married!" He shook his head and closed his eyes briefly. "Nonetheless, I watch over Lydia not out of guilt… well, not completely anyway, but because it is ethical and obligatory. She is your sister, and thus my family. I will not allow overt harm to come to her. If Wickham's behavior becomes unmanageable or hurtful, I have people in place who will remove her, forcefully if necessary."

He paused, a cloud crossing his features and tight clenching of his jaw apparent. Not for the first time Lizzy sensed there was more to his personal story of Wickham. The bits she knew from his letter and a few vague comments or short conversations like now did not fully compute. She remembered the rage on his face as far back as their days in Hertfordshire. If she hadn't been so angry with him at his insulting proposal she would have shrunk in fear from the fury evident when she threw Wickham's name into his face. And there were other unguarded moments when she had noticed expressions of profound disgust or anger when Wickham's name was mentioned. Curiosity to know more of their youth burned within, but some instinct warned her that it was likely worse than she imagined and perhaps more than she was prepared to handle. So she never asked.

He sighed faintly and shrugged imperceptibly, his face clearing as he turned toward her.

Darcy cupped her cheek, smiling in peace. "Let us make a new vow. I shall put the past affairs with Wickham behind me as best as I can, and we shall share our future knowledge freely. I cannot promise to embrace lengthy conversations on the subject, but I will not avoid them or wince overly. Deal?"

Laughing lightly, Lizzy kissed him in joy. "Have I told you lately, beloved, that you are the best man in the world?"

"Yes, but you may say it again if you wish," he offered with a grin.

She encircled his neck, drawing his forehead to hers. "You are the best man in the world, Fitzwilliam Darcy, and I love you."

SAMUEL OLIVER AND MARGUERITE Charbonneau were joined in Holy
Matrimony on September the third in the intimate Pemberley Chapel.
The groom wore a fine suit of black, dashing and elegant despite the
blush upon his cheeks and trembling hands. He was attended by a livery-garbed,
wigged, and smiling Phillips, yet leaning on a crutch and pale. The bride was
resplendent in a white taffeta gown, her golden hair for once not in a severe
knot but stunningly curled and piled atop her delicate head. She was attended
by her sister Dominique, a lady's maid at the inn in Matlock where Marguerite
had once been employed, wearing a lacy gown of rose organdy. Aside from a
few bouquets of late summer flowers and ribbons upon the pews, the chapel was
left unadorned, its natural beauty and reverent essence shining brighter than any
decoration would have.

Reverend Bertram, dressed in his finest vestments, performed the traditional ceremony. Marguerite was baptized a Catholic, as were most French,
but religion had not played a large part in her life. Therefore, she had readily
embraced the Anglican views and had met with Reverend Bertram several times
to familiarize herself with Samuel's chosen faith. Essentially it was the blessing
of God that was of vital importance to both of them. The entire household
staff, a handful of outside staff, a few other friends from the community, and
Samuel's father, a butler at Yeldersley Hall near Ashbourne, were present to

witness the union. Mr. and Mrs. Darcy sat in the front pew, adding their blessings to the solemn event.

All plans had proceeded as initially outlined a month ago. Darcy arranged for a coach to transport the newlyweds to Windermere, where they would holiday for two weeks. Samuel was consulted on all arrangements but offered little in the way of feedback, generally far too uncomfortable merely by being in his Master's study to even consider carrying on a collaborative conversation. Lizzy had better luck with Marguerite, although her involvement was minimal, primarily allowing her maid to do whatever she wished in regards to the wedding. Therefore, like most women throughout the ages, Marguerite and her bridesmaid organized the bulk of the ceremony's provisions, Samuel essentially required to simply show up at the appointed time.

Mrs. Langton and Mrs. Reynolds hosted a reception in the staff quarters with feasting and merriment. The Master and Mistress extended their heartfelt congratulations to the blushing groom and radiant bride, departing to the Manor and allowing the couple to celebrate at leisure with their friends. The Olivers would spend their wedding night in their new apartment on the Pemberley lower level, Samuel's mortification far too profound for Darcy to more than hint about providing a place of greater privacy.

Lizzy and Darcy ate a light repast in the dining room, the muted sounds of revelry drifting from below, and then retired to their sitting room for the remainder of the night. Of course, this was not unusual, but tonight they would essentially be on their own as the entire staff was likely to be occupied toasting the new couple for many hours to come. Despite Samuel's fretting to the contrary, Darcy managed perfectly well with performing his personal toilette and with only his wife to assist him in undressing. Lizzy, too, was quite capable and since they both actually rather enjoyed caring for each other, not having their individual servants attend them was not an uncommon occurrence. For the two-day interim before they departed to Yarmouth, Darcy would be served by Willis, a manservant from the Osprey Inn in Brawley, and Lizzy would be assisted by Marla, one of the maids. Darcy was still not sure whether Samuel was relieved to have his Master cared for or appalled at the concept of a strange servant handling Mr. Darcy's personal effects! Whatever the case, the Darcys released a huge sigh of relief to have their servants safely wed and on their way, the organizing frankly frequently annoying with Samuel blushing and stammering incessantly.

The fourth of September dawned brightly, Lizzy reaching sleepily for her husband only to find his space vacant and cool. He had not specifically mentioned leaving early for a ride or other duty, not that he necessarily was required to do so, but he generally did. Normally this desertion would have caused no dismay or perplexity; today, however, Lizzy was shocked to find him absent. Darcy had made no reference of a specially planned celebration for this day, but Lizzy had anticipated something, even if only a romantic morning interlude. Well aware of how sentimental her spouse was, Lizzy's expectancy had grown and her first waking emotion was crushing disappointment.

"I told you not to spoil me so, William," she murmured to the empty air. "You have set the standard impossibly high." She sighed, further chastising herself for being so foolishly saddened when overall he was far and away the best man on earth. The baby suffered no such sense of disillusionment, jumping about on her bladder and demanding nourishment posthaste as usual.

Crossing the threshold to her dressing room moments later, Lizzy's emotions were again assaulted, only now with soaring amazement and glee. Hanging on a hook placed above her vanity was the very dress that she had worn one year ago today when first setting eyes on Pemberley while visiting with her aunt and uncle. Laughing joyously, she reached tremulous hands to unpin the note secured to the bodice.

My dearest wife,

Surely you did not honestly believe that I would allow this gown to be discarded? My foolish, beautiful Lizzy! If I knew of a way to have it preserved forever, I would. Madame du Loire has altered it to fit your current shape. If I may be so bold as to insist you don this garment, for me?

I pray you entertained no doubts that I would revere this day, beloved. How could I not exalt the day my heart began to beat again? For certain you know where I currently wait, breathlessly anticipating beholding your beautiful face as I did precisely 365 days ago, with the same yearning desire unabated. Only today I shall kiss you as I urgently ached to do then.

Of course, I can never express my love for you simply, so I am sending you on a quest. Solve the riddle and follow the trail for the prizes earned. I shall await you at the end, my unfailing love your ultimate reward. Hurry, my heart!

Always yours,
William

Mrs. Darcy, my pearl
~ kisses by moonlight and starlight
~ coming home never so sweet
~ cold of stone and air eradicated by ignited hearts and lips
~ the flame of a torch dim compared

Lizzy smiled, instantly solving the riddle. Dashing through the time-consuming routines, she nonetheless freshened carefully with a splash of jasmine and gloss to her lips. The dress, supposedly disposed of months ago as no longer appropriate nor wearable, fit perfectly. The bodice seams were let out and altered with a lace insert to provide space for an ample bosom, the appearance mildly different but lovely with the creamy tops of her breasts displayed. The skirt was already adequately gathered and full, no adjustment needed to accommodate the swell of their child. She pinned her hair up in a loose bun as she had worn it then, with wisps of hair framing her face.

After a last inspection and pinch to her cheeks, Lizzy hastened to the balcony. Lying upon the bench where passionate kisses commenced on Lizzy's first night at Pemberley as Mrs. Darcy was a single red rose and folded piece of parchment. Attached to the rose's stem with a slim white ribbon was a velvet pouch holding two lustrous pearls.

Illusionary clouds and sky
~ horses run fruitlessly
~ familial chimes to count through the ages
~ a head in miniature lies abed
~ swaying rhythms under the power of love

Giggling like a child herself, Lizzy ran to the nursery. The room was sunny and cheery. As always when she entered this room, Lizzy paused on the doorstep, marveling at the joy which permeated her soul. Resting her palms over her belly, she gazed about the chamber, eyes alighting on each precious item.

The decorating was complete and the Darcys were delighted with the outcome. The entire wall opposite the three tall windows facing east was painted with an elaborate pasture scene. All in pastels, the scene was illusionary, as Darcy stated in his riddle, yet so incredibly detailed that one expected the pale green grass to smell and the brook of periwinkle to babble and pink sheep to bleat. Horses of white and grey grazed and ran amongst the sheep and multihued flowers. The lacy blue and yellow curtains Lizzy had sewn hung from rods of polished oak, falling in soft waves to brush the hardwood floor. Several plush rugs dotted the floor, spaced at careful intervals to mute heavy footsteps that might disturb a sleeping infant. The newly installed, modern Franklin stove waited to be lit, freshly laid marble tiles reflecting the gleaming metal. An enormous dresser with padded top sat against the right wall, the door to Mrs. Hanford's chambers to one side and the door to the small closet on the other. To the left, as in Lizzy's dream, stood the cradle and cushioned rocking chair. Above the cradle hung the cuckoo clock gifted on her birthday, pendulum swinging and ticking faintly. Darcy had refinished the rocking chair, it now glinting from where it sat beside the white satin and lace-draped cradle. Inside, resting on the tiny pillow was another red rose, pearls nestled in a sack.

> Constellations touchable
> ~ define the gods immortalized therein
> ~ paint your own designs, if you dare
> ~ passion flares beside tubes of metal
> ~ seeking eyes meet seeking hands

Blushing and laughing, Lizzy left the nursery, traveling down the long top-floor corridor to an empty chamber on the opposite side of the manor. Here, on the covered balcony, Darcy kept his telescope. It was a frequent game, especially during the long winter months, to pad silently in half-dressed states and gaze at the stars when visible on clear nights. Darcy instructed, Lizzy absorbing his knowledge, but ultimately losing the patterns in the jumble of heavenly bodies. She realized that she simply did not have the eye to discern the varied configurations, so would teasingly create her own. Initially Darcy had found this irritating, but over time he accepted it and enjoyed the humor of the situations. He reasoned that although his wife did not share his affinity for astronomy, she did adore stargazing in general, and as they possessed a plethora of common interests, one or two divergent ones made no difference. Besides, the lure of starlight and close proximity as he assisted her education inevitably led to far preferable amusements, often their lovemaking blissfully transpiring on the balcony's chaise. This is where Lizzy now found the third rose, pouch of two pearls, and next riddle.

> Military might slumbers
> ~ relative humor questionable
> ~ amusement and faithfulness assured
> ~ matrimony avoided, any ideas?
> ~ effervescent strength

Under the watchful eye of a rigidly poised Watson, she sedately walked down the stairs to the main floor's residence wing to the last door on the west passageway: Richard's chambers. The first time Lizzy had ever entered these rooms was during her beginning weeks at Pemberley, on one of those days when Darcy was busy with Mr. Keith so she utilized the time to wander about, learning her way. The vast percentage of Pemberley's guest chambers had a long disused quality to them readily discernible. This room, unknown as Col. Fitzwilliam's, had instantly struck her differently. She discovered later that Richard was a frequent visitor, actually residing more often here than at his ancestral home, Rivallain, and the mark of his ebullient presence seemed to have seeped into the very walls.

The rose lay serenely at the foot of the bed. Two more perfect pearls added to the others in her pocket.

> Hall of living stone
> ~ sightless eyes bore into your soul, loving you eternally
> ~ loneliness allayed forevermore
> ~ my beloved in perpetuity

Lizzy's heart leapt. She rushed from the room, slowing under the vigilant gaze of Watson, undoubtedly planted there to ensure her caution. She smiled at him brilliantly, dropping a curtsy. The footman bowed, his lips lifting slightly. At the corner she glanced behind, Watson's eyes upon her, and waved airily with a tinkling laugh before launching into a brisk sprint to the sculpture gallery.

Darcy's bust was the obvious answer to the puzzle, although the last phrase was unclear. *Her* beloved was in perpetuity, but Darcy was writing the riddle and referring to her. She had a guess as to the solution and rounding the corner gasped nonetheless when she found she was correct. While in London, Darcy had taken Mrs. Lathrop's suggestion to heart and Lizzy spent a few hours sitting for a sculptor. Darcy had made no further mention of her bust, Lizzy choosing to let the matter lie, knowing that he would prefer to surprise her in some manner.

Well, he had succeeded. Her likeness etched in cold white marble sat on a pedestal beside her husband's. Every detail flawless, her tender smile and glowing happiness magically captured. As when she gazed upon his bust, or any of the other amazing statues in the gallery, Lizzy was awed by the art form. She had blushed and mildly resisted having a bust made, but now that it was here beside her husband in this place where it would sit for generations untold, Lizzy could only feel deep pride. She paused a moment more, as she could never refrain from doing, and stroked his luminous cheek.

"I love you, William," she whispered with a smile, retrieving the rose, pearls, and note lying on a tiny table near the pedestals.

> Prose and poetry
> ~ classic and contemporary
> ~ silent contemplation amongst the dust
> ~ romance amid the historical
> ~ favored master retreat

No hesitation as she pivoted toward the far door and short corridor leading to the library. His clues were obvious, but the room was gigantic, offering any number of places to place a rose. She rather thought his chair a logical place, but was unsure based on the allusion to romance, which could easily refer to the time they made love between the shelves of history texts. Of course, they had made love several times in the library, she recalled with a blush and heavenly sigh, so he was likely being general.

She was correct in her initial assumption. The rose, pearls, and paper lay on his massive leather chair. Lizzy's stomach released a loud growl, tremulous hands reminding her that she had eaten nothing yet this morning. As delightful as his little game was, she sincerely hoped this was the last as she was famished. Alas, not yet.

A precious presence seen

~ heart awakens as eyes lock

~ a dream?

~ a delusion?

~ or the beginning of life lived abundantly and completely?

"The latter, my heart, the latter," she murmured, kissing the folded parchment. Fourteen pearls now weighted her pocket and her hands were encumbered with parchment and roses as Lizzy headed toward the terrace.

Memories flooded her as she hurriedly walked through the now familiar rooms toward the southern exit. Vivid recollections of her surprise encounter of Mr. Darcy a year ago with the subsequent invitation to his home.

First, the music room where visions of being introduced to his beloved sister Georgiana and hearing her play while a proud and relaxed Mr. Darcy smiled and laughed. Ah, his laughter! Such an amazing sound and sight that she had never witnessed from the stoic man of Hertfordshire and Kent. It had pierced her soul, Lizzy noting how beautiful he was, how carefree and joyous. *"You should always smile, Mr. Darcy,"* she had thought with emotions overwhelming, her spirit lurching at his evident happiness and then plummeting in the sadness of knowing he would never smile so for her.

Next into Darcy's study and out a side door to the wide corridor beyond. She passed through the vaulted archway to the broad stone terrace and was halfway down the stairs before she noted that Darcy was nowhere to be seen. She slowed, heart racing, and calmly crossed the stones toward the small table set for breakfast precisely on the spot where she had nervously attempted a bumbling conversation with Mr. Darcy all those months ago.

The round table was covered with a fine green linen tablecloth, an empty vase of Waterford crystal in the center, a china pot of tea, plate of sliced fruits, and two formal settings. Lizzy glanced around, fully expecting her husband to materialize from behind a potted bush or the lawn beyond, not that it is easy to hide a frame his size. She placed the roses into the vase, noting then the folded parchment propped against the glass.

Beloved,

A year ago today the road to my rebirth began. The interrupted journey of our destiny as one was resumed. Paths trod are frequently rend with hazards and washed away areas, but the wise pilgrim presses on and picks up the trail inerrantly. By the grace of God such are we, my wife. Fate shone and brought you literally to my doorstep. Never will I doubt the hand of the Almighty on our life and will forever be thankful for the mercy shown me. The quest, both the one that brought you to me then and that brought you to this note, are over.

I love you,

William

She released a breathy laugh, whirling about seconds later at the unmistakable sound of boot heels striking stone. Darcy was rapidly descending the stairs, dressed in the exact outfit worn a year ago from boots to cravat, only rather than an expression of stunned befuddlement and nervousness, his countenance was radiant with broad smile and glittering eyes.

Lizzy could only stare, an odd sense of déjà vu overlaid by vaulting ecstasy and love. How he stole her very breath away! His dimples flashed, teeth sparkled, eyes reflected the azure blue of the sky, and entire body exuded strength and energy. Purposefully he strode toward her, gaze never faltering, not pausing or slowing until a mere inch from her body. Without preamble he encircled her waist with one arm, pulling her into his chest while clasping her neck gently with his hand, leaning for a consuming kiss.

Lizzy moaned, hunger forgotten in the haze of instant passion as her hands slipped over his shoulders and twined into his hair. Darcy growled in his throat, kissing with ever increasing fervor, slow to be restored to anything remotely resembling rationality. Gradually the feverish kiss abated, Darcy brushing lightly over her lips, withdrawing to rest his forehead on hers with eyes closed in rapture and sighing heavily.

"Oh God, Elizabeth, I have been waiting for hours it seems with a rising need to kiss you! Whose foolish idea was it to send you scurrying about the house rather than running into my arms?"

Lizzy laughed shakily. "I shall not answer that question, love." She rose on tiptoes, nestling her cheek against his. "Mmmm, William, you smell delicious. Promise me something?"

"Anything, dearest."

"Always hold me securely when you plan to kiss me so marvelously so that I do not collapse into a heap at your feet?"

He laughed, kissing briefly before stepping back a pace. He caressed over her cheek, speaking softly, "You must be famished, my darling. I thought it might be nice to breakfast in style for a change. Sit and have some tea and fruit. I shall inform the kitchen we are ready to dine." He pushed her chair in, kissing the top of her head before disappearing into the house.

Lizzy did pour a much needed cup of tea and nibbled on a prune while she waited. It was not for long, Darcy briskly returning followed by Mr. Taylor and three maids, all laden with trays placed onto a small linen-draped sidebar. Lizzy was starving but found it hard to focus on food with her husband staring at her with fiery intensity from his seat mere inches away.

In due time the first course was set and the servants departed, the butler to loiter inside the doorway awaiting summons from his Master. For Darcy the interval of attendance was an agony of forced propriety when he wanted nothing as much as to touch his wife, a mission promptly executed the second they were alone. He leaned forward, lips gliding over her neck while he clasped one hand tightly and gently massaged over the bulge of their child with the other.

"Thank you for wearing the gown." His voice was husky and muffled against her skin, Lizzy shivering from the combined sensations. "I adore all your old gowns as they each spark such delightful memories, but this is my favorite." He lifted to kiss her lips. "Sweet. Delectable. I love you so, Elizabeth." He gazed into her eyes with pure adoration, Lizzy's eyes misty from the emotions elicited. "Do you know how often I dreamt of you in this gown?"

She smiled, running her fingertips over his face. "Apparently the answer is many times. How often, dear love, were you removing said gown in your dreams?"

He chuckled, unperturbed by the query. "Hundreds, although often I was at this spot in broad daylight articulating brilliantly all the proper phrases which *should* have occurred to me a year ago, and then I would kiss you precisely as I did a moment ago. So, dreams do come true." He kissed her again, deeply, clearly insatiable with the need to taste her entire mouth. A rumble from the vicinity vaguely under his hand erupted, Lizzy blushing but Darcy laughing. "I am keeping you from your nourishment, forgive me." He withdrew with a final pat to her womb. "Forgive me, my son, but your mother is irresistible." The baby answered with a well-aimed kick to his father's palm, Darcy's eyebrow arching in surprise. "My! Feisty, like his mother."

Laughing, they attended to their plates, Darcy likely hungrier than Lizzy, having been up for hours arranging his surprise with barely a few sips of coffee taken. Vastly differing from the afternoon being commemorated, they conversed easily about all manner of subjects, their clothing being the only similarity.

"William, your clever treasure hunt was inspired. How do you invent so many wonderful adventures?"

"Impressed, Mrs. Darcy, by the ingenious schemes from your admittedly dull-witted spouse?" he asked with a grin.

"You declared it, not I," she said with a smirk. "Yes, I am impressed, and delighted. I had a wonderful time, although I shall confess to being thankful the quest complete as your son was demanding food and I was aching to see your face." She reached across to caress his cheek, Darcy snatching her hand for a tender kiss to the wrist. "Thank you for the pearls. They are beautiful. Do you have a specific thought as to what I should do with them?"

He shrugged. "I had imagined a bracelet to accent your necklace. However, you may choose anything you wish. They were part of a shipment on one of my ships, gemstones and pearls from the Orient. My ears perked up, so to speak, when I read the cargo manifest. I acquired a pouch of diamonds and emeralds as well, if you want them to accompany the pearls. They would combine to create a beautiful broach or hair clip. They were a fortuitous parcel as I honestly did not have a planned gift for this day."

"Really? Perhaps my initial impression when I awoke was not far from the truth." She spoke teasingly with a caress to his hand.

He arched a brow in question. "What was your initial impression?"

Lizzy reddened slightly. "Well, I confess I was disappointed to find you absent. You have spoiled me, beloved, even further after today. I anticipated at the very least arising to have you staring at me and caressing with obvious intent. I hoped for that, I should say. Anything else would have been a bonus." She fluttered her lashes and he burst out laughing. "Therefore, when you were not in our bed I was crushed. I thought you had forgotten," she finished in a small voice.

"Elizabeth," he whispered roughly, grasping her hand, "how could you think I would forget one of the happiest days of my life? The pearls were an afterthought, but I have been laying plans and composing riddles for a week. You know how pathetically maudlin I am, thus you should never be surprised overly nor despondent. And as for caressing with obvious intent—that shall occur in a timely manner, I can assure you, several times if I have my wish." He grinned, bringing her hand to his mouth for well-placed kisses and nibbles.

Feeling rejuvenated after a full meal, Lizzy was ready for whatever her husband had planned for the day. Darcy rose from the table, assisting his wife from her seat. Lizzy's belly was not yet to the point where rising or sitting was laborious; in fact, her grace was unfailing; however, Darcy was prudent. A maid was sent to retrieve a bonnet and gloves for Mrs. Darcy, which Darcy placed on his wife himself, kissing and tenderly caressing throughout the procedure that should have only consumed a minute but instead lasted close to ten.

Lizzy smiled into his eyes, his fingers yet nestled under her chin, ostensibly straightening the bonnet's bow. "Where are we headed?"

He smiled enigmatically, offering his arm, tucking her securely against his side, and steered toward the steps leading to the grass. They walked at a leisurely pace across the manicured lawn, talking softly of the past.

"Often I have considered the various brilliant phrases and declarations I wished to say to you while visiting here, especially upon our initial encounter when you so surprised me," Darcy said as they reached the serpentine hedge and began weaving their way through the maze.

"What did you decide you should have said?"

Darcy laughed lowly, shaking his head. "I never did decide on a sure phrase. Oh, I came up with all sorts of clever witticisms or irresistible banter in my musings, none of which I would have remotely conjured at the time even had I not been nonplussed. Obviously if enchanting conversation were a forte of mine, I may not have been in such a predicament in the first place!" He squeezed her arm, Lizzy chuckling.

They passed through the vine-draped archway in the center of the maze. The central clearing was an exact circle of clover precisely thirty feet in diameter with an enormous elm tree in the center, trunk girded by a low brick bench. The entire maze spanned nearly two hundred feet with four entrances, north, south, east, and west. The paths weaved and twined with a combination of curves and angles, ultimately intersecting and leading to four equally spaced exits in the middle. All throughout the labyrinth were niches cut into the six-foot-tall hedges with statues or ornamentally sculpted bushes. Lizzy loved the maze. It had not taken her long to figure her way through all the pathways, probably aided by her superior sense of direction, and it was one of her favorite haunts.

She and Darcy strolled about the perimeter in contented companionship, smiling in remembrance.

Darcy continued, "In my imaginings I charmed utterly, but certainly not in reality. No, I stood there and moronically watched you walk away. For at least ten minutes I could not think coherently. If it were not for the lingering scent of your perfume, I may have convinced myself I had finally succumbed to my fantasies."

Lizzy stopped and was staring at him with skepticism. "You did not seriously smell my perfume?"

Darcy's brow rose. "Yes, I did. Lavender. It was in the air long after you departed." He leaned over, burying his face into her hair and inhaling deeply. "As I thought. Lavender. You splashed with jasmine," he nuzzled her neck, "but your hair wash is lavender, as it was at the Netherfield Ball." He paused to bestow a smattering of gentle sucks over her collarbone, Lizzy instantly shivering but also shaking her head.

"I cannot believe the details you recollect. Even after all this time you can yet dumbfound me, William. How did you note I used lavender?"

Darcy flushed slightly, taking her hand and sitting on the bench under the tree. "I noted everything about you, Elizabeth, both consciously and unconsciously. I caught whiffs while you dwelt at Netherfield, but the fragrance invaded my mind while we danced. Unfortunately I only had that one opportunity to get close enough to you, but I noticed your scent. It was intoxicating, but then everything about you intoxicated me, even your arguing, as it showed your spirit. At Kent I deduced it must be your favorite perfume as you always wore it." He caressed her fingers, staring at her hands entwined in his. "When I returned to Pemberley... after... I had the potted lavender outside my study window removed. I ordered Mrs. Reynolds to banish all lavender from the house. She must have thought me mad, although that oddity was the least of my peculiarities last summer."

He smiled wryly, glancing into her eyes. "You know the strangest part? Three weeks before you visited I was in my study, staring out the open doors as I do when cogitating. I was not thinking of you at that moment. I did, frequently, but was gradually finding the pain not as severe but more... bittersweet. The memory of your face and voice had become a part of me. The sadness of loss was as intense as ever, but had been tempered by the joy of having known you, even if superficially. Anyway, I was dwelling on a business issue, the very one that would take me to London, when I glanced to the patio stones and marked the stain from the pots of lavender I had ordered removed. Instantly I thought of you, your face as clear to me as it is now. As an epiphany it abruptly struck me that I no longer wished to erase you from my memory. I held no hope at that point but knew with certainty that I would never love another as I did you and I did not want to forget that feeling. So, I rang for Mr. Taylor and asked him to discover where the pots were and to have them returned. I felt... happier, somehow, once they were back, and the scent was comforting."

"Perhaps it was a sign," Lizzy spoke softly.

"That you would return to me as well? Perhaps. Although I still was flummoxed to see you." He laughed. "I do not believe I have ever been so confounded in all my life! As I said, I stood rooted to the spot, smelling lavender, and utterly at a loss as to the logical course of action." He continued to chuckle with the recollection.

"What did you finally do? I mean, I know you invited us to dine the next day, to my increased embarrassment and astonishment, but how did you reach that decision? It seems so unlike you."

He sighed. "Well, that is the crux of it, love. I had to do something radical. I was surprised and confused, but knew for cert that I was being offered a second chance. You were obviously nervous to encounter me as we did, but as I mused over your words and demeanor, you did not impress me as harboring hostility or distaste toward me. I refused to assume too much and your discomfort gave me pause, but I could not believe it an accident that you were here. Of all the manors in all of England, you were here! The probability of this occurring by random chance is astronomical. I decided it had to be by Design, an opportunity for me to mend the damage I had inflicted."

He turned to his wife with a beatific smile. "Of course, all those thoughts flashed through my mind in a chaotic whirl. The foremost sensation was quite simply a gut-wrenching surge of desire and need. It all was back in a gush of emotion. My love for you as desperate and intense as ever. How I stood upright yet amazes me as I could barely breathe, so agonizing my yearning to kiss you and hold you and tell you how passionately I loved you."

"Fitzwilliam," she breathed, reaching to cup his face. "How star-crossed we were! I had recently been gazing at your image with such aching hunger, if only you had known. You could have swept me into your arms right then and I would have melted, never to depart this place until I was yours completely."

Moving simultaneously, their mouths met. The spoken remembrances of craving igniting a tangible firestorm of passion as they devoured breath and essence. Lizzy climbed onto his lap, Darcy embracing tightly. Hands were everywhere, voraciously touching. For long minutes it continued, fingers mind-lessly beginning to release buttons and untie a cravat.

"Lizzy! God, I must love you, but not here. Wait, beloved! Please, come with me." He rose, lifting her from his lap and setting her unsteadily onto her feet. He palmed her cheeks, kissing lightly. "Come," he repeated, taking her hand and leading infallibly along the twisting path.

They exited the maze to the south, wending past the lily pond located before this opening, under the stone archway, and then across the extensive lawn rolling up the gentle slope beside the Falls to the Greek Temple. It was a significant distance, easily negotiated, but necessitating reining in the rushed pace. Lizzy was panting imperceptibly, at times the added weight to her slender frame affecting her. Darcy kept a firm grip on her hand, always a step ahead, but cognizant of his wife's struggles so he quelled his verve. By the time he parted the hanging branches screening the trail to the grotto, the worst of their flaming fervor had ebbed, although it was not entirely abated to be sure.

Lizzy released a booming laugh. Somehow in the midst of all his organizing he had managed to additionally assemble a romantic tableau of blankets and cushions over the soft grassy plain in the grotto. A basket sat on a flat rock, waiting.

"When in the world did you find the time to do this?"

"I told you I arose quite early this morning," he whispered near her ear from his stance behind her, hands resting lightly on her waist. "I have taken to keeping the blankets and cushions in the Temple since we inevitably find our way here now and again." He nibbled her lobe, initiating his travels over the long expanse of her glorious neck.

Lizzy sighed, leaning onto his hard chest and clasping his hands. Five times since returning from London in July they had managed to finagle time to visit Darcy's hidden sanctuary; twice planned but the other three spontaneous trysts as their feet veered toward the dell while walking. They were both coming to discover the delight of fresh air and balmy breezes over naked flesh irresistible and slightly addictive. The effect on their libido was remarkable, not that their mania for each other needed a stimulant.

"Do you require refreshment or rest, my love?" he asked, tone clearly indicating his fervid hope that the answer was negative.

Lizzy smiled tenderly, stroking his long fingers. "Nothing, my darling, but you. Always, only you."

Unhesitatingly, he resumed the unfastening of buttons, albeit leisurely now that they were alone with passion cooler. His left hand released the tie and clasps located on her left side, the other fingers laced with hers over their child.

"So tell me, my husband, how did the dress removal fantasy unfold?"

Darcy smiled against the nape of her neck. "Hmmm… A myriad of ways, in truth, my lover. In this position I imagined your body pressed into me with your dainty hands stroking over my thighs… yes, rather like that, Elizabeth. Then I would lavish your creamy neck with adoring kisses and nibbles. One reason I so admire this dress is the miniscule number of clasps securing it to your perfect body. See, just that easy and it is undone! It peels off so delicately, your skin revealed to my touch. Ah! A delight I had not anticipated… the cool air raising tiny bumps over your succulent flesh and your nipples hardening like little pebbles. Wonderful!"

"That effect transpires from your touch, beloved," she whispered hoarsely. "What next?"

He cleared his throat, resuming, "Then you stand in your shift. Of course, I had never seen a woman's undergarment except on Georgie once or twice when ill, so my memory was vague, but I rightfully imagined something lacy and mildly transparent. So incredibly feminine and soft, caressing your skin and silky under my palms. I can feel the warmth of you through the linen, the trembling as I arouse you and revere your body. Oh my love, how utterly beautiful you are! Summertime clothing is light and airy, so fewer layers, and no stays to encumber my access now that you are pregnant. So freely liberated is a shift, falling to your lovely feet handily. Now, here you are my precious wife, flushed and naked in my arms. Aflame with desire for me, because of me. My Lizzy, I love you so! I must make love to you!"

She pivoted in his embrace, leisure forgotten with resurgent yearning. The loosened, dangling cravat was pulled away, Darcy already removing his jacket. He encircled her again, grasping her bottom and pressing into his pelvis as she attacked the buttons of his waistcoat. Thus locked and entwined, they dropped to the blankets. Words were lost as mouths became occupied in sensuous pursuits. His shirt pulled off and tossed by Lizzy, who expeditiously moved in to kiss his chest while he struggled to discard boots and trousers.

Stretching onto the plush covering they paused, eyes riveted with seething desire and profound love. Darcy smoothed the loose hair from Lizzy's brow, bending to kiss her forehead then temple.

"Elizabeth, my wife. I love you."

His virile frame swathed her totally as he claimed her mouth in a thorough kiss. Beautiful rhythm as ecstasy rose higher with hearts fluttering. The warmth of September was diminished substantially under the thick branches and with breezes filtering through the brush over chill water; nonetheless, their bodies bathed in sweat from the exertion of intense ardor. Despite the fervid urgency of their mutual passion, neither rushed to attain fulfillment. Rather they danced with patterns of languid movements of extreme tenderness conjoined with periods of furious momentum. It was a prolonged, varied engagement of indescribable lovemaking culminating in due course with stunning rapture, their cries of sublime joy uninhibited and explosive.

They lay entwined on the pillows, as close as two bodies could manage, skin touching on every plane. Darcy lay on his side, cuddling Elizabeth into his chest with both silky legs trapped between his muscular ones, playing with her hair while watching their baby's lazy pushes. The sturdy kicks could now be visibly discerned as Lizzy's abdominal skin rose and rippled bizarrely. These humorous waves were a new development, first noted by a doting father two mornings ago while studying a slumbering wife. His infatuation and ebullience was infectious, Lizzy not sure what thrilled her greatest: the visual evidence of their child's vitality or her husband's giddiness.

Darcy pressed one finger onto a tiny bulge, grinning ridiculously. His animated face rested inches from Lizzy's, breath tickling her cheek when he spoke. "Do you think it a foot or elbow perhaps? Simply amazing! He must feel compressed, yearning for more space. Or merely exercising his muscles. Like either you or me, needing action and movement."

Lizzy lay her hand atop his, giggling at the wonder on his face. Darcy ignored her, mesmerized by the antics of their baby and the marvelous changes to his wife's body. Her breasts had not increased further for the past couple months, but were heavier, the nipples darkening slightly. Her belly had grown considerably, no gown able to hide the swell. The skin remained soft, supple, and void of marks, thanks to his uncle's ointment and Darcy's diligent massaging, but her navel was flattening and a faint shadowy line was visible from the umbilicus to groin. Her waist was thicker although the primary expansion was frontal, Lizzy still not noticeably gravid when viewed from behind. Her hips seemed a wee bit wider, and she occasionally complained of mild joint pain, a result, the book assured them, of muscles and ligaments preparing for childbirth.

Overall her health was as vigorous as always. The rare and thankfully minor contractions of the womb, faint twinges in her hips and lower back, occasional breathlessness if she overexerted, and infrequent heartburn were the only annoying complications thus far endured. What weight she had gained apparently all resided in her midsection and chest as the remainder of her frame was as slim, or bony as Lizzy teasingly called it to Darcy's irritation, as ever.

It was this very frame—sumptuous and toned and lissome to Darcy's eyes—that he now caressed with avid intensity and devotion. He quite simply never tired of touching and gazing upon his wife. Lizzy's idolization toward her husband's physique was as fanatical; therefore, she admiringly brushed over his chest and abdomen with the back of one hand while the other was lovingly clasped in Darcy's embracing one.

She turned her head and kissed him fleetingly, smiling into his blue eyes. "You did not finish your tale, my heart. You left off standing in a state of paralysis."

Darcy chuckled vibrantly. "How apropos of you to call it paralysis, love. It truly was. I think my brain even shut down as I do not recall what, if anything, I said to you. I do not honestly know how long I stood there after you had gone, but the stasis abruptly fell from me and I spun about and lurched up the stairs. I am certain I appeared the utter fool, all grace and dignity of station vanished. My only thought was that I could not let you go. Georgiana, bless her heart, was stunned at my appearance, likely thinking me again mad. After my actions earlier that summer I believe she thought I had mentally snapped!"

Lizzy was laughing at the vision as Darcy continued with humor imbuing his voice, "I was rambling and largely incoherent when I joined her in the music room. Somewhere in the midst she heard your name spoken. Of course, she knew the whole story of our relationship thus far, of my feelings toward you, but was highly confused by my behavior and unexpected arrival home. It took awhile before she deciphered my disjointed raving as meaning you were presently on Pemberley grounds. I finally bumbled some sort of explanation, enough that she gathered you were visiting with your aunt and uncle in Lambton, and that I intended to delay your departure and restate my feelings. You understand, Elizabeth, I had no plan, was largely inarticulate and mildly deranged. I dashed out of the music room, nearly bowled over Mrs. Reynolds in the hall, barked an order to resaddle my horse, and vaulted up the stairs with the vague intent to freshen up, as if washing my face and adding cologne would somehow cause you to fall into my arms!"

They were both laughing at this point, Darcy having rolled onto his back and wiping at his eyes. "I was wholly nonsensical. In truth, my irrationality of the moment led to the fortunate by-product of rapidly barreling up a flight of stairs and endless corridors rather than attempting to detain the three of you immediately. If I had, I am certain your uncle would have deemed me insane and vacated the premises forthwith! Instead, I reached my rooms wheezing and palpitating and had no option but to collapse onto the bed. I am athletic and vigorous, but I do think I was near to a heart seizure. While struggling to merely survive, cold rationality was reestablished. It was while I sat there calming that I decided to invite you and the Gardiners to dine. The logic of having you in my home with me and Georgiana for hours uninterrupted was beyond appealing and kept my heart racing despite my efforts at serenity."

He rolled back toward Lizzy, stroking her face. "You know the rest. I do believe I managed true gentlemanly decorum by the time I spoke with your uncle and aunt."

"Indeed you did. I, on the other hand, was a mass of churning nervousness and desperately begged them to leave."

Darcy arched his brows in surprise. "You did? Why?"

Lizzy reddened slightly, tracing her fingertips over his nose and chin. "I still felt so mortified and confused, I suppose. You had every reason to despise me or at least be indifferent. If ever one had given you cause to lose your good opinion, it was me! Like you, I had not sensed distaste in your words or posture, but I would not have predicted you wanting to dine with me or allowing me anywhere near your sister. I was truly shocked." She giggled suddenly, fingers on his lips. "By the way, I never told you my aunt's words. She said you were charming and that there was an agreeableness to your mouth."

Darcy blushed scarlet and Lizzy giggled, placing her lips softly on his. "She is correct, you know. I watched your mouth quite avidly all the next day, your smiles and laughter, and could not believe the thoughts rushing through my mind."

"What sort of thoughts?" he asked huskily.

"Let me show you," she murmured, proceeding to feather playfully over his mouth, utilizing teeth, lips, and tongue to great advantage. Darcy quickly lost all sense of anything but his rising fever, hands moving as he responded vehemently to her actions.

Darcy arched and groaned, voice a rough whisper when he spoke. "Elizabeth, I stand in awe at your imagination, but rather doubt you envisioned this or anything remotely similar merely by looking at my mouth!"

Lizzy laughed, kissing his pulsing throat and then capturing an earlobe between her lips. "I confess the specific details have evolved over time, my lover, but my desire for you was blossoming, aided in no small part by your sensuality and flawless physique. I may have been innocent then, Fitzwilliam, but I knew I wanted you. God how I wanted you! How I still want you, all of you, always."

He crushed her tightly to his chest. "You shall always have me, Elizabeth. Have no fear."

CHAPTER THREE

Toes in the Sand

EXHAUSTIVE DELIBERATION HAD PRECEDED Darcy's decision to go on holiday at the seaside resort town of Great Yarmouth in Norfolk. For hours he pored over maps of England and discussed the possibilities with various friends before deciding on the relatively unknown port town on the North Sea.

The seed of this excursion with his wife had been planted while yet in Hertfordshire. Between games at the billiard tournament in Meryton, Darcy and Bingley had engaged in conversation with Sir Lucas and a man named Houghton about the fad of seabathing and "taking the waters," which had risen to nearly fanatical heights since the 1750s. Spa towns, such as Bath and Cheltenham with their hot mineral springs and clean air, had been popular for centuries. The elite had long ago divined the healing aspects and pleasure gleaned from immersion in these natural pools, and an entire tourist trade had arisen. So much so that trips to Bath were an essential part of societal demands irrespective of the springs themselves. The open ocean, in contrast, was viewed with skepticism if not downright hostility and horror. The thought of willingly placing one's body into the cold, salty water of the sea was unheard of until the early 1700s when several physicians began writing of the curative properties of sea water combined with sea air; Dr. Richard Russel being the prime example. Cynicism was rabid in some quarters, but popularity grew nonetheless. This led to a wild emergence of seaside resorts, many no more than tiny fishing villages, attempting to profit by the craze.

Darcy had vacationed at numerous shoreline locales and spa towns both in England and in France over the years. He tremendously enjoyed the freedom and exhilaration of swimming in the cold water, the experience reminiscent of his youth when stripping naked with his boyhood friends and diving in Rowan Lake and secluded coves along the River Derwent was a regular summer pastime. He remained somewhat dubious regarding the rather lofty claims of miraculous healing from saltwater, but could not deny the sensations of vigor and health when merely standing on the sandy beaches, let alone the vitality engendered after a brisk swim.

A great part of Darcy's infatuation with the experience was the lure of the sea. He was not overly fond of ships and sailing. Sea voyages were a necessary part of getting from England to anywhere else, but not an undertaking particularly sought after by the landlubbing Darcy. However, the power and majesty of the ocean was entirely different. Nothing quite compared to the untamed wildness of the tides and waves and brisk winds and roars of the sea. Thus it was that when Sir Lucas and Mr. Houghton began talking about the mania sweeping through the country, Darcy began to contemplate taking Elizabeth. He was further convinced of the brilliance of the idea when a casual fact-finding remark to his wife revealed that she had never seen the ocean.

He seriously debated the matter, as is typical of the ever guarded and comprehensive Mr. Darcy. The coastal areas of southern England are warmer and provide the best shorelines in all the country. This was without dispute; however, the distance to Cornwall or Sussex was too great for Elizabeth to travel in her condition, in his opinion. Nor did he wish to visit a primary tourist destination. His desire to be alone with his wife for this perchance last occasion for years to come, now that their family was beginning, was too great a draw. Ramsgate was out of the question, Darcy probably never setting foot in that town for the rest of his life. From Pemberley to either the east or west coasts were roughly the same, travel wise. He considered Liverpool or Blackpool on the west coast, but, again, he wished to avoid highly trafficked areas, plus he did not personally care for the ocean to the west. Somehow the nearness of Ireland, although not actually seen, prevented it feeling like open waters. By process of elimination, this left the eastern coastline. Here is where the meditation and questioning truly began.

Darcy had visited none of the North Sea bordered towns except for Newcastle nearly ten years ago when Richard was stationed there during his training as a cadet. Yarmouth, or more precisely the hamlet of Caister-on-Sea three miles north, was his ultimate decision thanks to Mr. and Mrs. Henry Vernor. The elder Vernors had vacationed there the summer past and therefore knew the area well. Darcy conferred with Mr. Vernor, trusting in his recommendations, and listened penetratingly to Mrs. Vernor's gushing narrative, even jotting down her rambling comments. The accommodations described were perfect for the solitude and lavish holiday he desired.

The roughly one hundred seventy miles to Great Yarmouth on the eastern coast of Norfolk was a full two-day journey. Darcy refused to rush the pace, not only due to consideration for Lizzy's condition but also for the enjoyment of leisurely sightseeing. They departed Pemberley early on the morning following the anniversary of their reunion. As with the previous two times Lizzy waved adieu to her new home, the emotions were bittersweet. She leaned forward and stared until the Manor was complete out of sight, reclining onto her husband's waiting chest with a deep sigh of sadness. Darcy enveloped her, resting one hand over their child and caressing her cheek with the other, kissing her head, and saying nothing.

They rode in the coach, completely revamped and repaired from the Chesterfield bandit fiasco. The enormous carriage was plush enough normally, but Darcy had added several cushions just to be sure. Aside from gratefully accepting a small pillow to ease the mild strain to her lower back, Lizzy suffered no adverse effects.

At Derby they veered east on the same road traveled three weeks prior to Wollaton Hall. From there the route was new to Lizzy as they traveled through the southern edges of Nottingham to Grantham and then south to Peterborough, where they halted for the night. They paused frequently along the way, Darcy obsessively diligent to Lizzy's needs. She laughed at him, assuring that she did not require stretching her legs every twenty miles, but he ignored her and ordered stops anyway.

Darcy kept a running commentary as they rode, being moderately familiar with Nottinghamshire and Cambridgeshire from his University years, and did stop for a few sights along the way. They tarried for nearly two hours in Grantham, the town so teeming with historical significance and astounding architecture that they could not pass the opportunity by. They ate lunch there at the Angel and Royal Inn, a hotel over four hundred years old. The landscape, like most of the Midlands, was boundless rolling plains of green with innumerable rivers crossing the fields. Lizzy lost count of the bridges traversed and small villages passed.

They halted for the night at Peterborough. After dining they visited the Cathedral, a structure from the twelfth century that was truly beyond stupendous. The magnificent church of combined Norman and Gothic styles, although yet in a state of partial ruin from the 1643 English Civil War, was nonetheless an incredible sight, and the Darcys were tremendously moved. They attended a quiet service, Darcy especially never able to bypass a chance to worship and pray, and then viewed the burial place of Katherine of Aragon, Henry VIII's lamented first wife.

The second day dawned bright, Lizzy now fully reveling in the anticipation of journey's end. Darcy had ruminated over the route to take. Not knowing the region of Norfolk, he had asked the Vernors as well as several others of his friends for advice on the roads and coastal views. In the end, as long as Lizzy was physically managing the extended carriage ride, he decided to swerve to the north from Swaffham through Fakenham onto Cromer, where Lizzy would catch her first glimpse of the sea.

The carriage windows were open as they rode; the air noticeably cooler the closer they drew to the water. Darcy smiled indulgently at his wife's childlike enthusiasm, quite acclimated with the way she sat on the edge of the seat with her face almost out the window. It was endearing, this excitement she displayed, and he could not imagine even their children being more juvenile. He altered between reading while massaging her back and answering her numerous questions.

"Is it true that you can smell the salty air long before you see the ocean?"

Darcy laid his book aside, again, looking up at his wife's inquiring visage. "Yes, it is true. How far away depends on the breezes of the moment and obstructing landscapes. Also some areas have a stronger scent dependent on fishing activities or the roughness of the surf. Yarmouth is a major herring port, so the odor is reportedly strong. That is one reason the Vernors recommended Caister."

A while later, "Have you ever found a shell with the sound of the ocean waves inside?"

Darcy smiled. "Georgiana did. When she was four we traveled to Devon to visit my aunt and uncle. We spent a week at Sidmouth. My father thought the air and sea water might help my mother." He paused in mournful remembrance, Lizzy grasping his hand and caressing. He smiled and continued, "Georgie loved the ocean. It was her first time on the sand, and I remember she threw an absolutely horrid tantrum each time Father carried her away. It was she who discovered a perfectly intact conch, a huge thing with swirls of pink and turquoise. I am certain she yet has it in her possession. Anyway, you can hear the waves very well. We shall stay on the alert, beloved, eyes keenly searching, and perhaps you shall be so fortunate."

Another time, "Will we see seals and sea lions, do you think?" Darcy jumped slightly, thinking Lizzy asleep.

He glanced to her face where she lay on his lap, noting her eyes still closed. Chuckling and brushing strands of hair from her eyes, he answered, "I am positive we will. Hopefully we shall be so fortunate as to glimpse whales or dolphins upon the waves. There will be a vast array of wildlife unfamiliar, dearest. I confess that zoology and marine biology were not subjects I studied, so my working knowledge is minimal. I brought two books I found in the library as well as another on coastal plants. I thought we could learn together."

Lizzy had turned and was looking up at her husband with a smile. "Never pass up an opportunity to educate, William? Even on holiday?"

"Life is about growing wiser, Elizabeth. A true student should never bypass a ready chance to learn." He spoke with a tone of pomposity, Lizzy laughing aloud. Darcy ignored her, returning to his book with pursed lips.

Lizzy continued to giggle, fingering the gold etched title on the book binding. "*De l'esprit des lois* by Montesquieu," she read in butchered French. "Educational, Mr. Darcy? Or a French romance disguised as didactic? Of course, you could tell me anything and I would know no difference."

"You know very well who Montesquieu is, Mrs. Darcy. However, the concept of enlightenment engendered via a French romance should not be unwelcomed by you." He maintained his pose of haughtiness, but with shining eyes staring raptly at the pages.

Lizzy reached up to play along the edges of Darcy's cravat and lowered her voice. "Read to me in French, Fitzwilliam. That will be highly welcomed by me."

Darcy glanced at his wife, color rising to his cheeks. Clearing his throat, he began to audibly recite the text. Lizzy bit her lip, tugging on the dangling fabric of his neckcloth, truly affected by his resonant articulation. Darcy's reverberant voice thrilled Lizzy in any language, but there was a particular inflection he adopted when quoting literature that was especially lush and mesmerizing. She loved to tease him about his flair for drama, but the truth was that Darcy could have easily been successful as an actor, if he managed to overcome the whole being the center of attention facet! She had attended numerous plays in her life, especially most recently while in London, and knew that voice modulation and command coupled with theatrics was far more important than one's physical appearance onstage—not that her husband did not fulfill that feature adequately as well.

She listened, pulse racing, and wished fervently that they were not currently in a traveling carriage with open windows. Spellbound, she did not realize his cravat was undone until he faltered briefly when her fingers brushed over the hollow in his throat. He resumed, eyes riveted to the page with deliberate intensity, even when she rose and replaced her fingertips with her lips. Lizzy felt the vibrations created as he spoke, kissing tenderly over his neck and upper chest as buttons came undone.

Darcy's one hand held the book in a white-knuckled grip, the other about her waist, voice growing fainter with each word uttered until failing completely. "Continue, sir," she whispered into his ear, Darcy attempting to comply with limited success.

A smattering of French phrases later, one short paragraph finished haltingly and with poor enunciation, and Darcy renounced the endeavor. Instead, he tossed the book randomly, clasping her hair firmly to pull her away from his neck and leaning with a groan to assail her mouth. Once, while returning from London to Pemberley, they had made love in the carriage, initiated by Lizzy, but wholly welcomed by her adoring spouse. It was a strange experience with the carriage swaying and the awareness of persons hovering above them, but denying their desire for each other when it arose was never a feat either could adequately achieve. The bliss attained was well worth the slight discomfort in the location, and since making love outside their bedchamber happened rather frequently, both Darcys had learned ways to curtail their vocalizations of pleasure and muffle their culminating screams of happiness. Luckily the Darcy carriages were all constructed stoutly and well insulated, noises from both the outside and vice versa not transmitting unduly.

This solitary event flashed with alacrity through Darcy's mind, and fully intending on a repeat engagement, he bodily lifted his wife onto the opposite seat, turning rapidly to close the windows and lower the shades. This accomplished with due haste, he returned to his grinning wife.

"Do not utter a word, Elizabeth," he ordered in a terse whisper, Lizzy shaking her head with a smile. Darcy took the time to lavish kisses over his wife's beautiful neck and bosom, Lizzy's head thrown back in delight, while carefully and speedily removing all encumbering fabrics. Within minutes they were one, joined so perfectly, the rhythm of the rocking carriage aiding. They clung together, kissing and caressing, absorbing the joy and rampant electricity flowing through their bodies and felt in the other with even clothing not a barrier.

"Beloved, talk to me in French. I love your voice in French," Lizzy murmured breathlessly.

Darcy obeyed, hoarsely and sporadically interjecting an endearment in whispered flawless French. Lizzy shivered, mouth pressed tightly into his shoulder and hands through his hair. The sensations rose, heights gradually spiraling to astounding levels, both attuned to the reality that a peak of blinding rapture was nearing. Darcy released a sustained groan into Lizzy's neck when suddenly a sharp series of raps blasted through the carriage from above.

They both instantly froze. Darcy's face was twisted in an agony of interrupted desire, ragged breaths suddenly astonishingly loud in their ears.

"Yes, Mr. Anders," Darcy's voice boomed, startlingly normal and steady, given the circumstances.

"Sir, we are a mile or so from the seaboard," Mr. Anders informed, voice faintly heard from above.

"Thank you, Mr. Anders." Darcy responded in a clipped tone, a weak moan escaping. Lizzy was stifling a giggle, body shaking in mirth. "You are naughty, Mrs. Darcy! Pure evil, I daresay," he whispered tightly.

She met his glazed eyes with an impish smile, rapidly lost in a crushing kiss. Darcy shoved massively and in seconds they were replete, gasping and panting in each other's arms. With only minutes to tidy themselves, they laughingly and joyously assisted each other, lastly Lizzy retying Darcy's cravat, a skill she was now very proficient at.

"There," she declared, "as perfect as Samuel would do."

Darcy was beaming, smile broad as he leaned to kiss her ruddy lips. "Thank you, my heart, for everything. I love you."

She smoothed his rumpled hair, her own face radiant with love and satisfaction. "My pleasure, dearest. Anytime."

He laughed, reaching around her body to open the windows. The gust of fresh sea air was notable and their timing ideal. The carriage completed a wide arc over the sloping dune, stopping moments later onto a flat expanse beside the road. Lizzy gasped, hand rising to her mouth in sheer awe. Darcy glowed with pleasure at his wife's expression, opening the door and hopping out before Tillson, the footman accompanying them on this journey, had alit from his perch.

"Come, Elizabeth," he said, offering a hand to his wife, who took it rather absently, her gaze engrossed with the scenery.

They stood on a forty-foot cliff of combined sand and rock with clumps of gorse, lichen, kidney vetch, and heather about their feet. The varied colors and textures displayed by the array of vegetation were dazzling enough, but Lizzy would note this later. Her eyes were captured by the sea.

It was a clear afternoon, the evening fog yet at bay, with a sky of vivid cloudless blue. The dark blue-grey water sparkled and reflected the brilliant sunlight as a million flashing candles, endless to the horizon as the water rippled and roiled. Foam-crested waves of all sizes crashed, the sound loud upon their ears. Some waves reached the shore, tides pushing and pulling steadily over the white sands. The beach stretched for miles, dotted with clusters of dried seaweed and debris. To their left beyond the gently ascending and descending dunes, the cliff rose steeply with a sheer escarpment of chalk sandstone, massive boulders fallen amongst the naturally rock floor. Waves fed the stone, mosses growing in a thick blanket and the scurry of tiny crabs and clutching shellfish visible from their roost above.

Seagulls flew in screeching flocks over the water and beach, darting with incredible speed and accuracy to catch the unwary fish. Groups of nightjar and kittiwake rambled over the sands, bobbing and conversing as they too pecked into the rock clefts and sand for dinner. No humans were present although the faintly visible cluster of buildings off to the right indicated the nearness of Cromer and civilization in the lower valley.

"William, it is everything I imagined multiplied a hundredfold! No painting does the reality justice. I never accounted for the noise! It is like thunder." She trailed off, unable to articulate.

Darcy watched her with delight. As with sharing the beauty of Pemberley or any of the other sights they had seen together, his joy was boundless in experiencing it with her. She was aglow with happiness and awe, struck as Darcy always was by the impressive majesty of the roaring surf and vast expanse of ocean. Turning her incandescent countenance to him, his knees instantly weakening at her breathless beauty, she leaned toward him and clasped his forearms enthusiastically.

"Can we walk on the sand, William, please? I want to feel the water."

Darcy smiled indulgently. Glancing around, he noted that the road they parked beside veered left through the heath and sparse trees, beginning a gradual decline toward Cromer. The cliff elevation decreased until eventually disappearing into the sand at sea level some two miles before the town. Approximately twenty feet away from where they stood, he could see a rough trail twisting between the reeds and rocks down to the beach. It appeared safe enough, so he directed Lizzy to the trailhead, pausing to examine further. Lizzy, in her excitement, hesitated not a second, treading onto the sand path with surefootedness. Darcy grasped her elbow, pulling her back with a stern glare.

"Elizabeth! Be cautious. I know you are as a gazelle in your grace and confidence, but I would rather not see my wife and child tumbling down a cliff! I will go first and you can hold onto my arm."

Lizzy pressed her lips together but did not argue. The path was not steep, in fact was not a true path at all, but more accurately consisted of sandy gaps between the tufts of vegetation. Twice it was necessary to step over masses of flowering gorse, reacquiring the trail downward. Nonetheless, it was an easy descent, Lizzy not the slightest bit winded. Her booted feet sunk into the warm sand with each stride. She laughed, looking at Darcy with sparkling eyes.

"It is rather difficult to walk on and so warm! I can feel the heat through my soles. I was planning on removing my shoes but think not." She squatted, scooping a handful of the hot dry sand and trickling it through her fingers.

"Closer to the water the sand will be cooler, and firmer. You can remove your shoes then if you wish. I should warn you, the sand will lodge between your toes."

He was grinning happily, Lizzy leaning onto his chest with a coy simper and fingers at his cravat. "Will you remove your boots, William, so I can see sand between your lovely toes? I might even be impelled to tickle your gritty toes with mine. Would this please you?"

"I suppose I could be induced to perform in such a childish manner as long as we remain alone." He bent to kiss her as they were utterly alone, even Mr. Anders and Tillson out of view, but Lizzy pivoted and dashed toward the water line, her glittering laugh waving behind her.

Her sprint was not as speedy or graceful as usual due to the soft sand, Darcy rapidly outdistancing her with longer and stronger legs encased in tough boots. He halted on the hard sand, just beyond the tide's reach, hands extended to assist her final few steps.

"Very well," she panted, "it is official. I am a whale too ponderous to move across the sand! Grossly unfair, Mr. Darcy, and it is entirely your fault!"

Darcy chuckled, kissing her forehead and then kneeling to unlace her shoes. "I do believe you have something to do with the state you find yourself in, my love; however, if it pleases you, I shall assume all blame. Steady yourself on my shoulder and breathe deeply. The salt air will revive you. Other foot."

Lizzy gingerly placed her naked foot onto the sand, but Darcy was correct that it was cooler near the water, although warm. She wiggled her toes, smiling at the strange sensation. "It feels so different than dirt or river sand. So fine and soft." Her other foot was now bare, Darcy holding her boots and stockings, and she began to stroll, slowly digging her toes with each step while hiking her dress up to mid-calf. She headed toward the water line, the sand gradually cooling further with moistness apparent, as Darcy watched her with rising delight.

He experienced a sudden flash of memory.

Georgiana at four years of age, chubby legs striding with exaggerated steps over the sand at Sidmouth with her tiny face screwed up in perplexity, seriously debating whether she liked this odd sensation or not. Anne Darcy held her daughter's hand with a sunny smile, laughing her throaty laugh, while Darcy and his father stood several feet away observing the scene with pleasure.

"She is going to cry," a solemn sixteen-year-old Fitzwilliam said. "You wait. One of her infamous bellows that will frighten the seagulls clear to France."

His father laughed, clapping a hand onto his son's shoulder, already on the same level as his own. "Bet you a shilling she laughs."

Darcy looked at his father with a grin. "Deal!" They shook on it and not two minutes later Darcy was digging into his pockets for a shiny shilling to hand over to his father while Georgie chortled her babyish delight, tugging on her mother's hand in an insistent urge to become one with the cresting waves.

The scene on this deserted stretch of Norfolk shore was different in a myriad of ways, but the sight of his wife laughing as the cold, foamy water lapped at her ankles was strangely reminiscent. He did not fear her bodily launching into the sea, but her amusement and childlike zeal were not too dissimilar from Georgiana's. She glanced over her shoulder to her husband, who remained standing and holding her shoes.

"Are you afraid, Mr. Darcy? Fear the cold water may freeze your toes? Or that the tide may suck you in, a big fellow like yourself?"

Darcy shook his head, deigning not to answer. He looked about, spotting a rock five feet away. He sat and removed his boots and stockings, after another thorough search about to ensure they were alone. He joined his wife, already splashing her way toward the rocks, taking her hand as they strolled. He sighed deeply. "This is precisely as I imagined it. You and I strolling along the beach with the waves crashing and birds flying. Not a soul in sight."

"It will likely be busier where we are staying, so we should enjoy this time."

"Not necessarily. Mr. Vernor said the inn is secluded near a private cove. The guests are allotted individual periods to bathe, if desired, or merely gaze into the sea. Of course, we will be visiting other areas more public, but I chose this place for that reason. He also said the dining parlors overlook the ocean. We can dine and watch for sea creatures or ships passing." He paused, drawing Lizzy into his arms and leaning for a kiss.

They held each other tightly in silence, contentedly watching the surf and inhaling the fresh, crisp air as the sun lowered in the west.

W ILLIAM."

He turned at the sound of her voice, scenery of sunset over the water forgotten in a millisecond by the exquisite vision before his eyes. She wore a new gown of aquamarine satin, the skirt bordered with rouleaux of twining lace and roses; a velvet navy-blue spencer with short capped sleeves trimmed with wide, white lace accenting her bosom; gathers of satin falling in gentle folds over her swollen belly. The Kashmir shawl draped her fair shoulders, and a choker of blue velvet with a diamond pendant graced her slim neck. She was beautiful, glowing, and vibrant. Darcy was struck forcibly by how profound was his love and pride in squiring her as his.

He smiled, extending an arm with hand palm up. "Elizabeth, you are breathtaking. Come, beloved, watch the sun's setting glow upon the waves before it falls beyond the trees to the west." She joined him on the small balcony, Darcy encircling her waist and kissing her rosy cheek before resuming his study of the ocean.

A leisurely, halting drive along the coast had brought them to the enormous, sprawling building of rustic wooden beams and irregular stone that rested on a promontory roughly fifteen feet above the shore. Built over one hundred years ago, the lodge was once the seaside vacation dwelling of a now deceased viscount from Shropshire. Left without an immediate heir and financially depleted, the estate had been inherited by a distant cousin who wisely grasped onto the rising fashion of seaside bathing and avoiding Continental travel during the decades of wars. He transformed the gorgeous mansion into an elegant, opulent resort sought after by the gentry from all parts of England. Catering exclusively to the elite desiring a quiet recess from the cares of life, the woodsy seclusion, provincial charm, and luxurious furnishings created a wonderful combination highly praised among those wealthy enough to afford the accommodations.

Located a half mile south of Caister-on-Sea, the three-story-tall country house was nestled aside a sheltered stretch of beach secluded from the main shoreline by a natural rocky protrusion to the north and man-made wooden pier to the south. The pier was part of the resort, arising from an elevated, tree-lined bluff beyond the formal garden, and extending a hundred feet over the waves. The ornately designed formal garden and patio positioned near the pier also skirted the cliff's brink, providing a stunning view of the North Sea from the shade of canvas and leaves over plush chairs and settees. The bluff was surrounded by indigenous trees and bushes allowed to grow as nature intended with minimal purposeful landscaping interfering.

The individual suites were generous, well apportioned, and situated to grant adequate privacy from the fellow guests except for brief passes in the wide corridors. Ground floor public rooms that allowed for socializing and group dining if so desired were interspersed with intimate parlors and sheltered alcoves for personal privacy.

The Darcys had arrived late in the afternoon with no time to tour the elaborate environs or the opulent public rooms inside the house. With a planned sojourn of two weeks, they would have plenty of time to explore the resort's attributes. In fact, neither felt any rush at all, perfectly content to stand together on their ocean-facing balcony and observe the brilliant hues of scarlet, orange, and purple.

Lizzy rested her head against Darcy's upper arm with a sigh. "I have never seen such colors. Beautiful. Can we walk on the beach at night?"

"Certainly, although probably not wise in that gown. I would not wish to see it soiled overly. You are absolutely ravishing, my love," he finished in a low tone.

Lizzy slipped her arms over his shoulders, peering up into his face. "I love you, Fitzwilliam Darcy. Thank you for the compliment and you are welcome to ravish later; however, now I am famished."

The approximately fifty current guests sat in various-sized groupings throughout the dining parlors, some electing to eat at solitary tables sequestered from strangers, but some desiring to sit in larger companies of friends or new acquaintances. Darcy, never overly comfortable in a large crowd of unknown individuals, had opted to dine with his wife in one of the private dining parlors at a single table secluded near the wall-spanning windows overlooking the bay. The food was marvelous, service elegant and superb, and atmosphere divine. Lizzy and Darcy gazed at each other over the candlelight, softly talking as they ate, and filled to bursting capacity with unrelenting love. A number of evening entertainments were scheduled and offered nightly for the lodgers, but for this night the Darcys wished to be alone, departing immediately upon finishing their meal and returning to their room. There they would stay, primarily in the comfortable bed, snuggling and loving and sleeping intermittently until well after sunrise.

❦

"Need any assistance with removing your gown, Mrs. Darcy?"

"Stay over there, Mr. Darcy, as I am quite certain sea bathing would be delayed indefinitely if you aided my disrobing."

Darcy laughed, obeying his wife as he removed and carefully folded his waistcoat from where he sat on the narrow bench. Assist he may not do, but observe the stripping? Absolutely.

They were inside one of the resort's bathing machines Darcy reserved for an hour of private couples bathing. Naturally, despite his many excursions at coastal towns, this would be his first experience bathing with a woman, his adorable wife, the anticipation higher than any of the numerous times he swam with a troop of men.

He was impressed with the quality of bathing machine the resort offered. In point of fact, he was greatly impressed with all he had seen thus far, the remote and obscure tourist town well equipped and modern. The wide cove was divided into separate sectors for intimate bathing well away from the public areas for beach play. Furthermore, the machine usage was scheduled with segregated periods for married couples and for the individual sexes. Darcy planned to return later in the afternoon when the men bathed, already relishing what would be an extended span of intense swimming through the surf.

For now, however, he was thrilled to be here with Lizzy, introducing her to the joy of sea bathing. He only hoped he could control himself and allow her to truly enjoy the water. Watching her undress down to her shift and imagining how the thin garment would cling to her body once wet was not conducive to maintaining his restraint, Darcy swallowing and forcefully tearing his eyes away.

"I suppose he is safe and warm, untouchable by the cold water." Darcy glanced over, Lizzy standing with hands caressing her abdomen.

He smiled. "He is cocooned and protected, beloved, do not fear. The dippers all agreed, and you are not the first pregnant woman to bathe. Besides, the water is not all that cold. I think you shall find it refreshing. Are you ready?"

She nodded, eyes gazing over his naked form with equally decadent thoughts arising. "Are you certain we cannot be seen? I would rather no other see you in such a state."

Darcy laughed. "Fret not. I promise you, I would not permit you appearing in your shift if I thought there the slightest chance we would be visible to roving eyes! The canopy shall shield us. Now, sit on the bench and hold on while we move." She did as he instructed, Darcy pulling the lever to raise the outside flag. This was the signal for the driver to back the wheeled cabin into the water.

The so-called bathing machine had been around since the early 1700s, invented by Benjamin Beale. The concept was remarkably simple: a large wagon propelled by two horses with a canvas or wooden shed built on top; the interior generally consisted of shelves or closets to place one's clothing, a bench for sitting, and supplied with a stack of towels; one door in the front as the entrance, the backside open with steps to enter the water. A driver would direct the horses to back the wagon into the water then, in the case of private bathers, depart a safe distance until the flag was lowered as signal to withdraw the device from the water. Same-sex "dippers" were available to attend those persons who could not swim. This particular machine also sported an enormous tent off the back end to allow for added privacy.

Darcy jumped unhesitantly into the water, immediately diving completely under, swimming several clean strokes away, and surfacing with a splash. He turned to his wife with a grin, water running in rivers down his torso while he smoothed the wet hair off his brow. Lizzy waited on the top step, dangling one foot into the waves and admiring unabashedly. The water was waist high on Darcy, meaning that it would hit Lizzy well above her bulging abdomen. He waded back to her, snaking cold wet hands under her shift and clutching her inner thighs.

Lizzy gasped, jerking spasmodically. "You devil! Spawn of Satan as your aunt declared!"

Darcy merely laughed, grinning mischievously. "I thought you were brave, Elizabeth Darcy, fearless and adventurous. Was I in error in this assessment?" He climbed the steps, leaning his wet body against hers for a soggy kiss.

She squealed against his lips, wincing, but threw her arms over his shoulders and launched forward. Darcy was unbalanced in his surprise, both of them falling into the water. His strong legs stood fast on the sand, preventing Lizzy from being dunked, but the splashing water doused her adequately. She laughed and wheezed at the same time.

"Not that cold, he says! I beg to differ, sir!"

"Buck up, my lady. Be strong and..." His words halted by a forceful splash aimed precisely into his open mouth. Lizzy giggled and slithered away, walking on tiptoes over the shifting sand.

"Plainly unfair," he finally sputtered.

"Serves you right. Look, William, the bottom is so clear once the sand settles." She was staring into the water with rapt intensity, arms skimming over the surface. "I think I can... wait... let me see... Yes!" She bent slightly, reaching into the water and then raising her arm into the air with a shout of glee, a two-inch round rock in her hand. She looked at her smiling husband with pride. "Perfect balance and dexterity. Not bad for an obese whale. Here, a souvenir," and she tossed the small stone to Darcy, who caught it midair.

"What, pray tell, am I supposed to do with it?" He spread his arms widely, "If you have not noticed, I am unclothed. No pockets readily available."

Lizzy grinned, floating back to her husband, eyes raking over his form. "Oh yes, sir, I did notice you are unclothed. Of course, you are a man supremely noticeable whether clothed or not." She slipped her arms around his neck, nuzzling close, the rock discarded hastily as he enveloped her body. "Are you going to teach me how to float and swim, my beloved personal bathing instructor, or are we to continue discussing your nakedness? Either option appeals to me as they both involve your luscious body near mine." She nibbled his lobe, Darcy clutching her tightly with a heady sigh.

"Are you seducing me, Mrs. Darcy?"

"The thought did cross my mind, my lover. You assert we are utterly alone here."

"I cannot in good conscience renege on my vow to teach you to swim and float, however. All trust and confidence in my fidelity would be forfeit." His hands glided over her bottom, pulling her firmly against him. "I shudder to imagine what you would then think of me." He grinned, bending to bestow a thorough kiss lasting long enough to leave them both as breathless as if running a mile dash.

With a quick peck to her nose, he flipped her about, Lizzy instinctively thrashing. "Relax! I shall teach you to float. Surely you did this as a child in your pond, but the buoyant salt water makes it easier."

"Is the instructor expected to frighten the wits out of the student with rushed movements?"

"Only when said student is attempting to divert attention away from the lesson. Such behavior is considered cheating and would earn a sharp rap to the knuckles if we were in a proper classroom. Breathe shallowly, Elizabeth, but do breathe. I shall not let you go."

"Is this the voice of experience, William? The rapped knuckles, that is?"

"Absolutely not. I was a perfect student. Attentive and never in trouble." His tone was patently false with lips pursed. Lizzy chuckled, earning a tiny pinch to her bottom. "Concentrate, Mrs. Darcy."

She closed her eyes and relaxed, Darcy's arms under her back and upper legs. She had floated proficiently in her youth, even self taught a few basic swim strokes, but it had been years since her last rebellious foray to the Longbourn pond. The Pemberley grotto pond was far too shallow and small to attempt swimming, and the floating done in Darcy's embrace never lasted very long before preferable activities interrupted. This was vastly different. The gentle waves lapped around her, causing her body to bob and sway; the salty water was buoyant, the feeling of lightness delightful.

She sighed, a small smile of contentment on her lips. "For the first time in weeks I do not feel weighted down and off center. This is marvelous."

Silence fell, Darcy enamored. She was radiant in her happiness and, as suspected, the wet clinging shift left nothing to the imagination. His wife's incredible body with perky breasts and hard nipples, lissome legs, dainty feet and toes, precious swollen abdomen, delicate shoulders and collarbone all lay before his ravenous eyes. His arousal, well on the way since disrobing in the machine, was now complete. He cleared his throat, dragging his thoughts harshly away from the vision of hungrily loving her on the warm sand.

"Is it so burdensome carrying our child?"

She opened her eyes, gazing with overpowering love into the depths of his blue orbs. "Not in the least burdensome. The changes are odd, wearying at times, and I do feel awkward, but it is never a burden. Can I tell you something? I never imagined, since loving you so wholeheartedly, that I could possibly love someone as greatly, until now. He is not here yet, I do not know what he shall look like, or what his personality shall be, but I already love him with all my soul. It is rather strange, but so wonderful. How could I then deem his presence inside me a burden?"

Darcy had told her once that on occasion she said or did something that was so amazing to him that the emotions surging through his soul were nigh on unbearable in their intensity. This was such a time. As inadequate as it was, all he could manage was a brilliant smile, his eyes misting and larynx constricting.

Lizzy rolled out of his arms, turning about and clasping onto his forearms. "What next, teacher?" she asked teasingly, pulling herself into his chest with hands sliding down his back to derriere while wrapping her legs about his thighs. "Back stroke? Breast stroke?" Squeezing his rump firmly, she snared his lower lip and sucked, easy to accomplish as his mouth had parted open in avid yearning.

Darcy groaned, regulation and propriety forgotten. He cupped her face, applying fervid pressure to her mouth. Lizzy responded blissfully for a moment, startling him when she abruptly launched backward, using his body like a wall. Performing a number of perfectly executed backstrokes, she smoothly traversed the distance to the bathing machine steps. Her laughter floated on the air as he stood rooted to the spot. She settled onto the lower steps, body mostly submerged, observing his surprise with a naughty grin.

"As you can see, Fitzwilliam, I already know the backstroke. Perhaps you can show me the breast stroke?" She unbuttoned the top of her shift as she spoke, peering at him through lowered lashes.

Darcy grinned lasciviously, crossing the short space with a cleanly performed breaststroke, grasping onto the rails and pulling himself up until hovering over, muscles rippling and hairs black. He leaned in, lips brushing her upturned mouth, whispering huskily, "I love you, Elizabeth. God, how I love you! Please tell me I can make love to you here in this inappropriate place as I desperately burn for you and cannot return to the hotel in my current state!"

Lizzy reached to fondle him, Darcy moaning loudly, her legs drawing him closer. "I confessed I wished to seduce you, did I not? Love me, Fitzwilliam, please." Nodding curtly, he claimed her mouth, devouring in his thirst for her.

Releasing the rails for a far preferable grip to her breasts and bottom, Darcy united with his wife in one rawly penetrating motion.

On Christmas Eve they had first discovered the joy of making love in the tub, a blissfully rapturous interlude that they had repeated numerous times since. The sublime combined sensations of warm water surrounding their bodies while passion raged internally created a liaison of exquisite proportions. This assignation was both similar and yet superbly variant. Their bodies flamed, heat rising immeasurably until skin flushed; small bumps spreading over flesh fiery from within while chilled from the cold water and balmy air without, the fusion heightening the tactility of every touch and caress.

It was heavenly! For not the first time in their marriage they each wondered how it was possible for passion to soar to a higher pinnacle than yet attained. Darcy could not control himself, moving harshly within her in a frenzied voracity. Fleetingly he worried that he may be too rough, never wishing to harm her in any way, but she met his pace equally and propelled him on. The chill water swirled over their flaming flesh, surrounding and surging their most intimate regions as they loved. The racing sensations were inexplicably powerful.

Their culmination, when it finally arrived, swept through them in a torrent, shouts released in unrestrained ecstasy, only later thankfully recalling their isolation.

"Have fun, beloved, but be careful. I do not want to hear of my husband being caught in an undertow or snared in kelp."

"I shall be cautious. See you in a couple hours." He kissed her cheek and squeezed her hands before striding briskly toward the pier. Lizzy watched his tall, elegant figure until he disappeared from view, and turned toward the lodge with a sigh. She was not overly worried about him swimming in the open ocean, although the possible dangers were real. Mainly she recognized that she would miss him, but knowing how greatly he adored vigorous athletic pursuits, and swimming being one infrequently partaken, she could not deny him the activity.

The men bathed on the far side of the pier; the pier itself closed down for the afternoon to prevent any peeking, not that there was a woman alive who would admit to such voyeurism. Darcy had told her that most resorts scheduled male swimming in this manner. He said that most men preferred to swim in the nude; Darcy did, although some wore breeches or bathing outfits that were basically a type of long underwear of light wool. The vision of a company of nude men splashing about the waves was far too humorous to resist imagining, despite her embarrassment.

She sighed again. In truth, she would give anything to see her virile spouse with muscles contracting and tensing as he cut cleanly through the water. Granted the brief view of his strokes while with her that morning and well familiar with his manly physique, the picture was readily conjured and she shivered involuntarily. Stifling a highly unseemly moan, she entered the common room.

Those women left alone while their husbands or fathers bathed milled about conversing and sipping tea. Lizzy was greeted enthusiastically, her natural gregariousness rising to the fore. In no time at all she had formed numerous casual friendships and received a dozen invitations to dine at group tables. The array of women revealed a diversity of situations. Three young women were newly married like herself, one on her honeymoon and another pregnant with her first child as well. There were several unmarried maidens touring with families. The bulk of the women were older, enjoying holidays with husbands of many years or even decades. A final group consisted of the spinster sisters traveling with a brother; a widow and her companion; and Lady Eloise Underwood, a woman in her mid-thirties boldly traveling alone with servants only.

Lizzy had a delightful afternoon, tremendously entertained with titillating discourse, delicious snacks, and several games of whist. She returned to their chambers well after Darcy, who was already bathed and dressing for dinner. Not surprisingly, he had communicated sparingly with his fellow swimmers, learned only four names that he could effortlessly recall, and received no invitations to dine. He shrugged his shoulders, utterly apathetic to the lack of society, but more than willing to join a group table if it pleased his wife.

For their second night Darcy relented and they dined with a group of fellow visitors. He quashed with some difficulty the surge of possessiveness that reared, recognizing his wife's natural gregariousness that allowed her to make friends so easily and thrill in casual socializing. They dined in one of the larger dining chambers, elegantly furnished and softly illuminated by flickering candle chandeliers. Wide windows offered a view of the northern wood illuminated faintly by the moon. They were joined by Lady Eloise Underwood; the widowed Mrs. Alcastor and her companion Miss Stein; the Henner family, consisting of a husband and wife and two teenaged daughters; and Lord and Lady Stewart, a middle-aged couple with three children who were safely at home in Kent. Darcy was by far the most taciturn member of the assembly, although Lord Stewart was nearly as silent. The two men eventually discovered an equal passion for horses, a topic that would carry them through the evening.

The after-dinner recreation, aside from the usual games of cards, chess, and backgammon, was a silhouette party. Lizzy had read of the art form but never beheld the process. The fad of tracing silhouettes, or shades, began in France in the mid-1700s and was popularized by King George III with "shade parties" a favored amusement amongst the royal elite. The artist employed for the next three nights at the Caister Seaside Resort was a German who lived in Norwich and traveled up and down the coastal towns plying his talent.

Lizzy was thrilled by the idea of obtaining a tracing of her husband's profile and Darcy enchanted with having one of her, so they both consented to sit for the artist and purchase the portrait. Artists employed differing techniques and materials, but all focused on the profile. The concept was simple: A bright lantern was positioned near the subject's face, casting a shadow onto a white paper screen. The shade was then traced, to be later cut by hand onto black parchment or fabric, craftily embellished with slashed cuts for collars or jewels or other details, mounted onto a white background, and then framed.

The evening's diversion was tremendous fun, the German droll and cheerful as well as a gifted artisan. Darcy and Lizzy decided to place their shapes facing each other on the same picture, lightly bronzed and elaborately framed. It was a fine piece of art that would hang in their sitting room as a remembrance of this holiday for the whole of their lives.

It was late when they crawled into their bed, Lizzy already drifting into slumber when her warm-bodied spouse nestled against her back. He drew her close, wrapping limbs about her and kissing a bare shoulder.

"Good night, my heart," she whispered sleepily, twining her fingers between the longer ones lying on her belly. "Sleep well. I love you."

"I love you, Elizabeth," he answered with a gigantic yawn, kissing her ear and promptly falling asleep. Thus ended their first full day by the sea: sleeping deeply with cooling breezes and the muted sounds of crashing waves entering the half-open window.

❧

"Here you are, Elizabeth."

"Thank you, dearest." Lizzy smiled into her husband's eyes as she reached to take the tall glass of mixed fruit juice from his hand. "What do you have there?"

He placed the small linen-wrapped basket he held in his hand, the subject of her query, onto the little table between their chairs. Responding as he reclaimed his seat, "I thought while I was retrieving beverages for us I would also snare a snack. Completely selfish on my part as I did not wish to trudge up to the inn thirty minutes from now when you suddenly realized you have not eaten in two hours." He grinned while Lizzy rolled her eyes.

"Walking some hundred feet hardly qualifies as trudging, Mr. Darcy, and my increased appetite is all your doing, as we have established."

"As you wish, Elizabeth. I brought those pecan scones you like so much, some raspberries, and two bananas." He picked up his book, stretching long legs onto the lounger with a contented sigh.

It was their third day at the resort and thus far they had traveled no farther than the beach, pier, and pathways through the wood. Darcy had a whole list of local entertainments, most of which they did wish to visit, but the delight of leisurely hours staring at the waves and swimming was currently taking precedence. Both days they had risen later than usual, foregoing any bedroom activities to join the other guests for a lingering breakfast as the nightly mist departed. They had missed the sunrises, one of the items on Darcy's list, but the play of morning sunlight on the water and thinning fog was an enchanting backdrop while dining.

At some point in the day they utilized the bathing machine for an hour or two. Darcy did teach his wife to swim, the only stroke she was moderately proficient at being the backstroke. Modesty and safety prevented him steering her too far from the machine, even though they were well away from any potential prying eyes. Lizzy enjoyed the lessons and not merely because Darcy was the teacher. The water was colder then she would have preferred, but bracing and revitalizing nonetheless. Mostly it was the sense of balance and gracefulness she felt in the water that was appealing. Of course, they did manage to waste a great deal of time in horseplay with splashing, diving for rocks, tickling, and dunking. Inevitably the session ended with exquisite lovemaking.

Now they sat on padded, wooden lounge chairs located on the sand. An umbrella shaded them from the harsh sun. This area of the beach, the southern edge of the private expanse nearest the pier, was well away from the bathing machines situated to the left by the rocks. Numerous chairs and umbrellas were set to accommodate the guests. Several children frolicked in the surf, their squeals of glee mingling with seagull squawks and crashing waves. It was wholly relaxing, peaceful, and refreshing. The days were comfortably warm with the oppressive heat of Derbyshire left far behind; cooling, gentle breezes replete with the tang of salt and fish flowed intermittently.

Lizzy sipped her drink and nibbled on a scone while applying the finishing touches on a gown for their baby. Darcy read, naturally, Montesquieu having been completed so now he was studying the dry textbook on marine wildlife and vegetation with intent interest.

"Look here, love." He spoke into the silence, holding the page up for her inspection. "A drawing of those birds we saw yesterday by the rocks. An Arctic tern. I thought it was in the tern family, but the markings were different. They are indigenous to the polar regions, not seen frequently this far south. Listen to this: they migrate year-round from the Arctic to the Antarctic, making them one of the farthest traveling bird species known. They seek the summers in both places, rarely in their lifetime experiencing night. How fascinating!"

Lizzy smiled, displaying the appropriate amount of interest before resuming her own task. It was not that she found learning the names and habits of God's creatures unworthy, but her thirst for absorbing all knowledge to the tiniest degree was not as unquenchable as it was for Darcy. She was frankly flabbergasted that he could attend to the thick manual page after page as if riveting literature. What was even more astounding is that she knew he would assimilate and regurgitate eighty percent of what he read fifty years hence, his memory phenomenal.

The Henners wandered by, the thirteen- and fifteen-year-old daughters shyly glancing at Darcy, who was oblivious. "Mr. Darcy, Mrs. Darcy," Mr. Henner greeted with a bow, Mrs. Henner dropping a curtsey and softly greeting. "I pray your afternoon is progressing delightfully?"

"Very much, Mr. Henner. Thank you. Are you leaving the beach?"

Mr. Henner nodded. "The ladies are gathering for a swim. The menfolk will be meeting for faro in the game room. Will you be participating, Mr. Darcy?"

Lizzy stifled a laugh as a cough, Darcy ignoring her as he replied, "Thank you, but no. I will be bathing later, however. See you then, Mr. Henner?"

"Absolutely! Enjoy the sea air, Mrs. Darcy." They left, the girls giggling and whispering.

"William, if you wish to play cards, I do not mind. You do it so rarely that you should leap at the chance."

"I play rarely because I am hopelessly inept and unlucky, and I do not particularly enjoy the game. I may appeal to your magnanimity for a game or two of billiards this evening, however. Lord Stewart plays, as does Baron Noble. Would another short separation disturb you, dearest?"

"Of course not. I will miss you, but I am certain I can find some activity to soothe my broken heart." She reached over and squeezed his hand, Darcy smiling and squeezing in return. He returned to his book, Lizzy staring into the sea. After barely two days she felt as if they had been here a week. As enormously thrilling as their Derbyshire excursion had been, the fast pace had allowed little time for prolonged periods of relaxation. Here they spent inordinate amounts of time doing absolutely nothing, and it was fantastic. Lizzy would hesitate to admit it to her overprotective spouse, but her burgeoning body was gradually beginning to complain at the alterations! Personally she never would have imagined ever reaching a state of mind where lying lazily about was prodigious, but it was happening.

Lost in his text for God knows how long, Darcy was jolted to awareness by a piercing squeal from the water. It was only the children playing, Darcy smiling at their antics as he turned to his wife with a comment only to find her sound asleep. With a frown he realized that the sun had moved past the sheltering umbrella, the left side of her fair face dewy with perspiration from the direct rays. With a mumbled curse at himself, he rose hastily and readjusted the umbrella stand. He touched her cheek gingerly so as not to wake her, sending a silent prayer heavenward for his timing as the skin was unburned.

His eyebrows shot up when he noted the late hour on his pocketwatch, the time for men's bathing ten minutes away. He cautiously adjusted Lizzy's bonnet to further protect her face, studied the sun for a moment and moved the umbrella a bit more, only then satisfied enough to leave her napping. He knelt, gently rubbing over her abdomen and brushing the fingers resting there, leaning for a soft kiss to her head. Resisting the urge to kiss their child with difficulty, several loitering resort guests already peering at him oddly, he rose and crossed to one of the servants standing at attention by the beach edge.

"My good man," he began, pressing a five-pound note into the stunned servant's hand, "my wife is sleeping under that umbrella there. I am going bathing. I require you to watch the sun's movements and ensure she remains shaded. Wake her if this becomes impossible. When she wakens, inform her where I have gone and assist her to our room. Send for me if necessary."

His fears and concerns were for naught. Lizzy woke refreshed, well shaded, and with a cooling breeze wafting over her body. She instantly knew where Darcy was, not even needing to check her pocketwatch, the efficient servant merely confirming her supposition. They reconnected to mutual approbation in their bedchamber, both revitalized and dressed for dining. At the lower level landing, however, Darcy led Lizzy to the right and out the front doors.

"I know we have only been here three days now, but I am almost positive our dining room is to the left," she offered with a smile.

Darcy chuckled. "If you are not feeling faint from hunger, my love, I thought we could walk the beach at dusk. It is a peaceful time of day with the others engaged indoors and the birds calming for the night. I always love the serenity and beauty of the sea at dusk with the sun setting, casting remarkable shadows and deep colors onto the waves."

"You should have been born near the sea, William, although I cannot imagine you living anywhere but Pemberley."

"It is interesting, Elizabeth. In my travels I always gravitate to the seashore with eager enthusiasm. Yet, I am not fond of ships per se, despite owning four, nor do I care for sea voyages. I have met so many people who do live by the water and have discovered an odd phenomenon: those who live near the endless beauty of the ocean often take it for granted. They no longer notice the dazzling sunrises or sunsets, the surf does not move them, and they rarely walk the beach. I suppose we are all that way to some degree. I know that since sharing my homeland with you I have renewed my ardor for many of the wonders that I did not readily dwell on. It is as if I am seeing it for the first time through your eyes, and I love that you have provided me the opportunity. Therefore, I consider myself fortunate that I only view the sea every year or so, and from different perspectives. Keeps the experience fresh and ever changing."

He guided her warily down the dimly lit steps to the beach. They strolled in silence over the expanse of shifting sand toward the water line, the tide notably higher than when Lizzy departed that afternoon. The waning sunlight as it dipped below the western horizon did cast stupendous hues over the clouds and rippling water. With an essentially clear sky marred fragmentally with wispy strings of clouds, the rainbow tones of burnished scarlet, orange, gold, violet, blue, and a myriad unnameable massed together into a vivid display. They stood on the tide's boundary as the eastern horizon faded into deepening shadows; the terminal glimmers of sunlight on undulating waves slowly replaced with

MY DEAREST MR. DARCY

twinkles of starlight. A lone sailing vessel of indeterminate type passed gradually into the blackness off the world's rim.

All the while, Darcy and Lizzy stood with arms encircling waists, in silent contemplation of life and nature and the stunning majesty of the Creator.

CHAPTER FIVE

Magic Lantern

OVER THE FOLLOWING DAYS the Darcys altered their schedule some-what. They wandered into Caister-on-Sea, deciding to walk the half-mile, well-maintained, oak-lined trail from the resort to the small hamlet. The village itself was wholly unremarkable: quaint and tidy with a meager number of shops catering to the locals, small fishing boats in abun-dance, and a people universally rustic and hardy. The only true draws to the town were the church and castle, both of immense significance and interest to Darcy and Lizzy.

The Holy Trinity Church was in appearance like many other churches they had seen, architecture of the fourteenth century standard throughout the country. Of course, that is not to say it was not lovely. Built of grey brick with a tall castellated tower, high arched windows, and a long nave leading to an unusual pipe organ at the chancel. The organ pipes were split into two sets on either side of the aisle and appeared to lean toward each other as if whispering, creating a vague tunnel-like sensation entering the chancel. An ornately detailed hatchment with the royal coat of arms patently commemorated George III, yet it also showed cleverly painted-over markings for James I from two hundred years prior. The building was very old and deteriorating in subtle places, the modest community likely unable to contribute the monies necessary to sustain the structure. Darcy left a generous donation, feeling particularly charitable after a time of quiet contemplation both inside the sanctuary and strolling with his wife through the ancient cemetery and gardens.

Caister Castle was located near the church, a pleasant walk over the heathland. Sparse clusters of birch trees with a thick underbrush of gorse scrub and bracken with trailing vines of wild honeysuckle and bluebells adding a pleasing fragrance to overcome the faint but persistent odor of fish. Butterflies fluttered in abundance, unperturbed by the scores of bees attacking the fall blooms. The ruins of the castle sat rather forlornly on an expanse of wild land, the main pathway and road the only areas attended to. The moat had long since been drained and filled in with the debris of time, only the vaguest markings indicating that it had ever existed.

Built in 1432, the glorified manor house was notable for a couple reasons. One, the owner and architect was Sir John Falstaff, or Fastolfe depending on the reference, who was the inspiration for William Shakespeare's character of the same name. Luckily for Sir Falstaff, he was long since deceased before his name was immortalized in three of Shakespeare's plays as the depiction was not a favorable one. Secondly, Henry VI granted only five licenses to crenellate during his entire fifty-year reign, a legal necessity from the crown in order to build a defensible structure with battlements, moats, and gunports. Caister Manor, the home of Sir Falstaff, received this honor, allowing him to fortify his home with a ninety-foot tower, three-foot-thick bricks, and separate courtyards.

Lizzy and Darcy were two of a dozen persons wandering via the lush grounds and tumbling stones. The castle was actually well preserved despite the anomalous holes and general decay. The rusted chains to the absent drawbridge dangled beside the main entrance, the inner courtyard building frames were readily discernible, and the tall tower with sturdy spiraling stairway was easily navigable. Lizzy felt perky after so many days of lazing about, but did ascend the stairs in gradual stages with Darcy's hand as a rock on her elbow. The view from on high was well worth the breathlessness.

Another day found them comfortably settled into one of the resort's phaetons as they passed several hours meandering about the immediate coun- tryside with no distinct destination on the agenda. This was a highly irregular occurrence, Darcy being a man extremely detail oriented and organized with little spontaneity to his character! It was Lizzy's idea to set out randomly and Darcy blanched and spluttered at the concept, Lizzy laughing as she propelled him to the cozy carriage stocked with a picnic lunch, local map, and thick rug.

"Anywhere but east, Mr. Darcy," she said with lifted chin and imperiously pointing finger.

Darcy stared at her for a whole ten minutes, Lizzy maintaining her humorously commanding pose, while his mind raced with nearly audible clicks as the meticulous list of activities written in his firm hand were mentally checked. Finally he nodded, a tiny smile lifting the corners of his lips. "Certainly not east. Very well, Mrs. Darcy, as you wish. Ha!" The last to the horses and with a slap of the reins, they set off.

In truth, if one did not travel due south into Great Yarmouth, a destination for another day, or north where they had already traversed, west was the only remaining direction, and this meant touring the Broads. The extensive wetlands unique in all of England, given the name "Broads" due to the seemingly endless expanses of shallow lakes and connecting rivers, was honestly a sight to behold. Darcy drove the road north of the River Bure heading toward Stokesby. Within two miles they were on the fringes of the marsh, the ground notably soggier and air humid. Darcy cleared his throat, the usual precursor to an oration, but Lizzy spoke into the silence first.

"The Norfolk Broads," she began, in a strong lecturing tone as if reciting from a textbook, "an area approximately one hundred twenty square miles composed of seven rivers and fifty broads, most navigable. Home to a plethora of diverse wildlife, many believed to only reside here, and the necessary livelihood for the residents from Norwich and all the small burgs in the vicinity as the essential commerce route to Great Yarmouth and beyond. Most believe the vast waterways a natural landscape fashioned by God and time; others contend it at least partially a result of centuries of peat excavation. Whatever the case, currently the marshlands serve as a perfect habitation for farmers and fishermen. With vegetation naturally in abundance, cattle, sheep, and waterfowl flourish. The infinite quantities of hay, sedge, and reed are easily cultivated and sold."

She continued to ramble on as Darcy drove, his grin spreading with each passing word. When she had memorized the book he had brought with him, he had no idea, but his pleasure in her interest and recall was tremendous. He said little as they wheeled along the rutted tracks and across the numerous bridges, allowing his delightful wife to bask in her education and tease with her frequent inflections, gestures, and word usages, which were precisely meant to mimic him.

All the while they passed sprawling flatlands thick with reeds, rushes, fen orchid, ragged robin, and meadow thistle; all inundated with moths, butterflies, and dragonflies of truly astounding proportions and colors. Neither Lizzy nor Darcy had ever seen so many flying bugs. At times it was rather frightening, the masses of damselflies and gnats swarming about their heads. Twice they caught glimpses of otters slipping into the murky waters, and Darcy spied a red deer that agilely bounded behind a copse of sallow trees before Lizzy turned the direction of Darcy's pointing finger. The birds were as abundant as the insects, far too many to adequately identify. Even Darcy relinquished the endeavor, opting to purely take pleasure in the array of colors, shapes, and sounds.

Darcy kept the map on his knees, useful as a blanket shielding Lizzy's rubbing hand, but primarily to prevent him driving them astray. Unlike all their previous journeys where either Lizzy was supremely oriented, as during their frequent treks about Hertfordshire while engaged, or Darcy was knowledgeable, as in London and Derbyshire, here they were both utterly out of their element. The vague sense of unease never left him throughout the day, Darcy not comfortable in unfamiliar terrains. Lizzy had no trepidation whatsoever, giddily admiring the stupendous environs and trusting her husband's formidable competence as well as her own excellent sense of direction.

In the end, they suffered no mishaps. Aside from the reams of wildlife, people were also a constant. The river keels and wherries were interminable, not to mention the intermittent homesteads, all with congenially waving individuals aplenty. At Acle they veered northward to Thurne then turning easterly until reaching Hemesby, where they looped south to Caister. The landscaping remained stupendous and wildly diverse with wonders so numerous that they gave up even pointing or commenting, simply observing in serene awe.

By mid afternoon they were safely returned to the inn. Darcy escorted his wilting wife to their room, intent on tucking her in for a needed nap. Faint hopes were momentarily raised when she pivoted in his arms at the bedside, one arm slithering over his shoulder while tiny creeping fingertips fiddled with his cravat.

"Care to join me, my love?" she asked with upturned face and presented lips.

Darcy bent, accepting her invitation wholeheartedly, only to have her gift abruptly nullified by a jaw-cracking yawn. He chuckled against her mouth, withdrawing inches and caressing her rosy cheek. "Thank you for the offer, dearest, but I think I shall put you both to bed." He bussed her nose, whirling her about gently, and with a pat on the bottom assisted her into the bed. Sitting next to her warm body, he noticed not for the first time the increased inability to nestle snuggly against the front part of her. Not that he in any way was perturbed by this, joyously settling as close as feasible and resting a large hand over their child. He was extremely active at the present, kicking and jabbing his father's hand with great enthusiasm.

"I do not believe he appreciated the pickled herring," Lizzy mumbled, eyes already slipping closed. "He has been pummeling me since lunch."

Darcy laughed softly, leaning until his mouth rested over Lizzy's flattening navel. "Listen carefully, young one. Your father commands you to behave and allow your mother to rest. She promises to never consume pickled herring again. Be a good boy now and sleep." He continued on, Lizzy smiling at his silliness while the baby apparently disregarded his father's authority, exercise unabating. Internal calisthenics were not a deterrent to Lizzy's slumber after all, sleep claiming her within minutes. Darcy gently massaged her belly, sitting in serene contemplation for a bit before rising. After a soft kiss to her forehead and whispered *I love you*, he retrieved his book from the table and left the room.

The main patio was cast in deep shadows this time of day and nearly vacant. The men were bathing, but Darcy opted to enjoy the solitude. The book, *Moll Flanders* by Daniel Defoe, sat open on his knees, forgotten for the moment as he watched the waves and a group of children splashing.

"Mr. Darcy. I am surprised to see you here all alone and not bathing with the gentlemen."

Darcy glanced upward with a start, rising and bowing elegantly. "Lady Underwood. I trust you are well today and enjoying your visit?"

"Tolerably," she said with a smile, sitting gracefully on an empty chair across from Darcy. "It can be boring and somewhat lonely to travel unaccompanied, but I refuse to be a burden to my friends. Please sit, Mr. Darcy. No need to stand at attention." She smiled sweetly, fluttering her fan toward his chair.

Darcy hesitated, uncomfortably glancing about to ensure they were not alone, before resuming his seat. He sat with back ramrod straight, his bottom on the extreme edge, ready to spring up at the first opportunity for escape.

Lady Underwood laughed. "Relax, Mr. Darcy! I shan't bite, promise. Where is Mrs. Darcy, by the way?"

"She is resting."

Lady Underwood fanned her face, staring boldly at Darcy with a pensive expression. "Have you been married long, Mr. Darcy?"

Darcy stiffened even further, meeting her eyes with studied indifference. "Nearly a year."

"I must say I was surprised to see a woman so advanced in her pregnancy traveling. Few men would wish to squire their wives about in such a state. It is impressive and… touching."

Darcy remained silent, countenance impassive as he returned his gaze to the waves. Lady Underwood continued, "The two of you seem to have an unusual relationship. At least unusual compared to most I have observed. It intrigues me."

"Lady Underwood, forgive my rudeness, but I do not wish to discuss my personal relationship."

To his surprise, she laughed. "As you wish, Mr. Darcy. I meant no offense."

Silence fell. Lady Underwood eventually filled the quiet with casual chatter, Darcy responding in mostly monosyllables. Another fifteen minutes passed, Darcy wound tighter than a coil. Just as he prepared to excuse himself, Lady Underwood rose, lowering her voice seductively and leaning toward him. "Your wife is an adorable creature and I can certainly understand the attraction. Nonetheless, I know how difficult it can be for some men when their wives are in the advanced stages of pregnancy. Traveling unescorted does have its advantages, Mr. Darcy, but it gets lonely. Very lonely. Perhaps we can help each other."

The expression of disgust with flinty blue eyes leveled at her face caused Lady Underwood to retreat a step. Darcy said nothing, but his answer was clear. Still, she smiled, shrugging slightly. "Merely an offer, Mr. Darcy. Think about it. Have a lovely evening."

Darcy shuddered, rising quickly once she was gone, heart pounding with the need to touch his wife. He was not overly stunned by Lady Underwood's proposition, having been the recipient of similar sexual solicitations more times than he could recall, all of which revolted him and were never accepted. As disdainful as he considered the practice, he knew it was common. Nonetheless, he always felt dirty when accosted, but never more than now that he was married.

Elizabeth slept, face relaxed and gloriously beautiful. Darcy removed his jacket, waistcoat, and boots, cautiously nestling against her back. Lizzy sighed, murmured his name, and melted into his embrace without waking. He did not sleep, but held her close and tranquil for the next hour, renewed and cleansed in her presence. Only when she began to stir slightly with the familiar shifting cadence to her respirations indicative of pending wakefulness did he release the top buttons of her gown and slide a hand in to cup one ripe, warm breast. Squeezing tenderly and playing with a pert nipple, he feathered kisses along the nape of her neck. He was not yet aroused, instead merely delighting in the joy of holding her and knowing that eternally she would be his to love and talk with and share his soul.

Lizzy rolled in his arms with a heady sigh, sleepy eyes meeting his. His hand resumed its pleasure at her breast, the other stroking a now exposed shoulder. "I did not anticipate you being here when I awoke. It is a most pleasant surprise."

He smiled brilliantly in response, the dazzling smile only given to Lizzy with all his pearly teeth flashing and faint dimples appearing; the smile that extended into his eyes, blue orbs so crystalline as to nearly be transparent, sparkling, and shining so brightly that she could see a tiny image of her face in the mirror-like surface. Her breath caught at the boundless adoration and cavernous love reflected therein.

"I love you, William, with all my soul!"

"I love you, my Elizabeth. You are my soul, my blood and bone, my very life." He continued to stare at her, fondling her breasts but making no other moves, content to gaze at her for the present. Lizzy stared in return, hands slowly stroking over his body, as content as he to allow passion to gradually rise on the wings of idolization.

It could have been ten minutes, perhaps an hour, but eventually his shirt was discarded and her buttons were released with lips following the line of exposed flesh. Darcy tasted her, relishing the mildly salty flavor and musky odor of her skin. Mostly he thrilled at the soft mews of pleasure passing her lips and the rushing heat flushing her skin wherever he touched. Her breasts swelled and hardened under his hands and mouth. She tensed and shivered continually, the passage of time only heightening her response to his ministrations. Endlessly she murmured his name, driving him insane with desire and happiness.

Over the swell of their child, peacefully at rest, Darcy devotedly worshipped. He loved her belly, firm in its expansion yet remarkably soft; the outward shape changing as the baby shifted or as she moved. Each time they loved he asked if it was uncomfortable, especially with his large frame on top, but she insisted all was well as of yet. He gloried in this, fervidly excited by the sensation of their child pressed into his abdomen when they made love. If the growing bulk intruded somewhat, it mattered little to him, the emotional rapture in this tangible evidence of their love far superior. Now, he kissed over the perfectly stretched flesh, licking her navel and making her giggle, kneading gently before traveling lower.

Her legs were wholly unaltered. Strong, supple, toned; skin like finest alabaster or freshly fallen snow. Darcy could never name one part of his wife's body that he loved the most, all of her exquisite as far as he was concerned. Certainly there were specific areas that reacted to his touch with greater intensity, but as with her touch to his flesh, every inch was erotic and arousing.

Lizzy was lost in a hazy realm of purest passion. Remembering her name would be difficult, so crazily roused was she. Beautifully her husband transported her; hands, lips, tongue combined masterfully to provoke. Rhapsody grasped and waved through her head to toe as she screamed his name and arched in blissful surrender. Her muscles trembled, the sensations extending beyond what was humanly endurable as Darcy leisurely kissed, licked, and stroked his way back to her mouth, crushing her in a starved kiss.

His hands never ceased caressing, tenderly and lightly. He only allowed her to minimally calm, knowing that it would absolutely be only the beginning of the pleasure he could give her. "Beautiful wife, I so adore you. To love you is truly all I wish to do in life. If only all else could fade and I could endlessly rouse you. The satisfaction I derive from this alone is glorious."

She smiled, smoothing his rumpled hair and fingering over his radiant face. "How fortunate for us both, my heart, that I feel precisely the same. Loving you, watching your face as you attain your ecstasy with me, because of your love for me, is my greatest joy. How tremendously I love you, Fitzwilliam!"

Languid stimulation rapidly gave way to frantic need. Voracious yearning led swiftly to scorching delirium. Conscious thought rarely interjected when their mutual thirst rose to such unquenchable levels. Instead, they acted with pure animal lust, blindly moving as emotions guided. They fused as one with whispered endearments and promises uttered between pants. Indescribable flames of glory raced between their melded bodies, each feeling their partner's passion as intently as their own.

Each and every time they made love, whether playfully or hungrily, the sensations both physical and spiritual eclipsed what seemed logically possible. The thought of another never entered either of their minds; not a glimmer of curiosity or shred of wondering. How could it when paradise was achieved in each other's embrace?

Darcy held Lizzy for long minutes as they gasped for air and gradually restored clarity to blissfully fogged minds. Rationality always seemed to reassert itself with tender kisses along shoulders or necks or chests or wherever they found skin nearby. Fingers danced over perspiring flesh, involuntary writhing continued with neither wishing to break the connection hastily. Voices speaking softly, the individual words not nearly as important as the intonation.

Finally they collapsed to the bed, entwined and sated. Darcy did not speak of Lady Underwood. As deplorable as secrets were to him, more heinous would be hurting Lizzy. He honestly did not know how she would react to the idea of women propositioning her husband. Trust was absolute between them, so he knew she would never doubt his fidelity, nor would he doubt hers. If the situation were reversed, he would promptly kill the man, or at least maim him for life, à la Orman. As repulsed as Darcy was by Lady Underwood's solicitation, he was capable of shrugging it aside as a flaw to her character and of no importance to him. However, due to the forced proximity as guests of the resort, he thought it best to keep Lizzy unaware of Lady Underwood's interest. He wished for nothing to spoil their holiday.

He was thankful that he had alternate plans for dinner.

Mr. Vernor had directed his attention to an exclusive café in Great Yarmouth. Apparently extremely posh and intimate with spectacular French cuisine served as ordered from a menu of choices, the unique style of dining was born in France and gradually spreading throughout Europe and even to America. Conceived as a way to please the masses of France yearning for what was previously only available to the aristocracy, as well as providing employment for the suddenly adrift chefs and servants from the great houses, these establishments offering fine cuisine flourished.

For Darcy, a man who appreciated exotic foods and revolutionary ideals, the experience of dining with his wife in such a place was highly appealing. Especially since she had never been to France and despite Mrs. Langton's skill, pure French cooking was an art form only perfected by an authentic chef. Reportedly the owner of Tregois' Taverne de Yarmouth was exceptional, having trained under the famed Beauvilliers of Paris.

They dressed in their finest, Lizzy wearing her Twelfth Night gown. Her fuller bosom was displayed lusciously to an appreciative Darcy and the baby's bulge perceptible, but not large enough yet to tarnish the stunning beauty of how the gown flowed.

Darcy grinned, approaching his bewitching spouse with breathless enchantment. "Elizabeth, I... well, I truly do not have the words. You are beautiful, captivating, *magnifique, la femme plus belle dans l'univers, mon epouse, mon inspiration et survie...*" Despite his claim, words fell in a French torrent until trailing away at the crevice between her breasts.

"William, do we not have dinner reservations? I am rather hungry after this afternoon's exertions, and I distinctly heard a few rumbles erupting from your perfect midsection over an hour ago. Surely you are starved by now."

"I am famished, beloved, ravenous in fact, but not for food. God, Lizzy, how is it possible to want you so completely again?"

She laughed, pulling his face away from her décolletage and kissing him soundly. "Come, my dashing husband. I am currently famished for food, and I wish to be seen on the arm of the handsomest man to ever appear in Norfolk. Later, my lover, I will show you what it feels like to be wanted so completely." She sucked gently on his lower lip, the tip of her tongue caressing, only then clasping his arm and propelling him toward the door, ignoring his groan and faltering step.

Dinner was stupendous. The cozy café afforded an amazing view of the River Yare, the atmosphere so unerringly French that Darcy was transported to Paris and tremendously impressed. Lizzy had grown accustomed to French cuisine as prepared by Mrs. Langton, but this was subtly different. Darcy ordered several unique dishes never served at Pemberley, the sequestered table laden with far more food than they could possibly consume, even with Darcy's appetite. He wanted her to taste a bit of everything, getting a wee bit carried away with enthusiasm at the inclusive menu. Additionally, the wine cellar sported wines nearly unattainable even with the improved trade to France. Darcy ordered a rare Bordeaux from Château Haut-Brion dated 1796, eyes sparkling in anticipation.

They departed the quaint establishment, Lizzy assuming they were to return to the inn and rather partial to the idea as she quite frankly felt bloated and nearly ill from so much rich food. Darcy, however, steered her along the sidewalk toward a destination unknown.

"Surprises, Mr. Darcy?" she said with a tilt of her head.

He smiled, glancing sidelong into her face. "You know how I adore surprising you, Elizabeth. Next to making love with you it is undoubtedly my favorite pastime." Lizzy actually blushed, although no one was nearby to overhear.

They strolled slowly, Lizzy grateful she remembered to wear a shawl as the air was nippy. Darcy tucked her as close to his side as propriety allowed and attempted to increase the pace, but Lizzy held him to a stately speed. It was cool, but so crisp and fresh. Lizzy inhaled deeply of the salty breeze, the fragrance of the orchids and heather that grew in abundance mingling to create an oddly pleasant odor.

"It is strange to feel the mild chill here and know that home is probably sweltering." She paused to pick a sprig of heather, inserting it into his top buttonhole.

"It will begin cooling soon. Autumn is beautiful at Pemberley. Mr. Clark is a genius. He has the gardens planned so that they bloom in all seasons, but I do believe fall blooms are premiere. A final season to rediscover with you, my heart, then we will be entering our second year together and eagerly awaiting the birth of our first child."

He halted next to an enormous oak on the edge of a town square, the shops all closed except for a café on the diagonal corner. A handful of people wandered about, but they were alone where they stood under the faint gaslight. He grasped both her dainty hands in his, gazing into her eyes with his typical piercing intensity.

"Elizabeth, there is something I have wanted to ask you. I have been searching for the perfect moment and this feels right."

"Is everything all right, William?"

He smiled, stroking along her cheek. "Forgive me. I did not mean to alarm you. Everything is perfect. No, this is just a topic that has occurred to me from time to time, but especially since Marguerite and Samuel's wedding. I do not believe I ever told you, but every Darcy male, and many of the females, for generations unknown have been married in the Pemberley Chapel. It is one of those facts that simply are, without consciously holding much weight until the time comes to apply it. When we wed it was logical to marry in Hertfordshire with your sister and Bingley. I was mildly saddened to not say our vows at Pemberley, but it truthfully did not matter as I was so blissfully happy to have you." He laughed in delight. "We could have wed in a barn and I would have been deliriously ecstatic! Nonetheless, I have realized how deeply I desire to stand before Reverend Bertram, in front of the altar where my parents exchanged their vows, where I have worshipped all my life, where our children will be dedicated and baptized, on my ancestral land, and repeat my undying pledge to you."

He paused, squeezing her hands firmly, countenance serious but awash with devotion and love. "Elizabeth Darcy, will you marry me, again?"

Lizzy was speechless, her lips trembling and eyesight blurry with tears. She nodded and managed to croak a "yes." Darcy smiled brilliantly, bringing her hands to his lips for a hard kiss.

"Excellent! We can discuss the details later. I do so incredibly love you, Elizabeth." He bent and brushed her forehead. "Perhaps it can be a yearly event. Renewing our vows if for no other reason than to see you in your wedding dress again."

Lizzy chuckled, taking the proffered handkerchief to wipe her tears. "I doubt sincerely if it would fit me this year."

He extended his elbow, Lizzy snuggling close as they resumed their walk. "You can wear anything you wish, my love, as long as you promise to love me forever."

She looked up into his face, shaking her head. "Have no fear, William. That is a promise easy for me to make."

Darcy shepherded her toward the diagonal corner of the square, the café lively with numerous people sitting and standing, laughing and singing along with the minstrel band playing jauntily on the terrace. Darcy glanced at his pocketwatch, releasing a low whistle. "We need to step fast. I am afraid I miscalculated the time."

Past the café, down a busy avenue, and two blocks to the right brought them before a brightly lit theater. The building was clearly very old, probably built in the Elizabethan Era or shortly thereafter as it greatly resembled drawings Lizzy had seen of the famous Shakespearean playhouse, the Rose, in London. The original lath and plaster structure had been reinforced over the centuries with attempts to stylize and flourish the plain building obvious, giving it an amalgamated appearance of divergent architecture. Still, despite the mélange design, the theater was lovely, aided greatly by the modern gaslights, scrolling marquee, and gaudily painted posters blanketing the walls. The posters advertised the theater's entertainments, mostly of a musical or comedic variety rather than dramatic plays. Tonight's show was boldly declared on the marquee and on an enormous folded sign located by the door:

Professor Sciarratta's Magic Lantern Revue Presents
"Phantasmagoria"!

"Ooh! How fantastic, William! I adore magic lantern shows!"

"So you have seen them," he said. "I was not sure if any had traveled to Hertfordshire."

"Twice, at the assembly hall, as Meryton does not have a proper theater. The first was a repertoire of fairy tale stories, Aesop's Fables and Biblical tales primarily. The second was last summer, not too long after I returned from Kent. It was a re-creation of military battles from the Napoleonic Wars, complete with ships bursting into flames and cannon fire. Quite dramatic with accompanying sound effects and piano music; most patriotic and emotive. I have heard of *Phantasmagoria* though. Is it truly as frightening as written of?"

Darcy shrugged, handing over the coins to the ticket seller. "I do not know from firsthand experience. I have only seen three magic lantern performances, similar to your experiences. When I was eleven my family, including Lord and Lady Matlock with Richard, Annabella, and Jonathan, traveled to Paris. It was my first trip to the Continent. With the Revolution over and Bonaparte in control, it was deemed safe to travel." He paused to shake his head at that folly. "Anyway, Father bought tickets to see the original *Fantasmagorie* by Etienne Gaspard Robert. The show was all the rage then, the French not having had enough fright in their lives apparently." The last was spoken with dripping sarcasm, Lizzy also shaking her head.

"Of course, I was young and not fully aware of all the political intrigues, only wishing to see something reportedly so spectacular. Unfortunately, the day before the show Mother became very ill. It seems foolish now, but none of us considered the simple cause of pregnancy. My parents had given up on having more children so were caught unaware. Father insisted on staying with Mother until the physicians could diagnose and treat her illness; I would not leave although Father encouraged me to go, so the Fitzwilliams attended the show. Richard and Jonathan gushed on ad infinitum until I wanted to strangle them. Aunt Madeline found it too scary, Annabella had nightmares and refused to discuss it, poor thing, but Uncle liked it." He shrugged again.

They were inside the small lobby. Lizzy glanced about, noting the majority of the attendees to be common folk with simple suits and gowns. A minority was of a higher class and dressed in finer attire, and only a handful of those dressed as well as Darcy and Lizzy. She felt terribly self-conscious in her elaborate ball gown, but Darcy glided through the press of people as if at the Royal Theatre in London, heading directly toward the balcony stairs and confidently expecting all to part before him. The strange thing is that they did! A hush preceded their steps, a gap instantly created for Darcy to escort his wife through, and muted whispers of awe rose in their wake. Lizzy wanted to shrink into her skin yet concurrently puffed with pride at her husband's natural nobility and grace. Darcy was innocently ignorant.

The theater balcony did not boast individual boxes but rather was designed with long rows of seats, larger and more comfortable than the seats on the main floor. The low balcony afforded an excellent view of the black-draped center stage and two smaller curtained areas to the sides. The room was dimly lit although whether this was normal or as a means of increasing the eerie atmosphere for the performance, Lizzy did not know. The Darcys were ushered to seats in the first row, near the right side. Most of the seats were already filled, and the fever of excitement with palpable shivers of fear raced through the assembly.

Lizzy leaned toward her husband and whispered, "Will you hold my hand, William, so I will not be afraid?" She looked up into his face with a smile, but her eyes were mildly anxious. She would sooner be horsewhipped than admit it, but she was a bit frightened.

Darcy chuckled and took her hand. "I will protect you, my dear. No ghosts or specters will be allowed to molest you so long as I am here." He grinned and Lizzy laughed, slapping him with her folded fan.

Suddenly several of the dim lights were extinguished, throwing the already dusky room into deeper shadows. Numerous gasps were released, folks shuffling to their seats in earnest. A deep, sepulchral voice erupted into the hushed hall, startling everyone as the disembodied voice intoned without inflection:

"Ladies and gentlemen of the living, find thy seats hastily. The spirits are restless, desiring to arise in a dance macabre. None has the power to detain them. Do not be found wandering the empty aisles! This would be... unwise. Can thoust control the whimsy of the dead?"

The voice continued in the same vein as the final stragglers took their seats. The remaining lights were doused one by one until total darkness was achieved. As the final lights went out, slowly one by one, music gradually swelled. Music eerily brought forth by a glass armonica and accompanied by whining winds and clapping thunder. The gloomy voice grew fainter as it beseeched the dead to rise and begged for pity on the living until drowned completely by the wailing sounds emanating from the depths of the orchestra pit. Abruptly a deafening boom rent the air, succeeded by utter silence.

Lizzy was clutching Darcy's hand so tightly he winced, attempting to wiggle his fingers enough to restore circulation, but she would not let go. He bent to where he thought her ear was, whispering, "Elizabeth, I cannot feel my fingers." She started violently and then giggled, planting a kiss in the dark, which landed on the side of his nose, and loosened her crushing grip. He immediately encircled her shoulders and drew her into his side. No fear of inappropriate public behavior being frowned on here as no one could see them and he strongly suspected everyone would be tightly clenching each other before the show concluded.

The boom was rapidly followed by the appearance of a hazy red fog at center stage, the curtains apparently having been withdrawn. Out of the smoke a phantom appeared, growing larger and larger as it seemed to float over the gasping audience. The evilly grinning phantom was bathed in the red smoke, giving it the impression of blood, with a dagger in one hand and a severed head in the other. All instantly knew this to be the French Revolutionist Marat. Screeches pierced the void; fans could be heard fluttering wildly. Crazy laughter emanated from Marat's grin as he disappeared into thin air.

A collective breath was taken, but released in a rush as another apparition emerged. A woman in trailing garments, face beautiful initially but incrementally morphing into an old crone bent and wrinkled, her elaborate dress falling into rags as her old face decayed before their eyes until only a skeleton in strips of moldy cloth remained. She moved over their heads as she decomposed, skeletal form joining the now visible skeletons positioned all about the stage, or rather what had been the stage, but was now a cemetery replete with crypts and headstones. One by one the dead rose, walking on spindly legs, speaking from lipless mouths, empty sockets roving over the crowd.

On and on it went; one scene after another in rapid succession allowing no time to collect oneself. The haunting music rose and fell, ghostly voices droned, thunder and lightning crashed, specters and demons of all sizes materialized. Many of the scenes were familiar from literature or history: *The Nightmare* by Fuseli, *The Head of Medusa*, *Macbeth and the Ghost of Banquo*, other French Revolutionaries manning the guillotine, *The Opening of Pandora's Box*, *The Mysteries of Udolpho*, and more. Interspersed were the random bats, goblins, and ghosts, manifesting from all points on the main floor. The figures magically expanded to gargantuan sizes, hovering over the audience so closely that one felt they could touch them, and then shrunk before sinking into the ground as if returning to the underworld.

It was terrifying and fascinating. Fleetingly one would wonder how the effect was created, but generally the images and emotions engendered were so spectacular and realistic that coherent thought was eradicated. Lizzy, once past the introductory fright and comforted by Darcy's sturdy arm and warmth, calmed to a vague trembling and moderately heightened pulse rate. Screams were frequent, crying could be detected, and undoubtedly swooning occurred. The heat in the room increased from the combined press of bodies and raised body temperatures.

The crescendo was an appearance of all four Horsemen of the Apocalypse. The Biblical Riders trampled across the stage and into the crowd, swords and scythe brandishing, the clap of horses hooves echoing, while the original inhumanly bleak voice quoted from Revelations. With final bursting neighs and a resounding crash of cymbals, the Horseman rode through the back wall and precipitous silence fell, the room plunged into cavernous darkness for a full ten minutes.

The lights were lit all at once, revealing a tiny figure before the drawn curtains on center stage. The familiar voice again penetrated the quiet, although now it spoke with a bit more warmth and normalcy, "Ladies and gentlemen, I present to you the Illusionist Extraordinaire, Master of the Magic Lantern and Limelight, Creator of the Macabre, Professor Leonardo Finocchi Sciarratta!"

The tiny man bowed with a flourish, his grandly feathered tricorne doffed and swept theatrically as he blew kisses to the audience. The crowd erupted in applause and cheers, standing for a glorious ovation. Darcy and Lizzy stood as well, clapping enthusiastically. Her heart still raced and she was yet torn between loving the spectacle or hating it, but there was no doubt it was a stupendously artistic performance. Certainly one she would never forget, her fervent hope being that the ghosts did not resurface in her dreams!

CHAPTER SIX

Sunrise on the Sand

THE ROOM WAS SUNK into deepest shadows. It was that singular hour of the night when the moon and stars were fading, but the morning sun was still well hidden beyond the threshold of the horizon. Darcy snored softly, in his typical comatose state of slumber, blissfully dreaming, and wholly unconscious to his wife's gentle nudging and whispering.

"William, wake up. Dearest, please. William? Fitzwilliam Darcy!" Lizzy knew her husband to be a deep sleeper, but this was ridiculous. She did not wish to startle him, but the easy rousing was not working.

It was their ninth morning at the resort in Caister-on-Sea and Lizzy had determined that today they would not only finally rise early enough to view the sun ascend, but would be settled cozily on the sandy shore when it occurred. Thus she had forced herself to sleep lightly and had risen to the chill of pre-dawn, dressed in the darkness, and was now shivering beside Darcy's warm body. She sighed, gazing at his peaceful, handsome face and seriously reconsidered the wisdom of her plan. However, the vision of the very body displayed now before greedy eyes encompassing her on a blanket lying in the sand as the sun ascended and heated their skin was extremely appealing.

She lifted her skirts and nestled, kneeling, against his side. Bending over, she reverted to a form of waking known to prevail each and every time.

"William, my love, I need you to wake up," she spoke softly but clearly while bestowing firm kisses to his face.

Darcy groaned faintly, swiping at his face as if shooing a fly, then abruptly jolted awake and lurched up, nearly bashing heads with Lizzy, who fortunately had excellent reflexes. "Elizabeth! What is it? The baby? Are you ill? What…?"

"No, no! I am sorry, dearest. Please forgive me for startling you," she soothed with a giggle, stroking his dazed face and squeezing his hand. "I want to see the sunrise with you."

He stared blankly at her smiling face, illuminated by the single flickering candle on the bedside, very gradually and laboriously assimilating her words. "I have your clothes here, and a blanket, and I am certain it will be vacant down by the rocks. We can hold each other and watch the dawn." She paused, Darcy yet befuddled, and leaned in to touch his lips with hers. "It is on your list of things to do, Fitzwilliam. Additionally we can perhaps add another item to the inventory that I am positive has occurred to you but you were too polite to place in writing."

She accentuated her words with focused caresses, but it was not necessary as he was now fully awake and knew precisely what she meant. He smiled sensuously, staying her fondling hand but returning her kiss lustily.

"You are becoming quite proficient at these little surprises, my lover."

"I have learned from a master," she replied with a quick peck to his nose. "Now, get dressed, William! We have a sunrise to beat." She leapt up before he could halt her for more kisses, grabbing the pile of clothing on the foot of the bed and tossing them into his face.

Minutes later they were sneaking quietly down the dimly lit corridors and out the rear double-pane glass garden doors. A handful of servants were about, performing their morning tasks, but they ignored the Darcys as if they were invisible. It was quite dark on the pathway to the beach, but they had traversed it so frequently over the past week that their feet stepped confidently. The shoreline was deserted; debris and seaweed deposited by the high tides dotted the smooth sand, offering breakfast to the hundred birds pecking and fluttering about, which also ignored the Darcys.

Morning fog was minimal today, already drifted far out to sea where a thick blanket of clouds obstructed the black horizon. The sky immediately above their heads was crystal clear, the final visible stars extinguishing one by one as the sky began to lighten imperceptibly. Darcy spread the blanket on the firmer sand near the rocks. The waiting bathing machines provided additional cover from the possibility of prying eyes, although it was unlikely that anyone else would be about.

Their timing was perfect. The faintest glimmer of sunlight could be detected radiating above the massive fog bank, nearly indiscernible except for the hint of distinction between the rippling water and stationary cloud. Darcy was dressed in only a shirt and trousers with his large overcoat open and enveloping Lizzy, who nestled against his chest. Body heat emanated from his core, Darcy a true Englishman with internal furnace impervious to the cold. Lizzy wore a wool pelisse over her gown, so between clothing and husband, she was toasty. They sat in silence for the most part, Darcy gently caressing her arms and legs while Lizzy did the same, both content to enjoy the spectacle with nothing but the gently lapping waves as background music.

Like waiting for water to boil, the sun came up in timeless increments. Eyes burned with the strain of watching, but dared not close or look away in case that was the very moment she finally appeared in all her grandeur. Then it happened! No fanfare or blazing glory, but simply slipping above the clouds with majesty, completing a process performed millions of times in millions of ways in millions of places on the globe. Unconcerned with the mere mortals far below, she dawned, shining brilliantly with shades of gold unmatched on earth. All was illuminated and touched by her heat and beauty, the giver of life that she was, and all creation rejoiced at her coming. The birds flew higher and spoke louder, little crawling insects and sea crabs scurried about, flowers opened to receive the light, and the Darcys watched it all in awe.

Lizzy sighed, speaking barely above a whisper as it seemed somehow appropriate. "Not so dissimilar than all sunrises in the end, as they always move me, but I love how the waves glisten and the light outlines the clouds, showing all the layers. It is breathtaking."

"It varies so, the sun as it touches the clouds and water. At home the dawns and sunsets are essentially unchanged. Unless a storm approaches or snow blankets the ground, it is rarely differing. Beautiful, naturally, but the same. The ocean is something else. We could catch the rise each day and never see it precisely alike."

Warmth rapidly accelerated in the halcyon atmosphere surrounding them. Darcy rained tender nibbles along Lizzy's neck as she released a sound of pleasure.

"Perhaps you are correct about ocean sunrises, but I shall never tire of the dawn as seen from home. I love how the innumerable greens of the fields and orchards are gradually revealed as the sunlight spreads. It reminds me of spilled liquid gold as it touches the colors, covering all the valley and eventually the gardens and Manor in a brilliant blanket of light. Besides, we have our own rippling waters at Pemberley. The Cascade Falls and lakes with fountains shimmer and sparkle so stunningly." She sighed deeply. "I guess I am a bit homesick."

She turned in his arms, leaning backward against his bent knee to peer into his smiling face. Immediately he cupped her cheek, stroking softly with a thumb, pulling her tight into his body and surrounding her with muscular legs. Brushing her lips lightly, he then spoke, "Elizabeth, my heart swells when you talk of Pemberley with such devotion. I cannot express how pleased I am that you love your new home."

"The clichéd reply would be for me to say, 'How could I not love Pemberley as you are there.' Of course, this is largely the truth, but it is more than that."

"In what way?"

"I do not know if I can explain it, William. All my life, as much as I loved Longbourn, it never felt completely permanent. I suppose that is because as a female I knew I would someday marry and leave, but also because there was a sense of instability. We knew that if Papa died it could, and likely would, be taken away from us. Hardly a day went by that Mama did not lament the fact. It was home, but I remember feeling somewhat like the nomadic Arabs or American Indians." She shrugged and laughed, Darcy chuckling as well.

"I honestly gave it little thought, but I suppose I must have wished for a deeper feeling. Then again, I am fairly pragmatic, so undoubtedly figured experiencing emotions for a house impractical and silly. Whatever the case, when I saw Pemberley, something opened in me."

"How so?"

She sighed, staring blankly as she attempted to recapture those long-ago sensations. "Since reading your letter I had spent all summer replaying all our conversations, or rather the attempts at conversation. You know all this, love, as we have discussed it. Between my preconceived opinions and rudeness, and your awful communication skills, I had little to work with!" Darcy blushed slightly and Lizzy tickled him, both chuckling and unable to deny the truthful accusations.

"Anyway, after months of reflection, and extreme annoyance with myself in that I could not evict you from my mind, I came to the conclusion that I had erred horribly. Not in refusing your proposal, but in allowing my prejudices and independence to ruin the opportunity to get to know you. I cannot say I loved you, but I did recognize the good man you are. Yet never, not once, did I think of your wealth. Until I saw Pemberley." She reddened and Darcy lifted one brow with a crooked smile.

"Ah, mercenary after all, Miss Bennet?" He kissed her forehead and she playfully slapped his chest.

"Not quite that bad, but I am not completely stupid. We paused on the bridge and there she was. Oh, William, Pemberley is so beautiful! Maybe on some level it was because it was your home, but for a second all I could think was that I could have been Mistress of such a place. For the first time I truly grasped your station and the significance of your wealth. I laughed at what I knew every other girl alive would consider my extreme folly. I sat, still giggling, as the carriage resumed the ride up the drive. However, as quickly as those thoughts had come, they vanished. The closer we got to the house, and then when we did arrive and began our tour, all I could think of was you. Fitzwilliam Darcy, the man as I had begun to imagine you were behind the arrogant facade. I could see your elegance, grace, warmth, and taste in every corner of every room. Then Mrs. Reynolds began rattling on and on about what a fine Master you are, how all the servants and tenants revere you, what a doting brother you are, how generous and affable…"

"Mrs. Reynolds blathers too much and exaggerates," he interrupted with a hoarse grumble.

Lizzy laughed and reached for a kiss. "She loves you and only speaks the truth."

"Finish your tale, love, but save the flattery."

She slipped her arms tight about his neck, fingers in his hair. "How can I not flatter a man as perfect as you, Mr. Darcy?"

"I am warning you, Elizabeth!"

She laughed gaily, kissing him again. "Very well, in all seriousness. All my emotions swirled and coalesced, as you know, and I finally accepted the truth of my feelings for you. I do not think I can fully separate my love for you from my love for Pemberley as they are so intertwined. When I thought you were lost to me, again, I was devastated primarily at never being able to hold you and confess my feelings, but also with the reality that I would never see Pemberley again. Your home had surrounded me and entered my soul. I did not recognize just how much until after we were married. You remember how nervous I was as we approached the Manor after our wedding?" He nodded. "It was not merely because I feared being a good Mistress and making you proud; it was equally because I knew instinctively that Pemberley *deserved* an excellent Mistress and I feared myself not up to the task. I had already given her a personality all her own; she was as real as you or me and I did not want to disappoint her. It was then that I realized my love for a house! Over the next weeks it grew, and before our first month was complete, I understood what it truly meant to be connected to land and heritage."

He was softly stroking her face, smiling tenderly as they stared into each other's eyes. Lizzy reached one finger to trace his lips, speaking quietly, "Can I tell you something, dearest, without hurting your feelings?"

"Of course."

"When we get home, I do not want to go on any other adventures for a very long time. Naturally, it would be unwise," she said with a laugh and pat to her belly, "but mainly I want to abide, truly abide, at Pemberley. With you and Georgiana and our son and whatever guests visit, but always with the familiar walls around me and our bed to sleep in. For the first time in my life I truly have a home that is mine, will forever be mine, and I want to savor it."

"I promise we shall stay put, my love. However, I will remind you of your words when another long winter of snow and endless spring of rains causes you to lose your mind from the forced confinement!"

Lizzy laughed, again rubbing over her belly. "I think I shall have plenty to consume my time."

Darcy chuckled, lacing his long fingers through hers on the soft bulge of their child. He leaned for a kiss, pulling her further into his chest while gently reclining their bodies onto the sun-warmed blanket. The cushiony sand gave way under the weight, molding around their forms. Darcy's enormous coat covered them completely, shielding Lizzy from the whiffs of breeze as bare legs were exposed by a seeking hand.

Lizzy caressed over his chest, leisurely wending her way down his torso to groin, while kissing playfully with little nibbles and suckles as Darcy adored. He was dressed in his favorite gray overcoat, shirt open and no vest, his face stubbly and hair in sleeping disarray. Lizzy was always thrilled with his casual clothing and disheveled appearance, the combination of pounding surf and kindled daybreak enhancing the sensations.

"Hmm… William, I love you."

He withdrew from her lips with a faint moan, grasping her fondling hand. "Elizabeth, we should return to our room."

She opened her eyes in surprise. "I know you well, my lover. Do not tell me you have not dreamt of making love on the beach! I have seen your eyes rest on the sand when we bathe, with that singular expression I know indicates you are musing on making love."

"Decadent imaginings are not necessarily translated to reality, beloved. We are quite exposed here and I cannot allow my passion for you to overrule my judgment."

"Your judgment is flawed. It is barely six in the morning; no one arises this early, except for the servants, and they have no reason to come here. The bathing machines are not utilized until ten and shield us well. It is not yet fully daylight so our shadows will meld with the rocks, and your large coat will cover us. Since I rather enjoy making love to you clothed like this, it is an additional bonus for me."

She finished with a smug smirk, grabbing a thick lapel and pulling him roughly to her upturned lips. He relented for several blissful moments, hands intimately moving over her body. With a frantic gasp elicited by her purpose-fully stimulating hands, Darcy attempted to withdraw.

"Obviously you have given this serious contemplation, but I still deem it risky. Elizabeth! Desist!"

With a throaty chuckle and devious smile, she whispered, "You cannot return to the inn in your current condition anyway, Fitzwilliam. Therefore, you may as well search about to ease your mind as to our solitude, and then grant me what I demand. You know I shall prevail in the end anyway."

He stared at her, lips twitching as he attempted to maintain a stern glare. It was thoroughly impossible to do so when she was so beautiful and desirable with the rays of sunlight dappling her flawless face; lush, pert lips set in a succulent pout.

"What has happened to the sweet, innocent girl I fell in love with?"

"She married you, my marvelous lover. Alas, she is corrupted for life, naughty and wanton, a tigress by your own admission. Wipe the transparently false disapproval from your face, Mr. Darcy; the sun is rising higher and we are wasting precious time."

He caved, shaking his head and laughing as he rose. A quick scan and circuit around the machines proved the asserted fact that they were utterly alone. The majority of the beach and resort on the bluff above were yet sunk in shadow, only the few flickering lights visible at lower level windows. Briskly he strode to where Elizabeth waited, now sitting up and watching as he approached, coat billowing as he walked his uniquely powerful gait. He knelt by her knees, but before he could lay her back onto the sand, she encircled his waist with a firm clasp and squeeze.

Darcy grinned, lacing lean fingers through her trailing hair as she attended with devoted caresses. Of course, she was correct; he was helpless to resist her allurement and advances. The man of caution and towering regulation was shattered before the onslaught of her love. How she excited him and fulfilled him was infinitely beyond any dream he had ever entertained. He honestly believed the entire resort population could walk by and he would not notice, nor care.

"Fitzwilliam," she whispered as they loved, nibbling on an earlobe while his hot breath rushed over her neck in cadence with his tireless motions, "are your daydreams and fantasies being fulfilled?"

He lifted with a groan, arching and slowing until physically able to speak. "Truthfully? Oh God, Elizabeth! Wait!" He gasped, staring at her with glazed eyes. "I... I visualized us totally naked, rolling about on the hot sand in broad daylight. Completely impossible, naturally. This... Lizzy, my wife... every time is a gift with you."

Lizzy gazed up at her husband, resplendent with his morning face flushed and hair tousled, half dressed with flowing coat perfectly accentuating his masculinity. He was stupendous, abundantly gratifying every dream she conjured.

Several nearby birds squawked and flapped away in fright at the shouts emerging from the rocks, but no other life forms were aware of the rapture attained on the sand. The Darcys would be mistaken to assume they were the only couple to ever watch the sunrise and take advantage of the isolation. Luckily they were the only ones to pick this particular day, but the resort staff had more than once needed to discreetly steer a tiptoeing couple in an opposite direction.

Sneaking back into their room without being noticed was a bit problematic as more staff members were about. Still, the servants skillfully glanced in the opposite direction or busied themselves at some task until the Darcys passed by. Their faces were rosy with embarrassment, but both agreed the outing was worth any humiliation. Once in their room they laughed giddily like children, randomly dropped their sandy coats and the blanket, and commenced kissing and embracing with joyful enthusiasm.

"Elizabeth, I am as foolhardy and nonsensical as a youth when around you! And as amorous. Lord, what you do to me!" He grasped her bottom and pulled her tight, fingers traveling to the buttons down her back as he assaulted her mouth.

The zealous embrace continued until Darcy laced one broad hand through the wildly tangled hair on the back of her head, whereupon Lizzy frantically reached to where his fingers were with a gasp.

"My hair clip! It's gone!"

"Which clip?"

"The one with the pink flowers on it. Oh, I love that clip!" She was searching around the floor at their feet, Darcy joining the visual exploration, but it was nowhere in the room. "It is an old one of mine and not that important really, but I have had it for years."

"Shhh, relax, dearest. It is surely somewhere between here and the rocks. I will go look for it."

"I am sorry, William."

"For what? I have already had one of the best mornings in my life. I can wait to make love with you again for a few more hours," he grinned cheekily and kissed her lightly, Lizzy laughing.

"Thank you. I love you."

"I know," he said with an airy wave from the door.

The lost clip was discovered on the last step before the second level landing, a servant bending to retrieve it as Darcy rounded the corner. Darcy maintained his dignity, exchanged vague pleasantries, and thanked the servant who calmly handed it over.

Smiling happily and whistling cheerily, Darcy absently fiddled with the clip as he turned toward the stairs for the third floor where his adorable wife was awaiting his return, hopefully unclothed on their bed. Lost in visions so delectable, he did not notice a door opening until Lady Underwood was standing five paces away blocking his path. He halted abruptly, the silly grin erased instantly for a deep scowl.

In the intervening days since her disgusting proposition, Lady Underwood had made one additional overture toward Darcy. On the afternoon after the *Phantasmagoria* he walked along the garden pathway toward the wooden stairs on the northern side of the pier that led to the beach where the men bathed. She leaned casually against the trunk of a birch that grew on the edge of the path, the location clearly deliberate to waylay a walker as there was nothing in the area of interest. Darcy was not overly surprised to see her boldly lurking on the path since he had caught her eyes on him frequently in the ensuing days. She would smile in a mildly seductive manner, her eyes brazenly running over his body in a way that made him want to retch. Thus far he had managed to avoid her, but he knew her kind and figured she would renew her advance if at all possible.

Darcy did not slow his pace and instantly turned his gaze away after the briefest of eye contact in hopes that she would leave him be. Alas, it was not her intention to be ignored.

Her sultry voice pierced the placid silence, "Mr. Darcy, I have been expecting you. You are a creature of habit, I have deduced, as well as one who appreciates vigorous exercise." Her eyes dropped briefly below his waist although the double entendre was obvious nevertheless. "I can assist you in the latter and have been waiting patiently for your acceptance of my offer."

She stepped into the path, her hand already extended toward him. Darcy veered to the side, extreme fury rising so abruptly that he honestly did not trust his control if she touched him or obstructed his passage. Fortunately the hazard was deflected.

"Darcy! I hope you are up for a vigorous swim and muscle exertion as the surf is rough today." It was Mr. Henner, the older man suddenly visible through the thick bushes lining that portion of the curved path to the north. The irony of his innocent phrasing was not lost on either Darcy or Lady Underwood, her chuckle thankfully only audible to Darcy as she turned and smoothly hid behind the tree.

After that, convinced of her persistence and cunning, Darcy was extremely cautious. He angrily observed her false friendship with Elizabeth, who had no idea of her true nature or treachery as Darcy refused to allow her antics to invade their delightful holiday. He prayed that she would depart the inn, but each evening she was there in the salon, flirting and chatting. He strongly suspected that her claws had dug successfully into a couple of other gentlemen, noting oblique glances and touches, which sickened him, as one was a married man as well. Again, Darcy was not naïve, but the activity revolted him nonetheless.

Fortunately he and Elizabeth were almost always together and alone, neither desiring to socialize overly. But three times in the past two days Darcy was forced to change direction or abruptly engage one of the other guests in conversation to avoid Lady Underwood accosting him. He surrounded himself with other gentlemen on their walks to the beach or the few manly pursuits that separated him from Elizabeth. He was exceedingly careful, but now it appeared as if his luck had run out. With his mind on other matters his caution was forgotten, and the early hour meant that the corridor was devoid of anyone and likely to stay that way.

"Mr. Darcy, what a pleasant surprise." She wore a dressing gown and robe, her hair braided and hanging over one shoulder. She was a beautiful lady, no doubt, but also quite aware of her beauty and equally aware of the effect of her attractiveness on men, an effect she utilized as a spider did its web.

"Lady Underwood," he replied with a proper bow and eyes diverted, already taking a step to the left to pass her. "Good morning. Excuse me."

She moved as well, Darcy again forced to halt or bowl her over. "Your color is high this morning with vigor radiating. You are well, I can see."

"I am very well, but in a hurry. Good day, my lady."

"Oh, it shall be a good day indeed. I am very well also, Mr. Darcy. Improving by the moment, in fact. I heard your voice but waited until the servant left. I was beginning to doubt you would come to me. So much pleasure has been missed, but we shall rectify that, won't we?"

Darcy was stunned. Bold propositions he had seen, yes, but this transcended them all. For several seconds he was honestly speechless, staring at her lewd expression in frank amazement.

"Lady Underwood…"

"Yes, Mr. Darcy," she interrupted, her voice very low as she stepped nearer and lay one hand on his arm. "No need for discussion or further hesitancy. You should not stand about in the hallways. You would not want your sweet wife to know of our activities."

He jerked his arm violently away, supreme anger overcoming his surprise. "Lady Underwood, you are horribly mistaken. I am retrieving an item for my wife and merely passing by."

He again sidestepped to walk around her, but she reached out with a steely grip to his wrist, halting him and moving even closer until touching his body with her breasts. Her whisper was husky but with a hint of menace, "Come, Mr. Darcy. Be reasonable. A man like you needs his urges satisfied and I am willing. There is no logic in resisting."

Darcy's rage was monumental, only supplanted by his intense disgust. "Let me pass before I am forced to inflict harm upon you. You disgust me and I can assure you nothing will ever happen between us."

"You would be wise to rethink your refusal. I am accustomed to getting what I want and will find a way to secure my wishes. I would rather Mrs. Darcy not be hurt. She is a dear girl and would be crushed to discover that her beloved spouse seduces unescorted, fragile women."

Darcy's voice was icy, "I am warning you, leave Mrs. Darcy alone or the consequences will be extremely unpleasant. Now, unhand me instantly. A scene and subsequent scandal would not benefit either of us. Let us drop this unpleasant topic."

"Now you are mistaken, sir. The topic is a very pleasant one, for both of us. Please do not necessitate me causing trouble for you. I do have some influence, but would rather our relationship be mutually satisfactory, and voluntary."

Darcy was livid, face dark and rigid with an anger seldom experienced and rarely manifested toward an individual. Despite her bluster, Lady Underwood paled and instinctively released his arm and retreated a step. Darcy stiffened to his full height, towering over the petite woman as his entire body hardened with unmistakable menace. When he spoke, his voice was glacial, but terrifyingly composed and low.

"Listen very carefully, my lady. What you are asking will never happen. Furthermore, it is you who are unwise if you believe for one second you can threaten Darcy of Pemberley. I know who you are and know your reputation. I suggest you inquire of these 'influences' you state you have. You will discover the extreme error in your judgment regarding me and the power you think you have. I assure you that my power vastly transcends yours. In the meantime, stay away from me and from my wife, or it is I who will be causing the trouble. Are we clear?"

To her credit, Lady Underwood remained collected under her pallor, but her eyes were frightened and her voice faint. "Very clear, Mr. Darcy."

CHAPTER SEVEN

Up, Up, and Away!

UNDER THE CIRCUMSTANCES, DARCY was thankful to find his wife in her bath. By the time they reunited for breakfast his anger was dimmed to a simmering irritation and well buried. His joy at seeing and touching his beautiful Elizabeth was genuine and purifying to his soul. Lady Underwood was not about as they descended, fortunately; the Darcys breaking their fast and leaving shortly thereafter for a day trip into Great Yarmouth.

Once tucked comfortably into the coach with windows open, Darcy inhaled deeply of the tangy air, twined fingers with Lizzy as she turned a brilliant smile his direction, and felt the final vestiges of his chagrin dissolve. Aside from the sheer elation found in the presence of his beloved wife, there was also the anticipated delight in today's outing.

Great Yarmouth, or Yarmouth as the locals referred, was one of the few North Sea–located towns famous as a seaside resort. It held this distinction since 1760, when one of England's first seaside bath houses utilizing the chill water of the ocean was constructed here. The narrow strip of flat, sandy dunes situated between the medieval walled Rows east of the River Yare and the pebbly beach bore the unusual name Denes. Unique in all of England, the Denes had for centuries served as a haven for cattle grazing, for fishermen to dry their nets, and for the community to relegate other unpleasant tasks, such as criminal hangings, from the citizens safe inside the thick walls. This remained the status quo until wise and greedy city entrepreneurs recognized the financial advantage to cashing in on the seabathing phenomena by expanding on the existing wells and building a bath house. The mile-long expanse of finely churned sandy beach coupled with the wide barrenness of the Denes created the ideal environment. Great Yarmouth's economy subsequently exploded. Herring and mackerel fishing would endure as a primary industry, but tourism boomed. The ancient jetty near the bath house was rebuilt and reinforced until eventually extending 456 feet out to sea, providing both a stupendous view and exhilarating sense of the open ocean.

It was to this pier that the Darcys headed first. Despite their early rising and vigorous exertions, several days of lying about inspired each of them to wish for a brisk walk and full day of entertainment. Mr. Anders deposited them by the pier with instructions to park near the north gate of Nicholas Church. The streets were busy with the combined traffic of Yarmouth's twenty thousand natives attending to their daily activities and the massive number of visitors. The popularity of Great Yarmouth as a resort had rather surprised Darcy upon his investigation. He had heard of the city, naturally, but was only vaguely aware of the particulars. Quite obviously, as they crept snail-like through the streets, hundreds of English tourists were abundantly conscious of Yarmouth's charms.

The harbor and pier was clogged with fishing boats of all sizes replete with clamoring fishermen and straining nets of fish. The smell would have been overpowering if not for the constant easterly breeze capturing the wafting odors and transporting them far to sea. Nonetheless, it was unpleasant at times. Lizzy, as well as most of the women meandering about and a good number of the men, kept a perfumed handkerchief close in hand. Happily, the stench waned the farther one walked down the jetty. Darcy kept a firm grip to Lizzy's elbow as they walked the damp, uneven wooden dock. It was wide and very well constructed, intended to cater to the tourist desiring the excitement of invigorating ocean winds and pounding surf under one's feet; however, it was also a working dock with hardy men toiling and the risk of impeding ropes and fish innards blocking the path.

They made their way to the extreme end without mishap. It was a beautiful day, cloud-free and warm, the incessant air currents gentle but cooling. The majority of the boats preferred to anchor closer to shore for the ease in offloading their catch, which meant the far ends of the wharf were empty. Other brave folk were standing at the rail, Darcy and Lizzy finding a clear space with a stunning view of the endless waters north and east. They stood nestled close, Lizzy absorbing Darcy's radiating heat, with backs to the shore. The surf roiled and gulls screeched, the sounds just loud enough to drown any noise from the shore and moored ships, rendering a disconnected sensation.

"If the boards beneath our feet undulated it would be exactly how it feels on a ship," Darcy said. "I remember the first time I took a sea voyage, when we went to France, I could not quite decide if I enjoyed it or not."

"Did you get seasick?"

"No, fortunately. Jonathan did, poor thing, as did my uncle, although he would likely deny it if you asked him." Lizzy laughed. "They both retched horribly and kept to their bunks. Thankfully it was only a channel crossing. No, I always suffer a headache while aboard ship. My stomach has no upheaval, but my head splits." He shrugged. "I do not know why. Lying down makes it worse, which seems odd. I do best if I stay near the bow, feel the spray, and breathe deeply. Anyway, aside from that discomfort, I do love watching the waves, and there is nothing as stupendous as glimpsing the occasional whale spout or jumping porpoise. Yet at the same time the sense of helplessness, of knowing there are fathomless depths of water under and all about is disconcerting. Maybe that is why I get such a headache. I despise being out of control and having my entire fate at the mercy of other people and natural forces."

He shuddered and Lizzy chuckled, squeezing his arm. "Yes, I can see why this would frustrate you. I daresay I would feel much the same so am thankful for the firm foundation. Richard suffers no ill effects?"

Darcy laughed. "Richard is a born seaman. Honestly. I told him he was a fool to not join the navy, and he did consider the option, but decided the draw of the cavalry outweighed a ship. In the end it makes the most sense since, like me, he was practically born in a saddle. Still, I was a bit surprised as he perpetually extolled the exploits and virtues of Admiral Nelson with stars in his eyes, forcing me to play navy whenever possible. He was always Nelson and I some underling being ordered about to swab the deck or load the cannons."

Darcy smiled in remembrance. "Even then he possessed the air of command. I wish you could see Richard in this light, Elizabeth. He is so different. You would be amazed."

"Why did he not join the navy then?"

"By the time he finished at Cambridge, Nelson was dead. Napoleon was raging across Europe and soldiers were needed. It truly did make the most sense for him to be in the cavalry, and Uncle encouraged it. Richard rose quickly. He earned the rank of Second Lieutenant before he left for Russia in 1812. By the end of that campaign he was elevated to Captain. By 1815, at Waterloo, he was a Junior Major commanding two companies and distinguished himself brilliantly. He earned his Colonel's stars at battle's end."

"I confess I have not given much consideration to Richard's career. How remiss of me! I had no idea he was such a hero. You all must be so very proud of him."

"Assuredly. Although it was horrible during the long months with no communication. Aunt Madeline worried so. She had not embraced Richard joining the military, even though it is a typical career choice for second sons, and Richard would not be deterred. Still, I suppose all mothers are torn between pride in their sons for serving their country and tremendous fear. Each letter would be met with great rejoicing. We did not see Richard for nearly four years, but he returned with injuries minimal and medals abounding. We were blessed, so many families losing loved ones during those long years."

"Was he much changed when he returned? One hears terrible stories of what battle does to some men."

"Oddly, no. At least not too much. Richard has ever been gay hearted and humorous. Jolly, I suppose, is an apt word. Yet he is amazingly intelligent and focused. The casual acquaintance does not see that aspect of his personality. We spoke at length and seriously about his experiences at war, and he shared with Uncle, but few others will ever hear him talk of it without a ready joke or clearly embellished tale. Georgiana loves to hear him regale his exploits, wholly unaware that none of them bear more than a passing resemblance to the truth."

They wandered slowly up the pier, past the cluster of inns and boarding houses that surrounded the bath house, turning north onto the broad esplanade separating the beach from the Denes. The once restricted area outside the medieval town walls was gradually evolving from a wild wasteland to a developed part of the city, but the progress was sporadic and frowned on by many town officials, creating a pattern of intermittent buildings and empty spaces. The walkways leading to the beach underwent similar haphazard planning with proper development recently unfolding. Still, the rough avenues were not a deterrent to the mass of visitors. The beach was packed with blankets and umbrellas as people enjoyed the sun and sand, children by the dozens frolicked in the tide, and long lines of tourists rambled under the tree-lined boardwalk.

Lizzy and Darcy joined the strollers, arm in arm and slowly wending their way to the main avenue that would take them into town proper. North on King Street to the town marketplace wall to wall with chiefly locals buying and selling, they bypassed the crowds by veering to the left-hand sidewalk. The Church of Saint Nicholas, patron saint of fishermen, with towering gothic spires, was visible from a great distance. The enormous gated grounds were blanketed with thick lawn and shaded by innumerable ancient trees. Built in 1119 with the typical cruciform structure, the original edifice had been altered and added onto so many times in so many styles that one could no longer rightfully say the actual architecture. The building was gigantic, providing services for over a thousand parishioners and at one time boasting eighteen separate chapels catering to individual families and guilds. Currently the church was partitioned by three brick walls to allot individual places of worship for the Independents, the Presbyterians, and the Churchmen. This strange configuration was an oddity worth seeing, Lizzy and Darcy spending a pleasant hour investigating before meeting up with Mr. Anders and the carriage.

Lizzy requested walking to the southern end of the promenade, but Darcy insisted on the carriage, refusing to weary her overly. There were those moments when his over-protectiveness irritated Lizzy, this being one of them, but she bit her lip and did not argue. Of course, it would have been a fruitless endeavor anyway, Darcy being a man intensely stubborn in spite of a general desire to grant his wife whatever she wished. The press of the crowd meant that it undoubtedly took twice as long for the carriage to weave its way to the south Denes; however, the manifest affluence of the Darcy coach with emblazoned crest meant the crowds parted and Mr. Anders easily drove to the front entrance of the temporarily renovated training field at the Militia Barracks.

Today was a special day at Yarmouth. Precisely one month previous, on August 15 of 1817, the foundation stones were laid in the exact center of the military racetrack for what would two years hence be the first columnar monument in all of England raised to honor Admiral Lord Viscount Horatio Nelson. To celebrate, and to partake in the fever and publicity, a balloonist from Norwich was lifting off for a proposed flight to London.

As far as the monument was concerned, Darcy had a vague recollection of reading a couple short articles about the proposal, but the facts had escaped his memory until a week or so prior to their trip. Even then, it had been an offhand comment by Mr. Keith regarding the laying of the foundation that restored the memory. He had promptly added an inspection of the site to his list.

The balloonist, however, was a total surprise.

"William, did you hear about the balloonist?" They were in their room on the third night of their sojourn in Caister-on-Sea, having retired to the bedchamber after a pleasant evening of conversation and cards with the other guests. Darcy sat on the edge of the bed where he had rather impatiently awaited his wife's emergence from her dressing room, and was currently stroking and kissing the thinly satin veiled bulge of their child. Lizzy stood tolerantly, running fingers through his hair, smiling with pleasure at this necessary part of his day.

He glanced up at her. "A balloonist? Where?"

"Seven days from now near the site of Nelson's monument. A hydrogen balloon, so the leaflet says, to launch and fly to London. Can we attend?"

"It would be delightful, beloved. I have never witnessed a balloon takeoff, have you?" He resumed his attention to an active offspring, pressing his cheek against the insistent kicks readily felt.

"Five years ago we spent the Christmas season at Cheapside with Uncle and Aunt Gardiner when James Sadler took flight from Vauxhall Gardens. It was stupendous. I am surprised that you have not seen the spectacle, William, especially considering how captivated you are with strange inventions." She lowered onto his lap, leaning for a kiss.

He chuckled lowly, nestling her close and continuing the steady caresses to her belly. "Merely not in the proper place at the proper time. I remember the event you speak of, but was snowed in at Pemberley. Pity. Perhaps we would have encountered each other in the crowd."

"Sweet thought, my love, but I was sixteen and would have dismissed you as an old lecherous man even if you had cast a second glance my way, which is highly unlikely."

"I should be offended, but instead I believe I shall show you old and lecherous!" And with that pronouncement he clasped and carefully tossed his squealing wife onto the bed, proceeding to lavishly prove that lechery was an apt description, but assuredly not old.

The reality is that Lizzy was accurate in her assessed surprise at him having not seen a hot-air or hydrogen gas balloon. It was a tremendous delight to be treated to this rare occurrence, balloon flying still an extraordinary and dangerous undertaking despite being avidly pursued since the Montgolfier brothers first flew in 1783.

The rough ground of the Denes surrounding and including the Militia Barracks and Naval Hospital was gradually transforming into a developed region catering to the tourist. The construction of the track for horse racing built in 1810 aided the city planners significantly in their essay. Now, with the essential funds finally attained to erect the monument and the initial steps in building begun, public awareness beyond Nelson's birth land of Norfolk was spreading and the prospect of increased revenue was high. If the volume of people presently paying the modest fee and filing in to take seats was any indication, Great Yarmouth was in for a rapid explosion of progress.

Darcy gladly paid the steeper price for premium seats under the canvas awning, shade being an asset worth any cost. The gargantuan balloon could easily be seen from anywhere inside the makeshift stadium, and from a great distance without, but naturally part of the draw was watching the balloonist in action. This could only be observed from inside.

The fabric of the mammoth gas-filled balloon was woven with concentric circles of maroon, yellow, forest green, pink, black, white, and violet—all colors dazzling in the bright sun. Held securely to the ground by dozens of sturdy tethers, individually manned by burly fellows, the willow branch woven basket sat sedately on the dirt. There were so many people milling about the arena that until the exhibition commenced, no one could determine who the balloonist was.

"Ladies and gentlemen!" Barking in a powerful voice, a tall man dressed in a stunning suit of purple commanded silence and attention. In the hush that fell, he continued dramatically, raising the audience's expectation to a fever pitch, "Welcome one and all to Great Yarmouth and this extravaganza! Today all shall be witness to an aerial feat of magnificent proportions! Trusting to a liberal dose of mastery in the science of gases and atmospheric pressures, the balloonist is nonetheless an adventurer of astounding bravery! Ever at the merciful whims of nature and the Almighty, the courageous balloonist risks life and limb with each ascent! Who among you can claim such fortitude? Do you have the nerve? The sheer audacity to tempt fate? Nay, you confess? Well, allow me to introduce one who possesses all these traits and more! Ladies and gentlemen, please, a hardy round of applause for Miss Alita van Lingen!"

With wild applause following a brief caesura of stunned awe, the crowd greeted the impressive woman who materialized from the sidelines. Even from their seats high above the floor, Darcy and Lizzy could discern Miss van Lingen was easily six feet in height and probably as brawny as Darcy. As incongruous as it seemed, she wore a scarlet gown garishly adorned with lace and frills, a wide brimmed hat with ribbons and foot-long feathers, and a hem-length boa in white ermine. She waved her gloved hands grandly with florid bows in all directions, blowing kisses enthusiastically before entering the balloon's small basket. The announcer shut the door with a flourish, gallantly grasping Miss van Lingen's hand for a courtly kiss.

In point of fact, the actual ascension of the balloon was rather undramatic. One by one the tethers were released, the balloonist calculatingly emptied the hanging sand-filled ballasts as the balloon rose until well above the earth. So gradually as to be nearly indiscernible, the balloon began to glide horizontally as air currents were encountered. Necks arched and eyes strained with the effort to catch the infinitesimal alterations of the colossal device; time dragged as the ponderous contrivance gracefully and majestically soared until finally a mere dot lost among the wispy clouds.

All the while the people watched, collectively held their breaths and waved incessantly at the disappearing pilot. For long moments no one moved, as if under a spell difficult to break. Hypnotized, the audience began to stand and drift toward the exit. Talking was initially minimal, but progressively erupted in tiny bursts as total strangers shared in the awe.

Darcy avidly observed the spectacle with the singular twinkle in his eyes so familiar to Lizzy. She too was captivated by the demonstration, but having seen it once before she did manage to tear her eyes away and note her husband's expression. Lost in his reverie, apparently unaware that the balloon was far beyond even his keen eyesight, Lizzy squeezed his arm and leaned to his ear.

"I fear your busy schedule allots no time for you to take up ballooning as a hobby, love."

He turned to her with a sheepish smile, eyes still sparkling nonetheless. "That was truly marvelous, Elizabeth!"

"Let me guess. We must hasten to the nearest library to purchase books on the science of balloons and flight?"

He laughed. "No. We must hasten to the nearest pub as I am parched and famished. Later I shall acquire a book on the subject. Only for enlightenment, you understand?"

They did not need to travel far. The entire southern end of the sandy peninsula formed by the River Yare and North Sea was rapidly evolving from a primarily military habitation and ship docking quay into a tourist destination. All along the boardwalk small shops and eateries were practically daily opening. The previously rustic track had been widened and smoothed, with trees actively being planted to shade pedestrians. Large fields were leveled for carriage parking; naturally arenaceous beaches were meticulously combed and inspected for bathers and players; hotels were being built; grassy plains and cultured gardens were landscaped; and a modern wharf was being constructed.

In the middle of it all sat the racetrack. Some ten years ago the military men decided they needed a track to race their horses. Over time, what was essentially designated as a cavalry training field and arena for mild amusement among the militia grew into a full-fledged betting racecourse. Spectator seating, areas of concessions, and the all important booths for gambling had been built. Twice a week the track was taken over by breeders, owners, jockeys, and thoroughbreds from around the country for a sport that had been synonymous with England since the days of Queen Anne. Although this track and the racers exhibited could not compare to the Royal Ascot or Newmarket, nor were the purses as substantial, wherever there were horses traveling at fast speeds and money to potentially be made, folks would flock.

Since this latter description perfectly encapsulated Mr. Fitzwilliam Darcy, attending the races while at Yarmouth was an item high on his list. The truth is that of all the entertainments Darcy enjoyed partaking in, billiards being premier, watching the races ran a close second. He was not a gambling man by nature, so any betting was cautious and reserved for those animals he felt extremely confident in. As a longstanding member of the Jockey Club, as was his grandfather, as well as being a breeder who understood the animal as if one himself, Darcy was extremely knowledgeable regarding the sport. He could name every horse and jockey of merit throughout the country, was personal friends with the chief owners, and had patronized every racecourse of substance numerous times. Although the revenue Darcy had won through intelligent betting over the years was not copious, it far outmeasured the amount lost.

As for Lizzy, the world of horseracing was completely foreign. While in London Darcy had taken her to two events held at the Royal Ascot in Berkshire and once at Epsom Downs in Surrey. Naturally this was an essential for Darcy, not only due to his intense love of the sport but for business reasons as well.

Lizzy had approached the adventure with a fair amount of trepidation, frankly imagining being bored senseless and overwhelmed with choking dust and noise, but smiled and expressed delight with the prospect for her husband's sake. Darcy, of course, was not fooled in the least.

To her surprise, she found the sport extremely exciting. First off, both racecourses subverted her vague imaginings by being extraordinary in construction, opulence, comfort, and provisions. The seats afforded the Darcys were plush, shaded, segregated, and offered a fantastic view of the impeccable track. Secondly, and most amazing of all, the racing itself was exhilarating. Lizzy's six months as a Darcy, surrounded by some of the finest horses in the country and married to a man who nearly lived and breathed all things equestrian, had birthed in her an unrecognized appreciation of the majestic animal. Her enthusiasm and knowledge would likely never come near to Darcy's, but she discovered the entertainment fabulous fun.

Darcy, naturally, was thrilled at her embracing the diversion; so much so that he was only mildly perturbed when she insisted on betting for a particular horse because, "he has a nice name." Lizzy, unbeknownst to her spouse, had done so to tease him, confessing only after Sweet Whistler placed second!

"Look, Elizabeth," he now said, holding the program open and pointing. "Race one has a mare named Lovely Peacock. Sounds like a winner to me!" Lizzy harrumphed and swatted him away, Darcy chuckling.

Ignoring him for the time being, she studied the program carefully. Darcy had taught her the rudiments of calculating odds and the profile aspects of import. Of course he had the advantage by intimately knowing the pedigrees and racing histories of many of the horses. She pursed her lips, glancing at her handsome spouse who was currently avidly observing the prancing animals down below.

"Fitzwilliam," she began, Darcy raising a brow at the formal address, "I suggest a friendly competition. A challenge, if you will. Are you brave enough to match wits with your wife?"

"I believe I require further illumination, Elizabeth, as your wits frequently supersede mine. What did you have in mind?"

"I have fifty pounds in my reticule. If you will agree to limit your wagering to the same, we shall see who chooses the wisest by who wins the most."

Lips twitching, Darcy nodded sagely. "High stakes, Mrs. Darcy, especially considering I had no intention of being so extravagant."

"Is the idea too daunting, Mr. Darcy? Are you afraid?" Her eyes were twinkling, pert nose and chin lifted boldly in challenge. Darcy gazed at her, cursing inwardly at the restrictive rules of propriety that made it impossible for him to kiss her as he yearned to do with an agonizing stab through his gut. Lizzy knew him far too well, aptly reading the message in his eyes despite the controlled mien. Her smile widened as she waited.

"You know I never back away from a dare. Therefore, I accept your challenge, but shall grant no quarter, my dear."

"None shall be asked for, William." She leaned forward and lowered her voice, "I love you, you know. If I do win, I will expect you to reward me as I see fit."

Darcy took her hand and kissed her fingers lightly, eyes locked with hers, naturally resonant voice husky. "It seems that I shall win in either case then."

"Mr. Darcy, what a pleasant surprise!"

Both Darcy and Lizzy jolted. Lizzy flushed brightly, but Darcy recovered smoothly, standing with elegant grace to greet the older man smiling pleasantly from the aisle. "Lord Ellis. What brings you from Suffolk?"

"Sea air and horses, naturally. Likely the same as yourself. Mrs. Darcy, I trust you are well?"

Lizzy smiled. "Quite well, my Lord. It is a delight to see you again. Is Lady Ellis accompanying you?"

"Alas, she despises horse racing and has opted to shop." More random chatter ensued, Lord Ellis eventually leaving the Darcys to "continue their amusements" with a wink, Lizzy reddening again.

The afternoon hours elapsed. Darcy and Lizzy kept to their contest with playful seriousness, neither willing to tolerate defeat although it was equally obvious that neither would really suffer if the loser. Surprisingly, Lord Ellis was not the only acquaintance encountered. Probably a fifth of the attendees seated in the stadium section relegated to those of wealth and station were known to Darcy. Several were military officers introduced through Col. Fitzwilliam, but most were social peers familiar to varying degrees. Between casual conversations, thrilling races, a personally escorted tour of the Nelson monument site, delicious refreshments, the stimulating competition in wagering, and the incomparable joy produced by the presence of the other, Darcy and Lizzy were glowing by the time they settled into the carriage.

Lizzy promptly turned to her husband. "Now! Time to count the profits and see who the victor is."

Darcy laughed, but retrieved his money clip as Lizzy opened her reticule. Lizzy had been impishly secretive in her selections, insisting that Darcy stand away as she placed her bets so he "would not cheat." Darcy, in turn, had feigned confusion and dismay with much frowning and chin scratching. In between the blatantly smug articulations and theatrical heavy sighs, they mutually reveled in taunting each other.

Nonetheless, to Darcy's extreme pride, Lizzy calculated earnestly and won far more often than she lost. In the end, Darcy prevailed in their cordial competition, but by a mere four pounds.

"Game well played, Elizabeth. I am very proud of you. You chose horses wisely and it paid off."

"Thank you, William, but you have triumphed fairly. Name your desired reward, sir, and it shall be granted."

"Hmm… What a difficult decision this is! What can I possibly desire from you? Let me think a bit." He kept up the false musing all the way back to the resort, Lizzy sitting serenely beside him staring out the window as if wholly uninterested.

It was nearly six when they arrived. Lizzy, strangely, was not at all fatigued. Darcy had observed her circumspectly all afternoon, ready to instantly depart if necessary. To his increased pleasure she appeared hale with a becoming rosiness to her cheeks and mischievous glimmer in her brown eyes. Naturally Darcy had no problem deciding what his reward would be, the plotting initiated with instructions to have dinner served in their room.

Upon entering their chamber, windows open to admit the fresh evening breezes and everything cleaned perfectly, Lizzy walked to the middle and turned to await her husband. He stood silently by the shut door, watching her with a dreamily seductive smile on his lips. For a long while they stood apart, studying each other for the sheer pleasure of feasting hungry eyes. Slowly, with elegant poise, he floated toward her. Lizzy was breathless, already tremendously stirred from nothing but his brilliant azure eyes on her body and piercing her spirit.

He paused inches away, not touching for several seconds, and then reaching leisurely to her hair and began removing clasps and pins. Each tendril fell into his hands, slipping through caressing fingers. He toyed with curly tresses, pulling them gently as if springs, releasing with infinite care one by one the secured clumps of hair until wildly free over her shoulders. He uttered not a word. Lizzy panted in short spurts, a hazy part of her brain wondering how he consistently found ways to excite her to unimaginable heights by the simplest tasks. Now he laced long, slender fingers through the roots of her hair, massaging firmly over her scalp from nape to crown, only then lifting the heavy locks off her neck and combing tenderly until tangles unraveled. A dozen times he repeated the activity with studied meticulousness. Her lustrous hair crackled through his fingers, the varied hues of brown glimmering in the light with lavender rising to assault his nostrils.

Her eyes were closed in delight, hands clutching the edge of his jacket, and mouth parted. Mesmerized, he played lovingly with her chestnut mane as he scrutinized her expressions, groaning and briefly losing all control when the tiny tip of her moist tongue appeared to lick dry lips. He bent and kissed her unrestrained, tongue thrusting deeply, and hoarse moans caught in his throat. Blissful minutes passed, both succumbed to raging sensations. It was a singularly sharp squeeze to his derriere that jerked him to reality.

"Elizabeth!" He gasped. "Wait, please. It is my reward owed, you recall? I have a plan." He kissed to her ear, taking the lobe into his mouth for gently suckles. "We have hours and hours, best beloved. Trust me, we shall be satisfied." He pulled away to meet her glazed eyes.

"Fitzwilliam," she whispered. "I want you…"

"You shall have me, lover," he interrupted. "I can promise you that. All night, languidly and wholly I shall love you. This is my wish. Wait here." He pecked her nose, smiled, and left for his dressing room.

He returned quickly with a bundle in his hands, blushing faintly. "I brought this. It is my favorite. Will you wear it for me?"

Lizzy laughed, recognizing what he held. "William, you truly are too cute. Of course I shall wear it."

When she later returned from her dressing room, her husband was garbed in a figure-hugging black chambray banyan with borders of sage green satin. He was bent over the cozy table in the corner, now laden with several covered trays, lit candles, two place settings, and a vase of roses. A bottle of champagne sat chilling in a bucket nearby.

"What is for dinner?" Darcy pivoted, eyes grazing his wife head to toe as a grin of purest lust gradually spread over his face.

Approximately a month earlier Lizzy had woken with a pressing need to visit the water closet. It was nearly dawn, the faintest traces of light filtering through the curtains of their bedchamber. The room, however, was yet very dim and there was a slight chill to the air at odds with a Derbyshire morn in mid-August. Lizzy, naked as always and blessedly warm snuggled next to the inferno that was her spouse, had been struck by the cool room and blindly groped for the first garment she could find in the scattered piles of discarded clothing hastily tossed the previous evening. It was Darcy's shirt of finest spun silk with pearl buttons down the front. She drew it on, fastening the middle three buttons absently as she rushed from the room. Minutes later she returned, sleepily rubbing her face, and was brought up short by an audible gasp from the bed. Darcy lay propped on an elbow, eyes wide as he stared at her, an expression intimately familiar to her growing as was the evidence of his desire.

"You are wearing my shirt," he said unnecessarily, voice huskier than she had ever heard it and eyes aflame. "Come here." It was a curt command uttered in a tone that brooked no argument, not that it occurred to Lizzy to do so. What followed was a session of lovemaking closely rivaling, if not transcending, anything prior. The shirt stayed on throughout. Since then he had politely requested of her to wear it twice, amusing Lizzy as she would happily grant him anything especially as they were mindlessly aroused each time for reasons that neither could articulate.

The effect had not waned, Darcy now ogling with fists clenched at his sides. "Elizabeth Darcy, you are surpassingly sensual. Suddenly I am not certain how wise my request as I honestly do wish to proceed leisurely. God, how you tempt me!"

She approached, running one hand over the satin border draping his muscular chest. "As you declared, William, we have all night. Much can transpire in that amount of time. Of course, you are the master of the evening as the winner of our wager. I am at your disposal." The last muttered faintly against his lips while her hands moved freely over the quivering flesh of his torso.

Forgotten was dinner and champagne. Forgotten were preconceived notions of lazy loving. In a burst of energy he clasped her bottom with both large hands, lifting bodily, and aided by her wrapping arms and legs about him. Swiftly they were at the bed where Darcy knelt with Lizzy yet entwined. He ran seeking hands roughly over the voluminous silk swathing her lithe frame, even the swell of their child not filling the space. Why seeing her encased in his shirt thrilled him so he could not say precisely. Partially it was the way it fell to the middle of her rounded thighs leaving her long shapely legs completely bared. Additionally the shoulder width was nearly twice hers so the gaping fabric displayed tantalizing glimpses of her collar and breasts. But primarily the reason was indefinable, Darcy only aware of a visceral surge of primal eroticism in the vision before his rapacious eyes.

It was fortunate that Lizzy unerringly responded to her husband's miraculous touch with alacrity as Darcy was frenzied in his thirst for her, extended foreplay no longer an option. He captured her breasts through the fabric, suckling and squeezing while gently lowering her to the bed, pelvis pressing harshly against her. Practically ripping the robe off his body, Lizzy's hands instantly roving and trailing fire, he joined with her in a heated rush. They loved furiously, gazes acute and ensnared. Another protracted, consuming kiss ensued, ending when a harsh growl erupted from Darcy's chest.

"Lizzy! I need to feel all of you! Oh Lord, I love you so!" His voice faded into unintelligible articulations of glory as they plunged over the edge, blissfully united in their pleasure.

He collapsed into a slump, instinctively avoiding crushing her belly as his upper body fell to the side over her thigh. Gradually he peered up at her shining face, brown eyes slitted as she watched him and lazily played with his hair. "I love how you call me 'Lizzy' in your rapture."

"Would you rather I call you 'Lizzy' all the time?" His voice was yet harsh, naturally resonant tones always deeper in passion. Their son was rolling and kicking as he often did after they made love, Darcy absently chasing the movements with a hand.

"No. 'Elizabeth' is somehow proper coming from you, and I adore how your voice caresses my name every time. You never address me that it is not bathed with adoration and sensuality. You always have, if only I had had the ears to hear it. 'Lizzy' is uttered when you are completely undone, hence why I love it." She stroked over his perfect nose, resting on the dimple in his chin. "I love you, William."

He rolled, lying next to her and encasing her in strong arms. He did not speak for a bit, caressing tenderly and kissing through her hair. Finally, "I love you, Elizabeth. My Elizabeth, my wife."

After a time of cuddling and brushing kisses, she unexpectedly giggled, looking up into his eyes. "Well, now that we have that out of the way, perhaps we can proceed with the leisurely unfolding of the evening as you requested for your victory over me. Starting with dinner, as I now have heightened my appetite."

"I shall never consider making love with you as something to get 'out of the way'; however, food does sound appealing." He fingered the edge of his shirt where it lay over her thigh. "You will keep this on for me, dearest?"

"What if I become cold?"

"I shall start a fire."

"If I spill on it?"

"It can be cleaned."

"It is rather large, William. It may fall right off my shoulder into the plate!"

"You are filling it out better, Elizabeth, so I daresay that will not happen."

"It has a strange effect on your senses, love. Can you control yourself throughout the meal?"

"I shall endeavor to be a good boy; however, I seriously doubt you would argue terribly if I fail."

"Awfully confident you are, sir! Smug and arrogant."

"Yes I am, and I can tell by your expression that you are neither shocked nor dismayed. Shall I prove my conceit, my lover, or do we leave the bed for nourishment first?" He accented the challenge with a firm caress over one round swelling buttock, fingers probing, and grin wide.

Lizzy squirmed from his grasp, both laughing. Planting a glancing kiss to his lips, she stood, grasping his hands and tugging. "Come, love. Let me feed you before you faint."

CHAPTER EIGHT

Just Desserts

T HE AFTERNOON FOLLOWING THEIR Yarmouth excursion found them again reclining under the umbrella on the sand. Darcy read aloud while Lizzy sewed another baby garment. Caught up in their tasks, with the now familiar sounds and smells of the ocean washing through their subconscious, neither noted the servant approaching until he spoke.

"Pardon me, Mr. Darcy, Mrs. Darcy. These just arrived for you and here is today's *London Times* as you requested." He held a twine-wrapped bundle of parchment and folded newspaper in his hand, handing them to Darcy.

"Letters from home," he murmured. "Mr. Keith with updates. A letter from Georgie, one from Bingley, your mother, and Mrs. Lathrop." The latter two were taken by Lizzy, who opened Amelia's first.

Minutes passed in silent reading, Lizzy breaking the quiet first with a happy shout.

"Amelia delivered a girl!"

"Oh, how wonderful!" Darcy smiled with true feelings of joy, instantly thinking of Stephen while simultaneously imagining his own emotions when the time came. "Did all proceed smoothly? Mrs. Lathrop is well?"

"The baby was born three weeks ago now. They named her Fiona Heather. Amelia says she resembles Stephen, but has her green eyes. Oh, what a wonder!" Lizzy sighed, reading on with a smile.

"The birth… Does she speak of it?"

Lizzy glanced over to see him serious with a hint of anxiety in his pale eyes. She squeezed his hand, smiling tenderly. "She is well, love. The birth was long, she writes, as is expected, but there were no complications. Do not worry so, William. Everything will be fine, I promise."

He pressed his lips tightly together, jaw clenching, but he nodded and returned to his letter. At odd moments as the weeks advanced, Darcy would find his thoughts dwelling on the final birth process and possible emergencies. Lizzy was healthy and very strong, as was their child by all indications, but he knew well from stories and family traumas how horribly wrong it could end. The thought of losing their baby terrified him, but not nearly as much as losing Elizabeth.

A deep sigh from his wife interrupted the threatening stabs of fear. "I miss Amelia. I wish I could see her and the baby. Who knows when we will be able to travel again between winter and infants to care for?"

"We could visit on our way home, if you wish. Leicestershire is not far out of the way, and I am certain they would not mind."

"Could we? Oh, William! That would be so wonderful! You are brilliant and far too good to me."

He laughed and shook his head. "Thank you, dear, but I was only thinking of myself as Lathrop is the best billiard player after Hughes that I know." He picked up Mr. Keith's missive, feigning indifference while Lizzy chuckled.

Mr. Keith's letter was brief, stating that all was well with harvest beginning as usual, sheep being prepared for market, and the horses all responding according to the breeding plans. Georgiana delivered a rambling dissertation of her adventures sans any mention of Lord Gruffudd now that they had left his vicinity of Wales, to Darcy's mumbled pleasure. His uncle had included a short paragraph stating that they expected to return by the second week of September. Mrs. Bennet gave a typically detailed commentary of the local gossip, some of which actually interested Lizzy, noting in passing that Mr. Bennet and Kitty were well. Charles declared that all was in hand with the plans for relocation, the actual move to take place mid-October.

After the letters were read and shared, Darcy turned to the newspaper. Even on holiday he could not eschew keeping abreast of current events and business affairs. This compulsion was not only due to years of habit but also an obligation related to his station and influence.

"Ah! Look here, love. An entire article on Miss van Lingen landing her balloon on Hampstead Heath. She landed safely, not precisely where she planned to in the vastness of the park, but close enough that the awaiting spectators and reporters could relocate. Excellent!"

That evening they dined with a company of guests. The food was excellent, as always, and the lively conversation enjoyable, especially to Lizzy. Darcy was reserved, as was typical, his contributions limited and mostly confined to discussions of politics with a new resident of the inn, a barrister named Spade, who sat next to him. Lady Underwood was dining as well, but thankfully for Darcy, sat at another table. Nonetheless, he was uncomfortable, her presence and noisy laugh constantly reminding him of events he wanted to forget.

After dinner scheduled entertainment was a chess tournament for the men, although two brave women insisted on playing, and a fashion exhibit for the ladies. Darcy nervously separated from his wife, unable to resist casting a cold, warning glance toward Lady Underwood. She smiled benignly, her eyes hard. Darcy's irritation and trepidation increased, but there was nothing he could do.

Three modistes from Yarmouth brought living models to show the latest styles from abroad. It was wonderful fun with tea and refreshments offered, animated banter, and many of the accessories available for purchase.

Lady Underwood sat near Lizzy, seemed to take a special interest in her, in fact. Lizzy was flattered and sensed nothing amiss, honestly delighting in the older woman's charm and wit. Despite the gap in their upbringing and age, Lizzy felt relaxed and accepted.

The segregated portion of the night passed swiftly for Lizzy, but Darcy had difficulty concentrating on his game. Lizzy anxiously awaited her husband's reappearance, yet was content for the time being, enjoying the conversation and female entertainment.

When the gentlemen began filing in as their games ended, Lizzy kept an eye on the door from her seat at the settee where Lady Underwood sat beside her. Darcy entered, eyes immediately scanning the room for his wife, spying her seconds before she glanced up. Lady Underwood was currently speaking, her visage gay as all hung on her every word, one hand lying lightly on Lizzy's forearm. Darcy froze, instant rage masked from all in the room behind his regulated façade. Lizzy glanced up, automatically issuing a dazzling smile that wilted moments afterward at the constrained thunder in his eyes.

He crossed the room with minimal strides, entire body tense, bowing curtly to the assembled ladies and offering a brisk preamble. "Pardon me, ladies. Mrs. Darcy, it is time for us to retire." He held out his hand, Lizzy taking it with open mouth and scarlet cheeks. She murmured vague good nights, sensing Darcy's stress and impatience, further baffled and embarrassed by a brief but harsh glare directed at a triumphantly smirking Lady Underwood.

They did not speak until in their room. Darcy was seething and frantically wondering what he was to say to Lizzy after his precipitous rudeness. Lizzy was confused and worried and irritated all at once.

"William, what is the matter...?"

"Elizabeth," he interrupted, vainly struggling to soften his tone. "Please forgive me for that. It was rude and ungentlemanly I know, but I could not bear to see her talking to you so intimately."

"Who?"

"Lady Underwood." He avoided her eyes, his rage so intense that he did not wish her witnessing it. "Promise me you will not speak with her further."

"William, you are making no sense. Lady Underwood is a lovely person, kind and considerate, humorous and lively. She has done nothing untoward..."

He interrupted again with a barely controlled edginess, "Elizabeth, I will not discuss her attributes or character! I am ordering you to have no contact with her."

"Ordering me?" This time it was Lizzy who interrupted, bristling and seriously vexed. "You have no right to speak to me thusly, William."

"I am your husband, Mrs. Darcy, which gives me the right!" They glared at each other, anger in full sway on both sides with neither able to contain themselves.

"Is this how it is to be now? You barking commands without explanation? This is not like you, William. Tell me what is troubling you or I will make no promises of any kind."

"You have already promised to obey, if you recall." He flashed, immediately wincing inwardly.

She stared at him for a long while, Darcy sternly meeting her eyes but clearly deeply disturbed. "You are correct, Mr. Darcy, I did promise. I just never thought it would be lorded over me in such a manner."

His face fell and he reached for her slack hands. "You must trust me in this, Elizabeth. I know what is best."

His eyes were pleading, but she detected a distance not seen since long before their engagement. He was keeping a secret, she was sure of it, and the stab of pain to her heart was acute.

"I am going to change for bed," she finally said, withdrawing her hands. "Excuse me."

Darcy watched her leave, ripping at his choking cravat with a foul curse. "Blast, Darcy, you are a fool!" he muttered, throwing the unoffending neckcloth violently at the wall. He strode to her door, pausing at the last instant. *Give it a moment,* he thought, *calm yourself and think!*

He had worried so, not wishing to cause her pain by learning of Lady Underwood's advances. Yet he now suspected that his horrible actions had caused her far more pain than the simple truth. Furthermore, her comments strongly suggested that Lady Underwood had said nothing untoward. He suddenly wondered if she had not cunningly schemed for his outburst, realizing that she need only sit near Elizabeth to rankle her protective husband.

He threw his body onto the chair, hands running angrily in his hair. Now he had to rectify the situation, find the words to apologize profusely and on bended knee if need be, and then tell her the truth. He groaned, absently unbuttoning and removing coats as his mind whirled.

Whether planned or not, his natural need to shield her from pain had aroused his temper, in turn inciting her ire, and the two of them had clashed. Why is it that she rendered him in all ways impetuous? It had always been so, from their first unruly tête-à-têtes at Netherfield to the wild abandon found in their bed. She unhinged him in all ways, his organized mind disheveled constantly by her wit and verve. His passionate nature was unleashed and reckless. His love for her so consuming that rational thought flittered away with the supreme desire to please her and care for her.

He had asked her to trust him and knew that ultimately she would, without further questions. But he had seen the hurt in her eyes and knew it was borne of his distrust in sharing with her, not in the rude command. The wall thrust between them must be destroyed. He sighed, bending to remove his shoes and stockings.

She returned at that moment, hair braided rather than loose and wearing a plain gown with thick robe belted tight. She did not glance in his direction, but walked with lifted chin and stately poise to the bed. Darcy could not help but smile at her fire and not-so-subtle hints.

"Elizabeth, my love," he began.

"I am tired, Mr. Darcy. Good night." Her voice was firm, vexation apparent.

He paused, watching her roughly fluff the pillow and draw the blankets. Softly he spoke, "Remember how I told you once that women would offer themselves to me? Offers I never accepted, but grew somewhat accustomed to nonetheless?" She did not answer, but had stilled with her back yet to him. He swallowed and resumed, "Lady Underwood extended such an invitation to me, several times." Another pause followed by a deep sigh as he leaned back in the chair. "I should have told you and been honest, but I did not wish to ruin our holiday. I was in error. Please forgive me?"

Lizzy clutched the sheet, not turning. "How did it occur? What did she say?"

"The particulars are not important…"

"They are to me! What happened?"

Her voice was cold as Darcy had never heard it. He frowned but answered her. When he finished, she stood silently for a handful of minutes, the sheet edge crinkled under a white-knuckled fist. His frown deepened and he sat forward, opening his mouth to speak when she abruptly spun about. Her countenance was flushed with a rage he had never witnessed, not even at Kent. Eyes practically shooting sparks, she stormed to where he sat, Darcy involuntarily gripping the chair arms and sinking into the cushions by the force of her anger. She stopped before him, swaying slightly and leaning into his stunned face.

"Do not *ever* keep such secrets from me, Fitzwilliam Darcy!"

He nodded, but she was already moving away, striding vigorously toward the door in a manner vaguely familiar. It was just like him! Having no idea what she was thinking but truly fearful at the fury evident in every particle of her body, he jumped up and trailed after. The door was opening before he reached her, Darcy lunging forward and slamming it shut with one hand high over her head.

"Elizabeth, where…?"

"Out of my way, William!"

"No. I will not allow you to leave so angry and dressed like this. We must discuss this."

She pivoted, one hand still on the knob and pulling futilely against his superior strength, meeting his eyes with defiance. "She touched my husband! Pretended to be my friend while laying hands on you! She demanded to… to…"

Lizzy spluttered shrilly, waving her free hand briskly in the general region of his front side, "know you in the Biblical sense!"

Darcy fisted his free hand over the smile threatening to break forth as he coughed on the laugh that erupted. Lizzy's eyes narrowed dangerously.

"If you dare to laugh, William, I will hurt you! This is not at all humorous. If the situation were reversed, I know quite well how you would handle it! Pity there is not a sword or pistol about." And she actually visually scanned the room as if expecting and praying a rapier would materialize.

"Elizabeth, forgive me. You are right. This is not humorous. However, you are overreacting just a bit. Nothing occurred, naturally…"

"I know that!" she snapped, rolling her eyes and piercing him with a look of utter contempt. "I trust your fidelity, William, if not your reasoning and faith in trusting me!"

"I am not so sure my reasoning was flawed, considering your present irrationality."

She opened her mouth for a sharp retort and then clamped it shut as the partial truth of his softly spoken words penetrated her brain. Her eyes lowered and body relaxed into the solid door, finally releasing her tight grip on the knob. Not trusting her compliance completely, Darcy remained leaning into the door, sizeable frame dwarfing hers.

"How can a woman be so bold and… devious and immoral? Not that I cannot understand her excellent taste," she whispered, glancing up into his face. Her cheeks were ruddy, anger still evident by the fiery glints deep in her eyes.

"That is kind of you, Elizabeth. But I do not think such women are overly particular." He sighed. "I should have trusted you with the truth from the beginning, then we both could have avoided her and diverted this argument. You are justified to be vexed with me."

"Yes, I am vexed with you!" She flared anew, stalking past him to commence pacing and shooting daggers his direction. "And I am not overreacting in the slightest. Again and again she accosted you, these… advances occurring where anyone could have seen. And while I was pathetically unaware! You allowed me to pursue a friendship with her, knowing her character and what she had attempted with my husband. Do you not see what a fool this makes me? How she must be laughing at the stupid little girl? The pathetic child with the faithful husband who treats her as an infant."

"Do you honestly care what she thinks of you?"

"No! Yes! A little. That is not the point. Do you not see, William? Either what we have together is special and plainly revealed to all, or it is a lie. I *do* care what *you* think of me! No secrets, remember?"

"Yes," he whispered miserably.

"I am not a child. Nor a toy that you can play with and show off as your own personal property to protect and not treat with respect and equality."

"You know I do not think that," he began, but she continued as if he had not spoken.

"And why is it that you consider it your right to dash off risking your life to defend your claim and my honor, but I cannot do the same? Your possessiveness is not a mutually exclusive privilege, William. You belong to me as surely, and I am equally furious to think of another seducing what is mine! Yet, as offended as I am, what I cannot believe is that you would shield me in this way."

"Elizabeth, please, I am deeply sorry!"

"I know you are, William." She stopped pacing, suddenly weary and weak. "I also know you meant well, only wishing to spare me pain because of your love for me. I *am* naïve in so many ways and perhaps not fully capable of handling such things. But I never will learn if you do not trust me! Your job as my husband is not to screen me from life so that I do not mature in wisdom."

They stood in silence, eyes downcast as they wrestled with thoughts and emotions. Darcy was ashamed, recognizing the truth of all her words although he could not honestly imagine relinquishing the fundamental need to protect her from all pain or harm. Lizzy was mainly tired, yet a vivid vision of ripping Lady Underwood's hair out lingered.

"Have there been other propositions?" She spoke quietly, staring at the floor.

He looked quickly to her averted face, shaking his head vigorously as he rapidly crossed to her. "No others since long before we were engaged, beloved. But it does not matter in any case." He reached to clasp her shoulders but was halted when she lifted fierce eyes.

"It matters to me! I need to know if there are other 'friends' of mine who have privately desired or even unashamedly attempted to make love to my husband." Her voice caught on the final words, tears springing to blazing eyes.

Darcy studied her with deep remorse and concern. Her countenance was yet smoldering with resentment but also quite pale and pinched. She looked so fatigued and drained. Overcome with guilt and with heart constricting, he lifted gentle fingertips to her wan cheek, caressing slowly.

"We cannot control what others may muse on, beloved. I, however, can and should control my actions with improved wisdom. I made a horrible mistake in doubting your understanding. Will you please pardon me?"

"You are twice the fool if you honestly fear I would not forgive you any misstep," she countered with some asperity.

And then with a weak smile she fell onto his chest, Darcy embracing her tenderly yet with steely strength. All night he held her close, dozing lightly as he preferred to gaze on her face in the moonlight, noting the ease relaxing her facial muscles and the increasing health filling her cheeks as she slept. In the darkest hours of the night, it was Lizzy who roused and reached for her drowsy husband, pulling his body and lips onto hers. They made love in the shadows, dreamily bonding and stimulating with remaining four senses leading and heightened.

It was while Darcy waited patiently for his wife to join him in their chamber to descend for breakfast that Lizzy slipped out a side door on a mission of her own. She had slept well and her heart was whole. She understood Darcy's reasoning for maintaining his silence, and she did appreciate the compassion that drove him even if she did not agree with the decision. Hopefully he now recognized the reality that honesty and full disclosure between them was essential, even at the risk of hurt feelings.

Lady Underwood was another matter. Her anger toward that lady had simmered all night even in her dreaming state. There was no excuse, in Lizzy's eyes, for a woman to act in such a way. There were plenty of unattached men in the world for her to fraternize with, as disgusting and immoral as even that activity was to Lizzy. Yet certainly better than enticing married gentlemen, especially after they made it perfectly clear they were uninterested. Depravity warped into pure evil when one considered her threats to Darcy and counterfeit amiability toward Lizzy. This was not a lonely woman seeking comfort and companionship. This was a wicked narcissist bent on destruction.

Lizzy's knock was answered by a maid who admitted Lizzy and exited to inform Lady Underwood she had a visitor. Lizzy waited, experiencing a strange detachment. All night, even in her sleep, she had imagined what she would say or do, never doubting for one second that she would not confront the so-called lady in some manner. Pistols or swords were out of the question, but she now better comprehended Darcy's need for retribution. With well-laid plans intact, she evaded her husband and now waited.

However, calmly conceived ideas dissipated as rapidly as smoke in a stiff breeze the moment Lady Underwood entered the room.

"Mrs. Darcy. What a delightful surprise to see you in my room so early in the morning." She was dressed for breakfast, her hair yet unstyled, the smile on her lips only partially hiding the curiosity and trepidation.

Instantly the fury of last evening poured through Lizzy, with vivid pictures of this creature touching her husband invading her mind. She lashed out with every ounce of the bizarrely extreme strength she possessed in her svelte body and delivered a stunning slap to Lady Underwood's left cheek. The stricken woman staggered and cried out in pain, gasping in shock.

"That was for having the audacity to accost my husband," Lizzy said calmly, following her words with another ringing blow to the same place. "That was for evilly pretending to be my friend."

Lady Underwood whimpered, tears stinging her eyes as she peered at Lizzy with undisguised fright and astonishment.

"You are a disgrace to all that your title symbolizes and an ignominy to womankind. How you can live with yourself is a mystery. You should wither with the shame, but instead you persevere, which leads me to conclude you lack a soul and conscience. I pity you, my lady, I truly do. Yet my pity does not transcend my wrath. If you have even a shred of decency or, at the least, a modicum of wisdom, you will avoid my husband and me. I can do no more than strike you. Mr. Darcy of Pemberley can do far worse. You have been warned and would be very wise to remember that fact."

She left the room with chin held high. In truth she was trembling slightly from residual temper, but primarily felt exhilarated and satisfied. A flash of movement to her left caused her to glance toward the stairs leading to the ground floor where Darcy was in the process of descending in a rush.

"William?"

He halted and twirled about all in one motion, nearly tumbling down the stairs and grasping the banister to correct his imbalance. His face was suffused with distress, paling substantially as he glanced from Lizzy to the door she had just exited.

"Elizabeth, what…"

Words abruptly ceased when Lord and Lady Stewart appeared from around the corner. Pleasantries were conveyed, Darcy recovering quickly although he kept glancing to Lizzy, who acted as if nothing was amiss. In fact, she was particularly effusive. The second they were out of sight he turned to his wife, running hands over her upper body as if checking for injury. He noted the redness to her right palm before she had the chance to speak, eyes widening with sudden shock as he peered into her mildly embarrassed but triumphant eyes.

"I do not believe Lady Underwood will be as pretty as she usually is for several days. Perhaps that will inhibit her ensnaring any other innocent gentlemen."

"You... hit her?"

"Well, she deserved it!"

"Indubitably." He laughed shortly, taking her elbow and steering her to the third-floor stairwell. "I should scold you most profoundly, but I..." He laughed again, a bit hysterically, leaning his head back against the wall with eyes pleading heavenward. "Lord, why? I honestly did wish for a simple life. Was that too much to ask for?"

"Oh bother! Simplicity is overrated. Spirit and passion are preferential. Now quit whining and take me to breakfast. I have worked up an appetite." She tiptoed for a quick peck to his cheek, but he stayed her for a sober examination of her eyes.

"Are you certain you are well, Elizabeth? Completely, heart and soul? And our child? I truly was very frightened when you were gone." His voice caught, Lizzy doused with sorrow. She encircled his waist tightly, entire body pressed hard against him with their son protesting and kicking vigorously.

"I assure you we are perfect, body and soul. I beg your forgiveness, but it was something I had to do. Tell me you understand?"

He nodded, but his eyes were troubled. "I suppose I do. But you could have been injured, Elizabeth. Like it or not, it is my duty to protect you and handle physical confrontations."

"There are some matters that are mine to deal with, William." She looked up into his face, smiling comfortingly although her voice was resolute. "No woman will ever be allowed to touch you without hearing from me. Never!"

Lady Underwood departed the resort that morning, offering no good-byes. Speculative gossip abounded, but the Darcy name was never mentioned. As for the Darcys, they spoke no further on the subject. Lessons were learned, similar errors would never be made in the future, and thus the book was closed. Darcy would not completely forget. He was not a vengeful man by nature so did nothing permanently designed to punish Lady Underwood. However, his claim of power was not an exaggeration. There were ways available to a man of superior means, avenues open to exhibit one's clout and potential without actually doing anything. Suffice to say, Lady Underwood also learned a lesson and would be a bit more cautious in her future seductions.

CHAPTER NINE

On the Road Home

T HE REMAINING DAYS OF their seaside sojourn would pass exclusively at
the resort and were uneventful, comparatively speaking. By mutual
agreement they decided that sightseeing, although educational and
exhilarating, was not as preferable as simply lying about the beach and assuredly not as divinely stimulating as seabathing. Therefore, they reverted to the
pattern established on their first few days: sleeping late and dining late followed
by a time in the water; lazy afternoons on the beach; leisurely strolls along the
wooded trails or shoreline collecting shells; evenings in various pursuits with
the other guests; quiet contemplations of the ever-changing sunset; moonlight
walks on the sand or pier; and the occasional individual recreations.

One day it clouded and drizzled, but Lizzy insisted on taking their walk
regardless, to Darcy's initial discomfort. The nuzzling kisses enjoyed under the
close confines of the umbrella dispelled most of his unease; the rich aroma of wet
loam and pine allayed the residual. The storm worsened in the afternoon, causing
the surf to roar and upsurge dramatically. They sat cozily in the parlor sipping
hot cocoa before the fire and watched the impressive display all afternoon.

A hastily discharged missive to the Lathrops was equally hastily replied to,
the positive response arriving the day before the Darcys were to depart. They
were both very anxious to be home, but decided a short three-day visit to the
Lathrops' estate, Stonecrest, a perfect cap to a perfect holiday.

Their final night was passed on the end of the pier. Dinner was arranged by the resort staff, privately by candlelight as the sun provided a majestic living mural in its decline and the tides supplied the music. The fare was superb, but it would not have mattered as it was the atmosphere and communion that brought the greatest joy to their hearts.

"May I have this dance, Mrs. Darcy?"

Lizzy laughed, taking her husband's proffered hand and assuming a waltz pose. He did this frequently, surprising her at odd moments with a request to dance as he hummed a tune. Of course, the primary excuse was to hold her tightly, the formal posture of a strict waltz not maintained for very long. Darcy could not sing if his life depended upon it, but he could hum fairly well, or at least enough to set a tempo for the amusement. Over the course of time he had taught her a number of couples dances learned during his travels, most of which were far more intimate and livelier than the waltz. Lizzy was only proficient in the typical English country line dances, but was growing exceedingly fond of the duo dances popular in more progressive countries. Along the way they invented their own steps and movements, usually involving motions clearly sensual in nature and thus wholly inappropriate for public viewing, but quite scintillating in the privacy of one's bedchamber.

Here at the far end of a lonely pier they allowed themselves to cross a few boundaries, but did retain a dignified restraint. Darcy was as graceful and debonair as always, body fluid and flawless as he guided his wife and lover over the rough wooden planks. Lizzy experienced a slight awkwardness with bulging belly preventing total ease and refinement, but they enjoyed themselves nonetheless. They ended against the rail in the shadows after a lavolta lift and turn, Lizzy breathless in Darcy's arms with his face inches from hers.

"I did not think you would be able to lift me," she teased, seconds before his lips met hers with astounding passion. He cupped long fingers around her neck, thumbs caressing as the kiss varied in intensity and lasted for endless minutes. On and on they kissed with no sense of hurrying, both abundantly content to focus all senses on shared breath and taste. Lizzy's hands rested lightly on his waist, Darcy never left her slender neck or creamy shoulders. He withdrew for brief moments to caress her face with his eyes, never halting feathering strokes with delicate fingertips, and always returning to her mouth for more.

I love you whispered ceaselessly by both, kisses traveling unhastily over jaws to ears, passion bubbling, but overruled by adoration as moonlight shimmered palely.

"I am sure it is unnecessary, but I am compelled to verbalize to you how remarkable this entire holiday has been for me." His voice was low and vibrant, Lizzy shivering at the sensations educed. "Superlatives are jumbling in my mind, competing with each other to adequately convey my joy, but none do it justice." He paused for an interlude of fresh kisses and nibbles, knuckles lightly rubbing up and down her neck. "I love you, Elizabeth, with all my heart and soul. My happiness is higher than the heavens. I may live to be one hundred, and pray I do with you by my side, but I will never forget this time with you."

Claiming her sweet mouth yet again, Lizzy now encircling his shoulders with fingers running through his hair, he slowly glided downward, brushing over her breasts to the beautiful swell of their child. Tenderly, devotedly he smoothed and kneaded big hands over her abdomen, adoring the feel of taut flesh cocooning their baby. The wonder of it never failed to awe him. Daily she expanded as the product of their love grew stronger, miraculously nourished and harbored by his mother while adored by an eager father. Lizzy was well into the seventh month of her pregnancy, health generally excellent if a bit prone to fatigue and slight imbalance. She was lovelier to him than ever, glowing, robust, and with a peace emanating from her core.

"As anxious as I am to hold our infant I believe I shall miss this." He spoke softly, palms moving steadily on her stomach.

"As virile and amorous as you are, my love, I suspect the swollen belly will reappear frequently. I visualize Pemberley cluttered with rambunctious little Darcys."

He smiled, truly delighted at the vision and refusing to dwell on the risks of numerous births. A final walk along the beach by moonlight, Lizzy even convincing Darcy to remove his shoes and feel the cold water lap at bare ankles, was the culmination to their outdoor activities. The crowning touch was discovered when they returned to their room. Per Lizzy's instructions, servants had fashioned a makeshift picnic tableau on the chamber floor before the open balcony. Privacy was not assured on the balcony itself; other rooms situated without direct visual contact, but open windows too close for complete comfort. A thick blanket was spread with several large pillows, a platter of fruit and pastries, mulled wine in clay mugs, and two candelabras for illumination sat waiting. A low fire burned as the evenings were increasingly cool.

Darcy grinned happily at his smugly beaming wife, wordlessly taking her hand and leading to the blanket. Passionate lovemaking was the ultimate crescendo, but only after prolonged intimate conversation, frolicking, cuddling, feeding each other, and titillating foreplay.

~❦~

The ancestral home of the Lathrops, Stonecrest Hall, was located roughly five miles northeast of Melton Mowbray. The modest home of grey bricks sat in a shallow dell amongst a dense forest of ancient oaks and was surrounded by a broad expanse of compact grass and clover. There was a natural essence to the property, much as Hasberry possessed, which was relaxing and homey if not as grand as the formality and cultivation of Pemberley. Beyond the house proper were the extensive barns and fields amid the oaks where the cows and bulls roamed. The wealth of the Lathrop family was partially from the cattle market but primarily from dairy products, the cheeses produced considered some of the best in the country.

The Darcys arrived late in the afternoon, having decided to travel straight through from Caister. Lizzy was tired and her back ached, but the physical discomforts were offset by her excitement. Mr. Lathrop greeted them warmly, informing Lizzy that Amelia was with the baby. With a kind smile of complete understanding he directed a waiting maid to escort Mrs. Darcy to the nursery after the briefest of welcomes. The men chuckled once she was away, Stephen leading Darcy to the parlor for a much needed brandy.

Amelia was rocking and nursing her daughter when Lizzy was admitted. Kisses of true delight were shared while the baby obliviously fed on, eyes closed and tiny mouth working diligently. One delicate fist lay atop Amelia's breast, minute fingers kneading. Tears welled in Lizzy's eyes at the sight. Several of her friends, both in Hertfordshire and in Derbyshire, had children, but she had never witnessed a scene so intimately maternal. Her heart gave a massive lurch, one hand instinctively caressing her belly as she gingerly touched Fiona's downy cheek.

"Oh, Amelia, she is absolutely beautiful! How small she is! Oh…" Her voice caught and she swiped at her tears. Amelia was radiant, as all proud mothers are. Lizzy peered closely at her friend's face. "You look amazing, my dear friend. Are you fully recovered from the ordeal?"

Lizzy sat on a nearby stool, hands massaging her back while Amelia answered with a laugh. "Nearly. My bum still hurts and I am a wee bit sleep deprived, but it is a joy not to be carrying the extra weight!" Lizzy laughed, nodding as she rubbed aching muscles.

The following hour was spent in sweet companionship, both women sharing tales of motherhood. Amelia, in the forthright manner that she possessed, imparted detailed information of her labor and birth, Lizzy paling frequently but absorbing each point. Amelia commiserated with Lizzy's current travails, thankful that they were minor. She, too, had been blessed with a relatively easy pregnancy, but a certain number of aches and pains were universal. Fiona finished her meal, falling into the drugged sleep typical of the satisfied newborn. Amelia insisted Lizzy hold the slumbering infant while she freshened up for their guests, Lizzy not requiring too much persuasion.

Lizzy had held a few small babies in her life, but not since becoming a wife and soon-to-be mother. The rush of emotions was overwhelming. For the first time she experienced an intense urgency to hurry through the incubation process so she could gaze upon their son, as her prescient dream so many months prior had planted the assurance, and nestle him to her breast. For several minutes it was as if her spirit soared with an uncontainable need to flee this place for Pemberley, for home, where the focus would all be on final preparations for their child. The hunger to lay eyes on the nursery and all the waiting infant items was nearly painful and a sob caught in her throat.

Then Fiona stretched, releasing a weak gurgle as pink lips pursed and sucked on an imaginary nipple. Her eyes fluttered open briefly, a flash of greenish-blue before closing in renewed sleep. Lizzy smiled, stroking the soft cheek, and bending to smell the fresh fragrance that all newborns emanate. Her baby delivered a grouping of lazy kicks, as if to remind his mother of his viability and equal eagerness to be known. Lizzy chuckled under her breath, rubbing over his prodding limb. "Do not fret, my sweet, I love you best and will wait patiently."

The women joined the reclining men in the parlor. Amelia held the baby, Darcy's eyes instantly alighting on the swaddled bundle. Lizzy recalled with a smile that her husband had never actually beheld a very young infant. His careful regulation was slipping rapidly as they approached. The gentlemen rose, Stephen quickly crossing to assist his still sore wife to a comfortable chair. Lizzy squeezed Darcy's arm, eyes meeting with tender communication before he turned his gaze back to Amelia and the baby.

"Mrs. Lathrop, you appear well. Congratulations on your blessing."

"Thank you, Mr. Darcy. I am quite well, all considered. Now sit down and relax. My arms are frankly aching. Dearest," she looked to her husband with a wink, "perhaps you can assist me? Mr. Darcy, could I trouble you to hold the baby while my husband fetches Elizabeth and me some tea? Elizabeth, could you be a dear and plump up this pillow for me?"

With smoothly manipulated orders, Amelia fulfilled Darcy's wish without him needing to ask, which he likely would never have had the nerve to do. Fairly before he could take a breath, he found his arms blissfully encumbered with the blanketed, softly squirming baby. He sat stiffly, afraid to move an inch or even breathe lest he disturb the peaceful bundle or, heaven forbid, drop her. Heart pounding and inhaling shallowly, Darcy studied the diminutive life form in his rigid arms. She was so small! Every feature dainty in the extreme, wisps of pale hair, cheeks so round and pink, and incredibly light. Gradually he relaxed, sinking comfortably into the sofa and cuddling her close to his chest.

It was absolutely amazing. Never had he seen anything so tiny. Still, she seemed too large to actually reside inside another human being and with a sudden flash of insight he completely understood his wife's aches and complaints as their son intruded on internal organs and placed stress on muscles. Lizzy joined him on the sofa, reaching to gently pull the blanket away from Fiona's chest to unveil a petite hand.

"Easy, Elizabeth, do not wake her," Darcy chided in a whisper.

"Her stomach is full, love. A full marching band could troop through and she would sleep on. Here," she grasped his hand, "touch her cheek. She is so soft."

Darcy did, holding his breath and trembling slightly. "Unbelievable. I have never felt anything like it." He looked up at Stephen, who was grinning broadly where he stood next to Darcy, gazing at his daughter with insurmountable pride and bewitchment. "Lathrop, she is beautiful. An absolute miracle."

"Soon, my old friend, it shall be your turn. Nothing on earth quite compares, I assure you."

The three days passed in Leicestershire were tranquil. Lizzy and Amelia stayed near the house at all times, short walks about the grounds being the only excursions. Amelia was recuperating rapidly, the mild soreness evaporating as her body restored gradually. She lamented the additional bulk to her already full-figured frame, but did so with a giggle and shrug. Lizzy delighted in learning all she could about baby care. The days were highly informative and eased an inordinate amount of the foreboding Lizzy had not even been aware she bore.

Darcy and Lathrop were gone all day, each day, on horseback with rifles in hand as they tromped through the game-filled woods in the vicinity. Late afternoons and evenings were spent in the game room at billiards, primarily, but also the occasional chess challenge. Lizzy always rejoiced when her husband was able to truly embrace the various manly pursuits he enjoyed but often did not have the time or company to engage in. As fully as her masculine spouse devoured such activities for all the typical reasons, he also utilized the secluded moments to quiz his friend on infant-related topics. Mr. Lathrop was a strict traditionalist, so the concept of entering the birth chamber had never crossed his mind; therefore, his knowledge of the delivery process, from the first few pains to well after Fiona had arrived and all had been cleaned up, was nonexistent. Nevertheless, he was a devoted husband and father who happily shared what facts he knew, Darcy discovering the same easing of hidden anxieties as his wife did.

In between their individual recreations, the foursome reconnected for breakfast and dinner as well as early evenings reposing over drinks and conversation in the parlor. Darcy tactfully, and with transparently pleading eyes, asked to hold Fiona whenever possible. The Lathrops smiled at his sweet enthusiasm, and Lizzy positively beamed. By the end of their stay he felt fairly comfortable with the frequently wiggling baby, although the first time she screwed up her little face and released a truly astonishingly loud bellow Darcy blanched whiter than a sheet and clenched her so tightly in alarm that she halted instantly and pierced the big man with a wide-eyed accusatory stare. Amelia laughed, assuring the stricken man that it was merely feeding time as she removed the squalling infant from his shaking arms.

Darcy entered their bed late each night, Lizzy long since asleep, so it was morning before they were able to compare notes. Both felt the pressing urge to return home but also recognized the providential aspect of this visit. Excitement and enthusiasm coupled with book knowledge was wonderful, but nothing quite compared to firsthand experience.

When they said their farewells, the women shedding tears while they hugged, it was a moment of truly mixed emotions. They knew it would likely be months before they saw each other. It was not safe to travel with a young baby in the coming winter months, and obviously Lizzy would be going nowhere. Amelia's family was expected over the Christmas holidays, even if they had been willing to brave the elements.

"Come spring, my dear Amelia, we must visit! Either we shall come here or you to Pemberley. The season in London is much too far to wait."

"Pemberley is only a day away, love. We can easily arrange visitations. Mrs. Lathrop, thank you for allowing us to disturb your peace. It has been delightfully fun and instructive." Darcy bowed gallantly, delivering a friendly kiss to her fingers.

Amelia, however, lifted up and kissed him on the cheek. "William, you and Elizabeth are never a disturbance. Thank you for veering this way and for adoring my daughter. You will be a wonderful father."

Darcy's cheeks were rosy, and he smiled happily. "Thank you, Amelia."

THEY WERE HOME. HAPPILY ensconced in their familiar surroundings and gradually readapting to the regular pace of Pemberley.

To their surprise, Georgiana had returned home two days prior to their arrival from Leicestershire. She doubly astonished them, especially Darcy, by not flying pell-mell down the stairs and launching like a jackrabbit into his arms. Instead she stood sedately on the top step of the entrance portico, dressed in a very fashionable gown with her hair pinned up in a jewel-accented style. She smiled radiantly with eyes shining, but in all ways appeared a young woman.

Darcy did not quite know how to feel. On the one hand he was instantly struck by how beautiful she was in her grown-up poise and discipline, and his pride soared immeasurably. On the other hand, his heart was stabbed with an acute ache at the final vestiges of his baby sister apparently erased overnight. Then at the last second, as he mounted the final steps below her, she suddenly bounced on her toes, squealed, and vaulted into his ready embrace.

"Oh William! I missed you so!"

He smiled into her hair, recognizing the pure selfish happiness rushing through him in knowing that there were at least a few traces of the child in the woman he squeezed tightly to his chest. "My sweet Georgie. I missed you more."

She pulled inches away with a grin, delivering a quick peck to his cheek. "I rather doubt that, brother dear, as you had Elizabeth to assuage your heart."

"Yes, but there are some places even a beloved wife cannot touch." He kissed her forehead and then released her with a broad smile.

"Does your sister warrant such a greeting?"

"Oh Elizabeth! Look at you!" The two women embraced, Georgiana unable to tear her eyes from the significantly larger waistline.

Elizabeth laughed, placing both hands on her belly. "Yes, it is quite impressive, is it not? I found myself competing with the whales at the coast!"

Chatter and stories from all parties was rampant long into the evening. Georgiana was far more effusive than her brother or sister, as they were frankly exhausted, Lizzy actually falling asleep on Darcy's shoulder mid-adventurous tale. It would take days, but finally all gaps were filled and Georgiana too fell into the old routines of life at Pemberley.

The newlywed Olivers had also returned prior to the Darcys. Darcy and Lizzy found their personal servants attending to their duties and relatively unchanged except for the occasional dreamy expressions noted when happened upon unawares. Other than asking Samuel two or three general questions about the weather and sights around the Lake District, which his valet answered in short sentences, Darcy made no other inquires. His curiosity was not adequate to overcome the extreme mortification that would assuredly ensue if he did ask Samuel anything remotely personal. Marguerite was a bit more forthcoming regarding the various activities she and her new husband had partaken in, praising the countryside and accommodations, but gave nary a hint of anything intimate. Most information was gleaned from Mrs. Reynolds, who informed her employers that the Olivers were very happy and contentedly established into their apartment. It was further revealed that the previously stoic, excruciatingly bashful Samuel was looser now, both Olivers increasingly approachable and sociable.

Two days after returning home, Lizzy sat in the music room attending to the household ledger with mildly swollen feet propped up on an ottoman. Georgiana sat at the pianoforte providing background music. It was a quarter after four in the afternoon and pleasantly warm with a faint breeze blowing through the open patio doors. Darcy was away, had been since very early in the morning, observing the final wool baling and delivery preparations.

Phillips entered upon Lizzy's acknowledgement, bowing formally and announcing that there were two gentlemen in the foyer asking to speak with the Mistress as Mr. Darcy was absent.

"Who are they?" Lizzy asked with raised brows.

"They did not offer their names, madam."

"How odd," she murmured, rising with a shrug toward Georgiana, who also rose to trail along curiously.

"Madam, can we two lonely travelers intrude upon your hospitality for the fine Irish whiskey reputedly lurking in the liquor cabinet at Pemberley?"

"Whiskey, brandy, port, whatever you wish for, kind sirs, but first give us a kiss!"

Georgiana had already released a cry of delight and dashed to her favored uncle, Lizzy turning to a grinning Richard Fitzwilliam for a kiss.

"Richard! What a wonderful surprise! We were expecting this wayward traveler to breeze in eventually," Lizzy laughingly declared with a gesture toward George Darcy, "but you are an unanticipated albeit fantastic addition."

"He attached himself to me in London," George declared, "and I could not rid myself of him. Pathetic, really, so I dragged him along. Elizabeth, you appear to have swallowed an enormous ball."

"I wish it were that simple as then it would be lightly filled with air and not expanding further. Come, gentlemen, whiskey is secured in the liquor cabinet. Phillips, your penance for being roped into deception by these two mischief makers is to bring us a tray of comestibles for our weary travelers."

She linked arms with Richard, who said, "You look quite well, Elizabeth. How are you faring?"

"Very well, all considered. I have a husband who dotes most profoundly and a sister nearly as devoted, so I am not allowed to overtax."

"Where is the doting husband, by the way?"

"At the wool barn. I do not know when he shall return, but he usually arrives in time for dinner."

George laughed. "William miss a meal? Do not be ridiculous. Whiskey, Colonel?" he asked as he crossed directly toward the liquor cabinet.

"Please. Georgie, I want to hear all about Wales. Your letters were expository and Mother enumerated additionally, but I wish to hear more from your own lips. Especially, my dear cousin and ward, about this Lord Gruffudd you so eloquently chronicled."

Georgiana blushed scarlet. Lizzy chuckled, laying one hand softly on Georgiana's arm. "Richard, for shame! Do not tease your cousin so. Can a young woman not notice a handsome man and gush to a trusted guardian without being interrogated? Besides, ladies need their little secrets."

"Very well, I am properly chastised. Forgive me, Miss Darcy." He bowed gallantly her direction. "Skip past Lord Gruffudd to your birthday celebrations. I believe you were in Cardiff at the time?"

Georgiana overcame her embarrassment and launched into a detailed account of the merriment delivered by her aunt and uncle for her eighteenth birthday. Refreshments were brought and the small group exchanged stories for the next hour with much laughter ensuing.

Darcy was greeted to the distinct sound of revelry drifting down the hall as he discarded a dusty coat into the waiting hands of Mr. Taylor. "We have visitors?"

"Yes, sir. Dr. Darcy and Col. Fitzwilliam arrived this afternoon."

Darcy nodded, striding briskly to the parlor, and paused on the threshold to view the scene. Col. Fitzwilliam stood in the middle of the room with arms gesticulating as he related what Darcy quickly ascertained was a tale of foolish new cadets attempting to learn marching maneuvers. Lizzy and Georgiana were laughing gaily, while a grinning George sat sprawled on his deceased brother's favored chair with long maroon-covered legs crunched into the minimal space.

"I leave for the day and all manner of disorder arises. Pemberley apparently now hosts anyone who wanders by?"

"With such fine whiskey and beautiful, charming women in residence, it is only to be expected, William," George retorted with a follow-up sip of the amber liquid in his glass.

"I assuredly cannot argue the charming women, or the whiskey for that matter. Richard, it is wonderful to see you. I trust all is well?"

"Tolerably, cousin. I urgently needed to breathe fresh air and escape the adolescents lately come to my regiment. Besides, Dr. Darcy required a companion on the road. To keep him safe, you understand."

George snorted, Darcy chuckling as he crossed to his wife and sister. "Georgie dearest," with a quick kiss to her cheek before lifting Lizzy's fingers to his lips. "Beloved, you are well?"

"Perfect, dear. I have been marvelously entertained. Our guests seem to be bursting with amusing anecdotes."

"Passes the time, I suppose. Uncle, we have had no news since Devon. What have you been up to? And please tell me Darcy House is yet habitable?"

"No worries, William. The cousins all send their best wishes. We spent a week on the coast, then I departed to visit friends in Dorset. I actually was only in London for four days, which is why Darcy House is undamaged. Mrs. Smyth expressed her sadness to see me depart, but I longed for Pemberley. Nothing quite compares to the autumn here."

"I am discovering the same," Lizzy said. "William told me the gardens were particularly lovely in the fall, and he was not exaggerating."

"Of course," Richard interjected. "This is your first autumn here! I had forgotten. Mr. Clark and his staff are remarkable. My parents should allow him to train their gardeners."

"I arrived at the end of autumn past, but the rains and cold weather set in shortly thereafter so William had little opportunity to acquaint me extensively with the gardens. Except for what I could see from windows, that is."

"What a shame," George murmured. "Holed up inside with nothing to do all winter. How trying that must have been." He glanced slyly at his nephew, who was approaching with whiskey decanter in hand.

"Yes," Darcy intoned dryly. "It was terribly stressful, but we managed." He refilled his uncle's glass without meeting his eyes. "Of course, it was blessedly quiet. Virtually relative free until Christmas."

"Ah, Christmas at Pemberley." George dreamily stared into space, ignoring Darcy's playful slur.

"Will you stay for Christmas, Uncle?" Georgiana asked with a pleading tone.

"We shall see, dear. I am enjoying my leisure. By the way," he pulled a folded piece of parchment from his pocket, "it is a bit crinkled, I fear, but I have a missive from Raul. Have either of you heard from Miss de Bourgh?"

Lizzy shook her head negatively, Darcy responding, "Not for a month. I rather assumed she was otherwise entertained."

"Apparently quite so. Raja states that all is progressing smoothly. He is working at the hospital in Ashford as well as offering his services throughout the community as required. Lady Catherine is now singing his praises to all who will listen, probably questioning when he will officially propose and increase her prestige in society."

"Undoubtedly Miss de Bourgh wonders the same," Lizzy said.

"So he has not secured her hand as of yet? What is he waiting for?" Darcy was honestly surprised.

"Soon, I garner from his letter. He wanted to be established somewhat, earn Lady Catherine's undying respect and approval, and shower Miss de Bourgh with the full treasure trove of courtship rituals. I gather he has exhausted the arsenal of romantic tomfoolery, so with nothing remaining, engagement is imminent."

"Hopefully he has left a few romantic gestures in reserve. Women appreciate that sort of thing." Lizzy smiled winsomely at her husband.

"Is this true, Darcy?" Col. Fitzwilliam asked with a raised brow and smirk.

"I have found it to be so, yes. You would do well to remember the information, cousin." Richard shuddered, taking a quick sip of whiskey.

Lizzy laughed. "We must find a nice lady for you, Richard. You are far too wayward. Capricious, poor soul. You need a steady girl to stabilize you."

"Shackle, you mean," George spoke in defense of his friend. "Not all men are destined for domesticity, dear Elizabeth. Some of us prefer being footloose and fancy free! Although having a woman about can have its advantages, I suppose. Back massages, home decorating, darning socks, that sort of thing, eh, William?"

"Precisely, uncle. That is why I chose marriage," Darcy answered seriously, eyes twinkling and meeting Lizzy's.

"The day I darn socks will be the day the sun fails to rise. Back massages are acceptable, however." She and Darcy shared a brief, knowing smile.

Yet holding his wife's eyes, Darcy spoke to his uncle and cousin, "Speaking of matrimony, I am thankful that you both are here and do pray you intend to stay for a while. Elizabeth has agreed to marry me, again, in a ceremony at Pemberley Chapel."

Col. Fitzwilliam smiled delightfully, lifting his glass Lizzy's direction. George whistled and declared with a grin, "Romantic gesture of the highest order, indeed. Well done, William! How marvelous for me as I missed the official nuptials. When is the date?"

"We have not decided as of yet," Darcy answered, still gazing at Lizzy. "I was opting for November twenty-eight as a perfect commemoration of the happiest day of my entire life."

"I, however," Lizzy interrupted softly, "reminded my husband that I will be as enormous as a house by late November, if not in the actual throes of birth travails. Additionally it somehow seems irreverent to waddle down the church aisle to be wed while clearly nearly to burst with child!"

"I do believe, my dear niece, that it is far too late to hide that fact. Besides, I am sure God is privy to the fact that you two are already legally and spiritually bound, and shall withhold the lightning bolt."

Lizzy reddened but persevered, "All true, Dr. Darcy. I think we should wait until after the baby is born…"

"And I," it was Darcy's turn to interrupt, "refuse to wait that long. I have a burning urge to exchange vows with my wife in the Darcy family chapel. She has accepted my proposal so cannot renege on the agreement." He spoke with a slight edgy tone and clenched jaw, but wore a smile for Lizzy and eyes indigo with desire.

"Well," George boomed as he rose with a spine-cracking stretch, "I am free all next week. You, Colonel?"

"My docket is empty for a couple weeks," Richard shrugged. "A wedding is an adequate entertainment, I suppose."

With the family thus settled, the last weeks of September glided by with happy serenity felt all around. The weather held clement and sunlit during the day with a slight chilling come sundown. The gradual metamorphosis about the extensive grounds began as autumn colors invaded, leaves burnished with golds and reds. The emergence of the multihued dahlia, purple toad lily, marguerite daisy, calendula, nasturtium, rosemary, and salvias provided a fresh plethora of vibrant color and fragrance to the summer-fading blooms. The numerous bushes with variegated foliage accented the already dazzling displays. The gardeners were especially busy preparing the vast gardens for the winter freeze and spring flowering, bulbs arriving by the wagon loads.

Lizzy watched the digging for several days before gathering the nerve to ask Mr. Clark if she could assist with the care of the private garden to the east of the manor. If he was shocked or dismayed in any way by her request, it did not show. Thus it was that Lizzy could be found most days on her knees in the soft turf with two gardeners named Robert and Harry aiding nearby. Naturally the modest garden was already faultless, and Lizzy had no desire to radically transform anything. She merely wished to plant a few of her favorite plants and to fulfill a long-standing pleasure to work with soil and flora, gardening having always been a pastime she enjoyed.

Additionally, she resumed her duties as Mistress. She had not consciously recognized missing the simple household tasks while on her holiday, but once confronted with the pile of papers Mrs. Reynolds had carefully organized on her desk, she delved in with nearly as much gusto as Darcy. Naturally Mrs. Reynolds had managed all matters efficiently during her Mistress's absence, but she had no qualms with relegating authority to Mrs. Darcy. Rather she considered it her proper duty to do so. Thus the ledgers, purchasing notes, detailed lists of tasks completed, staff concerns, and so on were methodically perused in a series of meetings between the two women over several days.

Lizzy and Darcy rediscovered the contentment of evenings working side by side at their sitting room desks and in the joyful sharing of estate business. They naturally fell into the previous pattern of quietly attending to individual tasks or engaging in extended discussion of estate affairs. Darcy had accepted his wife's innate common sense that frequently opened a new avenue of thought regarding a subject or dilemma. However, in general he managed the business of Pemberley with minimal input, and Lizzy was unconcerned since she knew he did not need her participation. Plus there was still a large amount of his ventures that she simply did not comprehend. Instead, the dialogues were more for the joy of sharing.

Lizzy's curricle was utilized frequently as the fair weather continued. Darcy fretted, as always, but kept his fears mostly hidden. His only stipulation—stated softly but with an edge—was that she never travel too far and always have Georgiana as her companion. To this she agreed. Fortunately her dearest friends were in close proximity.

Sanburl Hall, home of Harriet Vernor, was less than two miles from door to door. She could easily walk the distance, and had numerous times during the spring and early summer months, but walking long distances was fast becoming a difficulty. Marilyn Hughes lived three and a half miles away, Rymas Park nestled on the edge of Rymas Brook and such a beautifully serene locale with the forest encasing the quaint house that Lizzy delighted in her visits there. The need to feel the wind upon her face and command the little carriage was too great to completely ignore, so even when a visit was not planned, Lizzy and Georgiana would commandeer the vehicle for a jaunt about the estate and a picnic.

Generally, however, her friends chose to visit Pemberley, all of them understanding the necessity for their pregnant friend to remain close to home. Julia Sitwell and Alison Fitzherbert, who lived near each other in the region north of Chesterfield, journeyed together for a stay of three days. Of course it pleased Darcy considerably to have his wife safe within Pemberley's walls, a fact not entirely lost on any of the women!

When not attending to business of some kind, digging in the garden, or visiting with her lady friends, Lizzy was usually with Georgiana.

"What song are you playing? I have never heard that one before." Lizzy glanced up from her embroidery, directing the question toward her sister-in-law, who was entertaining on the pianoforte.

Georgiana reddened, evading Lizzy's quizzical look. "I wrote it," she replied in a small voice, speaking louder at the dawning astonishment on Lizzy's face, "but you cannot tell William! Promise me."

"Why not? It was beautiful, Georgiana. I had no idea you had composed music. I am very impressed and know William would be as well."

"I do not think he would understand. And besides, it is merely a trifling thing. Not very good at all."

"I beg to differ. It was lovely. Perhaps not of the quality to worry Mr. Beethoven that he has serious competition, but certainly enjoyable to hear."

Georgiana laughed at Lizzy's tease. "No, I doubt any true composers need be threatened." She sighed, her eyes suddenly dreamy. "It was fun to try my hand at writing. Lizzy," she paused, speaking haltingly when she resumed, "do you believe, as Uncle says, that someday females will be able to... be more... be accepted beyond... not be frowned upon or chastised for pursuing... something else... or. Oh, I am making no sense!"

Lizzy laughed. "I understand you, Georgiana. Your uncle is a bit of a revolutionary, is he not?"

Georgiana nodded, giggling. "Indeed. Although I think he usually says radical comments just to see William's face and enter a debate. Still, it would be nice to have an option in life."

"Do you not wish to be a wife and mother?"

"Oh yes! Yes, I do!" Georgiana nodded emphatically. "Very much! But," she rose then, pacing with uncharacteristic energy, "there are times, when I am listening to music, or learning a new piece, when I will see notes upon a sheet in my mind. New notes, joined uniquely as the sounds play within my head, forming sections and whole movements. Cadenza, scherzo, ostinato, toccata. Melodies I have never heard before. Unfamiliar arrangements."

She stopped, sighing and shrugging. "So I write them down, sometimes. Wondering if they are truly my own ideas or lost remembrances."

"I see nothing wrong with you placing your musical visions upon paper, Georgiana. If this is a gift you have been granted, then explore it! Creating music, even if only enjoyed by a few, is a beautiful, worthwhile endeavor."

"You do not think it silly? A waste of time?"

"Of course not. Why is it any different than painting or weaving? If you enjoy writing your own songs, you should. I know I would love to hear more. How many have you composed?"

"Only a few sonatas, an impromptu, and I am working on a nocturne. All of a romantic bent, thus confirming my hopes in life and lack of wild inspiration." She finished with a laugh.

"What an accomplished woman," Lizzy whispered with true pride and awe. "Your brother would be immeasurably proud."

"Truly?"

"Without a doubt. He adores you, Georgiana, and only wishes for your happiness. You have no idea how proud he is of you. Play any of your tunes, especially the one you played for me, and he will probably burst from the joy."

"Did you know that women are allowed to enroll as students at the Conservatoire in Paris?" She glanced at a nodding Lizzy, her cheeks rosy and voice wistful. "It must be amazing to be surrounded by people desiring to learn nothing but music. To be immersed in music all day. To meet great musicians and singers and composers."

"You will travel to the Continent, Georgie. You know William plans for it. There you will encounter innumerable opportunities to enhance your skills. Paris is going nowhere and the Conservatoire will wait. Of course, this is provided you do not fall in love with the first man you meet at Almack's next spring."

"Oh, heaven forbid! William would surely have a heart seizure! I think he would sooner allow me to take the Grand Tour or dwell in Paris than that! Frankly I pray I am refused so I do not have to face such agony."

Lizzy laughed. "I am sorry to disappoint, my dear, but the odds of that are miniscule."

"One never knows, Lizzy. The Patronesses are whimsical in their approval. I heard that Angelica Cole was refused and Mary Ward!" Georgiana sat next to Lizzy, her face pale. "William would be devastated if I was denied, but then I am terrified of dancing with all eyes upon me. Oh my, I truly am a mouse as Richard insists!"

"Silly girl! First, Richard calls you his 'little mouse' because you are sweet, adorable, and mild. Second, no Darcy will be refused at Almack's. And third, you have had some practice dancing while in Wales, and after your presentation at Court, Almack's will be nothing."

Now it was Georgiana who laughed. "You say that because appearing at Court is what you dread!"

"Indeed I do," Lizzy shuddered. "One look at the gate before St. James's Palace and I knew I never wanted to walk through them. How can you be so complaisant? I was perfectly content to forego all the 'coming out' nonsense. Why does William insist I must?"

"Because you are Mrs. Darcy of Pemberley. He is proud of you and wants everyone to know how immensely fortunate he is."

"I shall trip over the formal gown and train, I know I shall. Or forget the proper phrases. The Prince will be insulted and I shall be mortified."

"Nonsense. Aunt Madeline will prepare us adequately, and besides, it is in and out within five minutes. I, on the other hand, will suffer the trauma of a whole evening being stared at and probably tripping over my own feet. It shall be torture!"

"Be cheered, dear sister. William will be there with you as chaperone, most likely glowering at every eligible male in the dance hall, so none of them will have the audacity to ask you to dance anyway!"

Darcy resumed his forays into the storage areas of the attic that had begun with the quest for baby furniture. Along the way he discovered numerous boxes containing a plethora of infant toys, memorabilia, school implements, childhood clothing, and more. Additionally there were the odd pieces of furniture, old clothing and trinkets, and assorted items that frequently sparked a memory. Darcy was overjoyed and rather amazed, the hours spent in investigating the past quite pleasurable. He knew his parents had amassed a large quantity of keepsakes, their penchant for saving valued items a character trait passed on to their children, he just had not realized the breadth. Of course there was also an enormous quantity of what could only be labeled junk: objects that were clearly decades old, moldering and decaying into dust. His organized mind shuddered at the rampant chaos, and although he did not need to add another chore to his docket, he ended up embarking on an extensive cleaning mission. The household staff wasn't exactly thrilled by the expedition but did their assigned duties, while dozens of families in the nearby communities benefited from the used clothing and furniture.

Therefore, what had begun as a simple retrieval of cradle and rocking chair ended up being a massive scourging and a chance to revisit past memories.

Thus it was common during those long days of autumn for Lizzy to discover her dusty spouse surrounded by boxes and scattered piles of oddities. One such day, not too long after their return from the Lathrops, she heard the ghost of his laughter reaching her ears as she approached the narrow stairs leading to the eastern attic where the family artifacts were accumulated. She smiled as she mounted the steps, grinning further at the sight of him sitting on the wooden floorboards with long legs crossed amid the cobwebs and chaos. Coats and cravat had been discarded in the stifling heat of the airless room, folded neatly over a threadbare chair, his fine linen shirt smudged with grime and hands filthy. He was reading a tattered book of sorts, grinning and chuckling.

"What is so humorous?"

He glanced up at his wife, motioning for her to come forward and clearing a space amongst the clutter by his side. "Remember I told you that when I was a boy I attempted to write a story about traveling to another planet? My mother kept it!" He shook his head. "I never spoke of it to a living soul so have no idea how she confiscated it. She kept everything! Every report I wrote, test I took, all my tutor's comments and marks, love notes to my family. Georgie's as well. Her boxes are over there." He waved to a group assembled in perfect order against a far wall. "I will bring those down so she can look through them." He shook his head in amazement. "Unbelievable. I fear I have not been so diligent with Georgie's school work, but think Mrs. Reynolds has as some of the items I saw are from well after Father died."

With barely controlled mirth Lizzy read the juvenile novel of a hero named Admiral Achilles and his red-haired companion Sergeant Hector conquering celestial planets. Darcy glanced at her face and nudged her side. "Go ahead, laugh. God knows I did. Give me some latitude, please, as I think I was eleven when I wrote that."

"And reading *The Iliad* at the same time?"

He shrugged, reaching into another box. "I always wanted to be Achilles. Handsome, nearly immortal, fleet, heroic."

"And how were you supposed to have arrived upon the shores of Mars?"

"I do not think I ever worked that part out. Look here, the puzzles I remember playing with!" He pulled out numerous twisted wooden and metal brain teasers such as those purchased in Derby. "Hmmm... I shall have to take these down and see if I can recall the mystery. Add them to the others that I have yet to solve. This whole box contains classroom apparatus: slates, abacus, a globe, old textbooks... Lord, these are outdated! Why keep such things?"

Lizzy had finished chapter one of the Martian tale, turning to an open box by his feet. The box was larger than the others, really a moderate-sized chest with elaborate scrolling, and had *Fitzwilliam* etched onto the lid in gold embossed cursive. "What is in here?"

"All my infant things. My grandfather built that chest. He was an incredible whittler. You recall the collection of miniature sailing vessels in the library that he created? Some of these," he indicated the interlocking wooden puzzles, "were designed by him. He was very gifted. Unfortunately neither my father nor I inherited the talent. Father built a similar chest for Georgiana, but it is more functional than ornate. Hers is in her room as was this one in mine until I moved to the master's chambers. I am not really sure why it ended up in the attic." He shrugged.

He watched Lizzy pull the various items out, both smiling as he reverently fingered each one. "I thought my mother foolish for keeping so many silly things. Until now, that is. As a soon-to-be father, I appreciate the value of every token, each one a testimonial of a precious moment lived and deserving of remembrance. I suppose when one is young, one imagines that all events are etched permanently upon the mind, but time has a way of eroding some memories, or perhaps the brain can only hold a finite amount of information."

Among the maternally cherished treasures were two tarnished silver and polished stone rattles; well-gnawed and cracked teething rings of rubber, ivory, and coral; several sets of dented, tarnished miniature dining utensils, cups, and bowls; a stuffed grey Irish wolfhound that was threadbare and lumpy, missing one button eye and floppy ear; three equally ratty, stained blankets; a pouch containing a mass of fine, light brown hair; a collection of bibs, bonnets, booties, and gowns likely special gifts from some relative or friend; a tied bundle of envelopes enclosing birth congratulations; a hairbrush and comb, both missing teeth and bristles; and a dozen odd toys perfect for small hands.

Lizzy had lifted the lid on a tiny silver case lined with scarlet velvet in which resided dozens of varying sized, pearly white teeth. She chuckled, grasping one of the tiniest between her thumb and index finger, "Yes, it is as you say, dearest, but much more." She placed the tooth onto the palm of his hand, continuing in a soft voice as he gazed at the miniscule white rock lost on his large hand, "It is so that years later you can do precisely what you are doing now, rumbling through old boxes covered in dust and filled with seemingly useless paraphernalia, and know that your parents loved you so much that nothing was deemed superfluous."

He smiled, rolling the tooth about on his palm. "They waited many years for a son and after losing my sister, I confess I was hideously pampered and a bit spoiled. Then there were all the long years until Georgie. Naturally I was loved, but I judge it was partially because my mother had no one else to dote on."

Lizzy laughed. "There is likely a great deal of truth in that. I know my mother kept very few of our childhood mementos. What souvenirs I have were kept by me. She was far too busy having more babies, not to mention definitely unsentimental."

"However many children we are blessed with, Elizabeth, they will be equally overindulged. I promise you that. What's this?" He withdrew a carefully sealed smaller box, placing it on his lap.

Lizzy gasped at the revealed contents, fingers immediately caressing over the delicate fabric. "Is it yours?"

"Must be, as this box contains all my keepsakes. Ah, yes, look here, my birth announcement: *Fitzwilliam Alexander James Darcy born to Mr. James and Lady Anne Darcy on November Ten of 1787.*"

"It is beautiful." Lizzy spoke softly, truly stunned by the gown of exquisite satin and Alencon lace overlay. It was white with short puffy sleeves, a lined skirt three feet long with the lace extending three inches to end in a scalloped pattern of leaves and bluebells, and minute pearls sewn over the bodice. "You wore this." It was a reverently whispered statement rather than a question.

"Apparently. I remember Mother saying she sewed a gown while expecting my sister. There is a box of belongings that were Alexandria's over there," he pointed to a lone box. "The awaited heir required something extravagant, she said." He smiled wistfully, eyes dim in memory.

"I cannot believe she created this herself." She bit her lip, looking shyly to Darcy, who was still lost in reminiscence. "Would you mind terribly if our baby wore this for the christening?"

Darcy snapped to the present with left brow raised in surprise, gazing at Lizzy in bafflement, "Why in the world would I mind? It is your decision, beloved, although I thought you planned to make a gown yourself. Would you not prefer our son to wear something new?"

Lizzy's cheeks were flushed and she ducked her head in embarrassment. "Well, I rather like the idea of him wearing what you wore. A sense of continuity and good fortune. But if you must know the truth, it is partially because I am not skilled enough to create a garment half this lovely, and your heir deserves the best."

He gently clasped her chin, lifting to meet her eyes as he leaned toward her. "Elizabeth, it is *our child* who deserves the best in all things, no matter the sex. I do not care what gown he or she wears when baptized, only that he is healthy and that the ceremony takes place. The choice is yours." He kissed her tenderly, caressing over the soft bulge of their son. "If you sew it, then it will be perfect. If you buy something or have it made, it will be perfect. If you wish to use this gown, then it will be perfect."

"Thank you, William."

He stroked over her cheek, leaving smears of dirt. "As for your sewing techniques or lack thereof, I married you even though you are so hideously flawed and I love you anyway."

He was grinning widely, Lizzy laughing and shoving forcefully so that he nearly fell over. They ended up dust covered, but happy and content when they finally left the sweltering confines. Arms were laden with items that were cautiously if hastily laid aside in the rushing need for a cleansing bath... together.

"Mrs. Darcy," softly whispered in her ear and accompanied by a tiny nibble and smattering of brushing kisses.

Lizzy stretched, arching blissfully into her husband's body and clasping the warm hand resting on her abdomen. "Rising so early, William. Something special about today?" She turned her head to reach his smiling lips for a glancing kiss.

"Indeed. We are a long way from Hertfordshire and the sun is barely cresting the hills. I have no need to converse with your father or any other Bennets, and can remain unclothed rather than formally attired. Thus I planned no rehashes of the day one year ago when you agreed to be my wife, but I certainly do not intend to forget it."

He rained tiny suckles over the nape of her neck, Lizzy shivering in pleasure, returning slowly to her ear. "I am as bewitched today as I was then, still desire to never be parted from you, and love you with an ardency multiplied a hundredfold. Thank you, my precious Elizabeth, for agreeing to become my wife."

"You are very welcome. And do not fret over the lack of celebratory dramatizations. I have a very good memory not to mention the painting to remind me of a significant event in our lives. All things considered, I would rather wake with you unclothed next to me in our bed. Besides, with another wedding fast approaching I am indubitably the luckiest of women in the area of special commemorations."

He chuckled against the skin of her mid back where he was bestowing all manner of oral delights while wending his way down her posterior side, one hand quite busy over her anterior. Neither would feel in any way slighted by their private choice in how best to honor the day in late September when Darcy proposed successfully.

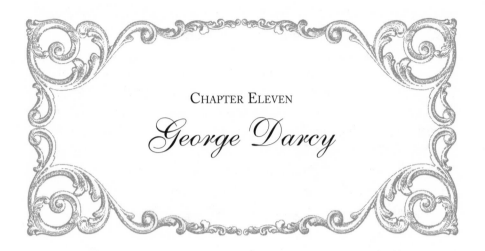

G EORGE CONTINUED TO TAKE his "holiday" very seriously. He spent
large periods of time in the vast library becoming personally reac-
quainted with each shelf. As at Darcy House, Darcy often gravitated
toward wherever his uncle was, not fully aware that his heart was seeking the
older man out. The relationship germinated over the summer months was
blossoming with each passing day. Darcy gradually continued to open up, sharing more of himself to the man who was so incredibly like his father. George
unconsciously did the same, the bond being forged with his nephew growing
daily deeper.

One such incident occurred two days after George's return to Pemberley.
They sat in the library enjoying the breezes flowing through the open windows.
Darcy sat at the small secretary located near one window composing a letter to
Mr. Daniels, while George leafed through the *London Times* from the enormous
Chippendale several feet away.

"Did you read this article?" George tapped a printed column on the
day's newspaper.

Darcy glanced up from the letter he was writing, squinting to see what
article his uncle was indicating. "Which article is it?"

"The one about William Blake's speech at the Guildhall in Cheapside.
More of his free love and religious mysticism nonsense." He shook his head in

disgust. "I may not be the best one to point fingers at another for disturbing the societal mores, but the man sees visions for goodness sake! They have a name for such people."

"I have heard him speak a couple of times. I concur that he is odd, but he does forward some positive notions regarding equality and abolition of slavery. His artwork is interesting, and I actually own two of his relief etchings. Of course, he has opposed our King and spoken out against many of the Church's tenets."

"Exactly!" George sat forward in agitation, fluttering the paper in the air. "The latter appears to be his primary theme these days as this is the second such expose I have read since coming home. It disgusts me."

Darcy was gazing quizzically at his uncle with head cocked. "Forgive me, Uncle, as I mean no disrespect, but I am frankly rather amazed at your vehemence. I would have suspected that your religious views had altered somewhat after your years in India."

George's left brow shot up, but then he fell back into the huge chair with laughter ringing. "Yes, I suppose that would be the natural assumption," he said, tugging on the edge of his blue silk tunic. "In truth the opposite is the fact of it, William." He paused, smiling with eyes distant in memory. "I confess that by the time I had finished my education my mind was far more centered on science and medicine than religious doctrine. Nonetheless, I was raised by your grandfather and you know how staunch he was. I think I was permitted to absent myself from weekly worship two or three times in all my youth, and two of those times was only because I had the mumps!"

They both fell silent, smiling inwardly with personal memories of the somewhat imposing but dear man who was the anchor at Pemberley for five decades.

George broke the quiet, voice calm and introspective. "It is interesting, William, to see how differently men deal with trauma and the ugliness of the world. During my studies and clinical employment at London's hospitals, I saw a tremendous amount of both. Yet I was still young, naïve, and hungry for knowledge, so I placed a shield about my heart, so to speak. Forced the realities of what I saw out of my ready consciousness and focused on the cold facts of science. Once in India I quickly became immersed in the culture, which I still adore to a great degree, but was rapidly sunk into the harsh brutality of suffering. It breaks men far stronger than me. Many leave after short enlistments or become so hardened they are stony of soul." He paused, shaking his head in sadness.

"How did you learn to deal with it?"

George smiled. "Ah well, I could impress you and say I am of sterner stuff, a better man than that." He met Darcy's eyes with a twinkle. "Primarily I made a choice. I chose to focus on the good I was doing. I chose to focus on the people themselves, to dwell with them, be friends, learn who they are, share their joys and sorrows. In essence I chose to expand my heart, let it encompass these people who are so wonderful and real regardless of their skin color or odd beliefs. Additionally I returned to the roots of my faith."

He paused again, staring at his folded hands with a flicker of old grief crossing his face. Darcy waited. Finally George resumed, "After Alex died I retreated from the world for a spell. On the day of the funeral, once it was over and before the guests had even departed, I packed up a sack of essentials and went to the cave. For two weeks I stayed there, alone, fishing for food, eating wild berries and such. I had no plan, you understand, unless it was a vague one of dying myself." He shrugged and laughed faintly.

"What happened?" Darcy, totally unconsciously, had risen and was now sitting in the chair across from his uncle, elbows on knees as he leaned forward and avidly listened.

"Your grandfather happened! He marched into the cave, bellowing at me to come out of the inner chamber as he was too big to squeeze in. I contemplated ignoring him for about a second, but one did not ignore my father. He did three things. First, he hugged me tight for about fifteen minutes until I finally broke down and cried. Then he abruptly pushed me away, patted my head, smiled kindly, but stated firmly, 'Enough, George. Time to get busy and move on.' Before two more days had passed I was buried in chores. He set me to working as a common servant about the Manor and volunteered my time serving the old curate, Reverend Halifax, and at the orphanage. It worked. Of course I would never forget my twin, but the aching grief ebbed in time and I learned to think beyond my own selfishness."

He looked at his nephew, eyes serious. "Faith became very important to me. Part of the reason medicine drew me was because of Alex's death, the perhaps stupidly misplaced belief that proper care may have saved his life. Yet it also was the desire to aid God's creatures, all of whom are loved by their Creator even if they do not know Him."

"You are a missionary, Uncle."

George laughed. "No, not hardly! Only a man of superior medical expertise. I rarely share my religion with others, so that precludes me from being counted a missionary, but it is a vital aspect of who I am. I admire all people, even if they do not admire or respect themselves, and I do not see it my place to upset them in their religious beliefs. If they are comforted in their gods, then who am I to take that from them?"

"So, your convictions were never shaken by Hinduism?"

"You still sound surprised." He grinned teasingly. "I am essentially a simple man, my boy. I do not like things too complicated, and the Hindu religion is far too complicated. Many tried to explain it to me and of course I do understand a great deal, but it only served to strengthen my faith. A dear friend loved to debate me on the subject, but she was never all that serious about converting me. Rather she preferred to stir me up for fun." A tender smile lit his face, eyes soft. Darcy watched him closely, but George snapped out of his momentary trance with a cough. "Besides, they do not eat beef! Are mostly vegetarian, in fact, so it would never work!"

Darcy could make no claims to theological proficiency, having never specifically studied the subject, but his years of regular church attendance, deep faith, and regular Bible reading had translated to what he presumed was a superior knowledge on the topic. Imagine his surprise through frequent conversations with his wayward uncle to discover the far wider breadth of the older man's comprehension. They debated upon occasion, but primarily Darcy found himself listening and learning. It was the launching point where many of Darcy's preconceived ideas regarding his uncle's character and morals were proven false.

It was not that he had an overwhelmingly negative opinion of George. However, he could not previously claim to really know the man intimately, and George's general air of flippancy and irreverence had translated to Darcy as disregard for what was appropriate and moral. He eventually realized that the old prejudices of his own character that he thought eradicated after nearly losing Elizabeth were partially intact. Even his repugnance for George's keeping of a mistress ended up not being the moral debasement that he imagined.

A few days later Darcy and George accidentally discovered themselves alone, sipping lemonade on the eastern edge of the terrace.

Lizzy was resting and Georgiana was practicing her music. Richard was currently at Rivallain visiting with his brother. A stack of work requiring hours with Mr. Keith had occupied Darcy's afternoon, finishing just as the sun lay low on the western horizon. Informed by Mr. Taylor that Dr. Darcy reclined under the canopy erected away from the harsh afternoon sun, Darcy decided to join him with fresh drinks and victuals.

"Ah!" George declared upon noting the laden tray in his nephew's hands, sitting forward from his slumped repose. "What have you brought? Gooseberry tartlets and sweet cream! Divine!" He snatched one before the tray was safely placed onto the table, biting deep with a sensuous moan of delight. "Oh, Mrs. Langton, you genius. William, no matter how prestigious it is to have a French chef, if you ever replace that woman, I shall turn you over my knee."

Darcy laughed, chewing with equal pleasure. "Have no fear, Uncle. I am a Darcy through and through, which means I appreciate excellent cuisine served in healthy proportions. If I want my son to grow as tall and hardy as me, then I would be unwise to restrict his diet to miniscule portions of rich fare. That only leaves one fat and lazy."

They ate in silence, enjoying the array of pastries provided. George Darcy, for all his natural jocularity, was much like his nephew in that he did not suffer the pressing need to fill the space with useless chatter. The men passed as much time together in quiet companionship as they did in conversation. They happily snacked while staring at the mesmerizing play of sunlight on the rippling waters of the lake and jetting fountains. The varied sounds of nature soothed their ears and lulled tired brains. It was quite some time before the hush was broken and then it was Darcy verbalizing unconsciously what he had been dreamily musing on.

"Elizabeth and I have discussed your recommendation that I stay with her during the birth."

"And?"

Darcy chuckled lowly, glancing at George with an arched brow. "You recall my shock at the notion? Well, for all the difference in our physical features, I do believe her expression mirrored mine. I did not bring it up forthwith but waited until late one night…"

"You deemed it wise to wait until she was adequately pliant and amenable?" George interrupted with a naughty grin and a wink, Darcy flushing but shaking his head in resignation.

"No, I needed to consider the matter and come to grips with the notion myself. Anyway, we agreed to the arrangement, although convincing Mrs. Henderson before she storms out in a contemptible rage may take some doing."

"Do not be ridiculous. You are the Master of Pemberley, Mr. Darcy of Derbyshire, etcetera. She has nothing to say about the matter and in the aftermath of your brilliance in the birth chamber will undoubtedly see the logic and spread the word, thus starting a fashionable trend that will benefit millions. It will be a revolution sweeping all England and then Europe. They will probably name it after you and you will be famous."

"Precisely another valid reason why I should *not* be there, but, alas, you have planted the seed too firmly."

George laughed. "Do not worry, William. I will break the news to Mrs. Henderson. Women are helpless against the George Darcy charm." He waggled his brows, Darcy shaking his head in resignation.

"Whatever you say, Uncle." He paused, George waiting as he sensed Darcy's seriousness and knew it best to remain silent until the younger man gathered his thoughts. With low, halting voice Darcy resumed, "Tell me truthfully, Uncle. Have you seen many men in the birth chamber and can swear that it is beneficial to the woman?" He stared fixedly at the distant fountain. "I will sacrifice my life for Elizabeth's comfort without hesitation, but I confess to not relishing witnessing what reputedly is a heinous trial for the woman I love."

"You are not all that fragile, William. As to your question, yes, I have seen many men attend and assist in birth. It is not so uncommon a practice in India. And, of course, doctors have been doing it for centuries. Personally I have always been rather affronted, pridefully insulted at the concept that childbirth is a woman's purview. As if a man cannot have the stomach for it! Besides, there is nothing more miraculous then seeing your offspring come into the world. It is beautiful."

He concluded in a bare whisper. Darcy glanced over sharply, noting George's faraway stare and the undisguised sorrow waving over his face. A rush of intense curiosity lanced through him, but he held his tongue. The months building their relationship had revealed a man astonishingly similar to himself, and if there was anything Darcy hated, it was prying. He was a fiercely private man and knew his uncle to be the same. If George wished to share what was clearly a painful subject, then he would do so without Darcy's urging.

Therefore silence once again fell, each man lost to internal memories and musings. Enough time passed that Darcy had almost forgotten the last words vocalized when George spoke.

"I was a father for a brief time." He looked into Darcy's surprised eyes with a grim smile and then he shrugged. "I have spoken of this to very few people. Raja does not even know. My daughter was born two months early and lived for a week. She was perfect. Bronze skin, black hair, tiny fingers and toes. We named her Bhrithi, which means cherished. I did everything I could think of, but she was too fragile. She would be ten years old if she had lived."

He paused to swallow audibly, eyes closing as he leaned back to rest his head on the cool stones of the Manor's outer wall. "Frankly I do not know why I yet hesitate to speak of these parts of my life. Years of maintaining secrecy are difficult to break, I suppose. James knew. He was my closest friend even with the distance between us." He smiled fondly.

"Uncle, you do not need to share this with me if it is uncomfortable."

"Quite the contrary, William. Surprisingly I do not feel 'uncomfortable,' but merely do not wish to burden you with my affairs unnecessarily. It is all past now, but I yearn for the honest relationship I sense building between us to continue. I know you are aware that I had a mistress. Previously I was unperturbed by your reaction to the fact. I do not suffer from embarrassment or the fear of disparagement." He laughed, opening one eye to peer at Darcy. "My towering self-esteem and arrogance is not a façade! If you thought less of me for living immorally, I honestly did not care. But, you see, this too has changed. Oh, I am still arrogant and likely will be until the day I die, but your opinion now matters. Quite annoying actually, but there you have it."

He closed the eye, smiling dreamily. "Jharna was the wife of my mentor, Dr. Kshitij Ullas, and daughter to a marvelous friend, Thakore Sahib Pandey. She and I were friends but nothing more until after Kshitij died, well after in fact. Jharna and Kshitij were a rare find in that they truly loved each other. He was far older and a widower for many years when he married Jharna. It was an arranged marriage, as most are there, Jharna given as partial payment when Kshitij saved Pandey's life. Of course, all this transpired long before I came to India. By the time I met them they were the parents of two young boys, happily married and in love. Jharna was supremely fortunate in that she had a wealthy, influential father who doted on her and a husband who arranged for her to be cared for after he died."

He sighed. "Hindu women have few rights, William, even worse than here, and their religion precludes them from enjoying life after being widowed. If not for a supportive family, Jharna would have been banished. Should have been, according to many, or encouraged to commit sati, suicide that is, when he died. Instead she retreated to a secluded house Kshitij prepared for her and lived as a recluse raising their sons. Our relationship evolved gradually.

My love for Kshitij and grief upon his death brought us together as friends comforting each other. Two years passed before either of us realized our friendship had progressed into love. What we felt for each other, the relationship we lived was wrong on many counts from both our cultural beliefs, but nothing has ever felt so right at the same time. I begged her to marry me and come to England, but she refused. Jharna was a Hindu and her place was there. I understood this, respected her bravery and viewpoint, but the immorality of our situation distressed me. Not for what other people thought, but for my personal principles. Maybe it was weakness on our part or perhaps superior strength of conviction. I do not know. It never bothered Jharna so much. She was one of those rare souls who accept the whimsies of life as freely as the trees accept the wind and rain."

"I wish I could have met her. She sounds remarkable."

"That she was."

"Tell me more."

George looked at Darcy's trusting face, eyes full of affection, and he smiled. And he did tell him more, then and in numerous conversations that would span the future time they shared.

While the friendship and familial bond between Darcy and George flourished rapidly, aided by these solitary intervals, Lizzy's attachment was delayed. She liked him instantly at the first words out of his mouth when entering Darcy House and his compassionate care for Darcy's shoulder. Her delight in his humor was instantaneous. However, true affinity and devotion was longer in coming due to the plain fact that they passed little time alone together while in London or at Pemberley during the summer. This began to change as the fall months progressed with fewer people to entertain and divert attention. Gradually their conversations deepened, the two upon rare occasions alone for a pointed engagement.

One such incident occurred one morning as Lizzy lumbered with mildly waddling gait down the peacefully quiet second-floor hallway toward the coolness of her parlor. Breakfast was over and Darcy was already gone on a jaunt about the estate while Georgiana was with her tutor. The persistent heat combined with an ever-increasing physical burden sapped her strength, necessitating afternoons at rest and any household chores requiring her concentration be done early in the day before weariness consumed her. Thus she was heading for her parlor where a stack of papers and ledgers waited on her small desk.

Her attention was captured as she passed the yawning expanse at the top of the grand staircase. George stood in the foyer focused on one of the three gigantic tapestries that lined the southern wall below the window embrasures. With a smile she diverted from her pathway, carefully navigating the marble stairs with hand tight on the banister, and silently joined him in contemplation.

"I cannot recall how many times I lost myself in staring at these, attempting to trace the interwoven lines and memorize all the names. Do you know we actually were tested on our family tree?" He turned to Lizzy with a grin and she shook her head. "Oh yes! You would think our tutors part of the family as vigorously as they enforced our ability to readily trace our ancestry. I was always gifted in rote memorization, but Alex was pathetically inept, poor soul. The first time, I think we were maybe eight or so, I told him to just toss in a ream of Alexanders and Jameses and Henrys and Roberts and he would fool the tutor." He laughed. "I was wrong, of course, and we both received lashes across our knuckles."

"The first time I visited Pemberley, with my uncle and aunt, we breezed through the foyer and I confess I was struck more by the ceiling and sculptures. It was the following day that William, Mr. Darcy as he was to me then, brought us here for a closer inspection at my request. I think he was a bit embarrassed, not wishing me to think him unduly proud of his home. He was trying so hard to impress me with his humility, you see, not realizing that I was already in love with him. He steered me to the opposite side, away from the tapestries, but I noticed them anyway."

The tapestries under discussion were enormous, masterpieces of weft-faced wool hung from four-inch-thick rods of polished oak. The first, woven in shades of forest green and gold, was ancient, tracing the Darcy family from Baron John D'Arcy in 1335 to the late 1500s. The second tapestry, maroon and silver, resumed the lineage, noting the elevation of Conyers Darcy to Earldom in 1682, a peerage that became extinct when Robert Darcy died childless in 1778. The Pemberley line of Darcys had long since diverged from the noble line when a second son, Frederick Darcy, had taken his inheritance and settled in Derbyshire to raise sheep in the mid-1400s. While the noble antecedents dwindled, the Darcys of modest wealth and prestige multiplied and financially prospered. The majority of subsequent lines were left unrecorded as the family proliferated and disseminated, but the uninterrupted chain from the current Master of Pemberley to that distant baron was explicit.

The final tapestry, navy blue and copper, was half filled with spidery lines and stitched names with dates. They stood gazing at the recent decades' entries with soft smiles elicited by the memories evoked.

"What were your thoughts?"

Lizzy laughed. "That I was woefully inadequate to ever imagine my name woven next to his. That the Bennets would be hard-pressed to trace their ancestry five or six generations, let alone nearly five hundred years! That Mr. Darcy must be thinking the same exact thing and wondering what insanity possessed him to propose to me in the first place. So many false and unimportant thoughts."

"And here your name is," he pointed to the embroidered *Elizabeth Bennet* now linked with gold filigree thread to *Fitzwilliam Darcy*, "and soon your child will be added. Families are all the same, Elizabeth. Filled with scoundrels, lovers, saints, sinners, noblemen, and paupers."

"Do you not experience a sense of overwhelming pride to belong to such an auspicious heritage?"

"Indeed I do, but then it does not take much for me to be overwhelmed with arrogance." He grinned rakishly, Lizzy shaking her head and chuckling. "Seriously, I recognize the eminence of belonging to an ancient legacy, but it is the living people who thrill me more profoundly." He encircled her slender shoulders, hugging to his side. "Without William, Georgie, and you, none of this," he swept a hand toward the woven genealogy, "would have any meaning. I love you, Elizabeth."

He kissed the top of her head. Lizzy blushed, ducking her face to hide the stinging tears but patted the hand resting on her shoulder. "I love you too, George."

Lizzy was incredibly moved by George's spontaneously offered declaration. Her affection for the older man had steadily grown in the months of his sojourn, but the frequent interruptions due to the individual travels undertaken along with the press of visitors had kept her from spending extended periods alone with him in serious conversation. Darcy managed to closet himself with his uncle dozens of times, equally for the express purpose of getting to know the older man and to avoid the unrelenting social fervor that had invaded their lives. Lizzy generally enjoyed his lively company in the presence of numerous others, rarely glimpsing the mature intelligence and earnest nature that her husband spoke of in their private moments.

This would change as the weeks of October and November unfolded. With the manor practically empty and Darcy often gone, George stringently applied himself to the dual role of manly protector and companionable entertainer. He took it upon his broad, if bony, Darcy shoulders to ensure the womenfolk were well cared for and entertained. Thus Lizzy discovered his lanky shadow looming every time she turned around. Thankfully she did not mind in the least, her affection growing until she felt as close to the good doctor as if he were truly flesh and blood.

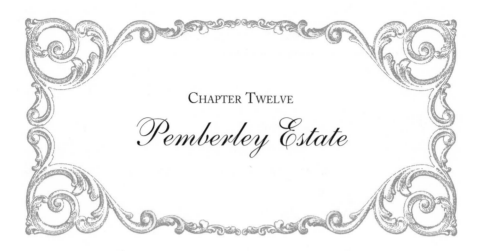

CHAPTER TWELVE

Pemberley Estate

D ARCY WAS QUITE OCCUPIED during these weeks, busily catching up on
the endless affairs that only he could properly and legally handle. He
relished the work, though, in truth, missing his wife during the long
hours either in his study or on his horse; nevertheless, the Master of Pemberley
thrilled in the occupation as a necessary part of life.

For Darcy, this time of the year was his absolute favorite. The weather
cooled, although such minor annoyances as excessive heat or driving rain never
bothered him all that much. Rather it was the constant activity as the estate
prepared for the stasis of winter that thrilled him. He could quite easily spend
the hours from sunrise to well after sunset engaged in some sort of outdoor
pursuit and frequently did.

Upon occasion George or Richard would join him when he left the
house on his horse. Neither knew much about the business affairs of
Pemberley, so when they did travel along it was for the exercise and fun.
Richard relished the action as much as his cousin, but he came and went,
often staying at Rivallain with his parents or visiting with Gerald Vernor
and the other gentlemen of the county whom he, like Darcy, had known
all his life. George tended to prefer quiet solitude in the library, so unless
his nephew was planning a casual ride to one of the tenant farms, he stayed
home with the ladies.

Mr. Keith was forced to accompany Darcy for certain jobs that required his legal or clerical input, but the steward was not as comfortable on a horse. It was a fact that may have precluded his acceptance as a steward to many large estates, but in the case of Pemberley it was a perfect arrangement as Darcy preferred to oversee the workings of the estate. Therefore, whenever Darcy was in residence, Mr. Keith could sigh in relief, settle into his office, and immerse himself in documents, ledgers, and mathematical figures.

But even Darcy knew his limitations. The management and mechanics of the fishery and wool mill were outside his full comprehension. He understood the basics but had long ago learned to trust the overseers and workers to handle the day-to-day. His knowledge of the harvesting facilities and crop maintenance was inclusive, and he made the ultimate decisions regarding what to grow and how to distribute, but it was the economic side of the equation that was his true purview. Therefore, he again trusted to the wise farmers, who in most cases were descended from generations of tenant farmers, who uncannily grasped the mysteries of agriculture as if the intelligence was written in their blood. Darcy's trips to these parts of his vast estate were generally brief, involving spoken conferences only with rare physical contribution. He kept his Master of Pemberley pose; the workers pleased to know their Master cared but relieved when he departed.

Of course, the stables were an entirely different matter! Mr. Thurber and all the grooms and stableboys were accustomed to seeing their Master walking among them, working alongside, and conversing with superior expertise. Obviously they treated him with the utmost respect, but it wasn't a shock to see him performing the same tasks as they, and he was readily approachable.

With his eventual elevation to the exalted rank of Master of Pemberley, he had easily assumed the pose of commander. In truth, the mantle of leadership, although arriving unexpectedly, had fallen upon his shoulders naturally. His inborn reserve, dominant competence, and estimable intellect had already given him an air of distinction long before his father's death. It greatly set him apart even when he performed mundane tasks like brushing Parsifal or breaking a horse.

Yet, for Darcy, it was necessary and intrinsic to undertake any physical, outdoor activity as often as possible. For this reason he was delighted when Mr. Keith interrupted his studied reading of a new contract from his shipping part-ners with the conveyed request to meet Mr. Burr at the dovecote. He mounted his horse with a barely concealed grin, spurred Parsifal into an immediate brisk run toward the gamekeeper's cottage two miles south.

The spread that consisted of Mr. Burr's modest home, the huts where his assistants lived, the falconry, numerous barns and pens for the animals, and the dog sheds spanned a wide-open area at the roots of the eastern forest. The entire complex was encased by a stone fence. Built into one wall near the iron-gated northern entrance to the compound and constructed out of the same gray and brown river rock was the dovecote.

The circular tower was over twenty feet high, the steepled roof deeply pitched with one narrow opening under the gable and the round hole at the point protected by an elaborate lighted cupola. This particular pigeon loft was very old, the origins unknown, but Darcy had always marveled at the beauty of the structure in comparison to most dovecotes he had seen. The roof was covered with interlocking tiles of slate, the colors different and forming a pattern extremely pleasing to the eye. The two-foot-thick bricks constructing the walls were also artistically selected to create a design of alternating colors with two wide supporting buttresses of aged oak. A ledge ran along the top, just under the roof's eaves, the pigeon roost also of hardened wood, although the intricate etching had long ago succumbed to claw markings and the scrubbing removal of bird droppings.

Mr. Burr sat on a low bench positioned against the stone wall, his legs stretched before him with two gigantic mastiffs lying on either side of his booted feet. He was smoking a pipe, his eyes half lidded as he watched his employer approach. He did not rise, instead silently observing as the smoke rings rose into the air. The dogs seemed equally bored although their ears twitched, Darcy not doubting for a second that the well-trained killers would launch into an attack at the merest word from their master. Fortunately he had nothing to fear, the massive animals finally rising with tails wagging to greet the familiar man once he dismounted.

"Vella, Raven," Darcy greeted, scratching behind their drooping ears. "Treats for you as always. Must keep those muscles strong." The raw chunks of meat, hastily confiscated from the kitchen and shoved into the saddlebag, were devoured in seconds, Darcy not even sure if the two-hundred-pound animals even tasted them. He ignored the saliva on his palms and the wet noses pressed against his body in hopes of finding additional food, continuing to pet the blocky heads as he turned to address the reclining gamekeeper.

"Mr. Burr. How fare you?"

"Well enough, Mr. Darcy. Still up before the sun and shooting straight."

Darcy nodded seriously, the standard greeting all he would ever get from the reticent man, so replied, "Can't ask for anything more. Problems?"

Darcy nodded toward the dovecote, noting nothing amiss, but well aware that Mr. Burr would not have called for him otherwise.

Darcy frequently visited the gamekeeper's complex, but for his own pleasure. Rarely was it to deal with problems or overtly question the master huntsman and breeder. Instead he came to interact with the dogs, picking ones to be stationed at the Manor; to hunt with the raptors, one of which he had trained as his own; or to enlist the company of a hunter when the mood struck him to hunt in the traditional shotgun manner. Occasionally he and Mr. Burr would hunt together, the gamekeeper an astounding marksman who had taught Darcy how to handle every firearm known to exist from the time he was old enough to pick up a shotgun. The two men were friendly but far from intimate.

Before Mr. Burr could answer Darcy's query, Mrs. Burr stalked through the gate, her gravelly voice lifted in anger.

"Damned scoundrel escaped! The tracks were lost in the river. Mole couldn't smell him after that." A string of expletives erupted as Mrs. Burr stalked directly toward the two men, Mr. Burr yet in casual repose; a lumbering mastiff easily fifty pounds heavier than the others walked at her side. She removed her tattered hat with an angry yank and threw it against the wall, cursing all the while. "Just you wait! I'll get my hands on the filthy rat and wring his scrawny neck! Mole will catch the bugger eventually and then we can fight over who gets to have him. Mr. Darcy," she finally acknowledged with an abrupt nod, not waiting for a reply as she turned to her husband. "You tell him?" She jerked her chin toward Darcy while tossing the leather sack draped over one shoulder to the ground with a thud, the Brown Bess musket more cautiously unslung and sat to lean against the wall.

Darcy stood unfazed, his years of acquaintance with the Burrs no longer causing surprise at anything they said or did. Mrs. Burr was six feet tall, as was her husband, almost as wide in the shoulders, and her husky frame was dressed as it always was in a loose men's shirt and trousers. Darcy had never seen her in a dress. Her iron gray hair was a wild mass of coiled curls cut short with no attempt ever made to style or control. Oddly, she was a very handsome woman in the face, her features angular and refined under the tanned skin with startling eyes of sea-foam green. Her hands were broad, fingers long and elegant—not the type of hands one would picture gripping a firearm with ready competence or slaughtering a pig with cool efficiency. Yet she could, and did, do all that and more. Mr. Burr was the head gamekeeper and prodigiously skilled, but everyone knew that his wife was every bit as formidable.

"I was about to," Mr. Burr replied. He finally stood up, stretching his limbs before continuing. "We have a poacher," he said matter-of-factly, his wife releasing another curse, "or most probably a duo or more. They have been plaguing us for a month or so now. Mostly small thefts. It took us awhile to figure out we were missing a number of deer and that the grouse and pheasant coveys were smaller than expected for this time of year considering the egg laying numbers and calculated growth-loss ratios. I got Lew and Sean tracking down numbers on the hare, turkey, and other game populations. We have had the dogs on it, but he, or they, are very clever. Last night the dovecote was robbed."

"They are getting too bold," Mrs. Burr interrupted. "To come this close to our house and the yard where the dogs roam is crazy. Next they'll be attacking the sheep. They took a dozen eggs at least and probably ten birds. We can't be sure as yet since the doves scattered and haven't all returned. Three were left dead on the ground, probably dropped when they ran from Hass and Jen who were prowling on guard that night."

Mr. Burr spat, releasing an evil chuckle. "Jen got one of them. Took a chunk out of his arse."

"But he still got away," Mrs. Burr grumbled.

Mr. Burr shrugged. "We'll get 'im. The dogs are as mad as you, so it's inevitable." He turned to Darcy. "Thought you should know and spread the word about. I had Ollie talk to Mr. Amos since Mr. Vernor's land is the next closest. He said they have noticed a few irregularities as well, but not enough to be one hundred percent sure it was a poacher. Now they'll keep an eye."

"I will talk to Mr. Murphy and Mr. Hughes," Darcy said, referring to his next nearest neighbors, "and let you know if they have encountered troubles. If we work together, I am sure we can catch these criminals. Have you set traps?"

"Yep, a few. I have some men setting up more today. Now that we are getting an idea of their tactics we can be more strategic. But I need more. That's another reason I sent for you, Mr. Darcy. Can I sign for ten of those new spring-traps that Ocktonlee makes? I can get them from the smithy in Matlock, but they are pricey."

Darcy was already nodding. "Of course. Whatever it takes, Mr. Burr. We cannot allow this to continue. I will have Mr. Keith speak with the constable so he can be prepared when the thieves are captured."

"If I let them live long enough to be hanged or shipped to Australia," Mrs. Burr rasped. "I make no promises."

Darcy smiled, not doubting the woman's declaration in the slightest. "As you see fit, Mrs. Burr."

She nodded once and then released a shrill whistle. Mole, who had wandered to the small creek some forty feet away, responded instantly, his massive body darting across the field with graceful power and stopping sharply at her side. "I'm going to search the west for a sign." She gathered her supplies, tucked the musket under her arm, slapped the hat back onto her head, and with another curt nod muttered, "Mr. Darcy," as she stalked away, Mole at her heels.

Mr. Burr had relit his pipe and was puffing contentedly. He was watching his wife walk away and for one fleeting, undisguised moment Darcy saw an expression of pride and love cross his grizzled features. Then his typical imperturbable mien returned, his untroubled gaze turning to Darcy.

"Mr. Holmes wanted to talk to you as well, Mr. Darcy. The fledglings have taken flight and he thought you may be interested."

"Indeed. Thank you, Mr. Burr. Keep me informed."

Mr. Burr shrugged in answer. Darcy smothered his smile, remounting Parsifal for the short ride to the falconry. He immediately decided to pass a pleasant afternoon with the hawks, not overly worried about the poachers as he knew the competent gamekeeper staff would deal with the problem as they had in the past. Considering the frightening determination of Mrs. Burr and the crushing strength of the mastiffs bred to protect Pemberley, he almost felt sorry for the thieves.

Almost.

The falconry was located farther south, on the extreme edge of the gamekeeper's complex. Mr. Holmes, the falconer, lived alone in a tiny cottage tucked under the trees outside of the walled-in area with the mews yards away and semi-attached by a covered passageway.

The Darcy family was one of a few who still practiced the art of falconry. An ancestor of Darcy's, Edward Darcy, had developed a passion for the sport in the early 1600s, when it was still a highly favorable royal pastime. It was he who built the falconry, captured and then bred the birds, and hired the men who served as specific caretakers. Edward Darcy was so enthusiastic about the endeavor that his exceedingly explicit journals with astoundingly precise drawings and diagrams were considered prized possessions among the Darcy family heirlooms.

The passion ebbed and waned over the centuries with not every Darcy learning how to hunt with a raptor or even paying much attention to the existence of falcons on Pemberley lands. Yet, the inhabited mews remained as an indelible aspect of the estate with a falconer always employed if for no other reason than to uphold a tradition.

Darcy's grandfather hunted with a falcon from time to time and did take his beloved grandson along on a few expeditions. Darcy held fond memories of the old man with a fierce peregrine or lanner on his arm. But his father was not interested in the hawks, and upon his grandfather's death when Darcy was twelve, he lost interest as well and did not embrace the sport. In truth, his energies were focused on the horses of Pemberley, his passion for hunting following the typical pattern of the day with the use of a firearm preferred.

It was not until his return from London the previous summer, still grieving and ill from his failure with Elizabeth Bennet, that Darcy began spending time with the hawks. It arose out of a request by Mr. Holmes to update some of the woefully ancient and decaying equipment and facilities. Darcy rode to the gamekeeper's yard, and after one afternoon talking with Mr. Holmes and observing the raptors in action, he was entranced.

In large part he knew it was a mental diversion from his ceaseless dwelling upon Elizabeth—and of course the concentration and commitment necessary to adequately train a young bird did effectively drive romantic thoughts away—but he also experienced a thrill nearly as strong as when he trained his horses. He quickly became addicted, spending hours every day with his chosen peregrine, Varda. Always a quick learner and extremely patient, Darcy and his hunting hawk rapidly built a successful relationship.

Parsifal took it well, the screeching bird no more annoying than a blasting shotgun. Running after a fast-flying falcon with his rider urging him to greater speeds sufficiently pleased the equine. Since his marriage, Darcy had not been able to spend as much time pursuing his new-found hobby as he wished, but the zeal and excitement remained present.

The majestic animals kept by Mr. Holmes were truly magnificent. Primarily peregrine and gyrfalcon with an array of other species added to the mix, all were bred for strength and speed. The falconer was a tiny man, barely five feet in height, with a beaked nose and fine-boned frame that rather resembled a bird. The largest of his falcons, when perched on a gauntleted forearm, looked scarily capable of snapping the limb in half or dropping him to his knees from the weight. But the diminutive, middle-aged man was surprisingly strong, and his rapport with the wild prey birds was remarkable.

One never could completely trust a raptor, of course. Incapable of being truly domesticated, feeling affection, or bonding with their master, they were not pets who desired to please. Rather, they were wild animals with independent wills and intense survival instincts. Life involved killing for the purpose of eating and very little else. The challenge was in learning to control the beast as much as possible and forging a working partnership. The thrill was in the hunt. It was a sport nearly as old as hound coursing and every bit as exhilarating.

For Darcy, who loved to hunt with his hounds, it was even more so as the birds are forever unpredictable. Working and hunting with them was never boring.

"Mr. Darcy, glad to see you," Mr. Holmes greeted, his voice as high-pitched as one would anticipate. "Burr told me you were coming out to see about the poaching problem. Terrible mess that is. I have been on the alert for days, barely sleeping, although I doubt anyone would be stupid enough to attack my hawks. Get a finger bit off, they would. Serve them right if they did. Maybe an eye gouged or earlobe torn. I know Pan and Shrill would not allow anyone to touch them. Varda either, Mr. Darcy, so you need not worry. But I have been alert. Set a few traps around the perimeter just to be sure. Burr said you would get 'im more so he did not begrudge me taking a few. Since the birds do not like the dogs about, I do not have that protection, so it was only fair. I am sure you understand. Of course, it might actually be entertaining to see one of those wretched scum try to take one of my birds! One swipe of Shrill's talons would damage more than Jen's bite."

He paused to laugh evilly, Darcy smoothly interjecting as he had many years ago learned was necessary to stem the verbal stream. "The fledglings have flown?"

"All but Zell. She may never be strong enough to train for hunting, poor sweet. But no matter. She can be a breeder. That makes four new hunters. Mr. Davington wants two, as we agreed, so I have sent word. Since Leo died, I thought to keep one as replacement. Did you have anyone interested in the other?"

They entered the mews—Mr. Holmes continuing to chatter about the newest hatchlings, eggs recently laid, the two latest young to be fledged, flight patterns, hunt statistics, and more in the same vein—with Darcy primarily nodding and commenting in short phrases.

The original mews were built of rubblestone with thick coats of plaster, the remnants of those two-hundred-year-old lofts now used for storage. It was these that needed the most repairing, Darcy endeavoring to restore without altering the unique style. The newer mews, built nearly seventy years ago, were far larger. Constructed of ashlar blocks with a combination of partitioned perches for each bird and open freelofts for limited exercise, these mews were lovely as well as functional. Darcy's grandfather had expanded the structure, keeping the sculpted appearance of the rectangular bricks but adding additional perches and nesting boxes to the already generous-sized mews. There was enough space to easily house three dozen full-grown raptors. Currently the census was twenty-two, most of the larger species of falcon but also a breeding pair of hobby and merlin falcons and a small collection of hawks. Mr. Holmes loved all types of raptor, although he naturally preferred the larger varieties.

Lizzy, on the three trips she had taken to the gamekeeper's facilities, found the whole concept fascinating and was intrigued by the blue-feathered merlin. At less than one foot in height, it was the perfect raptor for a woman to use. Mr. Holmes was instantly animated at the idea of teaching the new Mistress and thus crestfallen when she declined his offer. Unfortunately the fact that Lizzy did not ride made the possibility of hunting with a bird of prey next to impossible. However, she did enjoy observing the procedure, especially her husband with his Varda, a prime example of impeccable breeding.

Darcy greeted the peregrine now. Varda gazed at her master, black eyes steady and emotionless, waiting impassively for him to make the first move. Like many birds of prey, the females are generally larger than the males. Varda was no exception. She stood close to eighteen inches high, her body compact and strong. Mr. Holmes had chosen wisely between the three choices available when Darcy first asked to train a bird. Varda was intelligent, adapting to her expected behavior easily, and establishing a bond with Darcy as complete as one could hope for. Furthermore, her speed, size, and power enabled her to catch bigger prey, adding to the thrill of the sport.

Darcy smiled. "Well, my lady Varda. Since I am here we may as well have some fun. Hungry?" She lifted her black crowned head, yellow-rimmed eyes seeming to sparkle in answer. "As you wish, then," Darcy said with a chuckle, reaching for the thick leather gauntlet, jesses, hood, and bells kept by her cage.

No point in wasting the long ride out to the gamekeeper complex, Darcy thought with a grin. Varda released a screech, apparently agreeing.

⁓🦇⁓

A week later the small family gathered in the parlor after dinner. This was typical, of course, and it was also typical for Georgiana to entertain on the pianoforte. What was atypical was that the shy young woman had finally revealed to her admired older brother that she dabbled in minor musical compositions. True to Lizzy's prediction, Darcy was amazed but exceedingly proud. It had taken a bit of prompting, but Georgiana finally agreed to play her music in a miniature concert.

Thus they now reposed in the lavishly decorated yet somehow homey room and listened to the songs flawlessly played by the talented eighteen-year-old. Her blushing had finally ceased as she concentrated on the task, absorbed and filled with joy. Darcy stood near Lizzy, George was comfortably sprawled in a chair, and Richard acted as official page turner. All of them were entranced by the music. Honesty would require them to admit that the simple sonatas were far from brilliant, but the melodies were pleasant and well constructed. Clearly Georgiana was a novice, but the evidence of a blossoming talent was firmly apparent.

The applause was enthusiastic and genuine, Georgiana's flush reappearing with the effusive praise from her family. Such was the zealous attention that it was several minutes before Darcy noticed a patient Mr. Taylor standing by the door.

"Sir, Mr. Keith is in his office requesting an audience."

"Of course. Excuse me, please. Georgiana, keep playing your beautiful songs."

Darcy found his steward bent over his desk reading a folded parchment. Ollie, one of Mr. Burr's hands, stood by the window, nervously shifting from foot to foot and kneading his hat.

"Mr. Keith. Do we have a problem?"

"The opposite, sir. Ollie here has delivered a note from Mr. Burr. He received a summons earlier today from Mr. Lange, the surgeon in Rowsley. Apparently a man was dropped at his door in the late stages of acute blood poisoning from an abscessed wound on his right buttock. Upon cleaning the wound it became clear it was a bite inflicted by an animal. Lange had heard of the incident with the poacher—thank goodness for gossip swapped in pubs—and sent word to Mr. Burr, who rode to Rowsley to question the man. Apparently it was difficult as the man is near death, raving, and quite jumbled in his words. But he feels certain he learned enough to ascertain that the poachers are hiding in the abandoned limestone quarries at Cregg's Ravine."

"That is a dangerous place to dwell."

"Probably why they chose that as their lair. No one goes there anymore. Those collapsed caves and rocky terrain are treacherous."

"How many poachers are there?"

"He could not be certain. The man named at least three that Mr. Burr could be sure of, but beyond that it was indistinct. He isn't even sure where they are exactly as those mines extend for a good half mile, but the man made a couple of vague references that led him to deduce they are near Struve's Ridge, where the river once flowed before being dammed and diverted underground."

"Odd place. There isn't much cover there and no water."

"The stream is now aboveground," Ollie said. "The old dam broke years ago, and an avalanche off the ridge collapsed the ground so's that the stream now runs partially through the ravine, at least 'til Sawtooth Hill. Then it disappears again."

Darcy nodded. "Thank you, Ollie. I haven't been to that part of Derbyshire for well over a decade. If memory serves, there are a few caves, or at least semi-sheltered cliffs that could be fashioned into a dwelling of some kind?"

"Yep. That is what Mr. Burr suspects," Ollie continued with a nod.

"He is gathering his best men, and Mrs. Burr, and plans to attack under cover of darkness," Mr. Keith said, tapping the paper on his desk. "It is a good night with the moon at half brightness. Ollie here, as well as Lew, will be in front since they know that area best."

"We grew up just a mile away," Ollie explained, "and it was a sort of dare to hike through the quarries. Lew almost died when he was thirteen and he slid on some loose rocks. Mama forbid us to ever go again," he paused, his shrug and grin clearly stating how that order was disregarded. "That's how we know the stream is runnin' and that a few straggling trees and shrubs have grown up near there. It really is a good hidin' place, if you don't count the frequent rock slides."

"And flash floods," Darcy said, shivering slightly in memory of a horrific occurrence in his youth when some thirty miners were killed after a deluging rain high on the Peaks rushed through Cregg's Ravine. Not long after that the quarries were closed.

"That too. But the location is central. They can poach from several estates bordering, keeping the losses scattered. We figure this has been going on for some eight months now, but the takings were wide enough that no one gamekeeper figured it out. They made a huge mistake attacking the dovecote. That tipped us off for sure."

"That and bringing this man within Jen's teeth," Mr. Keith offered with a chuckle.

"So, what does Mr. Burr plan?"

Ollie shrugged. "A simple frontal attack. Should be easy. These are low thieves who probably have no idea how to fight. The man dying at Doc's don't look too healthy or kept up. We'll wait 'til after midnight, just to be sure they're sleeping."

Darcy considered for a moment, reading through the brief statement penned by Mr. Burr. "Very well then. Tell him to proceed as he sees fit. I will be joining in, but he is in command."

Ollie nodded. He wasn't at all surprised at Mr. Darcy joining the expedition. In fact, he would have been shocked if he hadn't. He put his hat back on and headed toward the door. "We are meetin' at the east gate in one hour. It is quickest to head through the narrow strip of forest there and then turn north. Mr. Darcy, Mr. Keith."

Three hours later the group of seven men and Mrs. Burr dismounted. The five mastiffs stood calmly at attention and the two bloodhounds pulled impatiently on their leashes. They were a quarter mile north of the area known as Sturve's Ridge. Or rather the section of rubble, small caverns, and graveled flooring below Sturve's Ridge, a sharp precipice thirty feet high. The ridge and narrow ravine below the crag was a treacherous place very difficult to navigate safely without a detailed map and light. Unfortunately they did not possess the former, aside from the imperfect memory of Ollie and Lew, and had to circumspectly utilize the latter. It was deemed best to enter from the north rather than attempt to scale the escarpment too close to where the poachers were probably hiding.

Each person possessed a tiny covered oil lamp, the screen to be opened only if absolutely necessary. It was doubtful that the thieves would post a lookout, but then again, they might be on a higher stage of alert after depositing their friend on the surgeon's doorstep.

Darcy kept to the rear of the group, a shotgun tightly clutched in the crook of his right arm and two loaded pistols tucked into his belt. He had wisely waited until he was in the stables before loading the firearms, Lizzy already fretting enough at his involvement in the venture. She said little, but the anxiety was discernible on her lovely face. He hated worrying her, but Darcy had never been the type of Master to sit back and let his employees do all the work. Besides, this sort of adventure was simply too much fun to miss, not that he would have said that to his wife!

Colonel Fitzwilliam, naturally, had come along. His expertise was valuable, although like Darcy he hung back and allowed the gamekeeper to command. Or rather the gamekeeper and his wife, since Mrs. Burr was stationed to her husband's immediate left, shotgun at the ready and Mole protectively flanking.

Lew withdrew the bloody, crumbled garments worn by the unfortunate poacher lying in Rowsley, if he was still alive, and held them under the noses of the two hounds. They each sniffed and slobbered over the clothes, taking less than one minute to firmly and irrevocably plant the scent within their nostrils before beginning the search. Noses pressed to the rocks and dirt, their leashes given plenty of slack to scout about, the dogs led as the hunters trailed behind.

It took about fifteen minutes. The dogs searched for the one scent among all the others detected, ranging over a fifty-yard span before finally finding the poacher's scent on a narrow trail winding through a dead copse of trees at the base of a shorter cliff a bit north of the taller pike. The silent black and tan animals gave no vocal indication of their victory, merely launching purposefully forward. Once on the hunt, nothing would divert them and their handlers were forced to trot at a rapid pace in order to keep up with the relentless pursuit.

The bloodhounds did not stumble, nor did the mastiffs. Their eyesight was keen and feet surely placed. The humans struggled more, no one escaping the occasional stumble, but gradually they advanced.

The wide valley closed in as the walls grew steeper and higher. Attempts were made to be as quiet as mice, but the crumbled chunks of limestone littering the ground prevented this. Thus, everyone was wary, each sense straining and vigilant. Eyes swept the environs constantly with peripheral vision locked onto the mastiffs, who would definitely detect trouble long before the humans.

The smell of water and sound of slow trickling over rock was noted before they reached the tiny creek and moderate-sized pond. A rapid assessment determined that the pond was not natural, a crude dam stopping the natural flow down the ravine's floor. It was their second indication—after the hounds' detection of the poachers' scent—that they were on the right track. The next question was how to determine precisely where they were hiding.

"Well. Look at that! They lit the welcoming light for us. How considerate." Richard's dry whisper reached Darcy, both men chuckling faintly at the sight of the flickering fire that answered the question.

The rock ring was located approximately four feet away from a gaping opening in the solid wall, the small fire casting uneven illumination over the clearing before the cave. But it was enough to adequately visualize the raggedly dressed man sitting in a slump before it. The sentry, presumably, although he appeared to be dozing and his rifle was lying negligently across his lap. The light was not bright enough to conclude there were no other caverns in the area, so they advanced with caution. Still, with minimal intelligence, the plan was fairly straightforward: a frontal attack.

At a hushed whistle identical to the call of an owl, Vella launched forward, her sleek body streaking across the space in a blur of motion. She leapt effortlessly over the fire, landing directly onto the chest of the sentry before he could inhale to scream a warning. Her massive weight knocked the man flat, air escaping his throat in a gush and rendering him incapable of speech. Not that he was likely to attempt it with a full set of razor sharp teeth less than an inch from his face. Vella released one short snarl, pitched low and profoundly menacing, her hot breath and saliva brushing over one cheek as she purposefully drew closer still until her wicked incisors rested against the man's jugular.

The Pemberley crew wasted no time. They moved forward, spreading in a wide arc with the dogs in front, sweeping the area visually for signs of movement or additional caves. A rapid scan confirmed two holes cut into the rock face of the cliff. A smaller opening some fifteen feet away showed no obvious tracks or signs of use, not that they would assume too much, while the one by the fire was clearly occupied. The bloodhounds were fighting the restraining leash in the mad desire to pursue their scented quarry into the large opening, and the numerous footprints and scattered debris surrounding the rough ground was further proof.

A faint light could be seen from within, but no motion or sounds were perceived. Darcy's heart beat a steady rhythm in his chest, his emotions controlled but the heat of excitement coursing through his veins. Richard's harsh respirations were an audible sign of his enthusiasm.

Vella maintained her position at the man's neck while Mrs. Burr knelt by the side of the terrified sentry, her attractive face set into a mask of fierce resolve. "How many?" she whispered, needing to repeat the question twice before the paralyzed man was able to squeak out the word "four" followed by a weak moan.

"Armed?" she asked.

"Yes... two... pistols."

She nodded. "Don't move or speak and Vella will let you live. Understand?" His answer was another moan.

Mrs. Burr rose, signals given to convey the message. She stationed herself on one side of the cave opening, Sean on the other. Lew, Ollie, Abel, Mr. Burr, Darcy, and Richard waited several feet away in a line with firearms aimed and the four mastiffs poised. Only then were the frantic hounds released.

They dashed into the cave, finally emitting deep barks as they searched for the owners of the scent embedded in their nasal passageways. Chaos ensued. Shouts and shrieks erupted, crashes and slamming echoed. The pale light was extinguished with the sharp shattering sound of glass. The startled sleepers were completely disoriented from the abrupt awakening into pitch black darkness. Curses rent the air, followed by the unmistakable smell of spilled lamp oil and the sudden snap of flames freely fueled.

Screams pierced the air. The fire lit the walls, showing the way out to the panicked poachers who darted toward safety, only to be tripped up by the dogs who had also decided that the cave was not the best place to be at the moment. They shot out of the exit, adroitly dodging the foremost poacher, who sidestepped in surprise and stumbled into a second frenzied poacher, both of them falling down in a heap at the feet of Mrs. Burr and Sean.

The remaining two avoided the tangle of limbs blocking the exit, running to what they believed to be safety but quickly deducing was anything but at the sight of six shotguns pointed their direction and four growling, slavering dogs waiting to pounce. They skidded to a stop, hands rising in the universal gesture of surrender.

The first two, still unaware of the realities, struggled to their feet. Only one step was taken before they too noted the threat. One man mirrored the actions of the previous captives, his arms lifting as he instantly halted his forward momentum. His partner was the only one who showed the slightest sign of bravery, or stupidity depending on the point of view, by grabbing the grip of the pistol tucked into his belt. His attempt at heroics was short-lived, however, as Mrs. Burr expeditiously reversed her shotgun and smashed the stock forcefully against the man's temple. He crumpled.

"Well, that was rather anticlimactic," Richard said to Darcy a half hour later as they mounted their horses for the ride back to Pemberley.

"Disappointed?"

Richard shrugged. "Somewhat. I haven't shot anyone in ages. I was looking forward to it."

Darcy laughed. "Please do not tell Elizabeth you were hoping for that sort of action, or she may forbid you assisting me in the future."

"Only if you promise that the next time will be a bit more exciting. I didn't even work up a sweat."

"I shall do my best, cousin."

CHAPTER THIRTEEN

With This Ring I Thee Wed

HARDLY BEFORE EITHER LIZZY or Darcy knew it, October was ushered in and the planned second wedding loomed.

Truthfully they had no serious disagreements regarding the reaffirming of their vows in the Pemberley Chapel. In fact, both would have happily planned and concluded what was essentially desired to be a simple, intimate affair within days of returning home from their seaside holiday. Lizzy theatrically teased by performing the wedding march with exaggerated waddling and thrusting her stomach out as far as possible. However, she honestly had no moral conflict with exchanging vows in a holy sanctuary with her husband, gravid state or no.

Only two elements gave them pause and delayed the exchange.

One: Georgiana, upon hearing the news, burst forth with schemes and expectations regarding everything from the gown to the flowers to the guest list. Initially both the bride and groom were flummoxed as they saw the cozy, understated affair they envisioned turning into an event. They managed to rein in the more extravagant ideas Georgiana invented, the white doves being a bit too much even for the romantic Darcy, but her enthusiasm was contagious, especially to the fore-noted hopelessly maudlin groom. Even the generally pragmatic Lizzy had to admit that a new gown was desirable.

Second: Lizzy and Darcy realized that whether modest or ostentatious, having as many family members as feasible around to witness the celebration was a pleasing prospect.

For these reasons Lizzy did lean toward waiting until after the baby was born, thinking that then her parents and Kitty would be visiting as well as the Bingleys settled nearby. Darcy pointed out that they could not count on Dr. Darcy still being in England. The truth is, he intoned with all the logic at his disposal, there would necessarily be several members of the family busy elsewhere no matter when they scheduled it, and he stubbornly persisted in his assertion that the ritual take place as soon as possible. The ultimate point of the ceremony was to please his burning need to wed in the Darcy family church.

This latter fact so moved Lizzy that she could not refuse his heart's desire had she wished it. She was well aware of the fact that the vast majority of women would be fortunate to find a man who longed to wed them once, let alone twice! The relationship they now shared meant she wholly comprehended how important being married in the Pemberley Chapel was to him. Therefore, October twelve had been set as the date.

George was in residence and Richard was an added bonus highly pleasing to them both. The elder Fitzwilliams were at Rivallain, as were Jonathan and Priscilla. A hastily scribbled note delivered on the morning of the seventh from Hasberry announced that the Bingleys had arrived the day before. Lizzy was ecstatic. She desired for them to be present but had not expected them as their last communiqué had alluded to a late October relocation. Within minutes of reading the note Lizzy rose, stating the intent to drive to Hasberry immediately. Darcy leapt to intercept her midway to the door.

"You are absolutely not driving in your condition!"

"William! That is unfair! I am perfectly capable of handling the curricle. I drove it just three days ago to Lambton!"

"Lambton is less than five miles away and a well traveled road. Hasberry is nearly fifteen and partially desolate. It is not a matter of you being unable to handle the carriage, love, as I know you proficient."

"Then why..." Her voice caught in a sob, Darcy gathering her into a firm embrace.

"Please placate my overprotectiveness just this once. I would worry so. Allow me a compromise: I shall send one of the grooms with a letter the moment you pen one and insist he tarry pending a reply."

In this way they received confirmation of attendance from the Bingleys before the day was over. That same afternoon Madame du Loire delivered Lizzy's gown for the final fitting, and word reached Darcy that the jeweler had finished the ring. All was set in motion for the renewal of their vows.

❦

October twelfth dawned crisp and cool, but cloudless and brightly sunny. Darcy woke with tingles of excitement racing through his body nearly as intense as on the morning of their official wedding day. Naturally there were a vast number of differences. On November twenty-eighth of 1816 he had barely slept a wink, dreams plagued with alternating enchanting visions of his glorious fiancée gliding toward him at the altar with dreadful images of the same glorious fiancée fading away in some horrible manner. His nervousness all throughout the morning had been extreme; he was at times virtually ill from the tension.

However, the greatest difference was that on this wedding day he woke with the luscious softness of his wife's body curled in his arms, knowing with blissful conviction that he would not be waiting until late in the evening to make love with her. With this delicious thought premier, he lightly kissed Lizzy's shoulder and commenced gossamer caresses over downy flesh.

"I believe we have erred, Mr. Darcy," she whispered sleepily.

"In what respect?" Kisses deepening along her neck.

"It is bad luck to espy the bride prior to the wedding, so I am told."

"I shall keep my eyes closed."

Lizzy giggled, turning abruptly and forcefully flipping him onto his back. With a grace truly astonishing for a woman eight months pregnant, she was astride his thighs and had his arms pinned to the sides before he took a breath. Despite his surprise both eyes were tightly shut, laughter escaping as her lips descended onto his.

She bestowed nibbling kisses and teasing suckles along his neck for several rapturous minutes before murmuring, "It is getting quite difficult to bend over, my lover. Your son insists on occupying all available space including a portion of my lung cavity, I believe. Typical Darcy, determined and insatiable."

"I have no idea to what you refer, Mrs. Darcy."

Lizzy lifted slightly, both to inhale deeply and to gaze upon her handsome spouse's face. She smiled at his pretend haughtiness and sealed eyes, thick lashes lying beautifully on stubbly cheeks. With elbows resting on his solid upper chest, she tenderly stroked her fingertips over his unshaven jaws.

"Open your eyes, Fitzwilliam," she whispered.

He obeyed, love radiating forth as hands initiated their adoring journey over her velvet knees and thighs. Passion rose naturally, neither consciously encouraging the rampant excitement nor able to halt the surging tide had they wanted to.

"I love you." The hush was broken simultaneously by low voices expressing an emotion tangible and critical to survival. Individual hearts no longer independent of the other; beats in synchrony and the impetus for each subsequent stroke. Skin as familiar to probing fingertips as the flesh covering their own body, yet never unscathed by the merest brushing glance.

Lizzy leaned to capture parted and waiting lips, the kiss serious with intent. Oh, the sweetness! How blissful a kiss with the one you love. Lips tingling, blood rushing, heat escalating, moisture shared, air of life mingling, and senses reeling from the intimacy.

Lizzy's lengthy tresses fell as a veil over Darcy's arm where he caressed one silky arm and neck. "God, how I love you," she exclaimed, trailing additional declarations between hard kisses all about his flushed face.

Lost in the sensations, Darcy's eyes slid closed in ecstasy. Their bodies surging together, buried deep physically and spiritually. Hoarse moans and guttural groans were unleashed as the excitement coalesced and burst forth through every nerve and cell, spines stiffening simultaneously with hands clenching hands. Eternal joy expressed in the most elemental manner.

"I love you, William!"

"I love you, Elizabeth!"

Lizzy lifted slightly, inhaling deeply and gazing upon her husband. Never was he more attractive than after they made love. His fair skin flushed, noble brow moist, lush lips ruddy, firm chest heaving, and pulse pounding in his throat. Yet it was not the readily visible signs of his pleasure that moved her the most. Rather it was the glow of utter elation and peace that suffused his countenance, eyes shining with total satiation, and mouth smiling with transcendent happiness and devotion. She did not require a mirror to know that her mien reflected the same as she could feel the gushing emotions through and on her skin.

Eventually he untangled his fingers from hers, tenderly grasping arms, and pulled her onto the bed beside him, instantly enveloping and burying his face between her breasts. "I would die without you, Elizabeth," he mumbled. "I fear my heart would cease to beat. Words do not exist in the English language to convey how deeply I love you. You are my life and breath, my very soul. Thank you for today."

Lizzy smiled, stroking through his thick hair. She had no need to reply, his articulations precisely stating her heart. The heart that belonged wholly to him and survived in him. All too soon they would need to rise and part for the day's scheduled event. For now they reveled in their sweet communion, allowing senses to be restored to normalcy at a gradual rate. Softly they caressed, speaking of love and marriage and children and Pemberley until the clock insisted they leave their bed and begin preparations for their second wedding.

Approximately a mile west from Pemberley Manor, along the avenue that connected to the main road leading to Lambton, nestled a small cluster of buildings amid a shallow valley in the midst of which stood Pemberley Chapel. The accompanying structures primarily consisted of resident dwellings for Pemberley workers in addition to a handful of simple business establishments. The tiny hamlet did not have a proper name, traditionally referred to as Pemberley Village or just the Village. It existed for the sole purpose of providing the most basic necessities for the tenants of Pemberley so as to avoid traveling the additional miles to Lambton during a busy day, and as a central meeting place for socializing. A modest assembly hall was located across from the church, and the orphanage was situated on the northern edge of the settlement.

For most Sundays during the warm months the Darcys walked to the chapel for services. Today, however, they would not only travel by carriage but would travel separately. Once parted for their dressing rooms, they adhered to the time-honored custom of remaining secreted apart until reconnecting inside the sanctuary.

The Bingleys had arrived the afternoon before. Charles was clearly harried and displeased to vacate Hasberry so soon after moving in, but the general air of frivolity that inevitably surrounded Col. Fitzwilliam and Dr. Darcy bolstered his spirit. They, naturally, were having tremendous fun with poor Darcy, regurgitating every pre-matrimony jest known to man up to and including giving intimate relationship advice about the wedding night; the latter especially ridiculous as neither were married. Before an hour passed Bingley's native gaiety was revived and he readily joined into the amusement. The evening's "bachelor party" was lively, Darcy unobtrusively slipping away sober and long before the other three.

Darcy owned several outfits of a highly formal cut and weave, allowing Samuel to pick one at random. The end result was nearly identical to what he wore for his official wedding day, or at least he thought so. The truth was he had taken no particular note as to his attire on that day either, trusting Samuel to provide the best. Darcy may have owned an obscene amount of clothing, but he honestly paid little attention to what he wore on a daily basis. Samuel chose a jacket and matching breeches of deepest blue wool, almost black, with a waistcoat of the same color, but accented with an edging of burnished auburn.

Darcy fingered the vest with a faint frown. "I do not recall this waistcoat," he mumbled, glancing at Samuel's inscrutable visage. "Have I always possessed it?"

"As you say, sir," Samuel replied flatly, avoiding his Master's eyes.

Darcy smiled inwardly, suddenly suspecting the color of his wife's gown, but making no further comment. The proffered white silk cravat also sported a faint glistening of interwoven auburn threads.

Richard wore his best dress uniform, Bingley in a fine suit of beige wool, and Dr. Darcy for once in full English gentleman's attire. His lanky frame was encased in a tailored suit of bluish-grey with long trousers to match, the reserved effect counteracted somewhat by the florid Kashmir scarf of innumerable colors utilized as a neckcloth.

"Dashing, Uncle," Darcy proclaimed sardonically upon entering the parlor where the men gathered. George grinned, lifting his teacup in salute.

"How is the groom this morning?" Richard asked. "Feeling well? No last-minute jitters? I am sure we could find a way for you to bow out gracefully."

"Hysterical. Have you been rehearsing these witticisms all week?"

"Only for a day or two."

"I daresay, Darcy, I am yet astounded that you of all people are purposely placing yourself on ceremony a second time," Bingley declared with a shake of his head. "I could never force myself to go through with it again."

Darcy smiled and clapped his friend on the shoulder. "It is not quite the same, Bingley. It would require a far stronger man than me putting a pistol to my head to induce me to stand before all of Meryton society a second time. This is vastly different. Although enduring these two jokers and their clever barbs for the past week has been torturous."

"It is becoming ugly in here, Colonel. We better get him to the church where the aura of God will halt his tongue. Besides, I am starving so we need to hurry along. Knowing Mrs. Langton, she has a special breakfast planned for after the festivities."

Lizzy, in contrast, was inundated with female approbation. Jane, Georgiana, Lady Matlock, and even Marguerite were effusive with praise for the dress, hair, jewels, and the entire concept. Lizzy's dressing room was a veritable hotbed of feminine giggles, perfume, and romanticism with the ladies exchanging sentimental musings of husbands and amour. Emotions were high and the air thick with excitement. Mrs. Reynolds played the part of commander, assuring the men were well away before Mrs. Darcy departed for the church.

Reverend Bertram had nearly collapsed from overwhelming delight when Darcy approached him regarding the renewal ceremony. Like Mr. Darcy, the good Reverend had also suffered an acute case of disappointment at having the marriage of his patron, a man he had known since birth, wed so far away. Naturally he would never have voiced this dismay to Mr. Darcy, but the intense happiness expressed left no doubt how he felt about the matter. Now he stood at the altar of his beloved chapel, wearing his best formal vestments, beaming at Mr. Darcy and the entire assembly. Outwardly he was sedate and composed, but the rosiness to his cheeks and broad grin revealed his enthusiasm.

The small chapel was decorated with a dozen bouquets of fall flowers and two large candelabras. No other adornments were necessary, the interior lovely as is. Aside from the family no other guests had been invited. After much debate, both Darcys wishing for several of their friends to be present, it was unanimously decided that if they invited anyone then all of Derbyshire would feel slighted. Neither wanted their private affair to become a countywide social extravaganza. Those of their closest friends understood. As a compromise, they planned a dinner party for that evening as a way to share the occasion with their intimates without causing an uproar.

The moment Darcy assumed his proper station to the left of Reverend Bertram, facing the gathering of his dearest relatives smiling at him from the richly polished oak benches, peace infused his soul. All niggling thoughts of the foolishness or inanity of his desire for this ceremony vanished. He gazed upon the beloved persons before him, and as if by magic he saw his mother and father sitting in their customary spaces in the front pew. There too was the vision of his grandfather, unruly grey hair and bushy eyebrows framing gentle eyes of midnight blue. He could feel the presence of all the long generations of Darcys etched into the very beams and floorboards of the sanctuary. Somehow he knew that just as surely as God Himself watched this holy ritual, so did the innumerable ancestors who had been baptized, married, and eulogized in this room. Peace, contentment, and supreme happiness were the ruling sentiments. None of the nervousness from before plagued him. Everything was different this time.

Until Elizabeth appeared on the threshold. Instantly Darcy was struck with the identical paralyzing awe and breathless wonder from November past. His heart constricted and the room faded as his eyes peered through a narrow tunnel focused exclusively on his stunning wife. Was she more beautiful than on their wedding day? Nothing would supplant the vision of Elizabeth Bennet in her wispy white wedding gown with golden ribbons braided through her hair.

No, it was the immediate surge of joy and rush of thanksgiving that blazed through his soul that rendered him mute and transfixed. She was everything to him. Suddenly the handful of minutes it took for her to glide gracefully down the aisle was an eternity. The need to touch her, smell her perfume, hear her voice, and gaze deeply into her astounding eyes was overpowering, causing his knees to nearly buckle and lungs to burst. Each step she took was an individually painted portrait hung in his mind's gallery alongside the array of Elizabeth portraits already residing.

Her gown was a deep auburn, richly woven of glossy damask with a fine pattern of lacy leaves. The color accented her chocolate eyes and lustrous brunette locks—hence why Darcy so adored her in brownish hues—and the understated embellishments of lace and ribbons suited their mutual taste for minimalism. Another Marguerite creation with highlighting gems displayed her glorious hair to best advantage. There was no hiding the swell of their child, and the maidenly blush was gone from her cheeks, Lizzy now a woman of elegance and maturity. This refinement manifest in all aspects of her bearing and mien. Darcy's heart grew further with pride and vaulting love.

Lizzy reached her incredible husband, hands clasped firmly and eagerly as she mounted the dais steps. She only had eyes for him, so regal and handsome with warmth radiating and abiding affection transparent. They stared at each other frankly, no hesitation or tremulousness. The seconds stretched, both lost in adoring gazes and startling slightly when Reverend Bertram spoke.

"Dearly beloved, we are gathered together here in the sight of God, and in the face of this congregation, to join together, once again, this Man and this

Woman in Holy Matrimony; which is an honorable estate, instituted of God in the time of man's innocence, signifying unto us the mystical union that is betwixt Christ and His Church; which holy estate Christ adorned and beautified with His presence and first miracle that He wrought in Cana of Galilee, and is commended of Saint Paul to be honorable among all men. Therefore, it is not by any to be embarked on unadvisedly, lightly, or wantonly to satisfy men's carnal lusts and appetites, like brute beasts that have no understanding; but reverently, discreetly, advisedly, soberly, and in the fear of God; duly considering the causes for which Matrimony was ordained.

"First, marriage was ordained for the procreation of children, to be brought up in the fear and nurture of the Lord, and to the praise of his holy Name. Secondly, marriage was ordained for a remedy against sin and to avoid fornication; that such persons as have not the gift of abstinence might marry and keep themselves undefiled members of Christ's body. Thirdly, marriage was ordained for the mutual society, help, and comfort that the one ought to have of the other, both in prosperity and adversity. Into which holy estate these two persons present come now to be rededicated.

"Fitzwilliam and Elizabeth have chosen this day to stand a second time before God in His Holy Sanctuary to consecrate their union, to express their undying faithfulness and devotion one to the other, and to receive the blessing. Their commitment to each other and to the institution of marriage as ordained in the Divine Scriptures is a testimony. I shall not ask if any know just cause for these two to not be wed, as that time has past. Assuredly the communal dedication they have shown coupled with the desire to suffer through another long-winded ritual proves their loyalty and seriousness."

The Reverend smiled, breaking from his solemn pose, as a soft ripple of chuckling ran through the assembly. Lizzy and Darcy laughed lowly, tearing their gazes from the other's face to glance with twinkling eyes toward the Reverend.

Clearing his throat and raising his voice, Rev. Bertram resumed, "Fitzwilliam, wilt thou have this woman to thy wedded wife, to live together after God's ordinance in the Holy estate of Matrimony? Wilt thou love her, comfort her, honor her, and keep her in sickness and in health; and, forsaking all others, keep thee only unto her, so long as you both shall live?"

Darcy's smile was faint, merely a tiny lift to the corners of his mouth, face awash with serene intensity as he responded in a firm voice, "I will."

Lizzy inhaled deeply, eyes blinking rapidly to abolish the tears threatening to overflow. Darcy squeezed her hands, and so mesmerized was she by the tender emotion saturating his face that she nearly missed the Reverend's words.

"Elizabeth, wilt thou have this man to thy wedded husband, to live together after God's ordinance in the Holy estate of Matrimony? Wilt thou obey him, and serve him, love him, honor him, and keep him in sickness and in health; and, forsaking all others, keep thee only unto him, so long as you both shall live?"

She wanted to shout her promise loudly with a ringing exultation, so enormous was her love and desire. Therefore, it was with some surprise that her words caught in a thick throat and she swallowed before able to utter in a husky tone, "I will."

Darcy smiled broadly, releasing a soft whistle while arching a brow. Lizzy flushed and giggled, pressing his hands firmly.

"At this time Fitzwilliam and Elizabeth shall declare their vows to each other. Per their request they have chosen to restate their promises with a unique melding of the traditional vows as well as personal sentiments."

Darcy stepped closer to Elizabeth, his hands completely encasing her smaller ones and eyes locked onto her face. Emotions overwhelmed him, but his voice was loud and clear. "I, Fitzwilliam, take thee Elizabeth to my wedded wife, to have and to hold, for better for worse, for richer for poorer, in sickness and in health, to love and to cherish, 'til death us do part, according to God's holy ordinance; and thereto I plight thee my troth. Elizabeth, you are my heart and soul. I promise to love you for all of eternity, trusting that even death shall not part us but for a moment. You have renewed my spirit, brought me purpose, and healed my heart. My gratitude is immeasurable and I vow to spend my life proving my thankfulness."

He paused, squeezing her hands before removing one to reach into his pocket. Clasping her left hand and gazing intently into her eyes, he said, "With this ring I thee wed, with my body I thee worship, and with all my worldly goods I thee endow. In the Name of the Father, and of the Son, and of the Holy Ghost. Amen."

The narrow band he slipped onto her third finger, nestling perfectly next to the one placed there nearly a year ago, was almost identical. His mother's engagement ring, given with extreme formality to Elizabeth on the afternoon after their engagement rendezvous in the meadow, was constructed of gold and adorned with a one-carat star sapphire of vivid blue, centered between two half-carat diamonds. Darcy's father had personally designed the ring for his mother. The tale told to his children was that he had searched all over England for the most exquisite sapphire he could find. Like many family stories, James Darcy embellished the tale for the amusement of his children, yet Darcy did not doubt his father's devotion to seek the very best for the woman he had loved and waited on for four years. Whatever the truth, the ring was magnificent and Lizzy remained awestruck that something so elegant belonged to her. The wedding band Darcy had designed for Lizzy was delicate; a slim band of gold in a braided pattern with three petite diamonds spaced with two small blue sapphires. For the sake of continuity he had ordered today's band fashioned similarly except with three sapphires and two diamonds. Placing it on her finger was not quite as profoundly moving as the first time, or at least he did not feel as lightheaded and dazed with emotion, but his heart skipped a beat and his fingers trembled.

Lizzy was momentarily speechless, tears welling and throat tightening. Darcy grasped her hands with a gentle caress, spontaneously lifting them to his lips for a soft kiss. Their eyes met, Darcy winking and smiling brightly.

Lizzy returned his smile, lifting her chin and speaking strongly, "I, Elizabeth, take thee Fitzwilliam to my wedded husband, to have and to hold, for better for worse, for richer for poorer, in sickness and in health, to love, cherish, and to obey, 'til death us do part, according to God's holy ordinance; and thereto I plight thee my troth. Fitzwilliam, the life I did not realize was empty became full on the day you married me. You have graced me with your love, your soul, and your entire being. I am complete in you, a woman because of you, and a mother as a gift from you. Eternally I shall love you, and forevermore I pledge to strive in all ways to foster your happiness."

Emotion threatened to engulf him at her words, vigorous breaths necessary as she completed her earnest vows. The modicum of calm he attained was assaulted seconds later when, with a secretive smile, she dipped into a hidden pocket of her gown, withdrawing a wide band of brushed gold. Turning his left hand upward, she slowly glided the warmed metal over his ring finger while reciting:

"Fitzwilliam Darcy, with this ring I thee wed, with my body I thee worship, and all that I possess I share with thee: In the Name of the Father, and of the Son, and of the Holy Ghost. Amen." She lifted the ring-clad finger to her lips, bestowing a tender kiss. "I love you, William," she whispered for his ears only.

"Elizabeth!" Darcy's mouth had dropped open in utter shock, shattered emotions strewn beyond the ability to reassemble. Thankfully Reverend Bertram sensed his stupefaction and looming collapse, smoothly assuming control by leading the assembly in a prayer. Darcy and Lizzy harkened to his words peripherally, captured by the other's concentrated stare.

Lizzy was beaming, quite smug at having astonished her husband so completely. Darcy thrilled at the sensation of the solid reminder of her promise heavy on his flesh. Men rarely wore wedding bands; it being a cultural custom not widely adhered to in England. Yet the feel of the metal on his finger was wonderful, and he wholly comprehended with stunning clarity why the visible, tangible evidence of matrimony was so vitally important to women. His heart soared and he knew without a doubt that he would proudly display her token of their unending love and fidelity for all of his life.

The Reverend finished the benediction, laying his hands atop Darcy's and Lizzy's clasped ones, intoning in a ringing voice, "Those whom God hath joined together let no man put asunder! Forasmuch as Fitzwilliam and Elizabeth have consented together in holy wedlock, and have witnessed the same before God and this company, and thereto have given and pledged their troth either to the other, and have declared the same by giving and receiving of rings, and by joining of hands, I pronounce that they be Man and Wife together, In the Name of the Father, and of the Son, and of the Holy Ghost. Amen."

The short conclusion was timely and adequate for Darcy to restore a semblance of coherency to his frayed sensibilities. The urge they felt to kiss each other was painful in intensity, but they resisted, managing to appropriately respond to Reverend Bertram's forceful declaration, "May I present, to my tremendous honor, Mr. and Mrs. Fitzwilliam Darcy."

The day's activities were jubilant. A delicious breakfast repast was served by Mrs. Langton, surpassing all expectations. Laughter was rampant, congratulations and well wishes abounding. Merriment and frivolity reigned, augmented as additional guests began arriving as the afternoon progressed. Lizzy and Darcy stayed as close together as feasible, deluged with innumerable requests to replay the vows and display their rings. The women universally wiped teary eyes, glancing speculatively at their husbands while the gentlemen feigned ignorance. It is doubtful that Darcy sporting a band would initiate a fashion trend, but more than a few of the younger men of their acquaintance privately thought the gesture romantic. None ventured a negative word and even George found no cause to tease.

The general air of gaiety was delightful, but eventually Darcy snapped. The need for even a minute of solitude with his wife multiplied to a craving hunger until he finally grasped her elbow, politely excusing themselves from the cluster of females surrounding, and led her to his study. Leaning against the door, he pulled her into his embrace as close as possible with bulging belly intruding, cupping her face with firm palms. Lizzy fully expected him to kiss her, had closed her eyes and pursed her lips in anticipation, only to open them moments later when the blissful sensation of his mouth was not felt.

He was staring with smiling, blue-eyed Darcy intensity. "William?"

"Elizabeth Darcy. I love you."

"And I love you, Fitzwilliam Darcy," she replied with a chuckle. "Was it all you dreamed of, beloved? Is your heart content now that we have married in the Darcy chapel?"

"My heart is content married to you, my love. Today's ceremony fulfilled a family tradition and provided me the opportunity to again express my undying faithfulness to you, my precious wife. I am grateful for many things, but especially that you still love me in spite of my mawkishness."

"Among your many stellar attributes that heighten my love for you, sir, your mawkishness is listed. I would not wish for you to be any other way!"

"Elizabeth, beautiful, sweet, sensual, clever Elizabeth." He caressed over her soft neck, lips brushing imperceptibly along her jaw. "I must tell you how incredibly I love my ring. I shall wear it forever, a treasure of you. What made you think of it?"

His lips had traveled to her ear, Lizzy rapidly succumbing to the allure of him. "Hmm... I wanted to make this occasion exceptional, to surprise you. I do not actually know what made me think of it. I guess it was you planning my ring, an additional token not really necessary as I told you." She withdrew, lifting his chin to peer into his eyes seriously. "William, you never fail to gift me with something special. You are far better at such things than me, despite your assertions to being uncreative." She kissed him lightly. "I wanted you to have a tangible remembrance of this day. To express how profoundly moved I am by all you do for me. William, I love you so very much!"

She kissed him fiercely, Darcy pulling her closer and responding with yearning. Seconds later she broke the kiss, eyes less than an inch away as she stroked softly over his face. "The ring is symbolic of our love. Strong as metal, precious as gold, brightly shining, and without end. I know you will treasure it, but I want you to understand that if it is uncomfortable in any way, you do not need to wear it. I know it is odd. I also know you; on or off your finger you will revere what it represents and cherish it."

Darcy was shaking his head with increasing vigor, finally halting her words with his mouth on hers. "Stop, Elizabeth! I love the ring and will wear it for all the reasons you stated. Nothing you give me in love could be uncomfortable or odd. In fact, quite the opposite. I rarely wear the Darcy signet, as you know, because the weight bothers me especially when I am working. This,"—and he held up his left hand, glittering gold band at home on his slender finger—"feels as if it belongs, as if it has always been there."

He grasped her hand, lifting for a lingering kiss to each fingertip. Then he grinned, "See how you have altered me. I am not the faintest bit embarrassed to flaunt my emotional qualities for all to gawk."

Lizzy laughed. "I delight in this, my lover. However, I rather like the severe, reserved man I fell in love with. Save the worst of your saccharine aspects for our intimate moments; otherwise, the boys on the play yard may torture you."

He laughed richly. "I always could prevail over the other boys, so I have no fear."

"Braggart," she teased.

"Yes, this is true. Darcy of Pemberley, prideful and arrogant. And now I have you by my side to heighten my conceit. Add a perfect child to the mixture and I shall likely be uncontrollable in my vanity. Whatever shall you do with me?"

"Unleash Dr. Darcy to restore your humility through biting sarcasm. First, however, I wish to passionately kiss my handsome husband for several minutes. Contain yourself as best you can, my lover, as we do have guests to attend to."

"I make no promises," he mumbled with lips already occupied in pleasanter pursuits than talking.

In the end they did manage to restrain their baser impulses… barely. The partying would continue late into the night, one meal melding into the next. Most of the guests would end up dwelling at Pemberley for the night, either because they lived a distance away, such as the Drurys and Sitwells, or because the gentlemen were too intoxicated and women too exhausted to travel. Pemberley had not hosted such a lively and large gathering for months, most of their previous dinner parties modest affairs. As typical Lizzy was extroverted, seemingly everywhere at once, and in every way the perfect hostess. Also typically Darcy was reticent, even the group of only friends and family wearing at times. Nonetheless, his happiness was apparent to all, the constant smile and glittering eyes belying his aloof pose. To this crowd of folks who had known Darcy the man for years, he was downright ebullient.

In point of fact, the Darcys enjoyed themselves immensely, Lizzy so weary she needed to be carried up the final flight of stairs and long hallway.

"One of the drawbacks to a manor Pemberley's size is how far apart all the rooms are," she muttered sleepily against her husband's neck.

Their second wedding was not consummated that night, but it did not matter overly to Darcy. After all, he had the remainder of his long life to make love to his adorable wife. And this was a mission he accepted gladly and would accomplish frequently with utter joy.

D AMNATION!" DARCY MUTTERED, THROWING the letter onto his desk and rising to pace in agitation to the window. He stood for a time staring sightlessly as thoughts whirled. Finally with a heavy sigh he turned and exited the room. Seeking the nearest footman, he was informed that his wife, as suspected despite the dreary weather, was in the garden.

It was a week after their renewal ceremony, the guests all returned to their homes except for Dr. Darcy and Col. Fitzwilliam. The two bachelors were currently riding, Darcy assumed, since they had asked him to join their excursion. Unfortunately a recently delivered pile of letters from Mr. Daniels was consuming all his time. Furthermore, the news from London would require an additional sacrifice that threatened to send him into a serious irritation, hence why he sought his lovely bride. Always her presence soothed him, but primarily it was to discuss the business at hand.

He smiled instantly at the sight of her dressed in a thick coat and old boots, wide brimmed bonnet shading her delicate skin, and bulging belly not inhibiting her from kneeling in the dirt and digging vigorously. She wore gloves as she planted the row of bulbs, but the smudges of dirt on her cheeks and neck illustrated her lack of concern for delicacy at the cost of fun. Darcy adored her lack of pretension as one of the hundreds of attributes that set her apart from all other women.

She glanced up at the sound of gravel crunching, lighting up immediately, and sitting back on her heels. "William! What are you doing here?"

"I needed to see your lovely face."

Lizzy laughed, brushing at the stray wisps of hair tickling her eyes before removing the filthy gloves. "I rather doubt it lovely at the moment, but thank you. Since you are here I shall request your assistance rising."

He gladly clasped the hands offered, pulling her up and leaning for a kiss. She withdrew slightly, halting him with a chuckle. "Kiss me and you will likely get dirt on your face."

"A little dirt never hurt anyone."

Several minutes later she was laughing again as she wiped his soiled nose and brushed over the specks on his jacket. "I did warn you."

"Sit, my dear. Aside from your delightful kisses, I do need to talk to you." Lizzy noted the tone of seriousness, turning to him the moment they assumed seats on the marble bench. Darcy clasped her hands, meeting her eyes with a faint, forced smile. "You know I received missives from Mr. Daniels." She nodded. "It is as I feared. I must travel to Town to attend to business matters. You know I hoped to avoid this, but never actually thought I would succeed. Perhaps in time I will manage to conclude all business issues from the distance of Pemberley, but not yet. For too many years I conducted a large quantity of my affairs from the city." He paused, softly stroking her pale cheeks. "I am rambling to divert the moment when I must face your tears and control my own. Elizabeth, I am so very sorry!"

She swallowed. "Hush, William. We knew this was a distinct possibility. You cannot ignore your responsibilities. When…" her voice caught, "when will you leave?"

"Tomorrow, early. The sooner I depart, the sooner I will be home. I dare not wait any longer for fear our baby comes early. As it is I am taking a chance and it kills me to imagine that I…" He stopped, voice also catching. He closed his eyes, pulling her dusty forehead to rest on his. "Oh God, Elizabeth! Tell me all will be well, please."

"All will be well, my love," she whispered. "George is here, Georgiana and Richard too. I am healthy and your stubborn son shows no indication that he wishes to vacate his warm cocoon anytime soon. He appears to enjoy pummeling my internal organs. Besides, if his manners are anything remotely akin to his father's, he will diligently wait until you return."

She too was rambling, avoiding the painful topic of her loneliness when he was away. She was not too fearful of their child's birth transpiring too soon, although anything was possible, her main heartache merely being the void created with his absence. "How long will you be gone?"

He sighed, standing to pace in agitation with fingers jerking at his sides. "No more than two weeks. Generally I spend a month or so in Town this time of year, but always that has included socializing, which I will happily forego. I have given this quite a bit of thought and am certain I can conclude my affairs in a couple weeks. I will likely drive Mr. Daniels's entire firm insane with my surly attitude and rude haste, but it cannot be helped. Additionally I will surely insult someone by rebuffing a dinner invitation. Nonetheless, I refuse to be parted from you for too long. Propriety be damned! I need to be here!" He whirled around, pebbles flying. "Elizabeth, tell me not to go and I will not. Say the word and I will find a way around this."

She bit her lip, staring into his troubled face. "I do not need to ask if you have considered all other options as I know you to be methodical in the extreme. If there was another way, you would have discovered it." She rose and crossed to where he stood panting and rigid, placing her palms lightly on his chest. "Later I shall tell you how much I will miss you, but for now I insist you go make the arrangements you need to depart tomorrow. Prepare your thoughts and papers so you can finish the tasks and return to us quickly."

"Elizabeth, I love you so very much." He kissed her deeply, withdrawing with effort and breathing slowly to calm. "Very well, I shall make the arrangements. Meet me in our chamber in one hour. I need to be alone with you." She nodded and he kissed her again, turning and walking briskly away without a backward glance.

It was only when he was assuredly beyond view that she collapsed onto the bench. They had spoken several times of the potential for a trip to London. It was absolutely out of the question for Elizabeth to accompany him. In some respects the separation would be easier to handle, having already survived their first and recognizing the necessity for such partings as a fact of life. However, the timing with their firstborn so near to arriving added a drama to the severance that was horribly painful, especially to Darcy. Lizzy would be home, safe with family and friends. Darcy, conversely, would be alone with guilt wracking him and, heaven forbid, if anything tragic occurred, he would assuredly never forgive himself.

Lizzy had wisely known that only through action would he prevent succumbing to his distress. A whirlwind of frantic activity ensued, Darcy barking orders immediately upon entering the house. If the servants were momentarily stunned by the discourteous commands and stormy visage of their generally polite and buoyant Master, they quickly ascertained the cause. Nodding sagely and with compassion, they carried out the instructions hastily. Of course the staff was abundantly familiar with their Master coming and going, more than capable to handle all arrangements for a rushed departure.

Nonetheless, it was closer to two hours before he reached their chamber. Lizzy had conquered her sadness finally, washing and changing into Darcy's silk shirt to await his arrival. Sitting on the sofa before the fire as she attempted to allay her melancholy unsuccessfully, her unhappiness led to a bout of tears and then exhaustion until she fell asleep.

Darcy entered shortly thereafter, Lizzy's cheeks dry, but red-rimmed eyes indicative of her grief. The instant lurch of desire at seeing her in his shirt was quickly cooled by the evidence of her tears. Kneeling beside and smoothing the hair off her forehead, he leaned for a soft kiss.

"Beloved?"

She turned sleepily into his ready embrace, murmuring his name as her arms snaked over his shoulders. "Hold me, William."

"Forever." Lifting her to their bed, he stretched beside, enveloping completely and tenderly caressing with only deepest love ruling. For a long while they held each other. Darcy was content to snuggle close, feeling her warmth and softness. He delighted in the occasional nudges of their healthy child. Burying his face and hand into her luxuriant hair, and smelling the heady aroma of her perfume was more than enough to pacify his heart. It was Lizzy who moved first, lifting her head from its comfortable rest on his inner shoulder to gaze upon and stroke his beloved face.

Everything slowed down. Time appeared to halt, or at least drag along gradually. Very few words were spoken as Lizzy incrementally undressed her husband. The familiar joy and passion was there with an undercurrent of sorrow tempering the usual rage of heat. As they kissed and caressed with the rising fervor muted, they realized that their prolonged adoration was as much about the yearning to express their mutual devotion and further burn the image of the other onto all five senses, as it was about the desire to make love in some unforgettable manner.

They moved about the bed in all directions, needing to touch each other and view each other from all angles. Darcy removed his shirt, desiring to bare his wife to feasting hands and eyes more than experiencing any heightened ardency elicited by his garment. In truth, nothing augmented his passion more than her natural state. He reached for the ointment, massaging reverently over her expanded belly while she sat astride his thighs and played with the downy hair on his chest.

"Will you do this while I am gone?" he asked softly.

"Yes, although it may remind me of every time you perform the task and the natural outcome."

She was attempting levity, but her voice broke at the end as the truth of her jest brought her sadness crashing down. Darcy frowned slightly, gazing into her eyes with disquiet.

"Elizabeth," he began.

"Shhhh…" She pressed her lips to his and shook her head slightly. "Say nothing, dearest, just love me."

"With all my heart and soul." His kiss was hard and intense, hands working diligently over her abdomen and dipping underneath the swell to brush over sensitive regions. Lizzy moaned, rocking into his seeking fingers, rapidly losing herself to rising sensations of pleasure. Both were surprisingly interrupted by a particularly strong kick from baby Darcy into his father's palm.

Lizzy giggled. "I think he wants a little attention from his papa."

"Can he not deduce I am otherwise occupied?"

Lizzy laughed louder. "He is a Darcy, thus demanding and persistent. You may as well give him what he seeks and trust me when I say he will likely not take no for an answer if he is like you."

Darcy grinned, gently pushing Lizzy onto the bed as he positioned his body between her legs, face and hands on the beautiful swell. Currently the ripples of an insistent and active son were playing over the soft skin, Darcy amazed afresh at how evident the baby was from so deeply inside. Lately he had noticed particularly strong pushes of what could only be a tiny foot pressing so firmly that Darcy fleetingly believed he could grasp the extremity between his fingers. He tried, nearly succeeding only to have the limb disappear and moments later reemerge elsewhere on his wife's belly.

"How does he do that? Is he not too compacted to travel about so rapidly?"

"One would think," Lizzy answered with a chuckle, fingers massaging over his scalp. "Yet I can assure you he manages to flip around easily, as I can feel him jabbing me everywhere."

Darcy was silent, mouth pressed against the soft flesh around her navel while his hands kneaded the slick oil tenderly into her supple skin, all thoughts of sexual stimulation forgotten for the time being as he diligently applied to the task at hand. He could feel every movement of his unborn child under his palms with fresh amazement. Suddenly he wondered if perhaps in the very slightest way the awe and transcendent bliss regarding all aspects of this pregnancy had diminished with even the joyous job of rubbing the cream becoming a routine step leading to greater pleasures.

And now he would be leaving, unable to daily talk to his child and perform the duty of caring for her stretching abdomen. Pangs of dismay and guilt for allowing his approach to become anything less than the greatest delight swept through him. He frowned, kissing softly over the rising skin.

"What is it, my love?" she asked softly.

He shook his head, laying his cheek on her flattened navel. "Stay inside, my son," he murmured. "Promise you will wait for me and be good to your mother. I love you, little one."

"Do not fret, William. All will be well."

As she spoke he transferred to lie beside her with body partially draped over and one hand yet rubbing the rippling bulge. He stared deeply into her eyes, propped on an elbow and toying with the loose strands of hair about her face. He was so serious, intently studying her face.

"What is it, my love?" she repeated. "Talk to me."

His answer was slow in coming, mind clearly contemplating his words carefully while Lizzy waited and tenderly caressed over all available skin. Darcy shivered at the sensations educed, finally speaking huskily, "I am afraid, Elizabeth. Afraid to not be here for you, afraid of my loneliness without you, and afraid of causing the same negative emotions in you. But primarily I am afraid that I have disappointed you by taking it all for granted. You and our child and the miracle of it all. I am sorry if I have been in any way less attentive than I should be."

Lizzy was staring at him with undisguised, wide-eyed shock, truly speechless for several minutes. "Fitzwilliam, surely you are jesting! Merciful heavens, no human on earth could possibly be more attentive than you! I doubt if there is a man alive more involved with his wife's pregnancy and unborn baby." She ceased her purposeful caresses to clasp his face firmly. "Dearest, erase those thoughts. They are not reality but merely your anguish clouding your judgment. I am in all ways satisfied and treasured and content in you. And our son shall be irretrievably spoiled within days of his birth. That is what I fear!"

She pulled his face to hers, seizing his mouth zealously and taking charge, showing him precisely what she wanted. Lizzy grasped him, face flushed and breathing labored with rapidly rising passion, drawing him harshly onto her with legs roughly encircling and body arching with clear intent.

Darcy groaned, fighting against her surprising strength to hold his heavy frame aloft. "Elizabeth, I will crush you!"

"Not today. I need to feel all of you, Fitzwilliam, please!"

It was pointless. He had no ability to resist. With a hoarse growl emanating from his chest, he embraced her tightly, falling onto her as they merged. Oh the bliss! She clutched him as if life depended, every plane of flesh adhered with the highly erotic sensation of belly and breast pressed under his torso. Increasingly over the past weeks the weight of his body was becoming uncomfortable for her, necessitating a departure from their preferred position of lovemaking. Naturally this distressed him not in the least, the joy of their union always blissful and intense in any position. Nonetheless, as they each agreed, nothing quite compared to the feel of her husband's virile figure pressed onto her and his wife's lithe frame wrapped around him.

It is perhaps fortunate that their mutual ardency was rampant as Lizzy had no chance to experience the slightest discomfort. The fiery passion rushing through them was powerful, racing swiftly to a crescendo that rocked head to toe.

Inexplicably, Lizzy burst into tears the minute she was able to catch her breath, Darcy cuddling her close to his heaving chest with trembling arms. He soothed her until she quieted, not needing to ask as his eyes were teary as well.

❦

As with their separation in June, they chose to refrain from speaking of it directly. George took the news with a solemn vow to guard Lizzy with his life and never leave her unattended. He was deadly serious and therefore mildly taken aback when Lizzy grunted and rolled her eyes.

"Lord, have mercy!" she said with mock pleading heavenward. "Not another one! I do not require a trailing hound dog, my dear uncle."

Darcy smiled. George arched a brow at his niece. "Very well, madam. I will refrain from dogging your heels, but will be in residence, likely the library, if ever you whistle loudly."

"And you shall come running with tongue lolling and tail wagging?"

"Precisely," he answered while the other three burst into laughter.

They passed the evening in quiet family communion. Georgiana, George, and Richard were fully cognizant of the anguish shared by Darcy and Lizzy, even if they did not quite understand it. All through the evening as they laughed and listened to Georgiana play, the three single persons were well aware of the frequent touches and glances meted out between the newlyweds in ever increasing allotments. The air surrounding the two where they sat squeezed into the very end of the sofa was electrically charged. Nothing improper occurred, both restrained in their tender caresses, but the clarity of mutual need and despondency was salient.

Lizzy was quieter than usual and Darcy was monosyllabic. Eventually even the energy of George Darcy could not penetrate the gathering gloom, so he rose with exaggerated yawning and stretching, proclaiming fatigue. If anyone thought it odd for exhaustion to suddenly strike them all at eight o'clock, it was not pointed out.

Lizzy refused to shed further tears and managed to retain command of her emotions. In actuality, once they were alone, comfortably dressed in robes and entangled before the fire, their spirits lifted. Both knew without the minutest doubt that they would be miserable beyond description for the next two weeks, yet they both vowed to handle the situation with maturity and strength.

The weather had gradually slid into the chill of autumn. The days were generally fair and the rains had yet to attack, but the winds were mounting and the nights were bitter enough to warrant a fire. The lovers reclined on the hearth rug and piled pillows, snuggled and warm, with passion at bay for the present as they discussed estate affairs.

"Mr. Keith will manage the day-to-day issues that may arise as he always has in my absence." Darcy spoke softly, but with the familiar undertone of authority notable whenever he addressed Pemberley business. "However, it is different now as you are Mistress. You have exceeded both our expectations, my intelligent love, and therefore, if you feel able, can attend to diverse matters that normally would await my return."

"Such as?"

He sighed, bestowing a kiss to her forehead before continuing, "Naturally all household issues are already handled by you, and if anything needs to be attained above the usual, you have the authority to procure it. I trust your judgment, Elizabeth, if there are any unforeseen problems amongst the staff or even the tenants. The senior staff knows you speak for me and will not question your decisions."

She gazed into his eyes, pleasure and uncertainty warring. "Are you sure this vote of confidence is wise, William? I appreciate your faith but would not wish to make any mistakes."

He smiled and ran his hand through her trailing tresses. "This is exactly why I have no worries. Not only are you intelligent and well versed in Pemberley's necessities, but you are prudent and will not hastily conclude a matter if you deem it beyond your scope."

She nodded, smiling brightly. "Thank you. I will assure all is organized and properly transacted so when you return you shall have nothing to do but love me! Oh, and celebrate your birthday. Ha! You thought to evade, yes?" Darcy was flushed and squirming, Lizzy tickling his ribs and giggling. "How silly you are, foolish man. Although please do not be expecting thirty gifts as I am not nearly clever enough to conjure so many brilliant ideas. I would exhaust myself at the endeavor!"

Darcy laughed, but her jest brought something to mind and he halted her probing fingertips. "Desist! I cannot breathe! Unfair that you are not ticklish." He gasped, clasping her hands tightly to his chest. "Seriously, listen to me, love. I order you, yes, I order," he glared and arched a brow, lips twitching, "that you not overtax. Your rest is essential. Promise me you will take care?"

"If you promise the same. I know you will be pressuring yourself to conclude your business so you can hurry home. I want you with me, Fitzwilliam, but not to the extent that you grow ill. Take your time but make sure you are home before the tenth."

"I am never ill, dearest, but I accept your chastisement. Let us both promise to behave, and I assure you I will be home well before the tenth. And while we are on the subject, please do not plan an extravaganza for my birthday. I would be perfectly happy to forget it altogether. I simply want to be home and the only present I desire is you, preferably naked on our bed."

"And tied with a big red bow?" She fluttered her eyelashes and pursed her lips, face offered and accepted handily. They made love by the fire, slowly and tenderly rousing the other. The subtle current of sadness was there, but the love they felt was profound and so intensely intrinsic, overruling the presence of dismay.

They fell asleep on the rug, limbs twined, with Lizzy engulfed by his larger body. It was the cold creeping over his back that woke Darcy, Lizzy deeply asleep and toasty in his arms. The room lamps were yet burning, casting a glow over her skin that was impossible for him to resist. He studied her, lightly running fingers, and inhaling of her fragrance: a mixture of lavender and sexual gratification and him. Their child slept, the bulge beautifully round and still. At times he missed her flat stomach, especially when making love and overcome with raging passion yet unable to release the concern for her altered shape and flexibility. But those moments were fleeting and rare. The miracle that was the product of their love lying inside of her body was astoundingly moving to his soul and strangely erotic.

"God, my Lizzy, I so love you," he whispered, bestowing a tiny kiss to her shoulder, additionally surprised at the sensation of her petite hand warmly stroking over his bare thigh. "I am sorry. I did not wish to wake you, but it is cold. We need to move to the bed."

She turned in his arms, sleepy eyes meeting his. "Yes. Our bed, my lover. Kiss me, William." There was no denying the yearning. All through the night they reached for each other, caressing on the edge of sleep, loving with every inch of flesh and every muscle. The last was as the sun crested the treetops, glow spreading across the fields and through the gaps in the curtain covered wide windows.

Darcy moved within his precious wife, fingers rousing and mouth stirring shivers along her spine. Every curve of her exciting, her heat and softness electrifying, moist depths surrounding and squeezing him thrilling, and articulations of delight enlivening. Wave upon wave of glorious rapture swept through, hearts and spirits soaring as their bodies succumbed to the elation of pure pleasure with shouts of loving joy.

Lizzy was soundly asleep seconds afterwards, a blissful smile on her gorgeous face. Darcy experienced a rush of fierce love and breathless peace. Leaving her was painful, but he knew all would be well as she promised. How could it not be with their souls intermingled? He kissed her several times, the drowsy smile widening, before carefully untangling his body from hers to prepare for departure.

The carriage ride to London was long, tiring, and uneventful. One thing it was not was boring. Richard ingratiated himself to accompany his cousin as he planned to leave in two days anyway. Darcy did not mind in the slightest, adoring Richard and knowing that his cousin's ofttimes irritating boisterousness would lighten the mood, provide entertainment, and stave off the gloominess sure to come. In this assumption Darcy was spot on.

The first hour or so was passed in silence. Richard surreptitiously observed Darcy's dreamy face, noted how he fiddled and caressed the ring on his finger, and heard the unconscious faint sighs. In honest curiosity he finally broke the quiet.

"What is it like, Darcy, to love as you do?" The impromptu question pierced the calm, Darcy's brows shooting up as he glanced to his cousin, and Richard coloring as he realized his private musings were vocalized.

There followed an awkward pause, Richard flushed and Darcy amused. "Why do you ask?"

"Forgive me, my friend, I meant no offense. It was impertinent of me to ask such a thing, so let us just forget the question."

"I am not offended and have every intention of answering your query, cousin. I am merely curious why you ask it. Do you have a particular lady in mind? Or are you seeking enlightenment for the furthering of your education in human interpersonal relationships?" Darcy was grinning broadly.

Richard grunted. "More the latter, I suppose, although you know I am not as ragingly consumptive of all matters educational as you are."

"Well that surely is the truth! How you managed to graduate University yet remains a mystery to me."

"Ha, ha." Richard intoned dryly. "Most amusing today, Mr. Darcy."

"Watching your discomfiture always increases my humor. You have yet to adequately answer. Why do you ask about love?"

Richard shrugged, gazing out the window. "Primarily idle curiosity. You have been so different since Elizabeth entered your life. I noted a change in your demeanor as far back as Rosings last, although I did not comprehend the cause. The oddity is that I thought you perfectly content before, yet now I observe the two of you together, and even how you fondle your new ring, and the happiness is transparent. Nauseatingly so." He grinned and shrugged again. "So I was curious what it felt like."

Darcy was gazing into his lap with a soft smile upon his mouth, self-consciously removing fingertips from the gold band. He did not answer hastily, finally speaking lowly, "I do not know if I can sufficiently place it into words. Perhaps that is why the poets wax eloquent with platitudes and analogies as mere common phrases do not suffice. All I know for certain is that almost from the moment I saw her she has filled my senses and my heart. There is joy with Elizabeth in every way and every moment, whether present or no. I feel light and buoyant, yet also grounded and secure. Giddy and frivolous, yet strong and steady. Childish and masculine simultaneously." He chuckled softly, closing his eyes and leaning back against the carriage wall. "Yet you know what the most miraculous part is, Richard? Greater than how she makes me feel is the miracle that she loves me."

He opened his eyes abruptly, staring at his cousin with full Darcy intensity. "Richard, there is no replacement for that. It is a priceless treasure, and I only wish all in the world could experience it."

"And this 'feeling' is worth the misery I note at times such as this, when you are separated?"

Darcy shook his head. "It is not misery in the way you imagine. Yes, I miss her terribly already and my loneliness will be profound, but our love sustains me and I have the constant joy of knowing she waits for me."

They were solitary with their thoughts for a spell, Darcy resuming the heedless caressing of his ring while Richard dwelled inwardly. Slowly Darcy began to chuckle. "Tell me, cousin, does any of this questioning have to do with Admiral Ulster's daughter?"

Richard's laugh was rich, an uncharacteristic ruddiness spreading over his cheeks. He glanced away, eyes downcast. "I admit nothing, especially to you who would tease me mercilessly. All I shall say is that the concept is not as repugnant as it once was, although God help me if I am ever as gushy and nonsensical as you, or completely lose sight of all propriety. Is that sufficient for now, Mr. Romance?"

Darcy laughed loudly. "It is a start!"

Once in Town, Darcy wasted no time in beginning the arduous process of concluding his business affairs. With the Darcy House staff under strict orders to remain mum regarding his residency, he entered the offices of Mr. Daniels bright and early the day after his arrival. For two days all went according to plan, Darcy quite pleased with the progress made. It was while sitting in the library the second evening after finishing a long devotion-imbued letter to his wife, brandy in hand and papers spread before him, that he began coughing. It was only a light tickle felt in the back of his throat, but it persisted no matter how often he attempted to drink or cough the itch away. More irritated than anything, he finally gave up working and went to bed.

Thus far the days and nights had passed rapidly with well-controlled sadness. He missed Elizabeth with an ache that was unrelenting, but the constant activity kept the pain at bay. Tonight he sat in the bed that was for many years comfortable and familiar as only for him, but was now glaringly empty and cold. He tried to read, but the prickle in his throat distracted, and he constantly glanced up toward her dressing room, positive he saw a shadow. Finally he gave in, dousing the lights and lying down in hopes that sleep would claim him quickly so he could dream of her.

Surprisingly, since he was not actually tired, sleep was attained rapidly, but his dreams were troubled. Elizabeth was nowhere to be found. Instead he floated dazedly through heavy clouds that occluded his respirations, thick cottony tendrils that invaded his nostrils, the air cool and damp. Then he was swimming in a hot spring, deep with the surface sparkling visibly above him yet he could not propel his weighted body to the promise of oxygen. He woke well before dawn, his sinuses obstructed and throat afire.

"Perfect," he mumbled scratchily. "Never ill, right, Darcy."

He forced himself to rise and bathe, feeling slightly improved once dressed and outside in the brisk air. However, after an hour closeted in the roomy office with Mr. Andrew Daniels and his eldest son Benjamin, his head felt to explode and the basic exercise of breathing was torturous. He ignored the unpleasant sensations as best he could until mid afternoon when the quill began to waver in his tremulous fist and a fit of coughing gripped him with alarming potency.

Mr. Daniels took charge, boldly facing the potential anger of his client by insisting on calling for Mr. Darcy's carriage and rescheduling the appointment for when his health was restored. Darcy considered arguing, but quite simply did not have the energy to do so.

It had been some five years since Darcy last suffered from the ravages of a common cold. At that time he had been residing at Pemberley, with Georgiana and Mrs. Reynolds fussing over him. It had annoyed him greatly, but he had to admit the constant female companionship and nursing was pleasant, not to mention beneficial in speeding his recovery.

Mrs. Smyth was not the least bit maternal and, aside from providing hot tea and edibles, had no idea how to care for the infirm. Therefore, Darcy was left to his own devices with only Samuel to make sure he did not wallow in his own sweat and disgusting bodily secretions.

Samuel, proficient with the vast array of masculine essentials, was utterly inept when dealing with an ill Master. The fact that Mr. Darcy had been unwell only twice since Samuel assumed the post as his valet did not furnish him much in the way of medical expertise. Nonetheless, even he could diagnose a frightening increase in infirmity by the third morning after falling sick. Darcy was difficult to rouse, blazing to the touch, coughing in wracking fits, and intermittently shivering and sweating.

The physician was sent for, rapidly assessed the situation, and assumed command. There was no question that the suspected cold was upgraded to influenza status. The prescribed medicines were obtained from the apothecary and detailed instructions were given to Samuel and Mrs. Smyth. Darcy was liberally dosed with a tea mixture of yarrow, peppermint, ginger, willow, and elder bark for general aches and fever. Further distillations of licorice root, elecampane, mullein, and honey were forced down his throat for the cough and chest congestion. Oil of lavender was burned to cleanse the air and promote sleep.

For five days total Darcy drifted in a hazy place of vague memory. His waking moments were brief and filled with stertorous, productive coughs that left him weak, gasping, and in pain. Muscles that he did not know existed in his body ached unrelentingly. The pervading odor of lavender reminded him excruciatingly of Elizabeth, and he knew on some level that time was passing without writing to her or completing the reams of paperwork that would bring him back to her, but then the thought would fade away as uncontrollable trembling assumed command.

The energy necessary to rise enough to utilize the bedside chamber pot upon those occasions his body required that type of relief was tremendous, leaving him utterly spent as he fell backwards onto the pillows in a heap. The room would undulate and whirl, his head throbbing, and more than once the endeavor ended with his stomach in wild upheavals.

He managed to drink some liquids beyond the curative concoctions offered, the cool streams of water soothing to his parched throat. Food was impossible, nothing able to stay settled in his stomach for longer than minutes before being regurgitated violently.

His dreams were randomly dark and disturbed or fantastical. Visions of people long since dead or not seen in years commingled with recent additions to his life, such as the Bennets. There was no coherency. His rational mind struggled to understand the purpose but was continually relegated to some far corner while the whimsical madness took control.

One afternoon he woke abruptly from a vivid but chaotic dream of Elizabeth crying for him. For several moments his heart pounded with the memory, but as the dream faded he recognized the current clarity of his thoughts. He was weary as never experienced before, but lucid. The bright sun streaming through the window pierced his sore eyes and his body felt as if he had been pummeled in a boxing ring, but he was cool and the bed was stationary.

"Well, finally back to the land of the living, are we?" It was Richard, grinning happily, but pale with an undertone of worry in his voice. Darcy opened his mouth to flash a sharp retort of some kind, nothing escaping but a faint squeak. "Eloquent, Mr. Darcy, as always. Here, cousin, drink this."

Darcy cringed, fully expecting another foul-tasting tea, but it was plain water. Cool and the most delicious-tasting beverage ever to pass his lips. Darcy was certain he could have consumed an ocean of the succulent fluid, but Richard forced him to sip gradually.

"God, I am tired!"

"Lazy old man. Lying about for nearly a week and you want to sleep?" Darcy smiled faintly, eyes closing as Richard reclined him onto the pillows.

"What day is it?"

"Tuesday. You have been ill for five days, not counting the time before Samuel called me. You gave us a bit of a fright. I knew you were too blasted stubborn to succumb to a mere fever, but Samuel has been as hysterical as an old woman."

Darcy's eyes had flown open and he was attempting to rise, quite unsuccessfully. "A week? I have work to do and must get home. Oh Lord, Elizabeth must be frantic. Richard…?" He fell back into the pillows, panting and coughing.

"Calm yourself, man, or you will have a relapse! Listen to me, William. Do not be stupid and exert yourself unduly. Elizabeth does need you home but that will not occur in a timely manner if you deteriorate again. I have taken the liberty to write in your stead and inform your beloved wife that you have a minor cold and requested I write for you. I know you hate dissembling, but I judged it proper in this case."

Darcy was breathing heavily, heart racing painfully, and the room was spinning again. Whether he liked it or not, he could not deny the logic of Richard's advice. "A letter… I should send… a letter… telling her…"

"Yes, yes, all in good time. Sleep again, William. You can dictate a missive to her later. She has written to you several times, which will surely boost your spirits." He stopped, realizing that Darcy was soundly asleep and snoring.

Lizzy stood on the Pemberley portico for ten minutes, allowing George Darcy's warm hands to rest on her shoulders and resonant voice to soothe, all far too reminiscent of her husband, before she wiped the tears away. Darcy's carriage was barely out of sight before Lizzy launched into a whirlwind of activity. She had decided with full conscious intent that if she must be alone she would keep busy so she could not dwell on it overly. Her first order of business was to begin planning for Christmas. The fact that it was over two months away meant nothing, as she wanted to have everything prepared before the baby came. With this at the forefront of her mind, she met with Mrs. Reynolds within an hour of Darcy's departure.

Thus began her days. As far as Christmas celebrations went, the plans were both easier and more complicated. It was easier in that she knew the tenants quite well now so deciding what to place in their gift basket was obvious. It was also easier because the guest list would be far smaller with focus on intimate family and the baby. Obtaining gifts was a bit more problematic, as Lizzy could not tramp through the shops of Lambton in her condition, so she needed to decide on what to present to her friends and family. Georgiana and Harriet Vernor assisted in this task, handling the shopping for her.

There was also the tenant Christmas feast to plan. Last December as Darcy toured her through the manor and first spoke of the holiday tradition for the Pemberley workers, Lizzy had briefly envisioned something grand. In the same way as the Summer Festival, she had wanted to reinstate the old customs with flair. Of course, those early plans had not taken into consideration the arrival of their first child. Not knowing how the birth might proceed, what her physical condition would be afterwards, nor when it would even occur, Lizzy decided it would be best to keep the event understated. Actually it was her husband who firmly declared that the dinner be a humble affair, allowing no room for argument, so Lizzy had no real choice.

Nevertheless, minimal or majestic, she wanted all to be perfect. Plus, it gave her something else to fret about besides missing her husband. Before the week was out the menu was determined, the necessary cleaning of the ballroom and formal dining room was begun, the date was set for a week before Christmas, a group of minstrels from Matlock was reserved, and the list of invitees was written with invitations ordered. A detailed timetable was itemized for the following three months so all issues would be handled with or without the Mistress's input.

In between Christmas scheming Lizzy attended to household duties with a vengeance. Mr. Keith consulted her on everything although Lizzy knew he did not have to. She spent large quantities of time at Darcy's desk usually for no real purpose other than for the comfort afforded. The massive desk chair was imprinted with the shape of his derriere and thighs, the desktop strewn with the odd trinkets that he fiddled with while he worked, and littered with random notes written in his strong flowing calligraphy. Darcy was highly organized, each document ever signed filed in a logical manner and the ledgers meticulous, yet strangely the surface of his desk was cluttered. It was all a ready reminder of her husband, and for the days he was absent she ignored her own desk in the corner or the one in their sitting room, preferring to sit in his chairs.

Her need to be close to him in even this elemental way ended up being educational. Initially she gave it no real consideration, but as she sat in his office she began idly reading through the carefully filed papers. At first when she came across something that made no sense to her or was written in a puzzling code she passed it by. But more and more she began to see a pattern, and curiosity overcame her. Mr. Keith seemed unperturbed by her nosiness, answering her questions and offering explanations. The files covering her husband's years as Master of Pemberley were separate from those of his father and grandfather. Mr. Keith informed her that past documents and ledgers were stored in a basement chamber, dating back well over a hundred years. Lizzy immediately noted the similarities and differences in the documenting techniques used by Darcy compared to his predecessors, not to mention the larger array of ventures delved into. Some of his recording methods were amazingly simplistic while others were wildly complex. And the number of business transactions, investments, and estate matters was vaster than she had suspected. All of it lent additional insight into the mind of the man she was married to while also increasing her grasp of Pemberley affairs.

Luckily no serious quandaries arose during Darcy's absence. The day-to-day required purchases of food, household items, provisions for the animals, and such were routinely procured and paid for. Staff wages were disbursed at the end of each week, all earnings tabulated and allocated by Mr. Keith to each person while in Mrs. Darcy's presence. Decisions above and beyond the usual were minimal. An overly abundant and earlier than expected harvest of barley provided an opportunity for Lizzy to receive a crash course in crop management and bartering. With Mr. Keith's patient assistance and the finely detailed notations in Darcy's files, Lizzy transacted a market exchange with a hefty profit and surplus barley storage for Pemberley.

She was quite proud of herself, but primarily she knew that it was the small things such as intact ledgers that would free up an inordinate amount of Darcy's time when he returned. Extending further, Lizzy completed a number of the tasks Darcy had left unfinished due to his hasty departure. She worked very hard to keep it all in the order that Darcy preferred and thrilled in imagining how pleased he would be to discover how well his wife had taken care of matters.

By the end of the first week, Lizzy had a new-found respect for all the business her husband handled. After eleven months she grasped most of the vast estate management of Pemberley but had remained ignorant of the day-to-day tiny things and those business dealings beyond agriculture and livestock. She recognized on a certain level that her obsession was as much to stave off her loneliness as it was to please her already adoring spouse, but she also tremendously enjoyed the challenges.

George Darcy took his role as protector and companion very seriously. He was never far from her side, forever interrupting her to check how she was or bring a snack, and pouring on the charm as he whisked her off for walks about the grounds. His presence in the manor was simultaneously comforting and disconcerting. Lizzy had grown accustomed to the uncanny similarities George shared with her husband, no longer consciously noting them. Until now. The timbre of his laugh, resonance of voice, piercing blue of tender eyes, and general height and posture, even in his extreme boniness, was nearly indistinguishable from his nephew. It unnerved her and intermittently escalated her desperation and soothed it.

Georgiana was nearly as persistent, ensuring that Lizzy was never bored. Her sweetly steady friendship and deep love for her new sister was genuine. They spent numerous evenings together in the Darcys' sitting room, giggling and sharing girlish stories while reclining in robes and nibbling cakes and sipping tea. It greatly facilitated the transition from busy day to solitary night.

Darcy's hasty exodus had allotted no time for her to prepare little notes or intimate reminders to tuck into his valise, so she wrote lengthy lovelorn letters each night to be posted every two days. Pouring her heart did ease the ache somewhat, as did his reply. Sheer exhaustion and the pressing demands of the baby allowed her to sleep deeply with delightful dreams of him, at least for the first week. His first letter arrived on their fourth day apart. Like her, he had composed it in the evenings over two days and it was far more sentimental and erotic then hers. Lizzy experienced slight trepidation over placing boldly intimate ramblings in indelible ink to then be carried across England by strangers. Darcy suffered no such inhibition, surprisingly, as the need to express his desires for her transcended the unlikely possibility of the letter falling into unknown hands.

By the end of the week she was beginning to sense some disquiet at a lack of additional correspondence, having written twice more to him, but assumed it was because he was busy. Then the scribbled note penned by Richard arrived saying only that Darcy was ill with a minor cold, offering a patently lame excuse of sneezing too much to hold a quill as to why he was dictating to Richard. Lizzy did not believe a word of it and was instantly catapulted into panic.

"George!" she yelled, her uncle appearing within seconds and nearly colliding with Lizzy as he bounded over the threshold.

"What is it?"

"Read this and tell me what you think."

He did, frowning. "Hmmm. Something does not seem right..."

"Not at all. William is ill, Uncle, I can feel it. I need to go to London. Can you help me with the arrangements?" She was already pulling the servants bell.

"Elizabeth, think. I absolutely will not allow you to travel to London so you can erase that thought from your head right now."

"But..."

"No, and that is final. William may be sicker than Col. Fitzwilliam claims, but that does not necessarily mean he needs you there..."

"But I am his wife!"

"Precisely... Thank you, Watson, but we no longer require your services." The footman bowed and retreated, George crossing to where Elizabeth stood fighting tears. He placed his hands on her shoulders, speaking in soft tones so akin to Darcy that the tears spilled instantly. "Listen, dear. William is very strong and hideously stubborn. I am quite sure he can fight off any malady. We know he is being well cared for between Richard and Samuel. If it were life threatening, Richard would be forthcoming, I am certain. William will heal faster knowing you are safe from harm. The journey is too risky and you cannot permit yourself to fall ill."

She was crying in earnest now, and George gathered her into his arms, patting with a whispered *there, there*. For two days she could barely think. Somehow she managed to attend to business as it arose, exercise regularly with extended, memory-packed walks about the gardens, and host a tea party with Harriet Vernor, Alison Fitzherbert, Marilyn Hughes, Georgiana, and Jane, who ended up visiting for three days to comfort her anxious sister. She wrote two more letters, begging for an update and for once not at all embarrassed at blatantly communicating her sorrow and yearning, sending by express messenger.

Finally on the third day after Richard's note, a longer letter arrived, also penned in Richard's feathery script, but clearly the words of her husband. Lizzy began sobbing before the salutation was read.

My dearest, precious Elizabeth,

My beloved, I do pray this overdue correspondence is read by a healthy wife, robust as always and yet encumbered with the blessing that is our child. I, as you have been informed by our dear cousin, have been ill. I fear he misled you on the full extent of my infirmity. He begs me, my dearest, at this juncture to apologize for his deception as done with only your well-being in mind. This I can assure you is the truth. I do believe I must take full responsibility for the calamity that has befallen me as I so arrogantly jested that I am never ill. Do you recall this boasting? It appears that fate has a sense of humor, or perhaps karma is true as the mystics proclaim. However, fret no further as I am speedily mending from the influenza that afflicted me. It was not a pretty sight, my beautiful wife, and I am abundantly thankful you were not here to witness my indignity. Rest assured that I am healing rapidly with, as Richard says, my obstinacy intact. I have no idea to what he refers.

Naturally my illness has set me back on concluding my business. Mr. Daniels has persevered with preparing all matters for me and we are resuming our meetings. Unfortunately they must transpire in my bedchamber sitting room for now and remain stunted as my strength is not yet fully restored. I do still hope to complete affairs and be home for my birthday.

Beloved, I cannot relate the whole contents of my heart as my secretary would likely refuse to write the sentiments. I trust that you understand the depths of my love for you and anguish I feel in being separated. Please, Elizabeth, I beg you with all my soul, do not worry! I am recovering, and there is no lasting damage. I love you forever,

William

Underneath were supplementary lines in a shaky script that was nonetheless clearly Darcy's:

My Heart, Forgive the poor penmanship, but I fear my hands are yet weak. I must be brief. I ache for you, my precious Lizzy! God how I want to see your face. Know that you are alive in every beat of my heart and the knowledge that you are safe gives me the greatest strength. Soon, very soon, my lover, I will hold you and kiss you and we will make love with all the passion stored. Dream of me as I dream of you. I love you, my Elizabeth. I love you for all eternity.

Your Fitzwilliam

The letter was dictated, shakily written, sealed, and posted the morning following Darcy's fever breaking. By the time Lizzy received it Darcy had proven his powers of regeneration and colossal strength of will by resuming nearly the same hectic agenda as prior to his illness. Richard returned to his regiment with a warning to moderate that he knew Darcy would ignore. In truth he was still weak, the cough abiding, and the need for afternoon rest periods undeniable. At least it gave him a legitimate excuse to decline the few invitations that arrived despite his attempt to maintain secrecy.

L IZZY RETURNED TO HER self-appointed duties with a relieved smile on her
face. She would not feel completely secure until she could feel his solidity
under her hands and gaze upon his healthy face, but her anxiety was allevi-
ated. While apprehension waned with subsequent letters written in an ever increasingly firm hand, desolation and melancholy flourished unabated. The pain in her heart
rose with each passing day, allayed somewhat in rejuvenating sleep and sweet dreams.

As the third week without her husband advanced, Lizzy and Georgiana
walked to the orphanage in the Village. They each carried a basket filled with
baked treats for the children, dressed warmly against the chill air. October had
passed into November, the last of the Pemberley harvests reaped and marketed.
The fields now lay tilled and bare. A light drizzle of rain had fallen last evening,
leaving the ground moist with shallow puddles in places, but today was clear
with the clouds lingering over the Peaks.

"If William were here he would predict the rains, whether they are gone for
now or to return." Lizzy spoke softly, gazing at the horizon.

Georgiana smiled, squeezing her sister's arm. "Yes, he always knows. It is
a gift I do not possess. Of course, if he were here he would likely forbid you to
walk, especially if he judges the rains to resume."

Lizzy laughed. "True, although I think I would welcome his overprotective
domination if it meant I could hear his voice."

"He shall be home soon, Lizzy. He will not miss his birthday. He knows how important it is to you, and nothing will keep him away."

"As desperately as I need him, I fear him overtaxing and becoming ill again." She sighed loudly and shook her head. "Enough! He has begged me not to fret, to trust him, and I will. His letter yesterday said all was proceeding expeditiously."

"Did he give any indication of when he would be home?"

"No, unfortunately. I think he is afraid to say much so as to not disappoint. In truth I do not expect him for another week, probably breezing in exhausted on the day before his birthday!"

"Why so long?"

"He had reckoned it would take two weeks at the least to conclude his affairs, and I think he was being generous at that so as not to increase my distress." She smiled at his ever conscious desire to assuage. "He was ill for a week, if my figuring is correct, then the slow recovery. I can still discern a weakness in his handwriting and weariness in his words. I am sure he is not able to work up to his normal stamina."

"Well, perhaps you are correct, and I suppose it best he take it slowly. Still, I know he will be here by his birthday! William always keeps his promises."

The children jumped for joy, delighting in the treats and affection from Mrs. Darcy and Miss Darcy. The joyful, innocent presence of the children never failed to cheer Lizzy, the afternoon hours spent very happily with only fleeting thoughts of her husband intruding. Toward the end of their visit, as the clouds were gradually blowing back toward the valley, Lizzy felt the preliminary twinges of pain.

She held a newer arrival to the orphanage, a girl of three years, as she stood watching groups of children playing hopscotch and jumping rope. One minute everything was roses, Lizzy laughing at the antics and blissfully snuggling the soft body against her breast, when the familiar vague contractions were abruptly displaced by a sharp stab of pain lanced through her abdomen rippling from back to front and down to her groin. It resembled the innocuous false labor pains that Dr. Darcy assured were normal and necessary, but was far more intense. She gasped, bending involuntarily as she rubbed over her belly. It passed as swiftly as it came, Lizzy breathing deeply and almost convincing herself it was not significant when an identical pain struck. She released a squeal, doubling over and nearly dropping the little girl, who was clinging to her neck in fright.

"Mrs. Darcy? Are you well?" It was Miss Seymour, the orphanage director, inquiring as she rushed to rescue the child.

"No, I think I need to sit. Oh!"

Rapid activity ensued, Georgiana calling immediately for the nearest carriage. In short order Lizzy was home, George carrying her to her third-floor chamber in an amazingly strong grip for such a thin man. The pains continued at an irregular rhythm and intensity. Lizzy realized once the initial shock was past that the pains were not horrible, but definitely more severe than normal. It was the stress of what they signified that sent her into trembling sobs.

"Calm yourself, Elizabeth. Georgiana dear, hold her hand and speak soothingly. Elizabeth, I must be allowed to examine you. Relax, all will be well."

His final sentence, uttered in Darcy's gentle tone, was more then she could handle. "George, I cannot... have this baby... now..."

"Well, he may very well have a differing plan, my dear, but we will not know until you settle down. This may be unpleasant and embarrassing, Elizabeth. I am sorry." He kept a steady stream of placating murmuring as he performed the intimate examination, Lizzy far too distraught to be embarrassed.

"Listen carefully, niece. At this point there is no internal indication that your baby wishes to be born." He laid his broad hands over her abdomen, palpating the intermittent muscle contractions. "The pains are not regular, which is a good thing. Mrs. Reynolds," he said, turning to the housekeeper standing nearby, "ask Mrs. Langton to brew a large pot of very strong tea, dregs included, of red raspberry leaf and chaste tree leaf. She has the herbs as I supplied them prophylactically. Elizabeth, focus on me, dear."

Lizzy was crying silently, enormous tears sliding down her cheeks, but she met his sympathetic blue eyes. "Listen, dear, very clearly to me. *If* your baby does decide now is the time for his birth, he is near enough to complete maturity that he will likely be healthy. He feels to be of a sufficient size." He pressed his long, firm fingers into her belly on both sides of the swell, palpating the shape hidden inside.

"You can ascertain his size?" Lizzy asked with surprise.

"It is not an exact science, but one develops a sense for these things over time. I am an excellent diagnostician, if I say so myself, and not half bad as an obstetrician." Lizzy could not prevent a tiny chuckle escaping, George smiling in return. "There, better, Elizabeth?" She nodded faintly. "Good. It is vital you remain calm. The tea I ordered may halt the contractions, but primarily you need to rest. My professional opinion is you have been given a fright and a warning. However, this could be a sign that you will not be waiting until December. Only time will reveal. In the meantime I am restricting you to your bed."

Lizzy was weeping again, Georgiana smoothing the hair from her brow as Mrs. Reynolds entered the room. "George," Lizzy whispered between soft sobs, "please, I cannot do this without William! I need him…"

"Shhhh… Be still. Say no more, Elizabeth, as I concur. Do not fear; I will send for him."

Dr. Darcy's summons, conveyed by one of Pemberley's own groomsmen on the fastest horse available after Parsifal, finally reached Darcy after first being delivered to Darcy House and then the offices of Mr. Daniels before discovering the addressee busily working up a vigorous sweat at Angelo's Fencing Academy. It was the only recreation Darcy had engaged in during the weeks in London and the only reason he had broken from his self-proscribed strict business agenda for this excursion was a raging need for physical exercise.

However, moments prior to the message's delivery he was beginning to seriously doubt the wisdom of his actions. The symptoms from his illness were essentially gone with the exception of a nagging cough and persistent muscle fatigue. He stood in the center of the floor facing his current adversary, Lord Miles Holt, whom he had prevailed over each time in the past, wheezing and six points behind! *So much for proving your potency and health, Darcy!* he thought with towering sarcasm and chagrin.

The interruption by the Academy's manager was abundantly welcomed by a frankly gasping Mr. Darcy, but followed by instant fresh sweat, this time of the cold variety, with the appearance of a Pemberley groom.

"Forgive me, gentlemen, for the disruption. Mr. Darcy, this man has a message for you." The groom nervously stepped forward, bowing as he handed the sealed parchment to his Master. Darcy removed his protective glasses with a slightly tremulous hand, murmuring his pardons as he exited the room.

William,

Forgive the abruptness of this letter, nephew. First, Elizabeth is well. However, today she began suffering with true birth pains. Even as I write this note the pains have lessened and the baby shows no overt signs of an imminent arrival; therefore, my medical opinion is that you will not be a father quite yet. Nonetheless, Elizabeth needs you. Tarry no longer, William. Do not be reckless, but come home.

George

Darcy's heart constricted painfully, lips pressing together in a tight line. Not hesitating for a second, nor allowing the fear to overwhelm him, he jumped into action. The hasty and rude orders barked at Pemberley were courteous compared to the rampage he went on once at Darcy House. The effect was as he demanded, though. Within an hour the Darcy carriage was clomping away from Grosvenor Square toward Derbyshire. He refused to halt until well after dark, resting at a cheap carriage inn for six hours. He was again on the road as dawn broke over the eastern horizon.

Weary with grey circles under his eyes, rumpled, unshaven, and jittery with anxiety, Darcy caught his first sight of the pinnacles atop Pemberley by early afternoon. Relief washed through him, tears stinging the eyes that automatically lifted to the southeast corner windows. Naturally from this distance he could see nothing of significance, the manor as beautiful and serene as always.

"Hold on, beloved. I am home."

꧁꧂

The relief to be at Pemberley was palpable, but only partially allayed Darcy's paralyzing anxiety. He sat in the stopped carriage waiting for the coachman to open the door rather than hurdling out as he anticipated doing for the simple reason that he was terrified at what he might find. The cold gust of air hitting his face when the door opened restored him and with a steadying inhale, he disembarked.

Apparently no one had witnessed his unexpected arrival, the footman Georges glancing up in surprise when Darcy walked into the foyer. He snapped to attention briskly, his greeting interrupted brusquely by his Master.

"Where is Mrs. Darcy?" His voice was firm, the fear at the answer well hidden.

"Mrs. Darcy is in your chambers, sir. Dr. Darcy and Miss Darcy are in the parlor."

"Thank you." He practically threw his overcoat at Georges with the stasis of dread vanishing in the liberation of his fears and the cavernous need to embrace his wife. Dignity be damned, he dashed up the grand staircase and turned left with long strides.

"Fitzwilliam!"

He pivoted at the sound of his uncle's voice. "Uncle! Elizabeth is in our chambers, yes?"

"I checked on her not fifteen minutes ago and she is sleeping now, William. Come into the parlor so we can talk."

Darcy stood in stunned alarm, trying to read his uncle's face. "Is she…?"

"She is fine, but she is asleep and she needs her sleep. Allow her to rest undisturbed, nephew, and have a drink with me."

"I am her husband and she needs me!" Darcy flashed angrily, face stormy.

George stepped closer, face sympathetic but determined. "What Elizabeth needs is a husband who is serene, stable, and informed. You are currently none of those things." He laid his hand comfortingly onto Darcy's forearm. "Come have a drink, William, just for the interim, and let your wife sleep."

Darcy glanced toward the far staircase, sighed, running a hand over a grey face as he nodded wearily. "Very well. Just tell me one thing first. Is she… is the baby…?" His voice broke, but there was no need to say more.

George smiled, placing an arm about Darcy's shoulders and propelling him toward the doorway. "Elizabeth is hugely pregnant and shows no signs of presenting you an heir in the immediate future."

Darcy sagged with relief, simultaneously sighing and coughing and laughing with an edge of hysteria. "Thank God!"

"Yes, indeed. Georgiana, look what the wind blew in."

Georgiana, of course, was dancing with impatience just inside the doorway and leapt at her brother instantly. "Brother! We missed you so very much! Welcome home. Oh, Lizzy will be so happy!"

Darcy clutched his sister tightly to his chest, desperately needing the love and warmth offered freely. George moved to the liquor cabinet, taking his time so the siblings could have their moment.

"Georgie! You have no idea how good it is to be home. How are you, my sweet?"

"I am well. You, however, do not look well at all. It is as Lizzy surmised." She broke the embrace, leading him by the hand to the sofa.

Darcy fell into the cushions with a heavy sigh, pulling Georgiana down beside him and under his arm. "What did my wife surmise?"

"That you would push too hard and not take care of yourself. Be prepared; she will scold you."

Darcy smiled. "I imagine I can tolerate her scolding quite happily. Thank you, Uncle." He took the offered whiskey, drinking deeply and ignoring his uncle's sharp gaze. "Are you examining me, Dr. Darcy, intending to inform me how terrible I look and rebuke me for not resting?"

"No point in stating the obvious. And I examined you out in the hallway. I was currently trying to decide which tonic would be best for your cough."

"I am certain whatever it is will taste horrible. Tell me about my wife and child." All jesting gone, he duplicated George's stare.

"Three afternoons ago now she began having contractions. They were not severe nor regular, which is, if you recall from the text and our discussions, the sign of true labor. Nonetheless, they persisted throughout the evening and were intense enough to warrant medical intervention. Upon examination I ascertained no indication of impending birth and her waters did not rupture. Georgie dear, if this is too graphic, perhaps you should depart temporarily."

"Thank you, I believe I will." She kissed her brother's cheek and exited, face flushed.

George chuckled, but Darcy leaned forward avidly. "Continue frankly."

"She has been a wonderful companion and comfort to Elizabeth, William. I have been quite proud of her maturity. Anyway, you understand of what I speak. As I told your wife, I was not overly concerned as the symptoms were tenuous; nonetheless, it cannot be taken lightly. I have her on a daily prescription of herbals that have some effect on inhibiting contractions. Additionally, I forced her to stay in bed until today."

He started laughing, eyes twinkling. "I checked on her this morning and the first words out of her mouth were, 'How long are you to keep me chained to this bed, Dr. Darcy? Until I atrophy and fuse into the sheets?' Well, that is always a sign of the patient improving. So I have allowed her to walk about the room, but no farther."

Darcy smiled faintly, but his eyes were troubled. "Are you sure she should be out of bed? I am quite familiar with my wife's temper and need for activity, but I do not want my child compromised. Nor would Elizabeth either, no matter her frustration."

"Here are the facts: If your baby is planning on arriving today or next month, there honestly is little we can do to stop it. The herbs and bed rest may aid temporarily, but are no guarantee. The detriments to lying in bed for the next four weeks, especially with a temperament such as Elizabeth's, would likely outweigh any benefits. Secondly, as I explained to her, the baby is near enough to complete maturity to conceivably be born healthy. He is a Darcy after all!"

His attempt to lighten the mood was disregarded, Darcy shaking his head. "Possibilities are not adequate. I will not gamble on my son's life. Whatever you deem the proper treatment, it will be done. If I have to tie Elizabeth to the bed I will!"

"Well, that would be a sight to behold. Yet I see no cause for such drastic measures. The truth is, William, your presence will be the best medicine. Promise me you will not chastise your wife because she does not need your severity but only your love and support. To a great degree her own nature is against her. She does not take leisure well, especially when driving herself to avoid sadness and to please you. Most importantly, she honestly is dependent on you for her serenity. You are a fortunate man, my boy."

Darcy smiled the first real smile since arriving, caressing and staring at his ring. "Yes, I am. It has been an hour now. Can I please wake her?" He spoke very softly, as a little boy pleading for permission, glancing to his uncle with beseeching eyes.

"Yes, you may." Darcy jumped up enthusiastically with a broad grin, but George stayed him with a hand. "One last thing, William. For reasons we physicians do not completely understand, sexual activity can induce labor. We should give it a few more days to be sure how she will respond to other physical exertions. I am sorry."

Darcy nodded, the grin in place. "No worries. I can control myself for the sake of my wife's health. Right now all I want is to see her face."

"Glad to hear it; however, it is not only you who must find control. Women can be persuasive and none, I judge, more so than Mrs. Darcy." He was smirking widely, Darcy actually flushing. Without another word, and to the sound of his uncle's laughter, Darcy left the room.

❧

He opened the bedchamber door gingerly, peeking through the crack. The bed was empty, but he did not require that evidence as Elizabeth was readily seen standing on the balcony. She wore his robe, the same one confiscated while separated from him in June; her back was to the door and her braided hair fell down her back. She stared south, watching vainly for sight of a carriage, hugging the robe tightly against the mild breeze. Darcy approached cautiously, not wishing to startle, utilizing the seconds to drink in every part of her.

To his continued amazement she still did not appear notably pregnant from the rear. Her daintily thin shoulders and narrow waist were nearly unaltered with only the faintest hint of widened hips and bulging belly visible from this angle. He knocked lightly on the open balcony door, speaking softly, "Elizabeth?"

She turned slowly, eyes widening in a delayed reaction when she realized it was not George Darcy. With a gasp and sob she cried his name, crossing the short distance as if flying weightless, and was into his arms. Pressing with steely hands on his back and face buried into the hard planes of his chest, she dissolved into tears.

Darcy embraced her with steady strength, hands caressing all about the trembling surfaces of her backside; his face embedded into her hair as he bestowed hundreds of kisses to her head. "Elizabeth, beautiful, dearest wife. Hush, love, I am home. I will not leave you. I love you, my heart. Please do not cry…"

On it went, Lizzy lost to salving tears. Darcy swept her into his arms, carrying to the sofa by the smoldering fire and sitting with her tightly clenched in his lap. Her face was nestled into his neck, fingers running through his hair as her weeping slowly subsided. He gave her the time she needed, hugging and stroking tenderly. Reaching gently to cup her jaw, he leaned back while pulling her head away, thumb caressing over her cheek, and met her eyes.

"Do not cry, beloved, please." He brushed over her lips lightly as the familiar jolt of pleasure rocked through his being. Her lips parted, insistently deepening the kiss. Darcy thought he could die of happiness right then. Embracing his wife, tasting her mouth and tongue, the intimacy of her womanly curves snuggled into his body, her tiny hands kneading and seeking, and the muted sounds of contentment escaping all conspired to overwhelm his senses.

The kiss broke, but their eyes remained closed with faces touching, cheeks fondling cheeks, noses grazing, foreheads in contact, and nuzzling kisses over all features while murmured endearments fell. Lizzy shivered at the blissful sensation of roughly whiskered cheeks and chin scraping the delicate flesh of her face, inhaled deeply of his woodsy scent, trembled afresh at the vibrantly adoring tones of his voice, and leeched the radiant heat always emanating from the sturdy muscles of his body.

Softly and huskily whispering into his ear between infinitesimal kisses, she said, "Dearest love, forgive me for forcing you away from your business, but I was so afraid. I should feel more ashamed of my selfishness and pathetic reliance, but I do not. I needed you here, and now I know precisely why." She withdrew a few inches to clearly view his beloved face, frowning instantly upon noting the lines of fatigue and marked pallor.

Darcy was attempting to wipe the drying tears with his handkerchief, his smile sunny. "I am at fault for ever leaving you, and if you are selfish or pathetic, then I am as well. We can be a matched pair of hopeless romantics."

Lizzy was barely listening, swiping at the handkerchief impatiently as she trailed fingertips over his face. "William, you look terrible. Are you still unwell?"

"I have been hearing this frequently lately. Very well, I shall confess to being tired beyond belief, consumed with worry, still a bit weak from my ordeal, and with a lingering cough. All of this will surely evaporate now that I can sleep in your arms, not to mention being dosed with some horrid concoction of Dr. Darcy's. Perhaps in a day or two I will again be the 'handsomest man of your acquaintance.'"

Lizzy chuckled lightly, still stroking over his face. "You are forever the handsomest man not only of my acquaintance but in the entire world, just a bit worse for wear at this current time. Now you are here for me to nurse you back to health."

"How odd. I was under the impression that I had come dashing home to care for you." He smiled, caressing over her abdomen. "Seriously, Elizabeth, how are you feeling?"

"No pains for the past two days. Well, other than the usual vague ones. He is active and apparently unperturbed by stressing his parents so profoundly." She swallowed, eyes moistening. "I was very frightened, William. Not so much by the pains themselves, but because you were not here. No one should see him before you. George says he would be fine if born now, but I do not want to take the chance."

"I concur. We will be cautious and do all he recommends. However, he did make one point we should bear in mind: if our son wishes to come, we cannot prevent it. I do not want his introduction to his parents to be anxiety filled. It *will* be a joyous welcoming, Elizabeth, replete with enthusiasm, hope, and love."

"This is why I need you here, my heart, to cheer me up and keep me focused."

Cosseted for the next two hours, they talked and kissed and nuzzled. The baby responded to his father's persuasion by rolling about and kicking. Lizzy, as Dr. Darcy intimated, was not pleased at the restriction in sexual activity, but she did not argue the logic. The yearning boiled under the surface, but as much as they desired each other, the desire for a healthy child was greater.

Lizzy was allowed to join the family for dinner, walking slowly on Darcy's arm. She felt not the least bit delicate or uncomfortable, frankly more concerned by the deepening circles under her husband's eyes, but he insisted she lean on him. It was tempting, but she did not tease him as to what she would do if he collapsed! George presented Darcy with a bottle of thick greenish fluid, which he did not ask the contents of, preferring not to know what bizarre extracts he was forced to imbibe. Whatever it was, his throat was instantly numbed, and the nagging tickle that kept him from attaining a deep sleep disappeared. Additionally, either there was some hidden ingredient that sedated or he was simply wholly depleted because he slept blissfully embracing his wife for twelve hours straight.

The days following Darcy's return passed in calm serenity. None of the four occupants wandered beyond the immediate garden pathways, and hardly even there as the weather was decidedly unpleasant. Lizzy experienced no further contractions of any notable intensity, devotedly drinking the foul-tasting tea four times a day as prescribed. She smothered her natural inclinations and irritation, resting frequently and walking short distances only. In all ways she was the perfectly obedient patient.

Darcy's cough diminished to a rare event of minor duration and strength. He was correct in judging that restful sleep and tranquility would restore his energy and health. The muscle aches and weakness faded rapidly, and the color returned to his cheeks as the duskiness vanished. His pleasure and frank relief at discovering all Pemberley affairs managed competently and completely in his absence was overwhelming. Mr. Keith only had a list of four items that needed to be discussed with the Master. Mr. Daniels sent a small packet containing the unfinished business, none of which were vital, allowing Darcy the time to attend it at his leisure. Slowly life was settling into the typical winter stasis with nothing of vast import looming, even the birth of their child an event to anticipate with nothing but excitement.

Darcy seemed to handle his uncle's interdiction to forsake making love to his wife with equanimity. If Lizzy noted a churning blaze in his eyes from time to time when he thought she was not looking, she said nothing. In truth, Lizzy discovered her sexual desire muted as the baby's weight pressed upon her body and increased her fatigue. At times the romantic feelings would surge, especially in the mornings when she was most rested and her husband traditionally his most amorous.

They slept together, as it was quite simply unthinkable to be apart, but Lizzy wore a gown and Darcy a nightshirt or breeches. The barrier of clothing did not prevent Darcy's desire to any great degree, but it was a tangible reminder for a fuzzy brain to be restrained. Feeling her husband's desire was stimulating to Lizzy as well although her craving was not as pressing. Nevertheless, neither was overly concerned about denied lovemaking as the infant's health was of prime concern. Dr. Darcy did not withdraw the ban, and they knew that each passing day allowed the baby to mature, possibly the difference between life and death. That idea was sobering and effectively squelched passion, even Darcy's.

The Bingleys arrived for a short sojourn to honor Darcy's thirtieth birthday. His wish to completely ignore the day was also ignored, but Lizzy had submitted to his request for a modest celebration. The plan was for nothing more than a private dinner party with a handful of their friends. The gentlemen had tentatively discussed a hunt if the weather permitted.

November the tenth dawned cold with a drizzling rain. No sun was forthcoming to wake the Darcys at the dawn so they slept late. Lizzy stirred first. As usual it was the call of a full bladder that invaded her restful slumber, care taken as she hastily but gently removed herself from Darcy's unconscious grip. He sighed sleepily, garbled something, and rolled to his back.

Lizzy returned from the water closet fully intending on pressing chilled feet against her spouse's shins as she returned to the land of dreams, but she halted at the sight greeting her. It was not at all unusual for her potent husband to wake in some degree of arousal, his morning amorousness generally greeted with delight and openness by an adoring, and fortunate, wife. Today was typical with Darcy asleep on his back, the evidence of his virility not hidden by the covers.

Remembering his first gift to her on the morning of her birthday in May, she smiled lasciviously and crawled under the blankets. Nestling close, she starting with moist kisses along his neck while reaching pointedly under his nightshirt.

Darcy jerked, instantly wide awake with thighs clenching and body rippling. "Elizabeth, what...? Wait, we cannot..."

"*We* cannot, my lover, but I can. Now lie back, relax, and enjoy."

Lizzy knew well the extreme gratification to be found in pleasing her husband. The long time without her did not afford him the greatest regulation, but enough to thoroughly enjoy all the wondrous thrills she bestowed upon his body. Lizzy's satisfaction in observing the man she loved so profoundly attaining satisfaction through her manipulation was excessive.

Seconds later, his body yet shuddering and skin ablaze, he pulled her into a sturdy embrace and captured her whole mouth in a penetrating kiss. The satiation achieved was immeasurable yet a mere fragment of the total desire he possessed for his wife. He pressed her harshly into his torso with hands caressing roughly in the need to show her his lingering hunger for her.

"Lizzy. Lord what you do to me!" He moved his hands to her face, panting roughly, and pressed his forehead against hers. For a very long while he held her in silence, his breathing and heartbeat gradually resuming regularity. When he spoke his voice was very deep and gravelly, "I was dreaming of you and I together under the trees. Thank you, my lover, for this morning. It was... you are... unbelievable. As satisfied as I am right now, my heart aches as I cannot return the gesture."

She halted his words with a long, teasing kiss. "Fitzwilliam, you are truly too wonderful and a bit of a fool. I am abundantly content to give you this gift. You give me so much, endlessly extending yourself in hundreds of ways to please me. I am blessed and exhilarated to have this opportunity to focus only on you. Happy birthday, William."

Darcy faced his birthday with a broad smile and spring in his step that was noticed by all, especially George Darcy, who in turn leapt to the wrong conclusion and kept a very close eye on Elizabeth. For her part, Lizzy was in a gay mood. She felt wonderful physically despite the consistent nags of advanced pregnancy, was emotionally joyous at the chance to honor her spouse on his special day, and spiritually thrilled by the peace she noted on his face. She was a bit smug about it, too!

The misty rain ceased by noon, the men folk jumping up instantly to take advantage of the break in weather for their hunt. Darcy, Bingley, and George were met by both Vernor men, Albert Hughes, and George Fitzherbert on the fringes of Pemberley's forest. The Sitwells would be arriving in the afternoon for the dinner party. Unfortunately the Drurys would not be able to attend as Chloe's pregnancy was far advanced and had not been an easy one. Georgiana spent the morning hours with her tutor, allotting Jane and Lizzy a block of time for sisterly companionship.

"Why did it have to rain?" Lizzy asked. She stood in her parlor staring out the window. "Now the walkways are slick and muddy." She sighed loudly, turning to join her sister on the settee.

Jane smiled. "I have never known you to be inhibited by the weather. Is Mr. Darcy's overprotectiveness wearing off on you?"

"Not completely; however, I must confess that in this instance he is wise. I am ashamed to admit it, but I have discovered a slight unsteadiness at times. All this weight on my poor hip bones, I suppose." She placed her hands on either side of her belly, smiling ruefully. "It is not worth the risk. Instead I wander up and down the halls where chairs are readily available." She shrugged.

"Considering the length of Pemberley's halls, it is likely more exercise than if you walked to the rock pond and back."

"Your tea, Mistress." Mrs. Reynolds entered with the pot of Dr. Darcy's prescribed brew, Lizzy wincing. "Drink it all this time, Mrs. Darcy. I will be checking. Mrs. Bingley, this is for you." She sat the pots down onto the table, bobbing a curtsy, and then departing after a pointed glance to her Mistress.

Jane began laughing the moment the door closed. "The fever of safeguarding appears to be contagious."

"I am carrying the Darcy heir after all."

"Pish! It is because she cares for you, Lizzy, any fool can see that. By the way, you speak of your weight, but do you remember Angela Harley? Poor dear was enormous. I seriously began to have doubts at the whole concept of matrimony and maternity watching her." Lizzy was laughing at the recollection. "You, dear sister, are yet svelte in comparison. I do hope I am as fortunate when the time arrives."

Jane's voice softened and she glanced away, Lizzy watching her with sudden speculation. "Jane, is there something you wish to reveal to me?"

Jane blushed brightly, staring into her lap. "I should say nothing yet, Lizzy, as we are not certain." She glanced up at Lizzy with a shy smile, continuing, "Oh Lizzy, I have been bursting to tell you! Charles and I may be expecting!"

Lizzy clasped her hands with joy. "Jane! How marvelous! I cannot believe that Mr. Bingley has managed to maintain his calm!"

"We only days ago began to suspect and cannot be certain. Please, Lizzy, say nothing, except to Mr. Darcy of course, but no other. I know you are not the superstitious type, but I do so want to present Charles a child and fear if we speak of it too forcefully it will prove false."

"Oh Jane, you are so silly! Nonetheless, I understand the necessity in waiting to be sure. I knew it would be lovely having you close. Now our children can grow together as playmates. Oh happy day!"

"Speaking of babies, have you heard from Charlotte?"

"Not for a month or so. In fact I was beginning to worry as I know she was due early this month. Her last letter assured me all was progressing normally. Mama's recent letter mentions nothing, so there must be no news to report or surely Mama would know!"

"Quite uncharitable of you, Lizzy, but I agree that it is true. Your tea is getting cold and you have yet to finish it. Tsk, tsk! Mrs. Reynolds may turn you over her knee. Here, have a scone. That may help the flavor."

⚜

"No, place it amid the curls just above her left ear. Excellent! Absolutely stunning. Once again, Marguerite, you have created a flawless masterpiece."

"Thank you, sir. With hair such as Mrs. Darcy possesses it is an easy task. I was assuming the amber necklace, madam? Does this meet with your approval?"

Lizzy shrugged. "Perhaps you should ask my personal fashion advisor."

Both Lizzy and Marguerite looked questioningly to Darcy's reflection in the vanity mirror. "By all means the amber necklace and earrings."

Marguerite disappeared into the closet, Lizzy gazing at her husband via the mirror. He stood in the doorway of her dressing room, dressed in a spectacular ensemble of dark gray pantaloons and jacket with waistcoat in silvery threaded purple, observing the final preparations of his wife with a happy smile on his lips. Lizzy wore the auburn gown from their renewal ceremony, her hair truly magnificent with a single clip of diamonds now nestled above her left ear.

Marguerite returned with the jewels, Darcy stepping forward to wordlessly take them from her. "I will finish here, Mrs. Oliver. Enjoy your evening with your husband."

Marguerite curtsied, with a faint rosiness highlighting her pale cheeks, and departed. Moving behind Lizzy, Darcy encircled her slender neck and clasped the necklace in place, fingertips brushing over her skin. He bent to bestow a tiny kiss to the nape of her neck, handing her the earrings and speaking roughly, "Earrings are beyond my expertise. Elizabeth, you are breathtaking. One of the best birthday presents in all my life, sans your bookmark, is the vision of you as you are now."

His hands rested lightly on her shoulders, Lizzy clipping the earrings on. "Thank you, my love. However, maybe this year's present will please you." She stood and took his hand, leading into the bedchamber. The wrapped gift sat on the sofa, Lizzy encouraging Darcy to sit and handing it to him. "Happy birthday, William."

"I will remind you that I requested no gifts."

"Surely you did not think I would obey such a ridiculous order? Be thankful I did not invite all of Derbyshire to pay homage. After all, it is a remarkably special day, your healthy birth the beginning of the pathway leading you to me. Now open."

He slowly untied the bow, pulling the wrapping away from the large, flat box. Lizzy was biting nervously on the corner of her lip, Darcy glancing at her with a soft smile. Inside under layers of tissue paper was a framed portrait. Darcy's breath caught and mouth fell open as with trembling fingers he removed the picture.

It was Lizzy dressed in one of his favorite gowns: a satin dress of navy blue with silver trim that beautifully accented her fuller bosom, capped sleeves off the shoulders exposing the creamy lusciousness of her flesh and swanlike neck. She wore his mother's pearl necklace and dainty drop earrings, thick chestnut tresses elaborately coiffed with tiny pearls woven into a strand of curls cascading over her right shoulder and wisps of hair brushing delicately along her temples. The artist had masterfully captured the vibrant sparkle of her eyes, faint twist of bubbling humor on her lush lips, and barely suppressed verve evident in the tilt of her head. The portrait was miniaturized, approximately twelve inches high and eight inches wide, but the realism was so astounding that the image verily leapt off the canvas.

"Elizabeth! It is unbelievable. When did you...? Who...?"

"I confess I deceived you, my love. Many of the afternoons you thought me shopping or visiting Harriet I was sitting for this. I think it good. Do you like it?"

"Good? It is stunning. You are stunning. I am at a loss for words! Thank you, Elizabeth!"

"I thought you could place it on your desk amid the clutter."

"It may distract me too greatly as the accuracy is remarkable. I will anticipate hearing your voice emerge from the frame. Besides, workmanship such as this deserves a place of honor."

"It is yours to do with as you wish. However, I did want it where you could view it frequently. Think of it as me watching over you." She reached to tenderly stroke his cheek, Darcy grasping her hand for a kiss to the palm while yet staring raptly at the painting.

"You know I require no tangible remembrances of you, but I will treasure this always. Yes, you are correct. I will place it on my desk, even clearing some of the mess to denote an esteemed locale. On the left corner, I think."

"You could remove that hideous statue of the bull."

"I like that statue! Oh, you are teasing me." He laughed, bending to kiss her pert lips tenderly and caressing her jaw. "Thank you, my dearest love. It is perfect. You never cease to amaze me. I love you, Elizabeth. May I share the painting with our guests?"

"As you wish."

Lizzy may have ignored his pleading for no gifts, but she did grant his wish for an intimate gathering. Aside from George and Georgiana, no other guests gave gifts. The focus was on fine dining and sedate entertainment. The Sitwells had traveled from their home near Chesterfield, residing at the Hughes's. In lieu of attending, the Drurys had sent best wishes for a joyous birthday.

All were in awe at Lizzy's miniature portrait, praising the artistry and sentiment. Darcy momentarily slipped away from his guests to reverently place it in his study, clearing a corner of the enormous desk with a smile as he imagined all the subsequent days spent at his labors with her beautiful face gazing upon him. He touched the gilded frame, chuckling happily as he freshly acknowledged the vast difference between this birthday and the last versus every other in his entire life. His mother and father, when he was young, had showered him with gifts, prepared his favorite dinner and dessert, and a handful of times in his youth held small parties with his closest friends. Then there were the grief-filled years after his mother died when celebrations of all sorts had practically ceased. His birthdays then were family affairs only with little in the way of gaiety. As he had told Lizzy last year, his adult birthdays had passed virtually with no recognition except for modest gifts from Mrs. Reynolds, Georgiana, and occasionally Richard.

Only once, when he turned two-and-twenty, was there a memory attached: Richard and Stephen Lathrop had conspired and surprised him at White's. The gents there had toasted to his birthday, his health, his prosperity, his future, on and on until the toasts declined to the realm of drinking a shot for his horse, his hair, his teeth, his boots, and so on. All he really remembered after that was waking up the next morning, shockingly actually in his bed at Darcy House, with the headache to beat all headaches. For the successive years he was blessedly content to forego any revelry.

This birthday was sedate, Lizzy certainly not physically able to tolerate an exaggerated affair and Darcy content to sip brandy while conversing and listening to his sister play and wife sing. All things taken into account, turning thirty was a blissful transition, Darcy glad to put the pain of his twenties behind and embrace the promised joy of his thirties and beyond.

CHAPTER SIXTEEN

November

T HE FOLLOWING WEEKS WERE quiet at Pemberley. The weather grew gradually colder with frequent sprinkling rains. The leaves continually fell from the deciduous trees, barren skeletons remaining dotted about the grounds. Little by little the autumn blooms faded and died, the colors about the house transmuting from vibrant to dingy. The excellent Pemberley groundsmen, under the tutelage of Mr. Clark, fabulously maintained the gardens and lawns, keeping all immaculate and as colorful as possible. Lizzy was actually quite amazed at how even the intermittent haziness could not totally subdue the picturesque landscape. Nonetheless, the gradual tapering toward the monochrome of winter occurred.

Dusk daily fell sooner, extending the evenings. What warmth was attained during the day was rapidly dispensed as the sun set, requiring the servants to light the lamps and draw the drapes earlier. Fires blazed nightly from all the inhabited rooms, allaying the cold that insisted on creeping through the thick stone walls and driving the chill into the hallways. Stored winter wear was pulled out and thoroughly cleaned. New boots and thick slippers were purchased as needed. Lighter weight pelisses and shawls were consistently utilized even during the remaining fair days.

There was the occasional day of milder climate when Lizzy and Darcy would take short walks about the grounds, but generally they remained secluded in the manor where it was warm and safe. Darcy's residual cough dissipated completely, leaving him as robust as prior. He resumed his typical activities with long rides on Parsifal leading the agenda, his uncle ofttimes accompanying. Work was minimal and easily finished, allotting him plenty of free time. He became fanatical about keeping the staff and his wife abreast of his whereabouts. Never did he wander farther than the immediate surrounds or into Lambton, and that rarely. Even his gallops followed a standard route so he could be swiftly found if necessary.

He observed Elizabeth's every breath, driving her insane at times, but it was a compulsion uncontrollable. For her part, she essentially felt quite well. Her back ached to some degree almost constantly; the mild, sporadic false labor pains escalated to a frequent phenomenon; her feet swelled slightly, enough to prefer loose shoes for comfort; and she was forever short of breath as the baby seemed to press farther and farther up into her lung cavity.

Mrs. Hanford moved into her newly renovated apartments on the far side of the nursery. Lizzy discovered the joy of sharing infant-related discussions with the kindly woman. The nanny was thrilled by the nursery, having never seen a baby's room decorated so elaborately, and delighted in all the delicately knitted and sewn garments and blankets. She humbly gifted Mrs. Darcy with numerous tiny articles that she had created over the past months, Lizzy happily adding them to the piles waiting in the drawers. Lizzy visited the baby's room several times each day for no other purpose than to touch the clothing and items sitting about. Darcy twice looked all over the manor for her, reaching a point verging on hysteria, only to discover her rocking placidly in the chair and stroking her belly.

Dr. Darcy insisted Lizzy drink the tea for three weeks, after which he figured the baby could safely be born if he so desired. George never asked outright if he could deliver the baby, simply assuming control of the situation. Neither of the Darcys gave it the slightest thought, frankly never having it cross their minds that he should probably have formally asked their permission or that they should have formally requested his services.

Mrs. Henderson, the midwife, was informed of Dr. Darcy's planned attendance, as well as Darcy's. Darcy and Lizzy fretted that she would feel slighted and outraged, and they did not wishing to insult the premier midwife of mid Derbyshire. But true to his prediction, the charm of George Darcy prevailed. He won her over with smooth flattery, swapping outrageous birth tales and medical expertise. It was agreed between the two that the physician would deliver the Darcys' baby with Mrs. Henderson assisting.

Lizzy was observed closely and regularly questioned on her current state of being. Only once more did Dr. Darcy examine her, about a week after the initial scare. It was only an external exam, his sensitive fingers carefully palpating over her bare abdomen. Darcy watched the procedure avidly. His diagnosis was that the baby was positioned correctly, of a sufficient size but not too large, and would likely soon lower himself into his mother's birth canal. Lizzy, especially, was thrilled about the latter as breathing was increasingly problematic. As the frightening symptoms of premature labor had not recurred, even with Lizzy resuming her usual activities, the physician's opinion was that all was safe.

Darcy presented the world with his typical calm demeanor, not even his wife fully aware of the rising anxiety as December approached. He read through the textbook entries addressing the birth process so many times that he had them memorized. As if magnetized he was drawn to the shelves in the library devoted to animal husbandry and medicine, vainly imagining that the one book with all the answers had miraculously materialized since the last time he looked. The fact that he planned on never leaving his wife's side once labor was initiated was not discussed in so many words, it, like Dr. Darcy's obstetrical service, simply a matter of course.

Roughly a week and a half after his birthday, Darcy and his uncle were mounted on their horses. The day was cool but clear, the soft fluffy white clouds scattered in the azure sky were stationary as the winds were nonexistent. It was an excellent day for racing and the two men had taken advantage of the respite. George, like any Darcy in recent generations, had been placed on a horse before he could walk steadily. Although his professional duties did not allot him the time to ride for pleasure, he managed to adequately maintain his aptitude. Therefore, the two greatly enjoyed these excursions when they could embark on friendly wagering as to who would reach a designated point quickest. It was all in good fun, Darcy the younger inevitably winning, but George's rusty equestrian skills were improving.

Today they crossed the northern bridge spanning the river, bypassed the Village, and headed due east across the moor in a flash of black and brown with coattails flying. The final destination, a clump of trees on a small rise, was reached essentially simultaneously with the good doctor ever so slightly in the lead.

"Ha! I finally beat you!" George declared breathlessly. "Good boy, Aristotle, very good boy." He rubbed his mount's sweaty neck, reaching into a pocket for an apple.

Darcy was grinning, face flushed from the cool air, the picture of health and happiness. Parsifal, on the other hand, appeared decidedly out of sorts, not at all pleased with being displaced by the upstart Aristotle. "Do not fear, old man," Darcy placated, stroking and administering treats. "You are still my favorite."

They dismounted, allowing the horses to wander a bit and graze. George pulled a cigar from his breast pocket, leaning against a tree to puff in contentment. Darcy absently picked up a branch fallen to the ground and peeled at the loose bark, his gaze fixed dazedly on Pemberley nestled across the valley. Silence reigned for a time, both men lost to individual thoughts. It was Darcy who broke the quiet.

"I was reading in the book yesterday," he began, no need to clarify which book he was referring to as these sorts of introductions were becoming common, "and it was talking about the final stages of the labor process and how irrational the woman becomes. Have you seen this often?"

"It is as I told you months ago, William. Labor is intense and very painful. Women often lose sight of rational thought toward the end. It is why having someone dear who can retain that calm is so vital. Are you sure you are up to the task?"

Darcy continued to peel the bark strips, tossing randomly as he thought, finally speaking very slowly. "I want to answer with an unequivocal 'yes,' but the truth is I do not know what to expect, either of Elizabeth or myself. I cannot well tolerate seeing her in pain. So, I vacillate between wondering if I will faint dead or dash away in fright, or be strong and the calming influence she needs. Normally I do not doubt my backbone, but it is all so different where my wife is concerned."

"Of course it is ultimately up to you, William, and none will think less of you if you opt to stay away as most husbands do. However, imagine it this way. You are in the sitting room or library or parlor, wherever, sipping brandy while your beloved wife is screaming and in intense distress. Pemberley is large with thick walls, but probably not thick enough. Even if you cannot hear her, your knowledge of the subject is too inclusive to not know what is transpiring. How would you tolerate that?"

Darcy shook his head, throwing the denuded branch away. "Not well."

"For what it is worth, nephew, I think you will be amazing. Additionally, there is no doubt in my mind that Elizabeth will want you there and will respond to your presence." He chuckled lowly. "You are becoming quite the trend setter, Mr. Darcy. Marrying for love not once but twice, wearing a wedding ring, sharing one chamber, and now attending your child's birth. Folks may write books about you!"

"Terrific. My life's goal."

George laughed in earnest, inhaling deeply of the cigar and releasing a satisfied sigh. "Ah! Nothing like the taste of fine tobacco. Comes from our former colonies, Virginia grown. Do not worry so, William. Elizabeth is very strong and all seems well with her and the baby. One can never be certain, but I do not foresee any major difficulties."

"Yes, she is very strong." Darcy spoke softly with a tender smile. "Nonetheless, I am very thankful that no further serious labor pains have reinitiated with her resumption of physical activity."

"Indeed. Including such activity of which I believe I recommended you two avoid."

Darcy spun around in shock, eyes wide. "We have not... that is I have not...! Uncle, I would never do anything that might harm my wife or child. Never! I am not a beast!" His face was stricken, blanched, and jaw slack, but eyes igniting with flickers of anger.

George, for one of the few times in his life, was mortally embarrassed and ashamed. "Fitzwilliam, forgive me! Of course you would never hurt Elizabeth. I should not have assumed anything."

"Why would you think this of me?"

"I do apologize, son. It is just that... well, if you must know, you and Elizabeth do not hide your physical attraction for each other very well." He paused, Darcy too confused and irritated to be discomfited by the intimate topic, but George abashed and reddening. He glanced away. "The poorly repressed desire notable when you returned from Town miraculously disappeared on your birthday and since. I... well, I concluded wrongly, obviously." His voice trailed away. It was an odd situation for the physician, normally being quite adept at holding blunt, personal conversations with patients. This was his nephew and niece, however.

Darcy flushed slightly, anger fading. "Yes, well," he cleared his throat roughly, "there are alternatives." His lips clamped shut, simply unable to continue. In no way could he verbalize the fact that his wonderfully giving wife gratified his physical yearnings. As blissful and relieving as it was to be loved in such manner by the woman he adored more than life, the activity was mixed with emotions of dismay as he could not fulfill her desire. Besides, nothing compared to making love to her in complete unity and his body ached to bond with her wholly.

He glanced at his uncle. George leaned against the tree trunk, cigar burning forgotten at his side as he stared downward. Assuming a neutral tone, Darcy spoke, "So, your professional opinion is that our child is healthy and could be born safely at any time?"

"Dates of confinement are not an exact science, William," George spoke in his most authoritative pitch, relieved to be on firm ground. "Based on the information provided as to Elizabeth's cycles, when you first suspected her pregnancy, and her current condition, the baby could be born anytime between now and early December. In fact, I think I will halt the tea as she hates it so." He chuckled, finally inhaling from the butt of his cigar. "Actually, I imagine we would all be thrilled to meet your firstborn as soon as he, or she, is willing to join the family."

Darcy laughed too. "I can confidently proclaim that Elizabeth is ready to *not* be pregnant."

George snuffed the cigar stub under his boot heel, not meeting his nephew's eyes. "At this point I would suggest embracing any activities that may elicit labor. I believe our mounts have rested. Race you back to the manor?" With identical grins they called to their horses.

Later that night Lizzy reclined on the sitting room sofa, propped comfortably on two plump pillows with her aching feet actively being massaged by her adoring husband. She read aloud while Darcy rubbed, squirming intermittently to ease the persistent strain on her lower back.

"Is your back paining you, my love?"

"*Your* son seems determined to kick me in the kidneys!"

Darcy laughed, patting her feet before he removed them off his lap. Falling to his knees aside the sofa, he scooted to her torso, placing his strong hands behind her back. He pressed hard, circular motions with firm fingertips over the lumbar regions next to her spine.

"Relax and close your eyes," he commanded gently, but she already had her head thrown back onto the pillow and was vocalizing sounds of satisfaction. He observed her with a happy smile, kneading steadily and leaning into her neck to bestow soft kisses. Nibbling to her earlobe, he murmured lowly, "Dr. Darcy and I had an interesting talk today about babies and delivery."

"Do I have you to thank for stopping the daily tea doses?"

"Partially, although he made that decision himself. His professional opinion, as he shared with you during dinner, is that our son could arrive at any time if he so desired. He even went so far as to suggest we pray for a speedy resolution to your discomfort and gave me ideas as to ways of hastening the initiation."

He withdrew from her neckline, meeting her eyes with a twinkle, one hand traveling from her back to breast with gentle caresses.

"Are you certain you understood?"

"Quite certain." He cupped one breast, holding tenderly as he continued, "Elizabeth, I love you so intensely and want to please you, and me as well I will admit. However, if you do not feel able or interested, all considered, I do understand. My only true desire is to show you my love for you in whatever manner, even if it is embracing you and nothing else."

Lizzy smiled, reaching up wordlessly to stroke his perfect face. She feathered over his forehead, brows, eyes, noble nose, to jaw and lips. Lightly grasping his chin with two fingers, she pulled him toward her until his lips were a scant breath away from hers.

"Fitzwilliam," she breathed, "love me."

He released a soft moan when she encompassed his mouth, searching and seeking possessively. How heavenly it is to love one's spouse wholeheartedly, body and soul, without encumbrances. Naturally accommodations were essential due to Lizzy's greatly expanded abdomen, but only in the final moments of their lovemaking. Before sleep claimed them, warm and blissfully satiated in their mammoth four-poster bed, they would love hard and with a joy of surrender.

Bare bodies nestled all night in the way it was meant to be, as far as they were concerned anyway. The reality that their child would arrive soon, whether as a result of this session of love or mere time, meant that the beautiful swell created by his presence would soon be gone. Darcy took advantage of the ability to caress freely in the days ahead, always enamored by the miracle of her stretched flesh as their baby moved. Their child would not be fazed by the vigorous activity of his parents, opting to stay cocooned and grow a bit more.

Lizzy's increasing girth, fatigue, and irritability were not always conducive to frequent periods of lovemaking, but they managed to satisfy each other frequently enough over the subsequent days for neither to feel ignored or ungratified. In many respects the prime joy was in the long cold nights when nude limbs were entwined with dainty bare back pressed into hard, naked, and very hot planes of a manly chest, fingers laced, and breath tickling shoulders as they talked quietly about diverse subjects and then slept deeply.

One such subject involved Darcy's uncle.

Georgiana's and Lizzy's sincere love for George had assuredly grown, and the thought of him leaving was increasingly a cause of distress. Yet neither could claim the intensity of emotion that Darcy now held for his uncle. Only Lizzy was privy to the innermost thoughts of her husband, and over numerous late night conversations as they snuggled he revealed the depth of his affection.

"I know it will not be precisely the same as when my father died," he said on one such night as they lay entwined, referring to George's probable departure once the baby was born. "After all, he will not be permanently gone. We can exchange correspondence of a far more familiar nature than we ever did before, and there will be the hope that he may return someday. I can prepare my heart in a way that I obviously never did with my father. Yet, on the other hand, I was still so young when he died. It was years before I fully grasped what I had lost and by then the pain was dulled and I had grown accustomed to his absence."

He paused, staring unseeing at the beamed ceiling and absently caressing Lizzy's arm, which rested over his chest. She observed his face in the flickering half-light and waited. "No, that is not the whole truth of it. It has only been *since* developing this relationship with George that I have come to fully grasp what I lost when Father died. It is not only that he reminds me of my father, because as akin as they are in many respects there are glaring differences. Nor is it that I desire a mentor or father figure in my life, although I do to a degree; but it is that I sense he needs me, needs all of us in fact." He turned to gaze upon his wife, fingering a lock of hair as he resumed in a husky tone. "For so long, when I allowed myself the luxury of dwelling nostalgically on Father, I always mused on what he meant to *me*. The benefits I would reap from his companionship, how wonderful it would be to watch our children with their grandfather, and so on. Always egocentric. I never looked at it from the perspective of what *he* lost by not knowing me, or you, or our children."

He kissed her forehead, nestling a cheek against her silky hair. "I know George misses his work and the many friends he has in India. He speaks fondly of Jharna's boys, who are grown men now, and expresses sadness at the distance now between them."

"Well, that would be expected, I suppose, as he helped raise them."

"Hmmm. He can be guarded at times with his emotions. Quick to blurt a quip when the subject grows sensitive, even with me. He sidesteps with a joke or broad gesture, but not always. Besides, he is too like me to camouflage completely. It is clear that it is the loss of loved ones that distresses him the most. The honest affection he feels for us has taken him aback, I believe, and he fears trusting it or giving in to it. I understand this as well as I experienced the same anxiety when I fell in love with you." He kissed her again before continuing.

"All his visits in the past have been no longer than a month and he was restless the entire time. He would be lax and nonchalant, but usually with a coiled energy that is not currently as evident. I am not quite sure what to make of it, but I hope it is because he is content and willing to stay for a while longer."

In truth, Darcy greatly prayed his uncle would stay forever. Not only did he now yearn for him to deliver their baby, but he also yearned for the camaraderie of the older man that unearthed long-buried memories and vacancies. His father had been mentally and emotionally absent from the time of Darcy's mother's death when Darcy was seventeen, and physically departed months after Darcy turned twenty-two. The empty years prevented the companionship and friendship Darcy knew would have evolved between he and his father if events had unfolded differently. As much as he cared for his Uncle Malcolm, there was a formality attached and, of course, Lord Matlock had two sons.

With George it was entirely different. George was so incredibly like James Darcy in personality that at times Darcy blinked and mentally shook his head at the sensations evoked. It was spooky. Yet deeply fulfilling.

"You should tell him how you feel," Lizzy gently encouraged. "Perhaps he needs to know how intensely you love him. He has been alone for most of his adult life, wandering without a family or home. And now Jharna is gone. Maybe he needs to know he is wanted and special."

"What you say is likely true, yet how does one say such a thing to another man? I am at a loss."

"You will know when the time is right. God will guide you in how best to express your love for him."

He pulled away, burrowing lower under the covers until at eye level with her. Smiling, caressing gently down her side and around to fondle the swollen expanse of belly, he continued in a familiar hoarse tone, "Such all-consuming, powerful emotions can be terrifying. Oh, but the bliss of potent love! Nothing compares and any eventual grief is tempered by the unsurpassed joy. George knows this, has experienced this, and merely needs to succumb to it happening again with us."

"Stop that!" she exclaimed with a giggle, swatting his fingers away from her protruding navel.

"But it is so cute and fun. Poking out and begging to be tickled." He nudged her hand away and resumed the play with a grin.

"Fitzwilliam Darcy, I am warning—" But he halted her with a kiss, fingers abandoning the springy flesh to roam lower. Discussions of complex relatives were forgotten for the time being.

Time seemed to drag. Nothing changed, aside from the weather, and every occupant of the Manor waited for early December when the new Darcy would make his, or her, appearance.

Lizzy tried to ignore the close scrutiny, but it frequently peeved her. She felt as if she were under a microscope. If she twitched or sighed or shifted suddenly, everyone in the room froze and glanced her way. They tried to hide the reaction and careful monitoring, but were largely unsuccessful. For the first time since marrying Darcy she breathed in relief when he left for some dangerous occupation in the stable yard. The footmen, once so amazingly talented at remaining invisible, were now conspicuously present at strategic locales like staircase landings. The maids strangely discovered filthy or tarnished furnishings in whatever room Lizzy happened to be occupying. Georgiana became a worse shadow than George, more of a conjoined twin in how closely she hovered.

The annoyance of it all, augmented considerably by how physically miserable she felt, escalated her foul temper. None were safe from her sharp tongue. Lizzy spent endless hours of the day in fervent prayer that her stubborn child, once so intent on arriving early, would again decide that December was far too long to wait. Frankly, the entire family was praying for the same and not only because they were anxious to meet the newest Darcy!

One night in late November, Darcy roused slightly to note his arms empty. He reached groggily, hands sliding over the faint indentation beside him. The awake portion of his brain fuzzily assumed she had risen to visit the water closet, a frequent incident, and drifted back to sleep. It was several hours later before he again rose from the clutches of comatose slumber to note the vacancy in his arms. An internal clock of some kind recognized that it had been far too long without her to be a mere trip for bladder relief.

Struggling against the tendrils of sleep attempting to ensnare him, Darcy shook his head and crawled across the expanse of cooled sheets to pull the curtains back. Peeking drowsy eyes through the crack, he scanned the room and finally noted Elizabeth sitting on the sofa before the fireplace, logs nothing but smoldering embers.

"Elizabeth?" he whispered, voice husky and barely audible. No answer was forthcoming; in fact, she did not move. Alarm bells began to toll in his fogged mind and with a jolt he was wide awake. He sat up further, impervious to the blast of cold hitting his unclothed torso, "Elizabeth," spoken much stronger.

No reply. Nothing. That was it! In a flash he was out of the bed and to her side, nakedness inconsequential. He knelt before her, hands on her knees, but she seemed unaware of his presence. She sat rigid, hands pressed flat on her thighs, eyes closed as she inhaled and exhaled with a steady rhythm. Her face was calm with a tiny crease between her flawless brows the only apparent indication of some sort of distress.

"Elizabeth! Speak to me!" He nearly screamed it, fingers digging into her knees. Elizabeth shook her head imperceptibly, continuing her deep breathing, and ignoring him. Just as he was about to shake her or run yelling from the room for assistance, she inhaled hugely, releasing the air with a rush.

Then she opened her eyes, staring directly into his troubled gaze a foot away. Her eyes sparkled happily, readily seen in the gloom, with faint hints of anxiety and pain evident. She reached up and ran her fingers through his hair, Darcy paralyzed with a host of emotions all warring for dominance and none prevailing.

"Are you prepared to be a father, Fitzwilliam? I do hope so as I am nearly certain today will be the day."

L IZZY CONTINUED TO RUFFLE through his thick hair, mussing it up even further as she smiled tenderly at the dazed expression on his face. He stared fixedly as the words rushed through his brain. A split second of panic was quickly stifled, Darcy instantly on the alert and fully in control.

He nodded once, bruising grip loosening from her knees. When he spoke, Lizzy was surprised at the command and calm in his tone. "I shall inform Uncle George. Wait here."

As if she planned on dashing off somewhere! Lizzy laughed, grasping his hand. "Dearest, put on your robe and slippers as you are shivering and turning blue. Then please stoke the fire. It is not yet dawn and by all accounts I will be at this for hours and hours, so there is no reason to wake the good doctor yet. Sit with me here, please? I want this time alone with you before all the craziness ensues."

He nodded again, face serious, but rose and did as she bid. The robe was a brilliant idea as he realized he was quite cold once the immediate terror passed. In minutes he had a fire blazing and retrieved a blanket to place around them. He nestled next to his wife, drawing her legs over his lap and covering with a second blanket, just as another contraction consumed her. Remembering to breathe regularly as George had shown her, she leaned into Darcy's inner shoulder and submitted to the necessary pain.

He hugged her closely, laying a palm onto her belly as his eyebrows shot upward at the extreme rigidity felt. He quickly learned that the muscles would relax imperceptibly seconds before the pain itself lessened. It was like a wave: starting high above her navel and traveling downward until the entire bulge was firm as a rock, the tapering occurring in like manner.

"It is logical, if you think on it," he said. "The muscles are attempting to push him out."

"Shame he does not readily comply," Lizzy responded with asperity. "If I was being shoved so forcefully, I would gladly leave the environment of hostility!"

Darcy laughed. "Well, there is more to it than that! Patience, my love, all will occur in its proper timing." To which declaration Lizzy gifted him with a snort of disgust and withering glare.

Unconsciously he assumed the pattern of rhythmic respirations Lizzy utilized to maintain her serenity, unaware he was doing so until she exhaled finally as the contraction ebbed. Her belly resumed its usual softness, the baby quiet. He kissed the top of her head, pulling her closer to his body.

"Is the pain so terrible?" His voice trembled somewhat, but not as greatly as expected.

"Not as of yet. It is tolerable although I am quite sure it will intensify as time marches on. Pity, otherwise it would be an easy process." She sighed, leaning her head back to see his face. "Can you believe we are going to see our son, William? I am so excited!"

He bent to kiss her lips, cupping her face gently. "I love you, Elizabeth, so utterly. You have made me the happiest of men. My wife, mother of my child." He again kissed her briefly and then placed her head against his shoulder. "When did your pains start?"

"I think I dreamt through the first few of them but woke around two. I lay in your embrace for a time, thinking them just the usual pains, but they seemed stronger, more focused. And they did not stop. After an hour I moved here. I did not want to wake you."

"You should have," he scolded lightly.

"To what purpose? Other than keeping me company and warm, there is naught for you to do. I reckoned you needed your sleep so as to be rested for later when I truly need you. Right now... wait." She gripped the fingers laced through hers on her shoulder, cadenced breathing initiated as another contraction began.

Therein started an arrangement that would continue until dawn was well past. They would speak softly of a myriad of topics designed to fill the five to eight minutes between each pain. Darcy held her in his arms, breathing as she did, softly caressing and kissing ceaselessly, murmuring words of encouragement, and never leaving except to add a log now and again. Lizzy dozed on occasion during the pause, supported by her husband's firm chest, and snuggly warm under the blanket and with fire roaring. If it were not for the unrelenting pains, it would have been a delightful, almost romantic interlude.

The sun rose gradually, faint twinges through the thick winter curtains signifying the start of a new day. "A day we will remember with clarity for the rest of our lives," Darcy whispered into her hair, Lizzy chuckling.

"I suppose there will be moments I will wish to forget but likely shall not." She paused, glancing at him with a serious expression. "William, promise me you will keep me awake and focused no matter what I say. I want to see our son the second he is born and remember the wonder of it. Promise?"

"I promise."

By seven o'clock Lizzy's methodically occurring contractions continued every several minutes without fail but had not increased in power. She sighed as the latest contraction waned, shifting on the pillow behind her aching back. Darcy smoothed the hair from her face, observing closely for any overt signs of distress. Lizzy smiled, eyes closing as she drew his fingers to her lips.

"Perhaps it is time to inform the household of what is transpiring. Jane needs to be sent for and Mrs. Reynolds will be seriously vexed if not involved from the outset."

Darcy frowned. "Do you feel it imminent, love?"

"Unfortunately, no. However, I do want to hear what my physician thinks. And I am thirsty." Darcy rose, settling her as comfortably as possible on the sofa, and crossed to his dressing room where he knew Samuel would be busily preparing his clothing and bath for the day.

"Samuel, please ask the nearest footman to inform Dr. Darcy that Mrs. Darcy is having the baby. It is not emergent, but we request his company once he is dressed. Then can you inform Mrs. Reynolds? I will need her here as soon as possible. Thank you." Samuel left the room with a brisk nod, Darcy standing in the middle for a minute. He took several deep breaths, allowing a wash of tremors to cascade through his veins. He closed his eyes, sending a prayer for strength heavenward. *One second at a time, Darcy,* he commanded himself, *be strong for her and do not let her sense your anxiety!*

Entering the room some ten minutes later, Darcy was again in charge of his emotions. Lizzy was reclining as he left her and immediately he noted that she was experiencing another pain, the furrows between her brows present and lips pursed as she concentrated on breathing. He knelt beside the sofa, taking her hand for tender stroking. She released the cleansing exhalation, squeezing his hand and smiling weakly. "I am so thirsty."

"Mrs. Reynolds should be here any... See, any minute." He stood to answer the knock at the door, greeting Mrs. Reynolds with a giddy smile. "Mrs. Reynolds, my wife seems determined to present me with our child today. Has Dr. Darcy been sent for? Excellent. First, will you notify Mr. Thurber to send one of the grooms to Hasberry for the Bingleys? I will pen a note to deliver. Secondly, ask the kitchen for a tray and tea, perhaps some juice as well. Let me think... what else?"

"Shall I inform Miss Darcy?"

"If she is awake, yes please. She can keep Mrs. Darcy company as soon as she wishes to. Whatever else you deem sensible; I trust your judgment at this juncture superior to mine. Oh, coffee, please."

She curtsied and left, passing George Darcy in the sitting room. He approached with casual strides, tea cup in one hand and muffin in the other, dressed in a flowing garment of canary yellow with green edging.

"I was informed that babies are birthing hereabouts? Elizabeth! You are still pregnant!" He stopped abruptly on the threshold, feigning shock.

"Yes, Uncle, we thought we would wait for you. Now that you have arrived, perhaps you can work your magic and speed the process along?"

"Alas, my dear niece, magic does not reside in these hands. Only staggering expertise and superior knowledge. William, you do intend on dressing and shaving? Your baby's eyesight will suffer if greeted by such a frightful vision."

"And your brash appearance is benign?" Elizabeth interjected.

"Babies love bright colors. Stimulates the retina." He had crossed to the fireside chair positioned across from Lizzy, sitting and extending long legs nonchalantly as he bit into the muffin. "So," he resumed while chewing, "tell me how we are faring, dear."

Lizzy launched into a briefly detailed synopsis of her contraction history while Darcy stood nearby, not sure whether he was calmed or irritated by his uncle's blasé attitude. Luckily he had no time to figure it out as another pain began, Darcy swiftly kneeling at his wife's side to assist and comfort. George ate in silence while Darcy stroked Lizzy's forehead and murmured soft encouragement until the pain passed, leaning for a brushing kiss.

He sat back on his heels, yet holding Lizzy's hand, and turned to his placidly masticating uncle. "What is the plan, Dr. Darcy? What is your professional opinion?"

"Elizabeth, I fear you are yet in the early stages of labor. I could examine you, but it is not necessary. Trust me when I tell you that you will know when the labor is causing changes and nearing completion. The truth is, as we have spoken previously, the birth course will be set by the baby and internal forces. However, there are some actions that may affect the outcome."

He sat up briskly, suddenly alert and businesslike. "Here is the plan. William, you will freshen up and dress, then go have a full breakfast..."

"You were serious about that?"

"Absolutely. Well, not about the baby's eyesight part, but you do need to take a few minutes for yourself."

"I am not leaving my wife!"

"Dearest, I think your uncle is right about this. No, listen. I will need you more later, and you need to be fresh and energized. Food is essential for you as you get grumpy when hungry." She smiled tenderly, caressing the hand clasped in hers. "And only I am allowed to become grumpy today."

"I will not leave her, William, and Mrs. Reynolds should return momentarily. We will call you if needed, but trust me in that nothing will change in the following hour, sorry, Elizabeth."

"Write to Jane and Charles, beloved, and take care of yourself. I will be fine." She halted as another pain enveloped her. Darcy assumed his role as comforter.

George rose to answer the knock on the sitting room door, revealing a tray-encumbered Mrs. Reynolds trailed by three equally laden maids. "Well, well!" He declared with a broad grin and snatched a blackberry tart, biting hugely. "Mmmmm... Oh my, this is heavenly." He sighed, eyes closed in ecstasy. "Mrs. Langton is a gift from God."

"I believe these were for Mr. and Mrs. Darcy, Dr. Darcy," Mrs. Reynolds said with a smile, "but by all means, help yourself."

"Thank you, madam. Actually, the father-to-be is ordered to break his fast with his sister, and none of these delicious edibles are appropriate for

Mrs. Darcy. She is restricted to liquids and perhaps fruits, if she can tolerate. Anything heavy will induce nausea." He turned to one of the maids. "Miss, we will require a steady influx of hot, sweet tea and juices." He continued his orders for the kitchen then enlightened the housekeeper on the current status of her Mistress.

Meanwhile, Lizzy's latest contraction ebbed with her husband by her side. He gazed intently at her face, smoothing over her brow as they simultaneously released the final breath. Lizzy chuckled lowly. "I appreciate the empathetic reactions, but you do not need to breathe with me each time. I fear you may faint!"

He shook his head, serious and troubled. "It is unconscious, for the most part, but I find it helps." He traced fingertips over her features, pausing on her lips, "Elizabeth, I am so proud of you already. You are so brave and in control whereas I am near to collapsing in a heap. I abhor seeing you in pain, even for the cause of bringing our child into the world. I feel helpless."

She pulled his head onto her breast, caressing through his hair and kissing his wrinkled forehead. "You are my rock, Fitzwilliam. I could not manage this without you. In fact, this morning, when my pains began, it was all I could do to not wake you! I love you and need you by my side. I was so selfishly happy when you woke up."

"Which is why I cannot leave you now," he stated firmly.

"Yet you will, because I will insist. Shhhh…" She pressed two fingers onto his parted lips, Darcy having lifted from her chest with a ready protest. "You will do this for me, to ease my mind. Write to Jane, bathe, eat, allow Georgiana to calm you, and return to me renewed. Then you can help me walk a bit. I am feeling cramped and edgy. The last few pains have hurt a bit more, but primarily I am thirsty and need to stretch."

Darcy assisted her rising, lending both arms to aid her waddling gait into the sitting room.

"Mrs. Darcy, I brought cold juice as well as hot tea. There is food if you feel able, although Dr. Darcy suggests consuming cautiously to stave off nausea." Mrs. Reynolds prattled on as she fluffed several pillows on the chaise, Darcy assisting his wife to sit comfortably while George poured a tall glass of juice.

Lizzy drank the entire glass in practically one swallow. Mrs. Reynolds busied herself preparing a cup of tea and small plate of sliced fruit, Darcy suddenly acutely aware of his attire. The housekeeper had certainly seen her Master in casual garb on numerous occasions, but the addition of another body into the room made him keenly aware of the number of people that would be shuffling through before the day was over. The idea of wearing full formal dress was unappealing, but staying clothed in merely a robe was untenable. On top of that revelation was the hollow emptiness in his stomach starkly awoken by the array of food on the table. All at once the thought of coffee was an immeasurable craving.

He glanced back at Lizzy, who was observing him with a tiny smile. "Go eat, but kiss me first."

He bent obediently and complied, softly and with reverence, brushing knuckles over her cheeks as he tasted the apples on her lips and tongue. "I love you, Mrs. Darcy, with all my soul. I will return quickly."

The respite was beneficial for both of them. Darcy wrote the note for the Bingleys, sending a groom to Hasberry posthaste. His plan was to then wash quickly, but Samuel had a bath drawn and the sight was far too inviting to resist. He bathed thoroughly, unable to avoid closing his eyes for a spell and allowing the soothing water to ease his tension. Not for long, however; the desire for coffee and food was almost as strong as the desire to return to his wife. Samuel, wisely and surprisingly, had chosen his Master's most comfortable clothes: breeches of soft wool, thin hose and house shoes, lightweight linen shirt, thin waistcoat, and summer jacket. All were quite inappropriate for this time of year yet somehow even the inexperienced valet knew his Master would be sweating before the day was over. A cravat was not offered nor would have been worn.

Resisting the urge to check on Lizzy one last time before descending, Darcy entered the dining room just as Georgiana was dishing up her breakfast. She glanced up with a smile, then eyes widened at the sight of her brother rather than her uncle as suspected.

"William! What are you doing here? It is not Sunday. And where is Elizabeth?"

"At the moment she is being attended by our Uncle George. She is going to have our baby today, Georgie!" All pretense at placid indifference vanished, Georgiana nearly dropping her plate in surprise. Darcy was grinning broadly, all the pent-up anxiety momentarily displaced by giddy happiness at his pending fatherhood.

"Oh William, truly? How marvelous! Is Elizabeth well?"

"So far, yes. It is early yet and I need to eat quickly to return to her side. This coffee smells divine! You know, my wife and our uncle forced me from the room. I was ill pleased at the notion, but now that I am here I comprehend the veracity. I am starving."

They sat together at one lonely end of the vast table, Darcy attacking his food with relish after a mouth-scorching gulp of coffee.

"Be cautious, Fitzwilliam, or you will choke yourself!" Georgiana scolded with a laugh.

"You sound just like Mother. I think she despaired of ever teaching me proper table manners."

"Well, if your son grows as rapidly as you did, I can imagine Lizzy suffering the identical despair. Father said you grew an inch each day."

"Not quite accurate, but close. Pass the salt shaker please. I must hurry, however, as I do not wish to miss anything of import."

"What is the typical scenario?" Darcy glanced at his sister sharply. "Yes, I know I avoided all birth-related conversations, but now I regret it. My sister is enduring a life-altering travail and I do not know what is to occur. Quite remiss of me." She spoke the last with a tone of guilt, looking down at her plate.

Darcy patted her hand, swallowing before he responded. "Do not fret so, my sweet. Elizabeth would not wish it. All you need know is that the pains will increase exponentially as the baby nears his arrival. I have been versed on the procedure a dozen times and have seen more animals birth than I can recollect, yet I am still unsure of precisely what to expect. You can visit with her if you wish. I know she would appreciate it, but understand that she will be interrupting conversation for frequent pains."

"How frequent?" she asked, face pale and eyes round in awe.

"They are occurring every five minutes or so now, but will grow closer."

"Oh my! How exhausting that must be. Are you sure she would care to see me?"

"Of course! Jane will be here soon, so you should spend some time with her before."

"How long will it all take?"

"No way to be sure. Uncle says first births can take up to a day and a half." Georgiana gasped, hand instinctively moving to cover her mouth. "Exactly. Let us pray to God that is not the case here. I honestly do not think I could tolerate seeing my wife in pain for that long."

"You can tolerate anything, William." Georgiana stated decisively. "You are the strongest man alive."

Darcy laughed loudly, tears springing to his eyes in mirth. "Your faith touches me, dear sister. Now I have a double challenge to live up to!"

Georgiana waited outside the Darcys' sitting room while her brother entered to see how his wife fared. Lizzy stood by the window, a bit hunched over and leaning into the wall with one hand tightly gripping the curtain. George sat nearby, watching her closely as he rattled on about a camel race across the desert, Lizzy clearly not listening attentively. Darcy crossed swiftly, encircling her waist as the contraction eased, Lizzy gratefully falling against the sturdy warmth of his chest.

He kissed her brow murmuring unnecessarily, "I am back, beloved. Georgie is outside if you feel up to visiting."

"Yes, that would be lovely. Help me sit first. I have stood long enough. How was your breakfast? Did you eat enough?"

"I am perfect. Just missing you. Uncle, any changes?"

"The contractions are steady. I have ordered Marguerite to prepare a bath as the warm water is relaxing to stressed muscles and often helps speed things along. If nothing else it is good for the psyche to be clean and refreshed, eh, William?"

"Very well, Uncle, you were right and I was wrong. Happy now?"

"Blissfully!" He grinned, rising and stretching with joints cracking. He left for a moment to speak with Georgiana, Darcy arranging Lizzy carefully on the chaise with a blanket over her legs.

"Did you eat something as well? You need to keep up your strength."

"A few bites of fruit in addition to the juice and two cups of raspberry tea. My doctor insisted, although now I feel a wee bit bloated. He definitely is correct about eating anything else. The very thought makes me ill. I do wish our son would hurry along. Perhaps his hesitancy to show himself is a sign that he possesses your reserved nature."

Darcy chuckled, kissing her lightly on the lips. "As long as he possesses some of your spunk and humor I shall be content."

Lizzy's fair disposition remained throughout the morning as she visited with Georgiana. The pains were unrelenting at nearly perfect five-minute intervals, allowing just enough time to rest and catch her breath and converse lightly. Occasional contractions were stronger, leaving Lizzy winded and with a hint of what was yet to come. Each time such a pain occurred she was torn between fear at the inevitability of what birthing her child would fully entail and hopeful excitement that finally the prodromal labor was at an end. The necessary but lengthy buildup as her womb gradually prepared to evict the baby was wearing, especially since Lizzy's natural disposition was not inclined for patience.

A prolonged soak in a hot tub with wonderful husband soaping and kneading aching back muscles was heavenly. Lizzy did feel revitalized and although the contractions persevered, the soothing water and massaging aided overall aches and pains.

George hovered nearby throughout, reading and eating the steady flow of victuals provided by the anxious kitchen staff. Mrs. Henderson was notified and arrived to assist Mrs. Hanford in preparing the nursery and Lizzy's heretofore unused chambers for the birth. Stacks of blankets and towels were brought in; the fire was laid and kept raging with several linens positioned alongside to readily wrap around a newborn babe; water was boiled by the pot full with buckets within reach for a hasty carry to the top floor; rags were freshly ripped for cleaning and binding; Dr. Darcy's instruments were carefully arranged on a small linen-draped table and covered while they waited; medications and herbal teas were mixed to be consumed as deemed necessary by the medical professionals; and the bed was warmed and protected from the mess to come.

Dr. Darcy's first extensive exam transpired after Lizzy's bath, her labor steady for roughly eleven hours. Darcy guided her to the smaller bed in the newly decorated bedchamber, settling her comfortably on the cozily warmed sheets, and nestling beside with her hands tightly clasped in his. His jacket had been discarded in Lizzy's bathing area, shirt sleeves rolled up past the elbows, and scattered damp patches drying rapidly in the heated atmosphere. The knowledge he possessed and experience gleaned from animal births lent a fair idea of what the internal exam of his wife involved; the mixture of anticipation at what the findings may be and embarrassment with the thought of observing such an intimate procedure warred for mastery in his gut, leaving him tense and lightheaded.

George was at his most professional, all jesting aside as he calmly spoke in his soothingly resonant voice, masterfully easing the tension in both patient and father-to-be. The exam was gentle and speedy.

"Good news. You are about halfway opened, my dear, and your womb is responding to the contractions as it should."

"How much longer, Uncle?" Darcy asked.

"It is still impossible to guess with any certainty. First babies can be quite stubborn."

"Is he tolerating the stress well? I have not felt him move in a dreadfully long time."

George smiled, running one hand over her abdomen. "Babies do not move during the labor process, my dear, so do not fret. All seems to be well, as far as I can determine." None of them voiced the obvious fact that there was absolutely no method of establishing what was transpiring internally. "Here is my suggestion. I can attempt to rupture your water sac, Elizabeth, but I would rather nature rule. Walking often helps. William, Pemberley's halls afford the perfect setting for your wife to receive some exercise as long as she can bear it. Niece, do not overextend and allow William to be your support, but stroll as vigorously as you can manage."

Mrs. Reynolds approached as Darcy led his wife out into the hallway, announcing that the Bingleys had arrived. Jane joined the slowly lumbering duo as they ended their first circuit of the square third-floor corridor. They stood at the southwest corner, breath in synchrony as the latest contraction built, Lizzy releasing soft moans of pain into Darcy's shoulder. His mien was composed, but very pale with flickers of anguish in his light blue eyes notable even to Jane who could not yet adequately read her inscrutable brother-in-law's face. He saw her over Elizabeth's head, gesturing with one finger.

Jane drew near, laying her hand lightly on Lizzy's arm. "Jane! I am so glad you have arrived. I was beginning to worry."

"A portion of the road was rutted horribly from the recent rains, requiring us to drive slowly. I feared I would be too late. How are you faring, Lizzy?"

They resumed their casual stroll as Lizzy, with interjections from Darcy, filled Jane in on the day's events. By the completion of the third journey Lizzy was weary, Darcy insisting she return to the room, but Lizzy stubbornly refused, compromising by resting on a corridor settee located near the stairs. She leaned into Jane's side, Darcy kneeling before her knees as another strong contraction overwhelmed.

"Where is Bingley?" Darcy asked Jane softly.

"I left him in the parlor with Georgiana. I met Dr. Darcy on the stairs heading that direction."

It took a fair amount of persuading, but Darcy finally agreed to leave the sisters alone while he enjoyed a needed respite with Bingley and George. Lizzy and Jane sat in silence as a pain completed its cycle, cleansing breath and shuddering muscles signifying the end. Lizzy sighed, leaning her head back onto the wall. "Is it so horrible, Lizzy?"

"It is not particularly enjoyable! I so want to hold my baby, Jane. It is all I can think of and that somehow helps to persevere through the pain. Mostly I am just tired. I have been awake since early morning and the pain erodes my strength. I do not know what I would do without William."

They spoke quietly, Jane lending her brand of serene support to the interminable travail. They spoke of inconsequential matters for the most part, the random converse perfect in distracting Lizzy's mind from the pain and fear of what was yet to come. Learning that her beloved older sister's expected pregnancy was now confirmed was a wonderful piece of joyous news. Even a particularly strong contraction did not dampen Lizzy's jubilant response. The idea of their firstborns being so close in age and physically near each other as they grew was cause for intense delight.

"Heavens, my back aches! I swear he is pinching every nerve in my lower spine." Lizzy arched, hands rubbing the spasms to her lower back, squirming as another contraction struck. "Oooh! This one is… harder and…"

"Breathe, Lizzy. Squeeze my hand and breathe." Jane grasped her sister's hand, gradual control attained and held for a minute as she concentrated on steady respirations, only to be lost abruptly as a gush of warm fluid flooded from between her legs.

Lizzy jerked in surprise, a sharp pain radiating from low in her abdomen. She gasped and released a small squeal, hands instinctively clutching her belly as she shouted, "William!"

Barely a heartbeat later Darcy was bounding crazily up the stairs, Dr. Darcy on his heels, both men instantly assessing the situation without pausing a step. Lizzy was lifted into her husband's arms, long purposeful strides carrying her to the bedchamber. His mien was grim: eyes tight with fear, jaw clenched, and lips pressed harshly together. Lizzy was panting and whimpering slightly at the pain gripping her belly, arms cinched over Darcy's shoulders.

George sprinted ahead, gesturing sharply at Mrs. Henderson and Mrs. Hanford. "The birth sac has ruptured," he declared smartly. "A warm towel, Mrs. Henderson. Mrs. Hanford, ask Marguerite for a clean gown for Mrs. Darcy. William, lay her on the bed. Elizabeth dear, try to relax and breathe. The pains will intensify now; it is normal to do so. Thank you, Mrs. Henderson." He took the towel and gently wiped her legs as he slowly lifted the saturated gown, continuing his calmly vocalized explanations. "Rest on your husband, Elizabeth, close your eyes and breathe as he is. This is to be expected and a positive development. It means your baby is nearing his arrival. Very good, dear. It is ebbing, yes? Excellent."

He pressed one hand onto her softening abdomen, the other unhurriedly toweling up her inner thighs while casually nudging her legs apart. "Allow me to ascertain what changes have occurred, if any. There's a good girl, lean on William and take your ease." He scrutinized and palpated carefully, assuring nothing had exuded other than clear water.

The pain had disappeared, leaving Lizzy trembling from the surprise. Now that it was over she felt rather foolish for losing control and yelling. She could readily sense Darcy's tension in the rigid muscles of his chest and arms as they surrounded her, and the raspy respirations echoing in her ear. Additionally she could feel the cooling wetness soaked into his vest and shirt from where he had held her. She peered up into his strained face, Darcy's eyes riveted on his uncle, reaching fingers to a pinched cheek.

"William," she whispered. "Forgive me for frightening you. I should not have shouted."

"Do not say that!" he snapped. "I want you to call when you need me! If you did not, I would be seriously vexed." He kissed the top of her head rather perfunctorily, attention again centered on his uncle as he asked tautly, "Is all well, Uncle?"

"You have opened a bit more, Elizabeth, and the baby is lower. The contractions will come quicker now and be stronger. You will need to stay in bed, but can move about however you wish, lying to the right side often the most comfortable. William, erase your frown before it permanently creases your face and assist your wife into a dry gown." George rose, crossing to the midwife and nanny for a quiet conference.

"Here, Lizzy, lift up and we will remove this wet gown," Jane spoke softly, voice as serene as always cutting through Darcy's coursing panic. He inhaled deeply, eyes closing briefly for a silent prayer before aiding Jane in dressing his wife. In seconds they had Lizzy settled comfortably, propped on several pillows and Darcy's torso, Jane departing to speak with Mrs. Reynolds regarding a fresh juice order.

"Beloved, you should change into dry clothing," Lizzy murmured. Another pain, far more intense than anything previous, had faded. She trembled slightly, faint and incredibly tired as she melted into Darcy's stalwart embrace, fingers laced with his and lying on the top of her swollen abdomen.

"It is insignificant. I will not leave you again, so do not ask." His grip tightened and he pressed his cheek into her hair. "I love you, my dearest wife. Are you certain you are comfortable?"

"As much as is possible," she laughed faintly, closing her eyes in an attempt to doze even if only for a second. "Comfortable" in any definition of the word became impossible as the subsequent hours unfolded. The contractions lengthened in both duration and intensity coupled with an increased frequency, which meant less time for her to recover in between. Those precious minutes were hastily consumed with ragged breathing and searing back pain. Somewhere in the midst she was incessantly plied with sips of water and cubes of sugar to keep up her strength.

Through it all Jane maintained her post to Lizzy's right side. Her placid strength, tranquil tone of speech, and gentle persuasion calmed Lizzy greatly. Since childhood Jane had been the steadying, rational voice amid Lizzy's ofttimes chaotic, impetuous nature. So it was now as Jane stroked her hand and forehead, murmuring pacifying sentences, relating memories of peaceful moments and places from their youth all designed to distract and soothe. It was successful to varying degrees as the afternoon waned into early evening.

Darcy kept his vigil to his wife's left side. Where Jane was the temperate tranquilizer, Darcy was the stabilizing stone. At times it was purely physical: his sturdy physique and capable hands essential for support and penetrating kneading to aching or cramping muscles. Other times it was his manly voice with resonant tones as he spoke of his love and pride, his soft lips brushing over her temples and knuckles, his fiercely kind eyes as he gazed with bottomless wells of adoration and encouragement. He seemed to instinctively know what she required at any given moment. If it was tenderness, then his voice and touch softened, stroking soothingly. If it was focus, then his voice deepened into the familiar ring of the Master of Pemberley, commanding her to concentrate and breathe.

"I cannot do it! Please make it stop!" Lizzy gripped his hand during one such incident, the spasms burning through the middle of her body in a fury. Her eyes were tightly shut, sweat beading on her brow, and head tossing to and fro while she whimpered.

Darcy grasped her cheeks in hands of iron, face inches from hers, voice low and resolute, "Elizabeth, look at me! You *can* do this and you *will!* Now, focus on me and breathe. Inhale deep, that is it, now exhale, good, and again. No!

Open your eyes! Focus on me! It will pass. Breathe again and one more is gone, all the nearer to seeing our son. Excellent! I am so proud of you, Elizabeth." And the litany would continue with kisses and caresses until the next pain.

None in the room sensed the internal struggle Darcy endured. A juvenile but persistent part of his soul wanted to scream in frustration, to rage against the impotence of a situation where the generally authoritative man of power was at the mercy of forces beyond his control. A small but very loud voice inside his head yelled at him to run, far away to some distant corner of the mansion where he could curl up into a fetal ball and hide from witnessing the agony suffered by the woman he loved more than life. Yet with typical, well-honed Darcy steel and discipline, he squelched those inner urges, recognizing them as childish and demeaning. Primarily he understood that despite his dismay at watching Elizabeth in her travail, there was in truth nowhere on earth he would rather be. As awful as it was at times, he knew he was providing a necessary service to his wife and partaking in a miracle. Always central in his mind's eye was the image of their baby, conceived in tremendous love, who would make his, or her, appearance to the world in due course. The thought of missing that advent was intolerable.

Dr. Darcy and Mrs. Henderson sat across the room, silent for the most part as they observed the unrelenting process transpiring on the bed. On occasion George would rise to assess Lizzy's progress, declaring with satisfaction that all was proceeding as expected. His dry humor, usually rather biting and sarcastic, was gentle with the perfect blend of wittiness and sensitive timing to ease the building strain. Mrs. Reynolds and Mrs. Hanford sat near the fire, keeping it blazing and rotating the waiting towels and linens. The housekeeper quietly communicated with Marguerite and Samuel, who loitered outside the room awaiting instructions for hot water or other supplies, and relayed information to Miss Darcy and Mr. Bingley. In fact, the entire household collectively sat on tenterhooks, no real work being accomplished as they awaited the news that all was well with their Mistress.

As dusk fell over the landscape, lamps lit and fires built, Lizzy successfully made the transition into the final stages of the birth process. Like all women down through the long ages since Eve, Lizzy instinctively sensed the subtle alteration in the contractions accompanied by an intense pressure felt low in her pelvis. Primarily it was an indescribable, uncontrollable urge to forcefully expel the cause of all her agony. It overwhelmed her reason, breathing no longer a viable option as the burning to her groin intensified torrentially; the heaviness demanding she hold her breath and bear down.

This she did, surprising her two companions who attempted in vain to persuade her to concentrate, but spurring her two childbirth professionals to jump up and lunge toward the bed. Darcy recoiled in shock when George sat efficiently on the end of the bed, spreading Lizzy's legs as he lifted the sheet. A quick probe confirmed what he suspected and after a nod to Mrs. Henderson, who turned to Mrs. Reynolds for instructions, he looked to Darcy with a beaming smile.

"Elizabeth is completely open now. Henceforth begins the real work, all else thus far leading up to this." His fingers were between her legs, carefully palpating as she began to relax into Darcy's waiting embrace. "Elizabeth, look at me. Very good, dear. Now listen carefully. Your baby is very low and ready to be born. You are as open as you can get, making room for his body. Still, as I have discussed with William and he has shared with you, this can take time. The infant still has some distance to travel and you must use the remaining pains to bring him forth. Do you understand so far?"

They both nodded, Darcy wiping his wife's brow and neck with a wet cloth while Lizzy panted. Dr. Darcy resumed, "The contractions will space out a bit, but when they occur you must hold your breath and bear down, hard, with each one. It will hurt, Elizabeth, but you must persevere. Breathe when necessary, but keep pushing toward your derriere until the pain halts."

"How long, Uncle?" Darcy asked in a hoarse voice.

"Let us wait and see how the next few contractions proceed."

A flurry of activity erupted in the room. Fresh buckets of water were brought, George washing his hands and soaking several rags. Additional lamps were lit for illumination.

The Darcys noted none of it. Lizzy reclined on her husband's warm chest, cocking her head to better see his luminous visage. She smiled, raising a hand to stroke his cheek, and Darcy almost fainted with a surge of breathless joy. Never had she been more beautiful to him than at that moment. Her hair was disheveled and loose from its braid, face flushed and slightly puffy, lips dry; yet she exuded a radiant happiness that transcended the particulars.

"I love you, Elizabeth," he whispered, cupping her face. "Thank you for allowing me to be a part of this miracle."

She laughed, eyes twinkling and for the first time in hours responding with the friskiness of his Lizzy apparent. "Well, Mr. Darcy, considering you were an integral part of the inception of the miracle, it is only apropos you are present at its consummation! I would not be in this predicament if not for you and could not survive it without you. Now, do your job and hand me that glass of water." She pursed her lips, blowing a kiss as she patted his smiling mouth with her fingertips, Darcy chuckling in a liberating release of nervousness as he reached for the indicated liquid.

The difficult task of laboring in tandem with forceful muscular spasms intent on expelling a somewhat pliable but bulky body through a physically much smaller space commenced. Neither Darcy wasted the effort at this juncture to marvel at the awesomeness of the operation. Instead, Lizzy embraced with enthusiasm the ability to be proactive for a change. The pain was intense, but at least she was *doing something* rather than lying inert at its mercy. Darcy quite simply could not think beyond the fact that he would lay eyes on his child in a matter of minutes. He was giddy with excitement.

Lizzy was serious and centered, not really needing the ceaselessly spoken encouragement now gushing from every mouth in the room, but appreciating it nonetheless. A half hour of concentrated effort passed, Lizzy exhausted and aching in every muscle, but strangely exhilarated and energized. Dr. Darcy kept to his seat, one hand on her abdomen under the draping sheet and the other stretching the flesh surrounding the birth canal. Mrs. Henderson stood by Lizzy's bent left knee, supporting and watching. Jane, per the midwife's teaching, did the same to the right leg. The sheet occluded full view, of which Darcy was thankful, and maintained modesty as much as is feasible in such a situation.

"Elizabeth, William, I can see the crown of your baby's head. There is lots of dark hair, not surprisingly. You are doing an excellent job, my dear. He is very low and it should not take much longer."

However, three marvelously executed pushes later and the baby had not budged. Dr. Darcy, face impassive, deepened his probing. Lizzy squirmed, feeling his fingers uncomfortably seeking. "Forgive me, dear, but I need to palpate the baby's head… Ah! Now I see the cause. Typical Darcy, always attempting to be unique and ostentatious."

Lizzy snorted, although she had no idea what he meant as far as her baby was concerned, while Darcy scowled. "Perhaps some Darcys I could mention," he said haughtily. "I, however, prefer to be inconspicuous and ordinary." Lizzy and Jane both laughed aloud, even Mrs. Reynolds hiding a snicker, to Darcy's confusion.

"You, my love, are the epitome of all that is *not* ordinary and at your height and with your presence are far from inconspicuous! We can discuss that later though. What do you mean about the baby, Uncle?"

Dr. Darcy was smiling at his scowling nephew, addressing the question seriously. "Your child is wishing to be born looking up at the ceiling when he should be facing the floor. What this means is, I need to attempt turning him or the final stage will take longer."

"Do you want the forceps, Doctor?" asked Mrs. Henderson.

"Absolutely not!" both George and Darcy echoed firmly. "Forceps will not touch my son's head unless it is a matter of life or death!" Darcy barked with eyes blazed, Mrs. Henderson retreating a step.

"Do not worry, William. I can manipulate him with my fingers or, if he is stubborn, deliver him as he wishes. It may be uncomfortable, Elizabeth, I am sorry."

She nodded, unable to speak as another contraction struck. The next several contractions were the hardest, Lizzy's discomfort increasing as the infant hesitantly responded to the physician's persistent direction. Mrs. Henderson was mesmerized, having never witnessed such a procedure, Dr. Darcy explaining the technique in quiet undertones as he worked.

Lizzy strained with the effort, releasing loud grunts and intermittent yells of pain. Darcy held his breath as she did, Jane also unconsciously mimicking the behavior. The room was quiet except for Lizzy's vocalizations and the sonorant urgings of Darcy. He held her enveloped in his arms with her back pressed to his chest, steady hands supporting her arms as she pulled on her thighs with each forceful squeeze.

"Stupendous, Elizabeth!" the poised physician commented. "Keep your legs open, give him room. The baby has turned and is coming! A towel, Mrs. Hanford, quickly! Harder, Elizabeth, do not stop now even if the contraction wanes. Push him out! Lots of hair, oh yes. Ears, nose, mouth… now breathe for a moment, dear, good girl, let me wipe the face, clear the mucus… Now again, Elizabeth! Let's get those broad Darcy shoulders out… the widest part of all… Yes! Here we are… Ha! A boy! Most definitely a boy!"

George's laugh was lost in the general mayhem bursting forth. Elizabeth collapsed onto her husband, tears of relief and joy springing to weary eyes. Darcy was laughing and crying, eyes glued to the draped knees of his wife while bestowing kisses to her head and hugging so tightly that if she was any more coherent she may have complained. Jane clapped with joy, Mrs. Henderson reached for the thick string to tie about the umbilical cord, Mrs. Reynolds proclaimed the time as 7:59 p.m. and bounced with delight, and Mrs. Hanford wept silently as she observed the initial movements of the newborn.

All of it was abruptly pierced by the lusty cry of a healthy set of newborn lungs, loudly protesting the overall treatment being inflicted upon him. George lifted the squalling babe glistening with birth fluid and streaks of blood, still partially blue and attached to his mother with forehead wrinkled in consternation and flailing limbs, for his first inspection by adoring and already hopelessly in love parents.

"Young Master Darcy, meet your mama and papa!" George declared with pride, holding the wailing and utterly irritated and uninterested infant aloft for another few seconds before placing him onto the waiting warm blankets held by Mrs. Hanford and tying the cord. He spoke aloud while attending to the crying infant, "He is perfect. All ten fingers and toes, color pinking nicely, male anatomy as it should be, head a bit pointed but not too bad, ears well formed, mouth intact… oh, good suck already, typical Darcy, instantly demanding nourishment. Here, Mrs. Hanford, take him."

Darcy buried his face into Lizzy's hair, body shaking as he sobbed and caressed her arms, hoarsely crooning, "Elizabeth, I love you so! He is beautiful, you are beautiful. Thank you, thank you, thank you… I love you. We have a son. A son! Our son… so amazing, you are amazing…"

Lizzy clutched his wrists, turning to capture his mouth for a desperately needed kiss. Their eyes met, radiant and overflowing with love. She smiled, kissed him again and then leaned onto his shoulder. "Beloved, go be with him. I want one of us to be near him giving comfort and it must be you. Please?"

He hesitated, glancing longingly toward the nanny then back to his wife. "I will stay with my sister, Mr. Darcy. Go to your son."

"Jane, after the events of today, do you think you may be willing to address me by my Christian name?" Darcy grinned, Jane blushing and lowering her gaze.

Lizzy laughed softly. "Please, go to Alexander. Kiss him for me."

"Of course." He cupped her face, delivering another lingering kiss before moving away, relinquishing her to Jane's ministering presence.

Mrs. Hanford and Mrs. Reynolds knelt by the low table situated before the fire on which lay the wiggling babe. His wails continued, currently augmented by the indignity of a bath. Darcy knelt, teary eyes avidly scrutinizing his son.

"Congratulations, Mr. Darcy. He is beautiful."

"Thank you, Mrs. Reynolds. May I touch him?"

"Certainly!" the nanny said with a laugh. "He is yours, after all."

Darcy beamed, hand reaching gingerly to stroke one finger over the baby's breastbone. Darcy caught his breath, freshly amazed at the velvet softness, personally never imagining any skin could be softer than his wife's. Laying his entire palm over the sturdy chest of his son, broad hand covering the whole breast and most of the abdomen with fingertips tickling under his chin. The frantic thrashing eased under the firm pressure, Darcy bending to bestow a kiss to the baby's damp forehead.

"Sweet Alexander, my son. This is your father speaking. That was from your mother, who loves you so very much. This…" and he kissed the downy cheek, "is from me. I also love you, my precious." He continued the gentle crooning, the baby having calmed at the loving caresses and sound of the familiar voice. Darcy lifted inches to discover a pair of wide, cerulean blue eyes staring at him with studied intensity, tiny creases between the brows.

Darcy experienced an electrifying jolt rush through his body and his mouth fell open. Alexander, as if by purposeful intent, encountered his father's little finger and wrapped one chubby fist tightly around. Darcy stifled a sob, blinking furiously as the baby remained locked onto his face.

"He knows you, sir," Mrs. Reynolds said. "Keep talking to him."

He did, voice rough with choking emotion. Alexander's gaze wandered frequently, but inevitably returned to his father's shining visage and brilliant grin. The women worked diligently, cleaning thoroughly over all skin folds and body parts, scrubbing the mass of curly brown hair until lying in silken waves. In between the singsong droning, Darcy closely examined his son.

Alexander possessed his father's blue eyes but they were larger and rounder than his, like Elizabeth's, and set under a mildly prominent forehead. The nose was not exactly buttoned as Elizabeth's, but not broad and long as his; time would tell how it evolved. The thick eyebrows were totally Darcy's down to the frowning wrinkles and left arch. He did not have his father's chin cleft, but the overall shape was masculine with a sharp jawline. His fingers were long and hands wide, the feet matching in size. In fact his entire body was long and lean with sturdily defined muscles encased by unblemished ruddy skin. Not a single mark marred his flesh, only the mildly misshapen head preventing him from being flawless.

Darcy grasped one large foot, smiling as he murmured, "No wonder I could almost grip your feet, my darling." He kissed the sole, nibbling briefly on the tiny toes, Alexander flinching and attempting to withdraw. "Ah, ticklish, are we?"

Alexander's answer to that inquiry was to release a forceful stream of urine, Darcy jerking backward and narrowly avoiding a blast to the face.

"What the…?" The women laughed loudly, Lizzy asking what was happening. "Our son tried to urinate on me! Well, at least we know that organ functions correctly." The room erupted in laughter.

"He is clean now, Mr. Darcy. We need to dress him, protecting his nether regions before more accidents occur. I am sure his mother wants to see him soon." Darcy's grin was nearly swallowing his face, turning to peer at his resplendent wife now in a clean gown and propped on fresh pillows while Jane brushed and replaited her hair. Their eyes held, volumes of unspoken emotion and sentiment passing between. In a few minutes the baby was diapered and wrapped loosely in a warm blanket sewn by Lizzy. Darcy carried him to Elizabeth, her arms extended in anticipation. Slowly the occupants filed from the chamber, Jane kissing her sister one last time on the temple and glancing shyly to Darcy.

"Congratulations, William," she whispered.

Darcy beamed. "Thank you, Jane."

Last was George. The proud great-uncle taking a moment to inspect the sleeping bundle of joy embraced against his weary mother's breast with jubilant and rather smug father encircling them both.

"Well done, you two, well done. He is lovely. Perfectly delivered, if I say so myself! William, ensure your wife rests. No staring at the baby all night in lieu of sleep. I will check on you later, dear. Notify me immediately if you feel strange in any way. Remember what we spoke of previously," he said, directing the last comment to Darcy, who nodded.

"William, once you are alone, assist Elizabeth in placing Alexander on her chest. Keeping him naked against her bare flesh is the best place for him to be. He will stay warm and be very calm. Enjoy this time while he is awake."

"When should I feed him, Uncle?" Elizabeth asked, not removing her adoring gaze from the rapt fascination with the baby's alert eyes.

"Just hold him for now, my dear. Let instinct rule. He will make his intentions known." The doctor chuckled, bending to brush the infant's cheek with a fingertip. He placed a tender kiss to Lizzy's brow. "Congratulations, niece. You were amazing. You too, William," and with a clap to his nephew's shoulder he departed, leaving the Darcys finally alone with their child.

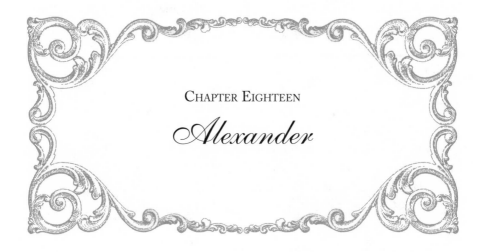

CHAPTER EIGHTEEN

Alexander

S ILENCE FELL. THE CRACKLING of the fire, ticking of the longcase clock, muffled murmurs of voices from without mingling with the familiar creaks from within the mansion's walls, faint whispers of a November wind beyond the curtained windows, and the harmonious heartbeats and contented respirations of the three Darcys the only noises.

Lizzy's gown was opened, Alexander nestled with his belly and chest pressed flat along her torso, his head pillowed upon one soft breast.

He was wide awake and for a very long time Darcy and Lizzy stared, plainly stared, at the beautiful face of their newborn son as he stared back. He moved occasionally, emitting soft mews, pursing full pink lips, delicate eyelids fluttering, miniature fingers grasping and releasing a parent's finger. His mouth would open, apparently seeking as his surprisingly strong neck turned a wobbly head toward her breast. But then he would pause, quieting as he resumed his inquisitive inspection of his parents.

Lizzy sniffled, wiping at a falling tear and sighing deeply. "Are you in pain, dearest?" Darcy asked, reaching to stroke her chin as she shook her head.

"No. Well, yes, a bit achy and very tired, but the tears are of joy. Look at him, William! Is he not the most beautiful baby you have ever seen?"

Darcy chuckled, chest vibrating. "As you know I have limited exposure, this is an unfair question. Nonetheless, I cannot fathom any other being handsomer. He has your hair, Elizabeth, and your eyes."

"His eyes are blue."

"Yes, but shaped like yours. And he inherited your nose, thankfully."

"It does not look like my nose, and besides, I adore your nose!" She turned her head for a peck to said proboscis positioned by her cheek. "It is easy to find for kisses in the dark."

"Indeed, it is. He is beginning to seek more diligently. Perhaps hunger is winning over the need for sedate cuddling." Darcy ran a fingertip over the tiny lips, Alexander instantly opening wide and searching.

"If he inherited his father's appetite, then this is likely true. Perhaps I should nurse him."

"It appears he has decided the same. Look how he squirms to reach your nipple, just as Uncle said he would. Marvelous nature!" Darcy declared in awe, both parents watching in amazement as with minimal aid from them, Alexander wiggled and bobbed his way toward his mother's bared breast. They laughed as they fumbled to help him, but it was not overly necessary. The newborn fortunately knew precisely what to do, only requiring the nipple to come within proximity of his gaping mouth.

Lizzy gasped and jerked at the strong suck, fresh tears springing to her eyes as emotions consumed her.

"Are you well, Elizabeth? Does it hurt?"

She shook her head vigorously, relaxing further into his warm body. "No, no. It is… blissful! I just… love him so much! And you… William, I am so deliriously happy!" He held her firmly, rocking gently as she cried, Alexander oblivious to it all as he nursed and held tightly to his mother's finger.

Gradually she quieted, lifting her eyes to meet Darcy's adoring gaze. He bent, kissing her lightly. "I love you forever, Elizabeth."

"And I you, Fitzwilliam. By the way, I know it yet a couple hours early but… Happy anniversary my darling. Do you like your gift?"

"I daresay I love both the gift and the packaging it came in. Happy anniversary, Mrs. Darcy."

Many hours later, well after midnight and nearing the dawn of November 28, 1817, another date of import, Lizzy woke. The unfamiliar room was dim, Lizzy momentarily befuddled by the strange and empty bed as well as the cramping leg muscles, burning arms, and throbbing bottom. The happenings of the twenty-seventh rushed through her consciousness, Lizzy smiling brightly at the surge of exultation, and then suddenly panicking as the vacancy in her arms stabbed her heart.

Her eyes flew open and she painfully attempted to rise, halting and relaxing with a gratified sigh at the vision greeting her.

Darcy lay asleep on the narrow, short sofa before the smoldering fire. His vest had been discarded and the linen shirt loose and gaping open over his bare chest with a blanket haphazardly covering his lower body. His feet were also bare and one long leg had fallen off the sofa onto the floor while the other was draped over the arm and dangling from the knee on. His beautiful face was turned toward the bed, lips parted, and he breathed in a deep rhythm. Lying on his ample chest was Alexander. The baby was swaddled and dressed, one arm free and hanging over his father's side. His tiny pink face was visible, full lips parted just like his father's. Darcy held his son securely, even in sleep, one large hand resting on the infant's rear and the other hand wholly encompassing the curly brown-haired head.

Lizzy lay awake for a long while watching father and son in peaceful slumber. It was a picture more moving than anything created by the greatest artist. The new mother studied the scene in the finest detail, reverently hanging it in her mind's gallery to be remembered for all of her life.

Alexander William George Bennet Darcy, Heir to Pemberley, Master Alex as he would be commonly known to the staff as he grew, was hungry and it was quite feasible that the entire household knew it! The future Master of Pemberley's character was yet unknown, his personality to undergo years of molding and development, but one trait that was instantly recognizable was his demanding persistence.

"Merciful heavens, my sweet, you ate barely two hours ago! I apologize most profoundly for being a bit fumbling at the procedure and for yet providing little in the way of actual milk. Bear with me."

"I cannot fathom where he comes by such a temper. Astounding, actually."

"Most humorous, Mr. Darcy. Make yourself useful and prop that pillow under my elbow. *Your* son is heavy on my tired arms. There you are, darling, that's my bright boy. Ouch! Goodness, I certainly know where he gets that talent from!"

"Be thankful as the ability to suck well induces the milk to produce rapidly, or at least that is what the book states."

It was mid-morning following his birth, the young master just over twelve hours of age. Despite Lizzy's playful teasing he actually had slept for nearly five hours nestled snuggly belly to chest with head tucked under his immeasurably proud father's chin and warm hand, lulled by the strong beat of a blissful heart beneath his ear. Darcy had awoken first, cramped and with no sensation to his left limb from the knee down, and a spreading wet warmth over his abdomen.

Both Darcy men had changed their clothing; elder Darcy with relief and baby Darcy with extreme indignation. Only the loving presence of his mother, and most especially her breast, had calmed him. He had eaten well, promptly falling asleep in Lizzy's arms, and woken two hours later apparently famished. In the meantime Darcy had called for coffee and tea, George had peeked in to assure all was well with the new mother, and the lovers had lost themselves in gazing at their son's face.

They were still lost. Darcy reclined with his wife on the bed, fingertips gently brushing over the wisps of brown curls while the infant nursed. Lizzy wore a smile unique to all mothers everywhere since time began, dreamily memorizing each twitch and curve, while allowing the sensations to course through her blood. Some were mildly unpleasant, such as the cramps elicited by his sucking, but most were joyous, such as the wash of intense love and happiness.

She rested her head onto Darcy's inner shoulder, sighing contentedly but wearily. "I think I could sleep for a week. After I eat the entire kitchen, that is."

Darcy kissed her brow, hugging close as fingers played through her hair while yet caressing the baby's fine locks. "As soon as Alexander is satisfied I will call for another tray and help you to freshen up. Marguerite is drawing a bath."

Marguerite assisted a stiff and hobbling Lizzy into her bathing room while Darcy stayed with the baby. He lay with him on the bed while Lizzy bathed, Alexander enjoying a brief span of contented wakefulness after filling his stomach. Father and son studied each other, Darcy again examining each feature and marveling at how tender yet sturdy the helpless infant was. He recalled a vague memory of his mother telling him not to fear holding Georgiana as, "She will not break, Fitzwilliam. Babies are tougher than most give them credit."

He could better perceive this in Alexander than he could as a young boy with Georgie. His legs kicked forcefully against Darcy's palms, the very bones firm inside robust muscles. He gripped Darcy's fingers or hair when it came within reach with tight fists that actually caused pain. His movements were random and uncontrolled, but strong, even lifting his head for short spells and arching his spine to the point of nearly flipping over! Of course, his stamina was transient, the hours-old infant sleeping more than anything. However, that was a delight as well. Darcy's tender crooning, arising from some internally paternal instinct he did not know he possessed, pacified Alexander, eyes drooping and limbs relaxing as his father whispered nonsense and devotion in a melodic voice.

Mrs. Hanford assumed her attendance over the sleeping infant while Darcy retreated for a thorough cleansing and a shave. He returned to discover his wife walking about the room, gently bouncing a soundly sleeping Alexander in her arms. Darcy scowled and grasped her elbows as if she were an invalid, ordering her back to bed.

Lizzy laughed, tiptoeing to kiss the creases between his brows. "If I lie in that bed a moment more, I shall scream. Sore muscles need to be exercised, as you well know." She rubbed the slowly fading wrinkles with a happy grin, Darcy gradually matching her expression, as she continued musingly, "Alexander has your eyebrows, nearly your whole face in point of fact. Shall be an advantage for me now that I finally know how to read the moods and thoughts so dramatically detailed in your eyes and perfect brow." She encircled his neck with one smarting arm, intent on indulging in a time of pleasurable kisses. Darcy blissfully submitted, hands flattening on her back as he tentatively pulled her close to his body, thrilling at the ability to do so. The soft bundle between their chests that was their swaddled son did not inhibit drawing her tighter than he had been able to do for the past several months.

Of course, nothing further could be accomplished so soon after giving birth even if Alexander had not decided to interrupt for another feeding. George visited several times throughout the day, but did not examine Lizzy. Rather he asked a number of pointed questions that caused her to absurdly flush considering the events of yesterday, to his great amusement. Since nothing appeared to be remiss, Lizzy actually feeling quite well aside from being extremely tired and sore, he left it at softly spoken reminders of what to watch for. And a new, foul-tasting tea concoction to ease the pain and augment her recovery.

Mrs. Hanford was stationed in the adjoining nursery. She was beckoned upon occasion, offering light assistance and words of advice, but mostly left the trio alone. The various family members paid short visits throughout the day, but they kept it brief as well. Partly this was due to the understanding that this time was special and should be spent alone. However, it was also because everyone knew that November twenty-eighth was not just the day after Alexander's birth, but it was also the Darcys' first wedding anniversary.

The Darcys' one-year anniversary was spent focusing on their baby rather than wholly on each other as they had tentatively planned, but neither minded in the least. Darcy had not arranged any wild celebration, knowing that Lizzy's condition, assuming she was still pregnant, would preclude anything extreme. Instead he had ordered the staff to prepare a lavish dinner setting in the conservatory. That was now out of the question. Even if Lizzy had felt physically capable of dressing and walking the long distance to the orangery, the thought of leaving Alexander or taking him on any excursions abroad was inconceivable. So, with a rapid shift in thinking, vases of flowers were displayed about their temporary bedchamber and a table was set for dining. Instead it was the Bingleys, also celebrating one year of wedded bliss, who would benefit from Darcy's devising!

The Darcys' commemoration of a joyous year's end was a quiet affair, the perfect cap to a busy day. Lizzy napped intermittently between nursing a demanding infant with a healthy appetite and visits with the family, but was still fatigued from her ordeal. They ate heartily of the stupendous cuisine created by Mrs. Langton for the anniversary, exchanged gifts that would be treasured, and blissfully returned to the comfort of the bed for cuddling and further staring at Alexander. Many anniversaries would be celebrated down the long years graced to them by the Almighty, some quite extraordinary for various reasons, but how could any trip to a foreign land or massive gala transcend the joy of their firstborn?

"My life has altered so dramatically this past year," Darcy mused. "It is fantastic and I could almost be convinced I am dreaming it all if not for the tangible touch of you and our perfect son." He leaned to bestow a kiss to Alexander's chubby fist tightly clenched around his index finger. The baby lay asleep on the bed between his mother and father, their bodies nestled as close as possible without smothering the contented infant. Lizzy's nose brushed the fine tresses as she inhaled his innocent fragrance and planted an endless amount of soft kisses. Darcy played with her lengthy hair spilling over the pillows, knuckles frequently caressing over her face.

Lizzy smiled through her weariness. Her body ached in unmentionable places and she was utterly exhausted; nevertheless, her happiness rushed through every fiber of her spirit as a surging wave. She spoke in a bare whisper, voice hoarse from the strain of birth and fatigue, "I do know what you mean. If anyone had told me fourteen months ago that I would be joyously married to the most amazing man in the world and with a child at my breast... well, I am certain I would have laughed! Now look at us, William. Together a year and blessed with a priceless gift. What was it you said once? 'A part of you and me, created by God through our union.'" She shook her head, "I still cannot believe you are mine, and now we have a baby! It *is* fantastic."

Alexander released a soft drowsy sigh, arching his head toward Darcy with petite lips sucking on an imaginary nipple. Thick lashes lay on rosy silky cheeks, his skin fair as was both his parents. The contrast of milky skin and chestnut hair was striking and so beautiful. Naturally his parents thought him lovely beyond any child alive, but the truth is Alexander was adorable. It was indisputable that he favored his father, but there was much of his mother about his features: the curly hair, diminutive nose, rounder eyes, and bent pinkie toes. His feet overall were long and broad like his father's, but the toe was a Bennet trait. Darcy was thrilled about the little digit, already delighting in ticklish nibbles; Lizzy was less than enthused, having always been embarrassed by what she considered a flaw, but her husband adored her feet—as well as everything else.

Darcy smiled at the joy elicited by the mere presence of their infant, leaned to kiss his forehead and inhaling deeply of his clean scent. "I smell the soap, but there is something indefinable about him. It is his very skin, his essence. He is so unbelievably sweet! I never imagined it possible to love someone so newly acquainted and largely unknown to this degree. He is a miracle, Elizabeth, and I cannot thank you enough." He met her glittering eyes, leaning to now kiss her equally as tender. "I love you, my wife, beyond measure."

"And I you, beloved. My heart is filled to overflowing. My soul is dancing a lively jig even if my body is too weary to respond!"

She yawned widely, Darcy chuckling faintly. "Close your eyes and sleep, dearest. Uncle says it vital you rest while Alexander does."

"Fitzwilliam, will you stay here with us? Please?"

"Of course!" He was genuinely surprised at the question and the tone of pleading it was asked in. "My place is with you, no matter the bedchamber. I would not leave even if you begged me to do so. When you feel ready, we will return to our favored bed, but until then you are stuck with me in this smaller one."

Lizzy smiled drowsily, eyes falling shut and voice a bare murmur, "Thank you. Should we move him to the cradle? I do not wish to, but I fear squishing him."

"He will come to no harm. I do not want him so far either. Sleep, Elizabeth," he whispered, drawing the blanket further over his wife and dreaming babe, stroking over her warm skin as she promptly succumbed to her fatigue. They slept all three together, Darcy awake long after his wife and child, watching over them as they rested with emotions unnameable alive inside of him.

The first days of parenthood were tremendous. Lizzy recuperated rapidly. Too rapidly as far as Darcy was concerned, his fears at her overextending falling on deaf ears. What she could not quite communicate to him was how marvelous she felt. Yes, her feminine regions were sore and swollen, her muscles were stiff and achy for a couple days, and it took her about a week to regain her natural vigor and no longer be stricken by fatigue, but these were minor irritations compared to the joy suffusing her soul. Additionally, the simple delight at suddenly weighing about twelve pounds lighter was stupendous!

Lizzy kept to her chambers during those early days of rejuvenation, Darcy leaving rarely. Upon occasion Alexander did sleep tucked into a ball on the mattress with a parent nearby, but the bulk of his early life was spent in some-one's arms. Neither mother nor father wished him out of sight, even the dozen steps to the nursery. Mrs. Hanford was constantly in residence, educating Lizzy and Darcy on the basic principles of diapering and dressing and bathing. Her knowledge was of a practical, experiential nature. Often it was the simple things that books did not teach that she readily knew and imparted with confidence that eased the Darcys.

For example, Alexander's first several bowel eliminations were decidedly odd and frightening, the new parents greatly relieved when the nanny assured them it was normal. For her part, the negligible time spent thus far at Pemberley had not fully prepared her for the intense interest both Darcys shared for all things regarding their son. Nothing escaped their notice, especially Mr. Darcy, whose eagle-eyed penetrating gaze frankly unnerved her initially, but speedily grew ordinary and was balanced by the tender devotion evident. All the rumors circulating since the Master's marriage were witnessed firsthand by the nanny, and her happiness with her new path in life was immense.

Alexander was alert more often than either of them had expected, his bright blue eyes penetrating and serious. It was a gaze, even in its infantile state, that was eerily like his father's.

Yet most of his awake-time was devoted to the all important chore of eating. There were a handful of slumbering stretches that lasted longer than three hours, but very few. The short nap followed by a voracious interlude at his mother's breast was a typical pattern during those initial days. By the end of the third day Lizzy's milk would be fully producing, allowing for longer reprieves between nursing, but for those first days he was never well satisfied. Naturally she minded not at all, generally holding him as he slept rather than placing him into his cradle. In fact, he would not sleep in his cradle for several days.

When Darcy was not present, which was rarely, and even a good portion of the time when he was, Jane or Georgiana, and often both, would be found placidly sitting nearby with a cup of tea or embroidery hoop in hand. These were episodes of pleasant conversation, one eye on the flashing needle and the other on Lizzy and new nephew. Both women possessed calm natures that pacified while also ready to jump up the instant she needed anything. Their constant vigil and serene presence soothed all of them and granted Darcy the relieving freedom to move beyond the chamber as required. Naturally the conversation often centered on Alexander and the soon-to-arrive Bingley baby, but general topics ranged wide as the women passed the hours companionably.

"I wrote to Mama and Papa a few days before I came here," Jane said at one point. "I told them about our blessed news. Caroline and the Hursts are arriving next week, so we will announce our blessing to them then."

"Are they staying for long?"

"Probably through the holidays. Do not make that face, Lizzy!"

"Forgive me, Jane, but I must confess I am happy it is you and not me! Although I suppose we shall host them a time or two. Caroline Bingley irritates me and the Hursts are boring. Sorry, but you know it to be true. Perhaps I can plead lingering post childbirth fatigue. Certainly I do not want a host of people handling our fragile infant, and William will absolutely forbid it. We have not discussed it, but what are your plans for Christmas?"

"Typical celebrations at Hasberry. I greatly anticipate a lively holiday in my new home. Yes, even with the Hursts and Caroline!" She laughed at Lizzy's harrumph. "But do not fret overly, dear sister. I assure you we will not willingly face the wrath of Mr. Darcy by invading your peace too radically."

"Don't be silly," Lizzy teased. "We want you and Charles here for Christmas dinner at the least. And for the christening in January. I can happily endure Caroline and the Hursts for a few days."

"We shall see," Georgiana muttered under her breath with a wink toward Jane that Lizzy ignored.

She continued, "Papa wrote and said they plan to arrive a week before Christmas. I think he wanted to be very sure *not* to be here during the birth, five previous times more than sufficient! I can only be grateful at that insight as I vastly preferred my husband by my side then Mama shrieking through Pemberley's halls." They all laughed, Lizzy shaking her head at the momentary vision of her mother attempting to "help" during her labor.

"Will Mary be accompanying Mr. and Mrs. Bennet and Kitty? I know she is currently at home pending her wedding in February," Georgiana asked.

"I am unsure. William and I extended an invitation to her and Mr. Daniels, although I believe the poor man will sooner tread over hot coals than reside as a guest here. We do hope Mary can persuade him."

"As do I. I miss Mary, and it would be fabulous to have Mary attend the Cole's Masque with Kitty and me."

Jane laughed. "I would not set my hopes on that, Georgiana. Mary despises dancing and would need to be chained and dragged there involuntarily."

The idle chat and laughter continued until interrupted by the menfolk.

Darcy did not go farther in those early days than the hallway, his dressing room, or sitting room where he would attend to his personal needs or relax with Bingley over a cup of hot chocolate. Two days after the birth, Darcy and Bingley engaged in a handful of backgammon games in the well-appointed game room. They conversed companionably and snacked on Mrs. Langton's excellent gooseberry jam-smothered biscuits and drank hot black tea. It was an enjoyable session, but eventually Darcy grew anxious, missing his family.

"Come, Bingley," he said to his friend. "Let us see what our beautiful wives are gossiping about today. Besides, you have not gazed upon my handsome son since early this morning. He needs to recognize the face of his Uncle Charles."

Darcy was already at the door, Bingley trailing with a chuckle and privately wondering if he would be as giddy upon the arrival of his firstborn. *Most likely*, he thought with a smile.

Jane sat on a settee before the roaring fire with needlepoint in hand, talking softly as Lizzy completed burping Alexander from the pillowed comfort of a second settee while Georgiana reclined on the chaise with a forgotten book on her lap. The men joined the ladies, Darcy crossing instantly to his wife for a tender kiss and taking Alexander from her sore arms as he sat beside. General conversation ensued, Lizzy leaning gratefully against the solid strength of her husband's side. It was Darcy, sleeping baby cradled in his arms, who broached an important subject in his typical forthright manner of speaking.

"Charles, Jane." They glanced over simultaneously, brows lifting slightly at the serious tone. "Elizabeth and I have a question of extreme magnitude to ask of you. It is essential you understand that we have given this a tremendous amount of consideration and are absolutely convinced of the wisdom in our choice. Although we would make every attempt to comprehend a negative response, it would be deeply distressing as we are confident in our judgment. We in no way want you to be obligated, however, if you feel just cause to decline."

"Speak freely, Darcy, without the extended preamble!" Bingley interrupted with a laugh, turning to his wife with a sidelong glance at his friend. "Mr. Darcy could run for Parliament considering how long winded he can be at times."

Lizzy chuckled from where she leaned on Darcy's shoulder, patting his arm. Darcy pressed his lips together, not angry but not as amused as the others in the room, continuing as if Bingley had not spoken, "Personality traits notwithstanding, Elizabeth and I wish to humbly request that the two of you consider accepting the position of godparents to our son."

Jane smiled softly, eyes tearing as she gazed at her sister. She had wondered if they might choose her and Charles, although Lizzy had extended no hint of such, nor had Jane mentioned the speculation to anyone, not even her husband. It was more a conjecture based on hope. Still, as greatly as she had secretly wished to be given the esteemed role in her first nephew's life, she was deeply moved.

Charles was stunned and it showed in the comic wide-eyed slackness of his face. As close as he was to Darcy, and perhaps partially because of his intimacy with the morally reserved man, he naturally assumed the choice would be a near relative or even one of his lifelong Derbyshire friends. Bingley well knew Darcy's strong religious convictions. Conversely, he had not been raised as rigidly, his lackadaisical father more apt to sleep late on Sunday morning suffering from a massive post-drunkenness headache than escort his children to church. Faith-based tenets were taught tenuously at best throughout his youth, and only in later years in his desire to break away from the waywardness of his early existence did Bingley begin to attend services with any sort of regularity. What he had discovered was a fount of peace and stability that he embraced, but not to the great degree of Darcy.

Darcy was smiling affectionately at his young friend, insightfully clarifying in his quiet voice, "You see, my dear friend, being a godparent is not exclusively about teaching Alexander the specific doctrines and theological creeds. That is what the Church and pastors are for. It is more about being an example of those Biblical principles, living them out within sight of his immature mind, teaching as a model of what is virtuous and acceptable. You and Jane exemplify everything that Elizabeth and I want our son to be in life."

"Of all the couples we know," Lizzy added, "not only do you breathe integrity and love and faithfulness, but you truly love him. We know you always will. It is vital to us that Alexander grows knowing that his godparents are not merely accepting a tradition or honored obligation but are performing a duty out of devotion."

Bingley glanced at his wife, throat tight as he swallowed the forming lump, their eyes meeting with instant communication. No hesitation or need to discuss the matter. "We would be honored, William, deeply honored," he finally squeaked out. "Lizzy, thank you. Yes, absolutely we will stand with you before God and commit ourselves to Alexander."

Charles and Jane departed two days later, but only because Darcy declared with obvious remorse that the innocuous-appearing clouds gathering over the distant Peaks portended a snowstorm. Jane peered at her brother-in-law with clear doubt at his assertion, but Bingley immediately began making plans to leave. Long association with his friend's uncanny ability to predict the Derbyshire weather, a talent he assumed was genetic, gave him no cause to pause.

The sisters said their adieus in the bedchamber while Darcy descended the stairs to spend the final hours with Charles in the billiard room. Jane held a sleeping Alexander, while Lizzy stretched a bit by pacing about the room.

"Jane, I cannot thank you enough for being here with me. I do hope I can return the favor when your time comes."

"Absolutely! I will need you there most assuredly. However, it is I who should be thanking you, Lizzy. Now I know most clearly what to expect and can attend to my thoughts for the following months and bolster my mental strength."

Lizzy laughed. "Knowing you, I doubt you will raise your voice even once, as I did, nor release a peep. Even worse, you shall probably have a four-hour travail and I shall never speak to you again!"

"If I am so fortunate, I think I could deal with never having you speak to me again," Jane teased in her quiet voice, Lizzy laughing so loudly that Alexander started in his aunt's arms. She soothed him, resuming, "When do you plan to leave these rooms for the rest of the house? Your pacing is a plain indication of your restlessness."

"Tomorrow. I intend to show Alexander the immediate rooms at the least, even if I have to barrel through William's body to do so! I cannot say I am ready to tackle too much, but these rooms are stifling me." She sighed, sitting onto the edge of the sofa next to Jane, fingers automatically traveling over Alexander's satiny cheek. "I redecorated these rooms and they are lovely, but I already miss our bedchamber. It just… does not feel right somehow." She smiled and shook her head, glancing to Jane with a faint blush. "I know I am being silly."

"No you are not. Be patient, Lizzy. I do not think you can fully trust your emotions so soon after birth. You will know in your heart when it feels proper to move. William is here with you so it truly cannot matter all that much."

"Thank you, Jane. Of course you are correct, and William says the same. I will miss you so very much! You and Charles must hurry back for a longer visit around Christmas, even if that means bringing the Hursts and Miss Bingley!"

The storm did strike late that evening, dropping four inches of powdery snow; nonetheless, it did not overly hinder the message that an heir to the Pemberley estate and fortune had been born. The news speedily disseminated throughout Derbyshire, the horrid weather not preventing gossip. The official announcements were not yet printed before congratulations were arriving to the manor, servants sent trudging through the snow and chill winds to deliver penned parchments by the dozens. It would be over a week before Darcy visited with the local gentlemen at the pub in Lambton, then discovering that it was Albert Hughes's father, Wentworth Hughes, who won the wager on nearly all counts. One hundred twenty-three pounds for guessing birth date, closest time, and sex! The gents toasted the new father, plying him with cigars and humorous words of parenting advice.

Back at Pemberley, as the weeks moved toward Christmas, life fell into the typical routines for this time of the year. Nevertheless, covering it all, threading through it all, and as a foundation of it all was Alexander. He was the star, the sweet center of attention, the innocent being that had every last soul wrapped around his tiny fingers. Lizzy did begin walking with him the day after the Bingleys left, Darcy at her elbow as they slowly traversed the endless corridors of the top floor. They took turns carrying him, pointing to various portraits or wall hangings, some of which were actually colorful enough to capture his brief consideration. Mostly he slept nestled onto a shoulder, the exercise being essentially for Lizzy's benefit.

Even the sporadically encountered footman or maid could not resist a spontaneous smile and warm gaze to touch the young Master's face. Lizzy was delighted to proudly show him to anyone, Darcy also overcoming a natural devotion to protocol by introducing him with a broad grin.

Georgiana and George joined the excursions from time to time. The dear doctor adored his grand-nephew, easily ensnaring the infant's serious gaze what with the garish outfits he wore, a voice exactly like his nephew's, and a natural storyteller's dramatic flair for enunciation. George found a captive audience to his wild tales, Alexander mesmerized by the theatric facial expressions and mimicking noises. "Aunt Giana," as she would become to the array of nephews and nieces to eventually join the Darcy family, seized every moment possible to bond with her first nephew. Her clear devotion to him and sweet disposition would prevail, forging a deep love that would last down through the decades.

IS HE ASLEEP?" DARCY asked Lizzy from the doorway as he entered the nursery.

"Yes. Mrs. Hanford, you will ring me if he wakens?"

"Of course, Mrs. Darcy."

"Do not fret, my dear. He has eaten well and should allot you at least three hours to dine. You need a full meal for a change." Darcy soothed his wife with a tender caress to the small of her back, bending simultaneously to bestow a light kiss to Alexander's forehead. The baby, hours away from being four days old, lay soundly asleep in his cradle for the very first time. His tiny mouth was parted in sleep, as Darcy's always was, miniature fists curled to either side of his head and round bottom lifted into the air as he snuggled into the cushioned mattress.

"Are you sure he will be warm enough? Perhaps we should add another blanket."

Darcy touched his cheek. "He feels warm, and Mrs. Hanford will ensure the fire stays lit. Come, love, all will be well, I promise." Lizzy reluctantly allowed her husband to lead her away, not realizing that the separation was no easier for him. Darcy shared a last glance with Mrs. Hanford, the understanding nanny nodding and smiling with reassurance.

Darcy had lovingly, but firmly, informed Lizzy that tonight they would dine with George and Georgiana. As difficult as it was to leave their son,

Darcy was craving a full-course, freshly served meal. Furthermore, he knew that for Elizabeth to regain her strength it was essential her diet improve beyond quick trays served in their chambers. Aside from the nutritional aspects of the decision, he judged that dressing in more than a nightgown, primping her hair, and wearing a few jewels would mentally aid in her total recovery.

Lizzy had tearily argued, Darcy embracing her and nearly relenting, but finally she had agreed. Now Darcy could only stare at his wife and the vision she presented. Marguerite had coiffed her hair in a basic, unadorned chignon with the strand of sapphires about her slender neck the only jewels. She wore one of the gowns designed for her by Madame Millicent in London for when she was early in her pregnancy, and already a mere four days since delivering she was slim enough to wear it, the creamy tops of her lactating breasts beautifully displayed.

He halted her in the bedchamber, Lizzy glancing up into his face with surprise and sudden hope. "Are we staying after all?"

Darcy smiled, cupping her face with his palms and shaking his head. "No, beloved. I intend to guarantee you eat until bursting, drink a glass of wine, laugh with your family, and unwind. First, however, I must tell you how absolutely stunning you are. God, Elizabeth! You take my breath away!" He encircled her neck, bending for a teasing and earnest kiss. "Delicious. Come, Mrs. Darcy, the clock is ticking, knowing the appetite of our son."

Lizzy was greeted with enthusiasm by George and Georgiana. Darcy, bless his amazing heart, had placed a goose down-filled cushion on the chair to his right, guiding his wife and lovingly assisting her to sit, a chore that was yet painfully accomplished. A large part of her heart and soul remained upstairs, but the warm welcome and dazzling brilliance of the appointed dining room calmed her. With the serving of the first course, a delicious roasted red pepper soup, Lizzy wholly relaxed into the joy of fine dining with dear loved ones.

"I received a letter from Raja today," George began as the entrée was served, all looking to him with rapt attention.

"Did he finally propose?" Georgiana burst out, flushing instantly at her rude interruption and glancing at her brother in expectation of his rebuke. None was forthcoming, however, as he was as interested in the answer as she was.

George continued with a chuckle, "Apparently so. Down on one knee with a bouquet of flowers to which was tied an engagement ring obtained from Spain, a family heirloom, he writes. Reciting poetry, no doubt, knowing Raul, although he does not say such. Anyway, Miss de Bourgh had to think on it for a few days..."

"She did not!" It was Georgiana again, but this time they all laughed as George shook his head.

"No, dear niece, she did not. He does not specify, but I can read between the lines. I rather imagine instantly leaping into arms or fainting dead away more the order of events."

"Anne is more the blushing and nodding sedate type, but there could have been some leaping involved," Darcy said dryly.

"Speaking from experience, nephew?" George winked at Lizzy.

"No leaping—although there nearly was fainting, from me." He squeezed his wife's hand. "Does Dr. Penaflor give any other specifics? Dates, perhaps?"

"Lady Catherine's reaction?" Lizzy interjected with an evil twinkle.

"I expect Lady Catherine has passed the recent months figuring how to incorporate royal Spanish elements into the de Bourgh family crest. Raja is ever the diplomat, not to mention a future son-in-law, so I cannot glean anything untoward. He has well established himself in the community as a worthy physician, already asked to be on the hospital board. I shall allow myself to take some credit in that as I *did* train him, passing on my superior expertise. Kent is blessed." He paused for a smug grin and bite of braised chicken.

"Anyway," he continued, "Raja says they are tentatively planning a February wedding. He and Anne desired an intimate Christmas ceremony, but Lady Catherine insists on her daughter and heir having an elaborate affair with probably all of England invited. I added the caveat there, but would wager the truth of it."

"Why does everyone insist on February weddings?" Lizzy moaned. "I do not think it wise to take Alexander anywhere during the winter."

Darcy brought her knuckles to his lips, speaking softly. "Do not fret. We will attend if possible, bringing Alexander if he seems hale enough, or we will not. In the end our son's health is of the greatest importance. Anne and Mary will understand this." Lizzy nodded, smiling bravely.

"Well," Georgiana broke the silence, "I think it is very romantic. So much love in the air. I cannot be happier for both Anne and Mary. Maybe we can even find someone for you, Uncle. Miss Bingley is yet unclaimed."

George literally spit his wine, Lizzy bursting into loud guffaws, and Darcy attempting to glare at his sister, but unable as he hid a smile into his napkin.

"Oh Lord forgive me, but bachelorhood has never conjured more appeal than at that vision! Shame, Georgie, shame."

"Do not be so hasty, Uncle. Miss Bingley will be visiting over the holidays so you can reconsider the notion at your leisure."

"Enough," Darcy said with a sharp laugh, "joking at another's expense is unattractive and uncharitable, no matter how humorous. Remember this, Georgiana."

"Yes, brother."

Lizzy patted her hand. "Speaking of hospitals and superior expertise, what of the hospital in Matlock, George? Other events transpired and I never heard the outcome of your interview."

George laughed. "Yes indeed, other events transpired." At dinner on the night Lizzy went into labor, George had casually mentioned that he was offered a position at Matlock Hospital. The burst of hopeful delight that flowed through each of their hearts was powerful. Questions had poured forth, but George became evasive after the declaration, skillfully diverting the topic.

"It was intriguing. The facility is fairly modern for a rural establishment. The board approved of my credentials, naturally, and personally I was a smash." He grinned then shrugged. "I was guaranteed a position, but have not decided for certain."

"You know you are welcome to stay at Pemberley as long as you wish, whatever your decision."

"Thank you, William."

"Alexander would miss you and I rather appreciate having a physician in residence." Darcy smiled at his uncle. "Additionally, the community could use a doctor of your talent, but do not let the praise swell your ego any further!"

"That would be impossible, I fear. In all seriousness, I confess I have enjoyed my time home more than I imagined I would. It is a difficult decision." His grave tone touched all of them. For months now they had all privately wondered what his plans were, hoping and praying that he would stay.

"Oh, Uncle! You must stay through Christmas at the very least!" Georgiana pleaded.

"That I can promise, my dear. I refuse to sail in the winter." He shuddered. "I am a very poor sailor and the Channel crossing is hideous in the best of weather. No, I fear you are stuck with me until spring!"

Georgiana clapped in glee, Lizzy stating, "That is excellent news! We Darcys are all quite selfish, Uncle, so garner no qualms. We desire your presence for as many months or years as you wish to grace us. And besides, my father would be crushed not to have another chance to triumph at a game of chess."

～❦～

The next day Darcy was sitting in his study attending to a short stack of papers that he could not ignore. It involved details on the horse breeding program, a lengthy report necessary to complete per the request of Duke Grafton. Darcy was poring over a comprehensive list of the current stable stock when an epiphany struck him: the perfect endowment—deeding the ownership title of Wolfram to Alexander Darcy. His heart began to race and within seconds he was dashing from the room to find his wife, skidding to a stop midway down the hall when additional enlightenment dawned: Lizzy may not be so overjoyed at the idea.

For a second, just the barest second, the old dominant arrogance flared and he thought, *Who cares what Elizabeth thinks? I am his father, after all!* However, this treasonous thought was rapidly smothered. Instead, he paced in the corridor for quite some time while running over the various ways to broach the topic and make it palatable to his non-horse-loving wife. In the end he threw up his hands, literally, and just decided to be honest. This approach worked the best in the majority of situations anyway.

Luckily he found Lizzy in the nursery actively nursing their days-old baby and wearing the beautifully wistful expression dominant when Alexander was at her breast. At moments like this he could probably sell her on anything! For a spell he lost himself to the identical exalted abstraction, forgetting why he had come in the joy of gazing at his son, but eventually rational memory reasserted itself.

"Dearest, I came here specifically to ask your opinion on a matter that I have been contemplating. It will come as no surprise to you, of course, to hear that my greatest hope is that Alexander, as well as all our children, would inherit my love of horses and riding."

"I doubt if that will be an issue to worry over."

Darcy smiled. "Well, I do pray for the desire to be imbedded in his soul as it always was in mine, but I do not wish to be presumptuous. However, with that supposition in mind I have an urge to gift Alexander a horse, but not just any horse. Wolfram is who I am thinking of. He was born on the very night that you came here as my wife, you have bonded with him to a degree, and as the offspring of Parsifal I know he is of the very best lineage and dear to me." He shrugged. "The latter reasoning is merely sentimental on my part, but there it is."

Lizzy was smiling softly, but her eyes were slightly disturbed. "I think it a lovely idea, but will not Wolfram be too old for Alexander to ride?"

Darcy laughed at her ignorance. "Oh no! A well cared for, sturdy thoroughbred can live for twenty-five to thirty years easily, often more although not ridable in its seniority. Wolfram will be in his prime when Alexander transitions from pony to horse. They will have years together. My first stallion, Pericles, was given me by my grandfather when I was nine and I rode him exclusively until I was twenty-one. He was my friend and loyal companion. He only died four years ago, but could no longer run as fast as I wished nor jump fences. Parsifal was of Pericles's lineage, his grandson actually, but still a colt. Nonetheless, I was in love. I rode various horses for a couple years until he was mature enough to carry my bulk in the demanding way I required." He laughed, closing his eyes in memory. "Mr. Thurber was nigh on to throttling me I think as I haunted the stables incessantly. He was new to the position of head groomsman and not yet familiar with my personal involvement. He grew accustomed to me in time. Anyway, I insisted on caring for Parsifal myself, no one else was to break him or train him or ride him, ever." He looked at Lizzy with serious eyes, one finger stroking over Alexander's cheek absently. "The relationship between a man and his horse can be a strong bond, Elizabeth. I want Alexander to experience that if possible. As for Wolfram, he is a special horse and will be perfect for our son until he is an adult and can pick a replacement as I did. Does this meet with your approval?"

Lizzy nodded, but her eyes were yet mildly troubled. Darcy chuckled, bending to bestow a light kiss. "I can read your thoughts, Mrs. Darcy. Have no fear. I will not be trudging through the snow with our fragile infant in my arms to be introduced to his future steed." He kissed her again and then kissed Alexander's hand before rising to leave. "Spring will be soon enough!" And with that final declaration and a roguish grin, he departed.

The proper documents were signed and notarized, ownership of one Wolfram deeded to Alexander Darcy of Pemberley. The new owner was unimpressed, not even opening his eyes when a proud father informed him of the transfer.

The first week passed blissfully. Alexander settled into a fairly regular routine, eating every three to four hours on the button all through the day, filling his belly to satiation finally enough to sleep for roughly five to six hours through the night. His parents had no comparison, but felt that he was overall a temperate baby. He assuredly *had* a temper, primarily displayed when he was hungry and when the, in his opinion, time-consuming silliness of diaper changing took precedence over his empty stomach. However, the very second the exposed nipple came within range of his seeking mouth, serenity and happiness as well as blessed silence descended. Once sated, generally handed to a waiting father for burping, Alexander was bonelessly lax.

"He is rather reminiscent of an inebriated person, limbs useless with eyes rolled backward and mouth widely open," Darcy stated with a warm chuckle. "Drunk on milk, my precious?" He held his son on his shoulder, garments well protected with a cloth after lessons learned previously much to Samuel's dismay, gently patting his back. The spellbound father swayed slowly, wisely not wishing to churn a stomach full of milk, wiping the corners of the infant's mouth where remnants of his meal pooled. Alexander released a satisfied burp and slept on. "There's a good boy. Such a strong lad you are, yes. So sweet you are, my little love, Papa's little man."

His tender murmurings continued. Lizzy observed with a smile from the rocking chair while reclasping her dress and adjusting her bosoms for comfort. Now that her milk production was fully established, Lizzy discovered the painful reality of a heavy breast, quite obviously not an issue ever encountered in her life! During her pregnancy the increased ampleness of her bosom, although extreme compared to her pre-gravid state, was far from the generous volume gifted to seemingly the majority of women. The normal application of gathers and inset stays to her gowns was more than adequate to support her altered physique. This was not the case now. Lizzy was frankly shocked at the affect of lactation on the size of her breasts, easily double her pregnant mass. The strain placed on her thin shoulder and chest muscles was considerable.

Luckily Mrs. Hanford had some experience in this matter. The nanny was not an overly large woman, and although beefier than Lizzy it was clear that there were similarities in bust to frame ratios. Sweetly and tactfully, she had approached her mistress with suggestions prior to Alexander's birth. An appeal to Madame du Loire had yielded an abundance of specifically designed gowns and stays for a nursing woman. The undergarments were fairly comfortable, prettily detailed, constructed of silky fabrics, and aided in restoring tone to her abdomen, but primarily it was the relief in having a support for her weighty breasts that was appreciated.

Darcy had extended no specific comments regarding his wife's lushly endowed bust line, but his eyes betrayed his thoughts. Obviously making love to her was out of the question for the time being, Darcy far too content overall to lament the necessary waiting, but his sleepy straying hands, which inevitably ended up cupping a breast, proved the train of his private musings. Watching Alexander nurse was elating for the delight in observing the natural activity of a healthy son, but also for the titillation of staring at her creamy bosom with imaginings running amok for when she was capable of resuming marital relations.

Darcy kissed the baby's head, sitting in the chair beside Lizzy and turning a radiant face to his equally radiant wife. "I do not think we shall hear a peep out of him for a while. He feels a bit heavier, have you noticed?"

"His cheeks are chubbier," she said, brushing over the mentioned body part with a fingertip. "Considering how much he eats I am not surprised. I can feel the difference in my breasts when he finishes so I know he is adequately fed." She laid her head onto Darcy's shoulder, sighing. "He is so beautiful. I never tire of gazing upon him. Did you read Papa's letter?"

"Yes. It will be a delight to have him at Pemberley. Georgiana was thrilled at the news of Miss Kitty and Miss Mary visiting. Additionally, I must also remember to thank Miss Mary for being a typically strong-willed Bennet and prevailing upon Mr. Daniels to join them."

"And Mama?" she asked with a twinkle.

"Please, dearest, do not tease me so. I am sorry I cannot claim affection for your mother, but I am reservedly pleased to have her as a guest. I am even preparing myself to magnanimously accept the inevitably ebullient commentary regarding Pemberley's well-appointed rooms and expensive furnishings!" Lizzy laughed, Darcy continuing with a mischievous gleam, "In all likelihood it is you, my heart, who will reap the greatest joy from your mother's enthusiasm with a plethora of maternal advice and assistance."

Lizzy playfully slapped his knee. "Beast! Watch your tongue, Mr. Darcy, or I shall inform her that you are hopelessly inept and require comprehensive instruction in basic parenting skills!"

Darcy winced. "Very well, madam, you win. While we are on the subject of your family, I have a thought that I wish for your opinion on. I had the notion of sending the coach to Hertfordshire for your family's transportation. With five now traveling and the weather unpredictable, I thought it may be more comfortable, not to mention safer. However, I was unsure what vehicles Mr. Bennet possessed, having only seen the landau, and I would never wish to offend by extending the offer. What do you think?"

Lizzy thought carefully, answering with deliberation, "Papa owns nothing remotely as grand as the coach, to be sure. In truth, he would probably be mildly offended if the offer came from you. If, on the other hand, it is *my* idea and I express my concern for Mama's nerves while traveling to the far colder regions of Derbyshire, I think he would be placated. Anything to divert a paroxysm of nerves during a daylong carriage ride will be welcomed, I can assure you! He may be slightly embarrassed, but his thankfulness will outweigh." She smiled at her spouse, beckoning him forward for a tender kiss. "You are the soul of kindness, William. Thank you."

Darcy blushed faintly. "It is a simple thing, Elizabeth. To change the topic, the birth announcements should be ready in a day or two. I have compiled a short list of friends and family to notify and Mr. Keith will send them once they arrive. The list is on the bed stand for you to peruse for accuracy as well as the envelopes for you to personally address. The post was extensive today. I received a missive from Richard as well stating he will be spending Christmas with his parents." He smiled happily, glancing a kiss to her temple. "And you sent the invitation to the Gardiners, yes?" She nodded. "It is rapidly transpiring into a full house of guests after all."

Lizzy frowned. "As delightful as it is to have family about, I do not want Alexander exposed to an endless parade of people handling him."

"I emphatically agree. We will be cautious. They can gaze upon his adorable face as he lays here in his cradle or wait until he wakes. By the way, I spoke with Reverend Bertram this afternoon and scheduled the christening for the Sunday following Christmas. Nearly all the family will be here so it is perfect, do you agree?"

"Absolutely." She peered up at his face with a grin. "That gives you one month to rethink naming him 'William' rather than 'Fitzwilliam.'"

"I do not need to contemplate the subject any further. There are enough 'Fitzwilliams' in this family. Annabella named her son Fitzwilliam and Anne can do the same if she wishes. That should appease tradition."

"What about appeasing Lady Catherine? She will be devastated."

"Perhaps it is time she learned to deal with disappointment, and do not pretend you are overly concerned for Lady Catherine's sensibilities, Mrs. Darcy. We have discussed it with serious reflection and I am satisfied with the names chosen. They are strong names all and pay tribute to those dearest to us as well as fulfilling tradition." He competently transferred the limp baby from shoulder to nestle in the crook of his arm, Lizzy tucking the blanket over naked feet after a kiss to tiny toes.

Darcy resumed, "Reverend Bertram is thrilled, as you can imagine. I tried to convince him we are planning a simple ceremony, but I have a suspicion he anticipates the whole of Derbyshire to arrive."

"And an angelic benediction for the heir to Pemberley?"

"Perhaps. He began talking about rearranging benches and clearing sections of the balcony." Darcy laughed, shaking his head. "My caution was unheeded. At least the chapel will be sparkling clean for the occasion. He did ask who we had named as godparents."

"You told him the Bingleys, obviously."

"Yes. He was concerned that we had not decided on the third godparent."

"We have time, love. I have a very strong suspicion the choice you wish for will soon be available. Be patient and trust."

"Words of faith and conviction coming from my wife?"

"Your strong beliefs are rubbing off on me, Mr. Darcy." She reached for a light kiss to his nose, Darcy chuckling.

"Mrs. Reynolds requested a meeting with you at your earliest convenience to discuss a few Christmas issues. Nothing too intense, as I have expressed our wish to proceed as last year. The groundsmen are already amassing piles of holly and mistletoe, and although I do not know this for cert, I imagine the maids are fabricating new kissing balls to ensnare the unmarried footmen. With so much scheming I wonder how any of them complete any real work over the holiday season."

"If my memory serves, the servants were not the only Pemberley inhabitants to profit from strategically located mistletoe. In fact, I clearly recollect you reaping the benefits, sir." Darcy grinned in happy remembrance, meeting his wife's eyes with a lusty twinkle. "New topic... I talked to Georgiana regarding delivering the tenant gift packages this year. She stammered a bit, but was agreeable. Perhaps Mary and Kitty can accompany her for moral support! By the way, your shy sister asked me to request a favor of you."

Darcy glanced over with raised brow. "She was too timid to speak with me personally?"

"Listen and you will understand. The invitation for the Cole's Masque arrived three days ago, as you are aware. Naturally we cannot attend, or at least I cannot."

"I certainly will not be attending without you," he declared firmly. "It is a pity. The image of you in my arms dancing the waltz is most appealing."

Lizzy smiled and chuckled. "Listen to you, Mr. Darcy! Suddenly so desirous of dancing and socializing! Who is this man I am now married to?"

"The same selfish one from years past, who wishes to squire the most beautiful woman in all England on his arm, spreading envy amongst the unfortunate, and increasing his arrogance. However, we already know my faults. You were speaking of Georgiana."

"Simply put, Georgiana expressed an interest in attending this year. While on tour with the Matlocks she danced at a handful of social engagements and enjoyed herself immensely; however, she knows how strict you are about the rules of officially 'coming out' and feared your censure."

Darcy was frowning, lips pursed in thought. "I did not know of her dancing while in Wales. Did she fear sharing this with me?"

"Only in the sense that she did not desire to disappoint you or incur your anxiety over her well-being. She knows how worried you were over Lord Gruffudd and abhors causing you any pain. She yet harbors guilt over the Ramsgate affair, to the degree of hurting you and earning your disrespect."

Darcy sighed deeply, speaking roughly, "I never blamed her for any of that and made my thoughts perfectly clear."

"She knows this, dearest, but her love for you is so great as to yearn only to please you. Surely you understand how tremendously high her esteem for you? You are all she has had in her latter years to admire and emulate."

"Until you." His countenance softened. "Thank you, Elizabeth, for being a friend and sister to Georgie. What do you deem wise regarding her attending the Masque?"

"Well, assuming she can be properly chaperoned by either the Matlocks or Richard, and since it is a local affair, I do not think it untoward for her to attend. The invitation did include her name, after all. Of course, I do not claim to be fully versed in all the finer nuances of high society, but if Lord and Lady Matlock allowed her to dance at balls while touring, it should not be an issue here in Derbyshire."

"I suppose I agree. An engagement or two over the winter will in no way effect her appearance at Court and formal admission to society at Almack's in the spring. Perhaps Miss Mary, Mr. Daniels, and Miss Kitty can attend as well. I can request Sir Cole include them on the guest list."

Lizzy laughed. "Unless her personality has drastically changed with the advent of love and impending matrimony, Mary hates balls and would likely cringe at the idea. Kitty, of course, is another matter entirely. Should I inform Georgie of your agreement or will you?"

"I will talk to her. I judge it the appropriate time for us to have an earnest brother-sister chat. If you do not object to my absence for an afternoon, I think I will escort her to luncheon and shopping in Matlock. It has been a while since we spent quality hours together and I am sure she has merchandise requirements, for Christmas if nothing personal."

"That is a brilliant plan! You should invite her for tomorrow since the roads have cleared and we have a spell of moderate weather. I can meet with Mrs. Reynolds. It is past time for Alexander and I to move beyond the top floor, is that not right, my darling?" She brought his miniature feet to her mouth for delectable nibbles, the deeply sleeping infant not even flinching. "Want to see the billiard room where you will be spending so much of your time, sweetheart? How about your papa's study? He sleeps like you, William, in a comatose state."

"It is the satisfied sleep of one who is utterly loved, and well sated, although for variant reasons." He kissed the top of her head. "Should we lay him down for now and join the others in the music room? Georgiana has a new song she wishes to perform for you."

"Yes, I suppose. Oh! It is just so hard to leave him!"

"Mrs. Hanford says he will have more awake hours as he grows, but for now sleep is crucial for his health. I do not imagine he would sleep as deeply being passed around and with the pianoforte pounding in the background."

Darcy rose, laying Alexander cautiously into the cradle to avoid waking, but the contented infant merely stretched, emitting a smattering of baby gurgles before resuming his pose of tranquil slumber. The blanket was smoothed and another added, both parents transfixed for another few minutes before Mrs. Hanford was notified and they departed.

Talking about Reverend Bertram's concerns over the third godparent was the impetus Darcy needed to finally make a decision and take action as he should have done weeks ago.

The selection of an infant's godparents was a solemn task undertaken with the utmost seriousness. The responsibilities of the adults who willingly assumed this role were critical and never taken lightly. On down through the ages the Church-instituted custom of assigning mature persons, at least two of whom must be the same sex as the infant, was approached with deep forethought. A godparent's place in the child's life was a vital one. He or she was ascribed the honored task of ensuring that the innocent babe grew strong in the tenets of faith, assisting in the teaching of Christianity as essential to one's existence so that one day the aware youth would consciously declare his belief in Christ for full salvation. Logically, therefore, the godparent needed to be a man or woman of faith themselves and in close enough proximity to the youth during his formative years.

The godparent was not a legal guardian, that station ascribed for variant reasons, although they could be deemed so if all parties wished it. In Georgiana's case guardianship had been granted to the two men closest to her who were the most mature yet also youthful and financially stable. James Darcy had stipulated in his will that if his son could not fulfill the duties of Master of Pemberley and primary guardian for any reason, the estate would be managed by Col. Fitzwilliam until Georgiana married.

However, since financial and physical well-being was not an obligation of the godparent, the role was not dependent on wealth, blood, or station. Thus, Georgiana's godparents were her brother, Aunt Madeline, and Mrs. Reynolds.

Fitzwilliam James Alexander Darcy was baptized by Reverend Bertram in the Pemberley Chapel thirty years prior with his proud parents flanked by James Darcy Sr., Mr. Henry Vernor, and Anne's sister Lady Muriel Griffin.

Naturally not all families placed extreme importance on the selection of godparents. The amount of prudence undertaken was directly correlated to the depth of religious faith within the family. In the case of the Darcys, faith was a major facet in their day-to-day lives, so the decision was seriously contemplated. Lizzy may not have been as strongly adherent to religion as her husband, but she certainly understood the importance to him and the prerequisite of choosing wisely. For several weeks prior to Alexander's birth they had discussed the options. Although they had felt strongly that their firstborn would be male, they still had to consider the alternative. They gravely considered everyone they knew, but their hearts and sound deduction inevitably returned to two names that without any doubt they knew to be perfect—the Bingleys always the clear front runners.

The Darcys were content with the Bingleys as chosen godparents. It truly had been an obvious choice and despite the formality demanded, neither had suspected a refusal. The choice for the third godparent transpired with far more circumspection and surprise. Georgiana was the easily agreed upon godmother, if their child had been a female. It is not that several other female family members and friends would not be wise choices, but the relationship between Darcy and his sister was simply too devoted to seriously contemplate naming another.

But the question of whom to name as the second male godfather had been a topic of debate for months. The Darcys had considered everyone, and with the wealth of upstanding, devoted male friends Darcy possessed, the answer was challenging because the choices were so numerous! A man of lesser character and meager religious convictions would not have struggled so, but this does not describe Darcy, so he agonized over the proper course.

Oddly, and to the surprise of them both, George's name gradually entered the mix and with each passing week the desire grew stronger. Initially Darcy was frankly stunned that he would even consider the option. Yes, he knew by this time that his uncle was strong of faith and not the moral reprobate he had assumed, but his capriciousness did not really qualify him for the post of godfather. However, this too seemed to be waning as his "holiday" was taking on a decidedly permanent air. Darcy, as typical, studied the idea from every angle. He approached the concept clinically and with logic, yet his heart continued to interfere.

Therefore, in a bold move not conventionally like Darcy, he decided to confront his vacillating uncle. It was long past time for honest communication and blunt ultimatums. Therefore, a few days after Alexander's birth and while a weary wife and son were sleeping, Darcy sought out his uncle, who was, not shockingly, reclining in the library.

In Darcy's chair. With long legs stretched onto a cushioned ottoman.

"Perhaps I should write to Mr. Chippendale and request he make an identical chair."

George glanced up at Darcy's grinning face. "Could you? This is by far the most comfortable chair I have ever sat in. Perfect for my frame."

"Precisely why I ordered it made to my dimensions six years ago. I was tired of being cramped into uncomfortable creations of hard wood and sharp edges." He sat in the opposite smaller albeit exquisite wing back Chippendale, folding his hands and closely examining the expression on George's face. "I am positive something could be arranged."

George smiled with genuine delight, moving his feet to clear space on the ottoman. "Take a load off, my boy. There is plenty of room."

"Thanks all the same, but I do not fancy assuming such a pose outside of the privacy of my chambers."

George laughed aloud, nearly snorting, and shook his head. "Oh William! You are such a treasure!"

"How fortuitous that you think so, and you have offered the perfect segue into what I came to speak to you about."

George lifted a brow. "Really! How serious you are, Mr. Darcy. Should I throw down a belt of whiskey to prepare myself?"

"If you believe it would bolster your fortitude, then by all means belt away. Just bring me one as well."

George laughed, rising and crossing to the small sidebar to pour them each a glass of fine Irish scotch. "So what has you seeking me out when you could be with your beautiful wife and adorable baby?"

"A topic that greatly concerns them, as a matter of fact. Thank you." He took a sip, waiting until George was settled before launching forth. With penetrating gaze fixed and tone sober, he began. "Uncle, you know that Elizabeth and I adore you. You and I have talked extensively about our kinship, so there is no need to reiterate our mutual accord. However, I think we have both shied away from verbalizing our feelings. My wife has encouraged me to tell you of the depth of my sentiments." He grimaced slightly then shrugged. "Women are far more effusive in vocalizing their emotions, but in this instance I suppose she is correct."

He crossed his legs and inhaled deeply, opening his mouth to commence, but was halted at George's chuckle.

"Let me spare you any emasculation, William. I love you and you love me. You have become the son I never had and I have to a degree arrogated the role James rightfully deserves. There, it is out in the open. Feel better now?"

Darcy smiled wryly. "Immeasurably. Elizabeth will be so pleased." He sipped his drink before continuing. "Very well then. All that being clarified, we have an important request to make of you. A requisite preface is forthcoming, though, so be warned. Apparently I can be long-winded at times, as a dear friend recently pointed out."

"I never have noticed," George murmured with a perfectly straight face.

Darcy ignored him. "Uncle, you are welcome to dwell at Pemberley for as long as you choose, for the rest of your life if that is your desire. I do hope you know that." George nodded, frowning slightly in confusion. "I have not asked your plans and we have tried not to sway you in any way as it is ultimately your decision. However, I need to tell you in the clearest words imaginable that the heartfelt wish of us all is that you would chose to reside here forever. Simply put, I do not want lose you. Forgive the cloying sentimentalism, but that is the truth."

George was momentarily speechless, swallowing and inhaling deeply to calm the abrupt rush of emotions. He nodded finally, voice soft when he spoke, "Thank you, William. You have no idea how I appreciate that, and since we are being forthright then let me say something." He leaned forward, bony elbows on his knees as he met Darcy's piercing gaze with an identical one. "I have purposely been evasive because... well, I guess I needed to hear you say what you just did. I have been gone for a very long time. When I left, my father was Master of Pemberley and I never questioned my reception if I chose to return. With James it was much the same, although I never considered the idea. I think I undertook this journey home with a latent desire to stay, but refused to acknowledge it because I had no clue what my greeting would be. So much had changed and the Pemberley that was my childhood home was no longer the ready refuge it had always been."

"But it is," Darcy declared firmly.

"Yes, I know that now." He sighed, sitting back into the soothing shelter of the enormous chair and smiling fondly at his nephew. "I love India and know it will forever be a part of who I am. But I have missed England and Derbyshire. I have missed family, my family. Jharna's death brought that world to an end for me and made me realize fully how adrift I was. I need to be here, William. I *want* to be here, so with your blessing I will accept your offer." He grinned, lightening the solemn mood as usual with a joke. "You can even banish me to the north wing or one of the servant's houses if I become annoying."

Darcy's lips twitched, but he shook his head and held a steady stare, intoning gravely, "I am afraid I cannot allow that, Uncle. After all, my son needs to have his namesake and, if you are so willing, his godfather near at hand."

George's mouth dropped open and eyes widened in amazement. Darcy laughed aloud, lifting his glass in salute. "To Alexander and his godfather. Lord help us all!"

❧

Gradually Lizzy returned to her duties as her energy was restored, but always with Alexander either accompanying her or Mrs. Hanford aware of her location. Since she primarily worked from her desk in Darcy's study or their sitting room, she was easy to find. The Indian silks gifted by Dr. Darcy were perfectly utilized as slings to hold Alexander against his mother's chest while he slept, enabling Lizzy to carry him easily and have her hands free. She looked ridiculous, and would never appear in public so adorned, but for meandering about the manor it was ideal.

Mrs. Reynolds had all the Christmas plans in hand, Lizzy only required to assist minimally and proffer input. They discussed the packages for the tenant families, the staff and tenant feast, any additional gifts Lizzy wanted purchased, the menu, and a few other incidentals. There truly was very little for her to address, Lizzy abundantly thankful as she vastly preferred devoting all attention to her precious baby.

Physically she rejuvenated rapidly. The occasionally intense cramps, a result so George informed her, of her womb returning to a pre-pregnant condition lessened daily and were gone by the end of the second week. She did nap most every day with Alexander snuggled against her breast after nursing primarily because it was so wonderfully joyous to do so. Her weariness was essentially gone within days to be replaced by the vigor of youth. The tenderness to her bottom persisted for quite a while, as did the scant discharge from her feminine area, but that too receded. She adjusted to some of the changes in her body: the large and cumbersome breasts that leaked milk frequently, and the wider hips that required several chemises to be altered. More problematic, from an egotistical standpoint, was the extra flesh over her abdomen.

Eventually this would disappear, Lizzy as svelte as always, but since this was a future development, she lamented this alteration to her physique. Logically she knew that her expectations were presumptuous and apprehensions irrational.

Her emotions were perhaps minutely a result of personal vanity, but primarily were for her husband. This too she rationally knew to be absurd as Darcy had proven time and again that his love and desire for her was not dependent on her shape. Nonetheless, her unease and embarrassment continued, Lizzy thankful that for now her moderately pendulous belly was hidden from view under a corset and gown.

"Enter," Darcy declared in response to the knock on his study door. The minor quantity of business that arose during the winter months had accumulated in a pile on his desk over the past week and a half, Darcy finally taking the precious time away from his wife and son to execute his duty as the Master of Pemberley. As important as the tedious issues were, he nevertheless was thrilled to see his wife and son cross the threshold.

"Forgive me, William, for disturbing you, but I have the final batch of announcements to post."

"I shall forgive you, beloved, if you kiss me and then hand me our son. Come to your father, my precious boy. There's my big strong lad. What are you and your beautiful mother up to? Hmm?"

Alexander was awake, bright blue eyes studying his father with an infantile hint of amusement. Darcy held him balanced on both broad hands, neck well supported as he made silly faces and conversed with the innate baby talk tonality that all parents seemed to possess. The baby squirmed and erratically swung his extremities, lips puckered, and stare riveted on his adoring father.

"Who loves you best? Your mama and papa do, yes, that's who! Give your father a kiss, milk lips. Ouch! Must you grab my hair each time?"

"Perhaps he is subtly enlightening you to the fact that you need your hair trimmed."

"Is your father a shaggy hound, wee one? Or is your grip just so strong you cannot prevent grasping anything in your reach? I think it the latter, yes I do, my sturdy little man, I do." Darcy buried his mouth and nose into Alexander's stubby neck, tickling and blowing as the amused newborn wiggled and burbled, nearly giggling.

Lizzy sat and watched her silly spouse play the child with Alexander, heart swelling with fresh rivers of joy. The infant's moments of wakefulness were minimal and seized upon wholeheartedly. Despite her familiarity with Darcy's humor and private frivolity, it still surprised her to observe how nonsensical he was with their firstborn. He would likely be mortified if a servant entered the room, or even many of their family and friends, but the delightful displays of merriment sprung from an inner fount of happiness that he could not contain. To say that marriage and now fatherhood had drastically affected the personality of the stoic Mr. Darcy would be a monumental understatement.

"I received a letter from Charlotte," she interrupted his jollities, Darcy lifting to meet her eyes with a wince as Alexander had a grip on his hair.

"You are smiling so it must be pleasant news." He untangled the tiny fingers from his locks, transferring Alexander into his arms for sedate stroking.

"She has safely delivered, over a month ago now."

"Why the delay in writing? All went well, I trust?"

Lizzy nodded. "Mr. Collins, if you believe it, is the father of twins! Two girls! Charlotte writes that the birth was long, two babies being utterly unsuspected." Lizzy shook her head, eyes mildly glazed. "I cannot fathom having to birth two. Poor Charlotte. Be that as it may, she says the recovery was swift. The eldest daughter weighed over seven pounds and was perfectly healthy. The second was barely five pounds and rather sickly, hence the delay in notifying friends. Apparently she was slow to grow and they all worried, but eventually she caught on to nursing and is improving. They feel she is out of danger. Listen to this: Lady Catherine insisted on employing a wet nurse to augment the increased demands of two babies! Paid for it herself! Your aunt can surprise me yet."

Darcy smiled with some surprise evident on his visage as well. "That is marvelous news. I do hope they encounter no further distress." He gazed lovingly upon his son, embraced so closely to his beating heart, speaking in a coarse whisper, "Nothing could be worse than losing a child, unless it is losing a beloved wife. Neither event would I wish upon my worst enemy."

Drawing Alexander's face near, Darcy bestowed numerous soft kisses, the babe calming until the tip of Darcy's nose brushed over pink lips. Instantly he opened wide, rooting for a meal. When that was not immediately forthcoming a loud bellow was emitted, the once placid face screwed in consternation.

"Apparently he is tired of me. Nourishment takes precedence over play or adoration, so it seems." He carried the upset babe to Lizzy, already drawing the shawl across her chest while releasing buttons. The process of positioning and latching was now accomplished rapidly, Alexander's cries stifled instantly as his mouth became active in pleasanter pursuits.

Darcy encircled his wife's shoulders, securing the shawl for privacy although no one would enter his study unannounced. He kissed Lizzy's temple, caressing Alexander's leg while he nursed. Never tiring of these moments of felicity, Darcy happily eschewed the work on his desk. Stacks of parchment, receipts, and invoices would regenerate no matter how diligently he applied himself; however, these precious interludes were a one-time experience to be savored. Yes, Alexander would eat again in a few hours and so on, but each day he matured in subtle ways, vague evolutions that meant he would never be quite the same. They may be blessed with a dozen children, each precious, but all unique in their personalities and actions. Darcy and Lizzy wanted to wholly absorb each minute with Alexander to be treasured in their memories and hearts for all eternity.

Darcy sighed, resting his head against Lizzy's. "I rather envy Mr. Collins, shocking as that is to confess. I would not be averse to spoiling two babies. Perhaps we can arrange something for the next pregnancy," he grinned.

Lizzy chucked. "Very sweet, but personally I prefer one baby at a time. And let us allow my bum to heal before we start planning further pregnancies. Unless, that is, we can figure a way for you to incubate one of them!"

Darcy laughed. "I am quite certain every woman on down through the endless ages has prayed for that miracle. Alas, the Almighty had a different plan. Very well then, one at a time is adequate, especially if they are all as adorable as our Alexander." He clasped one foot, toes automatically curling around the tip of Darcy's thumb where it pressed lightly the length of the sole. Alexander shoved against the pressure, causing his father to smile at his strength. The occupied infant opened one eye, shifted slightly, and momentarily lost his grip on the nipple. After a frantic search the nipple was found, Alexander casting a baleful glance at Darcy before attending to the serious business of eating.

"You of all people should know better than to disturb a Darcy while dining," Lizzy teased.

"Point well taken. Forgive me, my son." He bent to softly kiss the baby's downy cheek, planted a second kiss onto the beautiful flesh of his wife's breast followed by several others winding up her chest until reaching her lips.

The kiss was long, gentle, soothing, and loving rather than passionate. Darcy withdrew mere inches to gaze into Lizzy's sparkling eyes, hand and fingers stroking over her jaw and cheek. "I love you, Elizabeth, unbelievably so. You are beautiful and extraordinarily desirable to me. I know we cannot make love yet, but I do hope you understand my yearning for you is unabated. I will wait as patiently as you need, but when we can be together again, I will love you hard with all my soul pouring into yours. Nothing, not time or even Alexander, can usurp your place in my life. You are my heartbeat and breath, my beloved, precious wife."

They kissed again. Tenderness transmuting to urgency; passion growing as the kiss deepened; waves of desire swept through them both leaving them breathless. Lizzy moaned, hands gripping Alexander tightly, the infant oblivious as he ate. Darcy pulled away, his arousal well advanced, meeting Lizzy's glazed eyes with his own.

"Fitzwilliam," she whispered, as she always did when overcome by desire.

Darcy smiled beatifically. "Soon, my lover, soon. Anticipation is sweet, and believe me, my expectations are high so therefore it will be sweet indeed. I can promise you this, my soul." He kissed her again, temperately as passion was cooled, lingering teasingly over her lips before traveling along her jaw to then bury his face with a contented sigh into the delicate angle where slender neck met dainty shoulder.

Acknowledgments

THIS THIRD NOVEL OF THE Darcy Saga series is dedicated to my father, Edward Hudson, and my mother, Marge Shelly, who passed away in September. Naturally my existence is a reality due to their existence, but my thanks is for more than that. These two people have been a constant bedrock throughout my life no matter what tribulations troubled their own lives. Dad, I love you. Mom, I love you, miss you, and will never forget all you taught me. Next time I see you we will be free of all cares as we dance in Heaven!

Some special thanks: Deb Werksman for your patience, support, and friendship. Danielle Jackson for being utterly adorable and the best publicist on the planet. Simone van Lingen for your devoted friendship and for discovering Sourcebooks. Vee Stojcevski for your Aussie humor, proofreading skills, and being my #1 TSBO devotee. My husband and kids for loving me throughout the craziness. And above all, to my Lord and God for ceaseless inspiration.

Finally, and with all my heart, a huge thank you to my readers for taking this journey with me and the Darcys. The ride is just beginning!

About the Author

SHARON LATHAN IS A NATIVE Californian currently residing amid the orchards, corn, cotton, and cows in the sunny San Joaquin Valley. She divides her time between being a homemaker nurturing her own Mr. Darcy and two teenage children and working as a registered nurse in a neonatal ICU. Throw in the cat, dog, and a ton of fish to complete the picture. When not at the hospital or attending to the often dreary tasks of homemaking, she is generally found reposing in her comfy recliner with her faithful laptop. For more information about Sharon and The Darcy Saga series, visit her website at: www.darcysaga.net.

Mr. and Mrs. Fitzwilliam Darcy: Two Shall Become One
SHARON LATHAN

"Highly entertaining... I felt fully immersed in the time period. Well done!" —*Romance Reader at Heart*

A fascinating portrait of a timeless, consuming love

It's Darcy and Elizabeth's wedding day, and the journey is just beginning as Jane Austen's beloved *Pride and Prejudice* characters embark on the greatest adventure of all: marriage and a life together filled with surprising passion, tender self-discovery, and the simple joys of every day.

As their love story unfolds in this most romantic of Jane Austen sequels, Darcy and Elizabeth each reveal to the other how their relationship blossomed from misunderstanding to perfect understanding and harmony, and a marriage filled with romance, sensuality and the beauty of a deep, abiding love.

What readers are saying:

"This journey is truly amazing."

"What a wonderful beginning to this truly beautiful marriage."

"Could not stop reading."

"So beautifully written...making me feel as though I was in the room with Lizzy and Darcy...and sharing in all of the touching moments between."

978-1-4022-1523-0 • $14.99 US/ $15.99 CAN/ £7.99 UK

Loving Mr. Darcy: Journeys Beyond Pemberley
SHARON LATHAN

"A romance that transcends time." —*The Romance Studio*

Darcy and Elizabeth embark on the journey of a lifetime

Six months into his marriage to Elizabeth Bennet, Darcy is still head over heels in love, and each day offers more opportunities to surprise and delight his beloved bride. Elizabeth has adapted to being the Mistress of Pemberley, charming everyone she meets and handling her duties with grace and poise. Just when it seems life can't get any better, Elizabeth gets the most wonderful news. The lovers leave the serenity of Pemberley, traveling through the sumptuous landscape of Regency England, experiencing the lavish sights, sounds, and tastes around them. With each day come new discoveries as they become further entwined, body and soul.

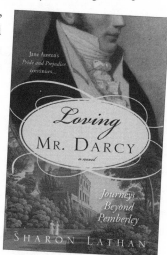

What readers are saying:

"Darcy's passion for love and life with Lizzy is brought to the forefront and captured beautifully."

"Sharon Lathan is a wonderful writer… I believe that Jane Austen herself would love this story as much as I did."

"The historical backdrop of the book is unbelievable—I actually felt like I could see all the places where the Darcys traveled."

"Truly captures the heart of Darcy & Elizabeth! Very well written and totally hot!"

978-1-4022-1741-8 • $14.99 US/ $18.99 CAN/ £7.99 UK